Praise for *The Good Brother*

"Chris Offutt's prose is lean, soulful, artlessly artful."
—Dan Cryer, *Newsday*

"[A] wonderful first novel. Offutt . . . is an original and mesmerizing storyteller."
—Katherine Guckenberger, *St. Petersburg Times*

"Offutt's first published novel shows the polish of long experience. He succeeds in creating almost unbearable tension, not from physical peril but from the protagonist's moral danger."
—*Roanoke Times*

"His lyrical prose could make tying a shoe interesting. Offutt's writing . . . can become very nearly addictive."
—Ellison Austen Walcott, *Lexington Herald Tribune*

"Offutt's surefooted first novel illustrates the potentially lethal crossfire between moral responsibility and familial duty, as a good man who starts out playing possum ends up a sitting duck."
—*The New Yorker*

"Mr. Offutt, an exceptionally good writer, . . . develops his story with a strong, yet admirably unstrained, sense of irony."
—Merle Rubin, *The Wall Street Journal*

"A beguiling first novel. Offutt's measured prose makes Virgil's moving story vivid."
—Adam Begley, *People*

"Chris Offutt is that rare author who can portray a place and its inhabitants so they're familiar and strange at the same time. Virgil is one of the more complex, capable characters in current fiction. [An] honest and moving novel by an extremely talented writer."
—David Galef, *The Memphis Commercial Appeal*

"Offutt is a writer well-worth tracking down."

—Frank Zoretich, *The Albuquerque Journal*

"*The Good Brother* is as close as a novel is likely to get to being The Great Western American Novel."

—*Salt Lake City Tribune*

"A quintessential American story. *The Good Brother* is an engrossing story that carries us into dangerous territory and leaves us with more knowledge about ourselves than we may wish to know."

—Wade Hall, *Lexington Herald/Leader*

"Offutt's portrayal of two mountain settings is rich in its delineation of character and landscape. Offutt is a tremendous storyteller with an uncanny ear for dialogue. He understands the milieu in which he travels."

—Brent Kilewer, *The New Mexican*

"*The Good Brother* is a classic tale of violence and retribution spawning only more violence and retribution, a centuries-old story powerfully recast by a tremendously gifted storyteller."

—Rob Spillman, *Salon*

"[A] first-rate tale of loyalty to family and land."

—Fabiola Santiago, *The Miami Herald*

"*The Good Brother* is a smart, engaging story of two different cultures that turn out to be more than a little similar under the surface."

—John Barron, *The Chicago Sun Times*

"Chris Offutt's *The Good Brother* is prose poetry."

—Florence Gilkeson, *The Pilot*

"If you are searching for a new author to read whose writing ability will sustain your interest for the next few decades, the author of *The Good Brother* should suffice."

—Larry D. Woods, *Nashville Banner*

"The character [Offutt] creates in Virgil Caudill . . . is a frighteningly accurate portrait of the American Everyman."

—David Breeden, *San Antonio Express News*

"*The Good Brother* brings complex modern history to life with blood, guts, dark humor, and a seething hatred that suggests real love."

—Eric Beaumont, *Milwaukee Journal Sentinel*

"Offutt is a fine writer . . . especially good in describing the hills and inhabitants of Kentucky and capturing their voices. The more strange and remote the people, the more brilliantly he renders them. *The Good Brother* is a complex book that captures rural voices, tells a compelling, contemporary story while asking difficult questions about the nature of freedom and revenge."

—David McLean

"Beautifully written." — *Library Journal*

"The skills evident in Offutt's earlier writing, including his pitch-perfect rendition of the vivid, terse, often droll character of the spoken word, and his talent for vigorously, precisely describing rural blue-collar culture . . . are once again on display. . . . As a portrait of a good man's life shattered by violence, and as a meditation on the persistent attraction of violence in American society, [*The Good Brother*] is persuasive, original, and disturbing. The work of a sizable talent."

—*Kirkus Reviews*

"In reading *The Good Brother*, I found myself utterly beguiled by the vividness of Chris Offutt's world, the thorny, particular music of his voice, and the power of his storytelling. Already one of the best writers of short fiction in his—or any—generation, he has now proved himself a remarkable novelist, in possession of narrative gifts equal to his humanity and wit."

—Tobias Wolff

"With his first novel, Chris Offutt surpasses the promise of his stories and memoir. *The Good Brother* is the moving work of a first-rate storyteller soaring at the height of his power."

—Annie Dillard

"Chris Offutt takes the rough-and-tumble of our national underlife and polishes his characters into unexpected gems. The dark journey of *The Good Brother* from trouble in Kentucky to catastrophe in Montana is a devilishly fine cat's-cradle of our national tensions."

—Ivan Doig

ALSO BY CHRIS OFFUTT

Kentucky Straight

The Same River Twice

The Good Brother

Chris Offutt

SCRIBNER PAPERBACK FICTION
PUBLISHED BY SIMON & SCHUSTER

SCRIBNER PAPERBACK FICTION
Simon & Schuster Inc.
Rockefeller Center
1230 Avenue of the Americas
New York, NY 10020

First Scribner Paperback Fiction edition 1998
SCRIBNER PAPERBACK FICTION and design are trademarks of Simon & Schuster Inc.

Designed by Jenny Dossin
Manufactured in the United States of America

1 3 5 7 9 10 8 6 4 2

The Library of Congress has cataloged the Simon & Schuster edition as follows:
Offutt, Chris.
The good brother / Chris Offutt.
p. cm.
I. Title.
PS3565.F387G66 1997
813'.54—dc21 96-53348
CIP

ISBN 0-684-80983-4
0-684-84619-5 (Pbk)

Excerpt from "You Can Have It" by Philip Levine reprinted by permission of the author.

The author gratefully acknowledges the Iowa Arts Council, the National Endowment for the Arts, the Guggenheim Foundation, the Whiting Foundation, and the American Academy of Arts and Letters for generous financial assistance during the writing of this book.

For Rita,
Sam, and James

Give me back my young brother, hard
and furious, with wide shoulders and a curse
for God and burning eyes that look upon
all creation and say, You can have it.

PHILIP LEVINE
"You Can Have It," *7 Years from Somewhere*

The Good Brother

1

Virgil followed the rain branch off the hill and drove to the Blizzard post office. The mail hadn't come yet and he continued past, giving a general wave to the crowd that gossiped in the glare of April sun. He drove up a steep hill to the county line. It was only two miles from the house he'd grown up in, but he'd never crossed it.

He parked by the edge of the cliff. The color of the air was brighter at the top. Clay Creek ran through the hollow with purple milkweed blooming in the ditch. When Virgil was a kid, he and his brother had walked its slippery bank, gathering enough empty pop bottles to buy candy when they reached Blizzard's only store. Virgil wished he and Boyd could do it again but people had stopped throwing pop bottles away when the deposit rose to a nickel. The store closed when the owner died. Boyd was dead now, too.

Virgil tried to imagine the land when it was flat across the hilltops, before a million years of rain chewed the dirt to make creeks and hollows. Clouds lay in heaps like sawdust piles. He figured he was seeing out of the county and he wondered if hawks could see farther, or just better. The world seemed smaller from above. The dips and folds of the wooded hills reminded him of a rumpled quilt that needed smoothing out.

Cars were leaving the post office, which meant the mail truck had arrived. A titmouse clung to a tree upside down, darting its head to pick an insect from a leaf. Pine sap ran like blood from a wound in the tree. Virgil drove down the road and parked in willow shade beside the creek. A tattered flag dangled above the post office, fastened permanently to a hickory pole. Every morning the postmaster, a white-haired man named Zephaniah, dragged the flagpole from the post office and slipped one end into a hole in the earth beside a fence post. He buckled a leather belt around the flagpole and the post. At day's end he stored the pole inside.

Instead of a system of organized boxes, Zephaniah had laid out a few narrow tables to correspond roughly with the surrounding terrain—two hollows, a hill, and a creek. He arranged the day's mail in stacks that represented the location of each family's house in the community. Virgil leaned on the narrow shelf that protruded from the arched hole in the wall where Zephaniah worked. The shelf's edge was round and smooth from years of use.

"Flag's looking kindly ragged, ain't it," Virgil said.

"Government never sent a new one this year."

"Can't you tell them?"

"Could."

The screen door banged as a man from Red Bird Ridge came in.

"Mail run yet?" he said to Virgil.

"Just did."

"I ain't seen you since . . ."

The man adjusted his cap, looked at the floor, and rapidly scratched his sideburn. The last time they'd met had been at Boyd's funeral. Virgil didn't know how to ease the man's discomfort.

"Well, a long while went by since I seen you," the man said.

He stepped to the window and looked through the mail that Zephaniah had gathered for him.

"Write me a order, will you, Zeph?"

"How much?"

"Ten dollars even. Mamaw owes the doctors that much a month."

"Which doctor?"

"I don't know, that clinic in town. The one everybody goes to."

"Rocksalt Medical?"

"Reckon."

Zephaniah filled out the form, printing carefully. When he finished, he waited, and Virgil knew that Zephaniah would stand there all day rather than insult the man by asking him to write his name on the money order.

"Go ahead and sign it for me, Zeph."

Zephaniah wrote the man's name at the bottom of the money order, and asked for eleven dollars. The man placed three fives on the shelf.

"Buying money sure ain't cheap," he said.

"Best to have a checking account," Zephaniah said.

"None of my people have fooled with banks and I ain't about to start now."

"Need an envelope?"

The man nodded. Zephaniah wrote the address on a pre-stamped envelope and made change. The man went outside and spoke to Virgil through the screen. "Come here a minute."

Virgil went to the door. The man pressed his forehead to the screen, his skin pushing through the mesh in tiny squares. "I knowed your brother," he said. "You tell your mama I'm sorry."

Virgil never knew what to say back. The man looked up and down the creek before speaking in a ragged whisper. "It was a Rodale done it. Billy Rodale."

The man walked swiftly to his truck.

Virgil leaned against the wall and inhaled as deeply as possible. He let the air out in a long slow breath. Across the road, green tendrils of forsythia bushes dragged the creek.

"Virge?" said Zephaniah. "You all right?"

"Yeah. Just sick of it."

"Of what?"

"You know. Boyd and all."

"People feel bad."

"You didn't hear what he said."

"I heard. Ears is the last thing I got left that works."

"Well, I'm sick to death of it. I know who it was. The whole damn creek does, and I don't need everybody telling me. They figure I don't know since I ain't done nothing."

"A man like him ain't worth worrying about. He's the reason for the flag problem."

"What?"

"I ain't asked for a new flag because I don't want to draw attention. When I retire, this post office will shut down. Only reason it's open now is folks buying money orders. Half this creek pays their bills through me. We're showing a profit here, which ain't exactly something the government is used to."

"So why close down?"

"Because profit ain't what they go by."

"What is?"

"If I knew that, I'd be President."

Fifty years ago the post office building had housed the company store for the town of Blizzard. The community had run on scrip issued by the mineral company. Now the mines were empty and the town was gone, along with its barbershop, saloon, train station, and doctor. Most of the families were gone, too. The remaining people still walked off the hillsides for money orders, another form of scrip.

"If they shut this down," Virgil said, "there won't be much left of here."

"Church and grade school," Zephaniah said. "I've throwed hours of thought at it. Blizzard's old and wore out, and the government's getting rid of it. They ain't too many to care about us. I'd say even God was right mad the day he laid this place out. It's as slanty a land as ever was."

"Maybe you could get a petition."

"Who'd sign it, Virge? You can't turn in a petition full of X's. They'd say if these people can't read or write, what do they need a post office for? No, Virge. Blizzard's done."

Zephaniah stood with his shoulders slumped, his arms hanging straight as if held by weights. He suddenly seemed what he was—short and old.

"I could retire now," he said. "I'm tired enough, but I'm the last man with a job. That's why I keep working. If I stop, the town stops."

"Well."

"It burnt my daddy up that I never left out of here. He died still mad over it. I know they's some saying you ort to take care of that Rodale boy for killing Boyd. More say it than don't, my opinion. But I say get yourself out of here, and I don't mean Rocksalt, either. There's Mount Sterling to think on, even Lexington. No sense going to the state pen over your brother."

Virgil couldn't imagine leaving Blizzard. He'd lived here thirty-two years. Boyd was the restless one, the wild brother, the one who'd leave one day. Virgil had grown up letting Boyd do the talking and later the running around acting crazy. He drove fast, drank hard, played cards, and chased women. Finally, Boyd had done the dying.

The narrow hall seemed to squeeze Virgil and he felt a need for breath that he couldn't quite get. He was thirsty. He stumbled outside and smelled honeysuckle vine along the creek. He drove down the road and up the steep dirt lane of his home hill. In his mother's house, he turned on the faucet and let it run to bring water from deep in the earth. He drank two cups fast. His body recognized the water, its cold taste the most familiar sensation he'd ever known. He breathed through his nose as he drank, his chin and shirt wet.

He was drinking his fourth cup when he noticed his mother and sister watching from the doorway. He set the cup in the sink.

"Mom," he said. "I ain't going to that post office no more."

His mother's face didn't change, but the expression of her eyes did. Virgil recognized it as the look she got when Boyd said something outrageous, but she had never regarded Virgil in this manner. He leaned on the sink and looked through the window. It was cracked from the beak of a cardinal that had repeatedly attacked its own reflection.

"Where's the mail at anyway?" his sister said.

"I left it."

"Well, shoot, Virgie." Sara turned to their mother. "I'll send Marlon directly. I'm glad I married somebody who's got some sense, even if it's just to pick up the mail."

"I just don't like hearing that old gossip down there's all. You go, Sara. You'd talk a bird out of its nest."

"What were they saying?" Sara said.

Beside her, their mother waited without speaking. She had spent most of her life in just such a stance—silent in the kitchen, waiting for news that was invariably bad.

"You don't really want to know, do you?" Virgil said.

Sara nodded.

"They say that Wayne girl is pregnant," he said.

"No!"

"Sure is."

"Which one?"

"Up on Redbird Ridge."

"I know that," Sara said. "They ain't but one bunch of Waynes. I mean which girl?"

"The littlest."

"Lord love a duck, she ain't but fourteen."

"Well," Virgil said.

"Whose is it? Anybody say?"

"They's no question of that."

"Well, who?"

"I hate to be the one to tell you, Sara. But it was your Marlon done it."

Sara's face changed color. Her breath rasped into the air. Their mother glanced at her as if to make sure Sara wasn't going to collapse, then studied Virgil carefully.

"Sara, honey," she said. "I believe he's telling a story."

Sara grabbed a sponge and threw it, bouncing it off his chest and leaving a wet mark on his shirt.

"If you went for the mail," Virgil said, "you'd know true gossip from wrong."

"If you can't fetch mail," Sara said, "you at least can mow the yard."

Boyd had taken care of the yard and retrieved the mail. Four months after his death, the family was still trying to divvy up chores.

2

Five days a week Virgil drove to Rocksalt for work, crossing water at hard turns as the road followed Clay Creek through the hills. In summer the creek dried. Men filled trucks with the flat rock and hauled it to dirt roads. Spring rains returned the rock to the creek.

The road's official name was County 218, but everyone called it The Road. If they needed to be specific, people referred to it as The Main Road. It had two directions—toward town, and away from town. Every turnoff was a dead-end hollow.

Virgil pulled into the parking lot for maintenance workers at Rocksalt Community College. He left the keys in the ignition to keep from losing them. On one side of the lot were the blue trucks that the crew bosses drove. They were promoted from the crew and usually held the job until death or retirement. Men on salary wore a blue uniform with their first name sewn above the pocket. Virgil was due. Since working full time, he'd put in one year as a utility man, floating from job to job, and three years on the garbage truck. He hoped for a promotion by spring. Virgil dearly wanted his name on a shirt.

The cars in the lot were ten to twenty years old and American-made. They sat low on one side or high on the other. Mufflers hung by wires. Some cars had cardboard taped in place of missing windows. Several were two-toned from salvaged doors, hoods, and quarter-panels that matched the make and model but not the color. The back seats were filled with tools and toys.

Virgil joined a crowd of men in caps who circled a car, drinking coffee from thermos cups and smoking cigarettes. A pup sat on cardboard in the front seat. Rundell Day leaned against the hood. Hair grew from his ears like gulley brush.

"By God, boys," said a man, "that's one set-up pup, ain't it."

"I had his job I'd quit mine," said another.

"I'd not give a man two hundred dollars for a pup," said another.

"That ain't just any old dog you're looking at. Hey Rundell, what's it do for that kind of money? Tricks? Roll over? Punch the clock for you, what?"

"It'll flat tree," Rundell said.

"Shit, that dog couldn't tree a leaf."

"I ain't for sure that is a dog, boys. My opinion, that's a possum in a dog suit."

"It might have some possum to it."

"Boys, I don't know, now. I believe what it looks like ain't possum a-tall. Take a good long gander now. See them ears. See that mouth hanging open whopper-jawed. Boys, if you was to ask me, that's one dog looks a lot like Rundell Day."

"Shoot, I see it."

"What are you doing, Rundell? Trying to get your kin on the job? Best take it in to see the Big Boss, ain't you."

"It's a dog," Rundell said. "And it'll out tree ary a dog you fellers got."

"Boys, watch out now. Rundell says it's a dog."

"Can he guarantee it?"

"Two-hundred-dollar dog ort to live in a tree."

"I got a three-legged dog that'll out-tree that pup."

"By God, there's something to brag on. A man keeps a three-legged dog around."

"It's the kids' dog. Old lady won't let me kill it."

"What else won't she let you do?"

"She don't much care."

"Listen at him. His own wife don't care. By God, mine was to hear me say that, she'd cut every ball on me off."

"She'd not need but a butter knife."

"Time is it?"

"It's time."

The men began moving toward the main building where the time clock was. Rundell opened the passenger door and the pup sprang to him, paws sliding on the vinyl seat. Rundell leaned his face for the pup to lick.

"You be good, now," Rundell said. "Don't you pay no attention to them boys. You're a good old dog, yes sir, a good old dog."

He kissed the dog on the face and locked the door. He and Virgil walked across the lot. Surrounding the town were high hills, their tops in mist.

"You really give two hundred for it?" Virgil said.

"Why, no."

"What did you give for it, Rundell?"

"You in the dog buying business?"

"No."

"Then I'll tell you, Virge, but don't say nothing. I found that pup on the road this morning."

"Just giving them something to think on?"

"When I go to sell it, I'll get a hundred and they'll think it's a real deal."

They opened the blue door of the maintenance building. The men were strung in a line down the hall, at the end of which hung the time clock. It ticked and the first man dipped his card into the slot and went out the door. The line moved forward.

As each man left the building, he went to the crew shop where the boss assigned the day's work. The hierarchy placed electricians at the top, followed by carpenters, painters, landscapers, and garbagemen. Off to the side and on their own were the custodians of individual buildings, quiet men who moved slowly, ignored by students and faculty. Virgil headed for the garbage dock. He cut through the main building instead of going around, walked down a hall, and came out a seldom-used door. He closed it very quietly. He stepped around the corner and stomped his feet. Two men turned quickly, half-rising from their seats. Footsteps from that direction could only mean the Big Boss.

"Don't get up, boys," Virgil said. "I know you all are studying on important stuff."

Rundell spat coffee. "I wish to hell you'd not do that, Virge. Damn near woke Dewey here up."

"I ain't asleep," Dewey said.

"You were asleep and you know it. You're the only man I ever seen who can sleep standing up."

"I don't talk the wax out of a man's ears," Dewey said. "Now let me alone."

Virgil opened the door to the garbage crew's tiny office. Inside was a desk, three chairs, and an industrial coffee machine that had been salvaged from the trash. He filled a styrofoam cup and went outside.

"You're on wheel, Virge," Rundell said.

Rundell had run the garbage crew for twenty-three years and divided all aspects of the work equally. Four men could fit in the cab of the truck, and each week they rotated among driver, cabman, outside man, and gearshift man. Rundell was set to retire in a year and he'd marked Virgil as his successor.

"Where's Taylor at?" Virgil said.

"Ain't here yet," Dewey said.

"I can see that. But is he on the job?"

"Well." Dewey gave him a sly look. "His card got punched."

"Then we got to wait on that sorry son of a bitch."

"He'll be here."

"Now I ain't trying to tell you what to do, Dewey," Rundell said. "But you'd best watch punching him in that way. If you know he's coming late, it ain't nothing. But that Taylor, he's likely to be in the jailhouse as in the bed. Get caught fooling with his card and you're out of a job. I've seen it happen, boys. More than once."

Across the back of the lot, Taylor came slipping through the gate.

"Look yonder," Virgil said. "If it ain't the old girl hisself. Watch this."

He ducked into the office and hid all the styrofoam cups but one. He used a finishing nail to make a series of small holes around its brim and set the cup by the coffee machine.

Taylor came slowly across the lot, walking in a stiff way to keep his head level. His clothes were wrinkled and dirty. He hadn't shaved in a couple of days and his lips were cracked.

"Boys," he said. "Somebody shoot me. I can't stand this no longer."

He went in the office and closed the door. He kept a half-pint of whisky inside, but as long as Rundell didn't see a man drinking on the job, he could deny it. Taylor came out of the office upright. The whisky had given his face some color, his eyes a little life. "Who's got a smoke?" he said. Dewey tossed him a cigarette and Taylor put it in his mouth and pulled out a Zippo. He leaned his head away and tilted the lighter at an angle opposite his head. The flame shot six inches into the air. Taylor sucked hard and capped the lighter. "My hat on fire?"

The men chuckled and shook their heads.

"Boys," he said. "I feel like I been shot at and missed, shit at and hit."

He sipped the coffee. It came out of the holes onto his chin and a few seconds passed before he registered the burn. "Goddam you son of a blue-balled bitches. Every one of you!"

He jerked the cup away from his face, sloshing coffee onto his hand. He passed it quickly to his other hand, but held on to the coffee because of the whisky he'd dumped in it. He lifted the cup and bit off part of the rim to get rid of the holes. He spat the styrofoam and drank, lifting his eyebrows to Rundell over the cup.

"What are we waiting on?" he said. "Time to hit a lick, ain't it."

Dewey smiled, dark gaps speckling his mouth where teeth should be. Rundell clamped his lips like two bricks because his laugh was a high-pitched giggle that embarrassed him. Taylor choked his laughter off, lifting his hand to his forehead, his face twisted from the pain.

"Don't," he said. "Damn it. You boys are harder on a man than a preacher. I knew I shouldn't have come in."

"Why did you?" Virgil said.

"Hell, I wrecked my car last night. I woke up still in the ditch and I was closer to work than the house. I just come in for a drink to feel better."

The men laughed on the cement dock, blowing white gusts of breath into the chilly air. The sun showed above the eastern hill. After a few minutes, they began drifting toward the truck. Virgil climbed behind the wheel, marveling at the way they moved as a group with no clear sign from Rundell, like a flock of geese. Other crew bosses had rituals that told everyone it was time, such as looking at a watch, or standing, or simply a nod. With Rundell it was an attitude. He assumed an air of resignation, as if he didn't want to be the one to say, but he had to, which prevented him from having to speak at all.

Virgil used his old driver's license to clear frost from the inside of the windshield. The dashboard was covered with items of potential value that the men had found in the trash, including a headless Barbie doll and a one-legged GI Joe that Taylor put into sexual positions. Virgil shifted to first and the truck jerked forward.

Taylor finished his coffee. He held the brim with his teeth so that the cup covered his nose and mouth. He nuzzled Dewey, grunting like a hog. Dewey slapped the cup away, flinging coffee dregs through the cab.

"Goddam it, Dewdrop," said Taylor. "You got something against hogs?"

"No. Just that you ain't one's all."

"You saying I ain't a hog?"

Dewey nodded.

"Then what am I?"

"You know what you are."

"He's a cuckolder," Rundell said.

"Did you call me a cuckolder?" Taylor said.

"Sure did."

"Think I ort to let him get away with that, Dewey? Calling me a cuckolder, by God."

"I don't know," Dewey said. "Maybe not if he called you it twice."

"He's a cuckolder," Rundell said.

"He done it," Taylor said.

"I'd not let him call you three cuckolders," Dewey said. "He's lucky it ain't me he's calling one. I ain't never held nobody's but my own."

"No," Virgil said. "The world's lucky you ain't one."

"What is one anyhow?" Taylor said.

"Well," Rundell said. "A cuckolder is what you're give up to be half the time."

"Hell, it must mean drink whisky," Taylor said.

"No," Rundell said. "It more or less means a man who fucks another man's wife."

Virgil rounded a curve and junk slid along the dashboard. Last year's leaves still clung to the hardwoods, while the maples were beginning to bud. Ground fog rose as if drawn by a fan.

"Well," Virgil said. "Nobody here's married except Rundell, and I'd say Taylor ain't got him worried too bad."

"That's right," Rundell said. "The old lady'd shoot him for looking at her funny."

"What does she use to shoot with?" Taylor said.

"Ever what's laying handy."

"Good woman," Taylor said. "They mostly favor them small calibers that ain't good for naught but beer cans and squirrel."

"You know why that is?" Rundell said.

"Weaker sex takes a puny pistol, I guess."

"For a man says he knows as many women as you do, you sure don't know a lot about them."

"What are you saying?"

"Reason women shoot little guns," Rundell said, "is it's men who teach them to shoot. Not many a man wants to give his woman a gun that'll put him down. Me, I trust my wife and she can handle any gun in the county."

Virgil turned at a long building that housed married students. A narrow lane behind it held rows of overflowing garbage cans. The men left the truck and Virgil eased forward until Dewey signaled him to stop. He and Taylor emptied cans into the hopper.

Rundell walked ahead of the truck, checking the garbage for buckets of paint and old motor oil, neither of which they picked up. His primary job was to set the pace. This was dependent on the condition of the men—the worse off they were, the faster the pace. The trick, he'd explained to Virgil, was in figuring out how to cover your own ass while covering the men's, too. That was the whole key to being crew boss, he'd said, that and making them work.

Virgil had spent two years taking courses while working part-time at maintenance, but hadn't fit in with the students. An hour after sitting in a classroom, he'd be on his knees in front of the same building, painting the curb yellow. The majority of students came from the surrounding counties and tried to conceal their hill-bred traits, a doomed enterprise since everyone recognized not only the habits but the attempts to hide them. Virgil's presence was a reminder of what they wanted to leave behind.

His decision to quit school and stay in garbage perplexed everyone. What Virgil enjoyed was that no trash man could pretend he was more than what he was. Education was like a posthole digger, a good tool, very expensive, but worthless unless you needed postholes dug.

Rundell was moving fast and it wasn't just because of Taylor being drunk. Emptying dumpsters was the sole chore for the day, which meant the sooner they finished, the sooner they could loaf. Garbage was impossible to fake like other jobs, because once it was picked up, you were done. As Dewey said, "If folks don't want to put out their garbage, you can't stop them."

People left the apartment building for school. Each time a woman drove past, Taylor smiled and waved, but couldn't draw a glance. An old Nova went past, its big engine rumbling. A suspension kit had been added and the back end rocked gently over dips in the gravel road. Chrome mags flashed silver inside each tire.

"A loud-looker, ain't she," Taylor said.

"Wonder what's under the hood."

"I was talking about the driver," Taylor said. "I'd eat a mile of her shit just to see where it came from. Wouldn't you?"

"Don't reckon."

"Why? You got something against eating shit?"

"More or less."

"What are you, stuck up?"

"Yeah," said Virgil, "I'm the first stuck-up garbageman to ever walk the earth."

"There wasn't nothing snobby about your brother. You ever hear about the time me and him went to the bootlegger for a couple of half-pints?"

Virgil shook his head. This was the first time that Taylor had talked about Boyd since the funeral. Virgil knew they'd buddied all over the hills for a spell. Boyd had a way of using people up. He ran with a man until he'd out-wilded him, then he'd go on to the next restless boy from the darkest hollow or longest ridge. Every season he extended his range, like an animal hunting food. His former running buddies included the incarcerated, the dead, and the recently religious.

Taylor talked around his cigarette.

"It was me and Boyd and another boy name of Hack Johnson. Nobody much liked Hack on account of him dropping a tree on a man while they was logging. But Boyd, he just never went in the woods with him. I was up front with Hack. Boyd sat in the back with a brand-new coonhound that Hack was afraid to leave at home and get stole.

"We pulled up to the bootlegger and around the corner come the biggest German shepherd you ever did see. Blacker than the ace of spades. Hollering to beat hell. It was jumping at the window, tearing at the side of the car. That coonhound went right back at it. It was standing in Boyd's lap, just filling the car with racket. I thought the window was going to bust out.

"We didn't know what to do. We couldn't get our whisky with that dog out there. Boyd told Hack to let the dogs fight, but Hack said no. Said that dog had cost him a hundred bucks and a good .38 to boot, and he wished he had that pistol now, he'd shoot that shepherd. He asked if me or Boyd had a gun but we didn't.

"After a while, that coonhound started slowing down its barking in the back seat. So did the shepherd. When the coonhound stopped, the shepherd went back to the bootlegger. I looked back to see what made it stop, and there set Boyd jacking that dog off. Calmed it right down, by God. I started laughing, but Hack, he got mad. Said it would ruin the dog for breeding.

"Ol' Boyd, he got mad right back. Told Hack, he said, 'Go fetch that fucking whisky before I have to reach up there and do you like this dog.' Well, Hack jumped out of that car like he'd got set on fire.

He came back with the whisky and Boyd said to put that dog in the trunk. Hack didn't want to. Boyd told him now that he'd gotten a taste for dog, he might just want some more, and Hack started driving fast, saying let's get away from that shepherd first. He pulled over at the first wide spot. That coonhound was laying in a circle asleep and there set Boyd with half his liquor gone already. He had that big grin on him. Hack picked up his dog and Boyd looked at it and said 'Bye, honey' and Hack got so tickled he like to dropped that damn dog. He put it in the trunk.

"We finished that whisky and went and got some more and drove all over hell and back and finally Hack asked Boyd what made him think to jack that dog off. Boyd, he just sat there a minute. 'Give me a cigarette and I'll say,' he told Hack. Hack was the only one with smokes left and he didn't like to give them up. He'd served two years in the pen over killing that man with a tree and the only change in him when he come out was getting stingy with a cigarette. Well, he gave me and Boyd both one and that was like a flat miracle for Hack.

"Boyd opened his second pint and threw the lid out the window. He took a pull. He lit that cigarette. Said one time he'd been over to Mount Sterling drinking in a rough little bar and there was a boy wanted to fight him something awful. The boy was bad drunk. Nobody liked him. Said this old boy just kept swinging and missing and staggering, and Boyd hit him a couple of times but it was like hitting a cow. Didn't do no good. Then the boy got a lick in and made Boyd mad. Boyd, he picked up a beer bottle by the neck and busted it and held the jagged part out at the guy. The bartender came up then and said to Boyd, 'Hey, there's people in here barefoot.' Boyd set the busted glass down and somebody took the little drunk outside. Boyd said he couldn't sit down because he'd got a hard-on like a prybar jammed in sideways and hung on his underwear. Said when that dog started barking, he remembered all that. It just made sense to help the dog out that way.

"We ended up wrecking that night. Run into the creek and not a one hurt. Killed the dog, though. Drowned it. Hack never did blame your brother. He knowed it wasn't Boyd's fault, same as Hack falling a tree on that man wasn't no fault of his."

Taylor stood by like a clock run down from all the talking. His clothes didn't fit right and he was moving inside them, his body twitching like a horse shaking off flies. There was a lit cigarette in his mouth and he started to light it again. The pupils of both his eyes were big.

"What are you on?" Virgil said. "Trucker pills?"

"You want some?"

Virgil shook his head.

"Boyd didn't like speed either," Taylor said. "He was an acid man. You know what he said to me once. Said 'I want to improve reality, not see more of it.' Best buddy I had. Crazier than a three-balled tomcat."

Virgil drove to the next dormitory on their route and waited for the crash of garbage cans. About ten men had told him that Boyd was their best buddy. At first Virgil thought it was just what got said when a man died, but after a while he understood that they really meant it. Boyd's directness endeared him to people who'd become accustomed to being discarded, but he'd never had a best friend. The closest was Virgil when they were kids, and that was an accident they'd both got stuck with.

They'd shared a long, narrow room in the attic of their parents' house. Virgil thought monsters lived up there, and Boyd always went first, racing up the steps to the light switch, spinning rapidly at the head of the stairs to dispel the monsters and ensure his brother's safe passage. Even then, Virgil had been glad that Boyd was the oldest and such chores fell to him.

After their father died of emphysema brought on by a lifetime of breathing coal dust beneath the earth, Boyd had never held a regular job. He stayed at home with their mother. It was as if there were two Boyds. One obeyed his mother, hauling water and splitting stovewood, supplying fresh meat in fall and fish in summer. The other Boyd existed away from the house. He never came home drunk, bloody, hung over, or mad.

The sun moved into the lane of sky between the hills, spreading heat along the hollow. Rundell increased the pace in order to finish before breaking to eat. Like hunters, the men functioned best on empty bellies.

In midafternoon, Virgil drove off campus to the Dairy Queen on the edge of town. Taylor drank pop and ordered French fries for Dewey as a reward for having punched his timecard. The other men ate sandwiches brought from home. They sat at a picnic table in the warm sun, watching the occasional car go by. Beside them trees grew at angles from the steep-sloped hill. A dove called.

"You know," Taylor said, "my mamaw could hear an owl of the night and tell you who was going to die and when. She was part Choctaw."

"Which part?" Rundell said.

"You know what I mean."

"Yeah, I do," Rundell said. "I never worked with a man yet who didn't claim to be part Indian. How about you, Dewey?"

"My papaw always said he had a little Indian in him," Dewey said. "When I was a kid, I begged him to show him to me."

The sound of an engine grew louder. The men looked toward the road, where a pickup stopped abruptly, its tires leaving long skid marks on the blacktop. The driver poked his arm from the window, fired a pistol three times in their direction, and drove away.

"What in the Sam Hill?" Rundell said.

"Oh, shit," Dewey said.

"Anybody know that truck?" Virgil said.

"Warning shots," Taylor said.

"Had to be," Rundell said. "I can throw a rock straighter than he shoots."

"By God," Dewey said, "he's lucky he ain't killed me. I'd a killed him back, by God."

"Boys," Taylor said, "I reckon I know what all that was over, and don't none of you'uns have a thing to worry on."

"Who does?" Virgil said. "You?"

Taylor ran his tongue behind his lower lip, making it swell like a fuzz worm. He lifted his cap and settled it back to his head, clamping hair from his eyes.

"Yup," he said. "I carried a girl of his off like a cat does a kitten up to Jeff Mountain. Reckon I was lucky not to get her drawers down."

"Goddam, Taylor," Rundell said. "I don't know what to think about a man gets his work buddies shot at and sets there eating lunch big as day."

"Yeah," Dewey said. He shoved his meal off the table to the ground. "Them bullets took the belly timber plumb out of me."

"You ain't going to eat that?" Taylor said.

"I couldn't eat pie right now."

"You act like you was town-raised."

Taylor retrieved the container of French fries from the dirt. He picked through them like a carpenter gleaning lumber, holding them to the light, tossing some aside, keeping the good ones. When he chewed, the bill of his cap moved up and down.

"We ort to find another hiding place," Rundell said. "Getting shot at sort of hurts this one awhile."

"How about the ballfield," Virgil said.

"Ag farm," Dewey said.

"Freshman girls' dorm," Taylor said.

They debated their favorite places to park the truck and wait out the day until Rundell made the decision and they went to the landfill. At the end of the shift they drove back to their loading dock, where the Big Boss appeared as if dumped from a boot.

"Got a call from the sheriff," he said. "Said shots got fired at the Dairy Queen. Said you and your men were there. Said it was oh-two-hundred in the after-damn-noon."

"We took a late lunch," Rundell said.

"Who was it shooting?"

"None of my men."

"Where were you?"

"Outside eating."

"How many men are at work on this crew?"

"Oh," Rundell said, "about half."

No one spoke. Each man found something to study—his boots, his hands, the hilltops beyond the lot. The Big Boss finally chuckled.

"I don't believe the Dairy Queen is a suitable place for lunch," he said.

Rundell nodded and the Big Boss walked away with one hand clasping the other behind his back. He reminded Virgil of a kid trying to hide a cigarette. As soon as he was gone, Taylor spat.

"Short little fucker, ain't he," he said.

"You best keep your timecard in good shape," Rundell said. "He'll be watching us now."

"He can go to hell. I never met a boss I liked."

"He ain't near bad as most," Rundell said. "You're the first I ever heard of who got shot at on the job. Maybe you should ask for hazard pay."

"We all should," Virgil said. "I don't need no bullets hitting me. How about you, Dewey?"

"I done been shot once," Dewey said. "Bullet cut a crease in me big enough to lay a finger in."

"Where at?" Virgil said.

"In the ass," Taylor shouted. "Go ahead, Virgil. Lay your finger in it."

Expecting retribution, Taylor backstepped rapidly and stumbled into the cement block wall. "Damn it, boys," he said. "Just when I get over my damn hangover, I have to go and make my head hurt again. You're right, Rundell. Just working with me is a hazard on my ownself."

The men laughed and Rundell rose from the loading dock. As one, they walked around the building to punch their timecards.

3

A fierce hailstorm in May marked the boundary between spring and summer. Ice fell from the sky in blurs of white that beat tobacco beds to shreds. The storm's passage left hailstones pooled in low spots of the earth. A few hours later the sun returned and summer began. Kentucky turned thick and heavy with green, as if the world weighed more.

At his mother's house, Virgil entered the old smokehouse that was now a shed. The faint smell of pork still emanated from the dark walls. On an oily workbench sat a car battery, the head of a rake, and a pan full of nuts and screws. Scrap lumber leaned in a corner. He dragged the mower into the yard, jerked the cord, and the engine settled into a steady cycle. The muffler rattled against the engine housing. When Virgil tried to tighten the muffler, it came off in his hand. The threads were stripped. He figured Boyd had some private technique to keep it fastened, a wire in the right spot, or a delicate turn of the threaded end. He found wire in the shed and spent thirty minutes rigging the muffler in place.

The afternoon sun lay above the humped horizon of the hills. Virgil heard a car with an automatic transmission coming up the hill. The sound faded into the curve at the top, then increased along his mother's ridge. The county sheriff parked at the property's edge and strode across the high grass. Troy wore an official hat and jacket with a badge, although the rest of his clothes were casual. The last time he had visited was six years ago, courting Sara.

"Hidy, Virge," he said.

"Troy." Virgil nodded once in greeting. "Any news?"

The sheriff shook his head.

"Your mom home?"

"She stays home, Troy. Don't hardly go nowhere but church. Sara takes her."

"I've seen that before," Troy said. "I'm not much of a churchgoer myself."

"No."

"Me and your brother, we ran together some."

"You were pretty wild before the badge."

"Yeah, buddy. I always remember Boyd telling me what Jesus said to the hillbillies before he died."

"What?"

"'Don't do nothing till I get back.'"

Troy looked up the hillside, where road dust settled onto the brush, forming a patina over each leaf. He wiped his forehead and spat.

"You sure you can't just talk to me," Virgil said. "And let Mommy alone."

Troy stared into the treeline. His tone of voice shifted, as if backing away.

"It's got to be her. Official."

Virgil led him up the plank steps and across the rain-grayed porch.

In the front room of the small house a bare bulb lit framed photographs of Boyd and their father. On the other walls hung pictures of Sara, Marlon, and their children. There would be no pictures of Virgil until he produced kids or died.

Sara came into the room, blocking light from the kitchen.

"I warn you, Troy," she said. "I ain't going peaceable."

The sheriff laughed.

"How Debbie could stand being married to a man mean as you I don't know," Sara said. "Has she had that baby yet?"

"Three more weeks, Sara. She's doing fine."

"And you?"

"Same."

"I meant about having kids."

"Don't bother me," Troy said. "I told her we'd quit whenever she wanted."

"Sounds like you changed some."

Troy's face turned red and he closed his mouth. When he spoke, his voice had shifted again, as if he'd stepped behind an invisible wall.

"I'm here to see your mom, Sara. Need to talk to her direct. You all can be present, but it's got to be her."

Sara looked quickly at Virgil, who shrugged. She brought their mother into the front room.

"Mrs. Caudill," Troy said.

"Hidy, Troy. You're too late. She's been married nigh five years."

"Could be I'm up to court you this time."

Her face softened briefly.

"Law says one at a time, Troy. You get the divorce, then come back."

"Yes, ma'am." He removed his hat. "I just wanted to tell you that the investigation is open and ongoing. At this time we have no suspects. We have no evidence and no weapon. What we have got is more rumor than an oak's got acorns, and it all points to a man named Billy Rodale. He's been questioned. He denies it. There's nothing I can do."

The sheriff slowed his words, careful to look only at Virgil's mother.

"No one is willing to testify, Mrs. Caudill. You know how it is.

People keep their mouths shut in a situation like this. If something happened to Rodale, people would stay quiet on that, too. If there's no witness or weapon, I couldn't do nothing about him, either. The person who did it would probably not get hisself caught."

He stood and held his hat in both hands.

"I'm speaking for myself now, Mrs. Caudill. I feel terrible about it. All of it. But the law can't do a thing."

Virgil followed him to the porch. The sheriff avoided his eyes as he walked across the yard. He drove out the ridge and Virgil watched the road dust rise like smoke.

In the house, Sara and his mother sat on the couch. No one spoke. Virgil saw in their eyes what they wanted him to do. He left the house.

He started the mower and worked slowly because the grass was high, lifting the front wheels to prevent stalling. He mowed steadily, following the pattern he'd learned from his father—mark the perimeter first, then work inside it. He'd learned to paint a wall the same way. He wondered where the urge came from to delineate the edges of everything, to make maps and build fences.

He eased the mower along the edge of the hill, swerving instinctively for a tree that wasn't there. He wondered if someone had cut it down, but there was no stump. Sweat stung his eyes and his wet shirt clung to his back. He got his bearings, which seemed ridiculous in his own yard, and saw the tree. It was in front of him, four feet over the hill, surrounded by ground cover. The tree was bigger but he recognized the angle of its growth. As a child he had pushed the mower on the other side of the tree, but now there was no grass near. He was stunned to realize that the hill was falling slowly away.

He shut off the mower and rested in shade. The raucous sound of the engine had hushed the birds, and the abrupt silence made his ears ring. The acrid smell of the septic tank drifted on a breeze. If the very earth could shift, anything could.

The sound of a car engine drew his attention, and he placed it as Abigail's big Ford. He'd known Abigail all his life. They'd dated in high school but she had married the star quarterback of Eldridge County High and moved to Ohio. He drank and beat her, a secret she'd kept until the day she arrived at her mother's house with a carload of belongings. She'd taken a two-year course in accounting and now worked in the payroll department of Rocksalt Community College.

For the past four years, everyone in Blizzard figured she and Virgil would get married. Virgil went along with the idea. She would marry him if he asked, and they'd talked about it in an oblique fashion, but he didn't ask. He couldn't, although he wanted to. He wouldn't ask until he knew what held him back in the first place.

He tightened the muffler and returned the lawnmower to the shed. A bobwhite emitted its three-note call. He inhaled the scent of dusk, the coming dew. Katydids creaked like old bedsprings. Lightning bugs made a trail of yellow specks in the dimming air. He and Boyd used to wait until they blinked, then pull their bodies apart and smear the glowing mush on their faces.

Virgil leaned against the back door, dreading entry and supper. From inside came the rising laughter of Abigail, his sister, and his mother. It struck him that half his life happened when he wasn't around. While he washed his hands for supper, Marlon arrived, having left the kids at an aunt's house. Virgil stood in the kitchen door and watched him with the women. Marlon had more of a place in the house than Virgil did.

Sara noticed Virgil in the doorway.

"There he is," she said. "Poop-head's here."

"Yard mowed?" Abigail said.

"You know the hill's going over the hill out there."

"No," Abigail said. "I didn't know that."

Everyone waited for him to continue.

"This house," Virgil said, "is a good six feet closer to the edge of the hill than it used to be."

Marlon stomped on the floor, frowning as he gauged the walls.

"Foundations ain't twisted," he said, "or the windowglass'd be broke. I'd say the house'll last awhile yet."

"But will the hill?" Virgil said.

He sat at the metal-rimmed formica table. The ceramic salt and pepper shakers were a hen and rooster that leaned against each other.

"You sure get funny thinking in that head of yours," Sara said. "Reckon when the hill went over? Last night?"

"No. Sort of slow and steady for twenty years."

"We all been going over it for twenty years."

"Yes," their mother said, "and it'll be going over us for many a year more."

Abigail removed a tray of cornbread from the oven. The smell washed through the room like mist.

"Glad I ain't from off," she said. "People from off don't know how to do."

"I wouldn't know," Sara said. "You're the only one here who's left out of here."

"Worst thing I ever did was leave."

"Well, you came back. I know one man's glad of it."

Sara looked at Virgil with an expectant expression.

"I'm real glad," he said.

"Set and eat," their mother said. "You'uns put a bottom to your stomach."

They gathered at the table, which held pieces of fried chicken lying on the brown paper of a grocery bag. The heavy plates were veined by a network of fine cracks. They ate without talk, as if at work, and Virgil remembered that the back and neck had been his father's favorite pieces. The family rule was that whoever ate them also received the delicacies—liver, heart, and gizzard. Everyone took a second piece and Virgil's mother served the neck to Marlon. Virgil wished he were in his trailer eating a frozen pot pie.

"Any dessert?" Marlon said.

"Not tonight," Sara said. She patted her hips. "I don't need no extra."

"Just more to love," Marlon said.

"Kids sure packs the weight on," Sara said. "You all fixing to have any, Ab?"

Virgil could feel heat rush to his face. Abigail pitched her voice slightly higher in order to appear casual.

"We haven't done any talking along those lines."

Marlon was clearly confused. He looked from Virgil to Abigail and back. "You all go and get married?"

"No," Virgil said. "Folks do that for different reasons."

"I was pregnant," Sara said.

"Sara!" her mother said.

"Well, I was. The whole hill knowed of it. I told Virgil first, before Marlon even. If our family's got secrets, you can't prove it by me."

"She always did talk worser than a jaybird," their mother said.

"Nobody's pregnant," Virgil said. "Unless it's you."

"We're done, ain't that right, Marlon. I'm thinking on getting my tubes tied."

"Sara," their mother said, "you're at the table."

"It's on TV, Mama. And I ain't no jaybird, either. I'm the only liberated woman on the creek. I cuss in my own home and Marlon don't care if I do."

"Around here," their mother said, "they ain't no liberated nothing. Why, even these old hills got laws put to them anymore."

"My opinion," Virgil said, "Abigail's on the liberated side. She works and takes care of her own car."

"And lives alone," Sara said.

"That's right," Virgil said. "But she don't go around talking about getting herself spayed, either."

"Leastways, I'm thinking on doing something I should."

"Meaning I ain't. Is that what you're trying to say?"

"Take it any way you want."

Virgil stood and went outside, leaving a tense silence behind him. The sky was gray between the hills. He wondered what kind of person his family thought he was. Perhaps they'd never had him right. He realized with a terrible twist in his chest that they wanted him to be like Boyd.

He lay on his back and studied the sky. The Milky Way spread overhead like the partial covering of spring frost. Some stars were so far away that by the time the light got to him, they'd already burned out. Boyd was like that. Even dead, he still threw energy into the hills.

Darkness grew at the head of the hollow and filtered down the creek. The air between the trees closed. He stood and kicked one of Boyd's old liquor bottle lids. It rolled in a circle like a crippled dog. A hundred years from now some kid would find the cap and make up its history. Virgil wished he could invent a new history for himself, or even better, a future.

The screen door rasped and he recognized Sara's tread on the porch.

"Hey, Virgie," she said.

He waited in the dark. He'd discovered long ago that the less talking he did around his sister, the more he learned.

"You out here pouting?" she said.

There was nothing for him in that except bait. He stayed quiet.

"Now, Virgie, honey. It ain't but us now. We got to get along."

A whippoorwill's call floated along the ridge. Sara moved into the yard.

"I should have been born a man," she said. "Then you could knock the shit out of me and everything'd be fine."

"That's easy talk," Virgil said. He immediately regretted having spoken.

"I know what's right."

"You don't know the first thing about it."

"I've laid awake many a night thinking on it."

"Me, too," Virgil said. "I ain't a murderer."

"That ain't what it is."

"The hell it ain't, Sara. That's exactly what it is. You know it, Mommy knows it, even that damn Troy knows it."

"If you don't," she said, "I know someone who will."

"You'd do that, wouldn't you. Just throw Marlon away. A man with four kids."

"You heard what Troy said."

"I ain't talking about the law."

"The rest of them Rodales, you mean. Well, you never can tell. Maybe they're more like you."

"You're full of talk, Sara. You know that? You just sit in your house, watch TV, and not do a goddam thing else. Just talk. You're the same as you always were only now you got Marlon and the kids to run. Well, you ain't the boss of me, Sara. Get that in your head."

"I thought maybe you'd want Marlon to help you out, is all. You always let Boyd do the doing for you before."

"That's not what I want. I don't want nothing like that."

"All right. Marlon don't know about any of this anyhow."

"No, I don't reckon he would."

"Ain't no sense in you getting stubbed up over it, either. I was thinking of you. Trying to spare you."

A dove called through the woods.

"I guess it's good you ain't a man," Virgil said. "I don't believe I'd like you much if you were."

"Maybe not. But liking never had much place in this family. All we ever did was love."

"And the best of us is gone."

"That's the way it always is, ain't it. The biggest tree gets hit by lightning, and bugs chew the prettiest flower. It's the way of the world."

"If it's so natural, then how come you're wanting me to do something about it."

"Because that's natural, too."

She had answered gently, as if speaking to a lover or a child. She stepped into the house, boards creaking beneath her feet. The night enveloped him like a tent. A barred owl called, his favorite bird, and Virgil mimicked the sound. Boyd had taught him to follow the rhythm of "Who cooks for you, who cooks for you all," as he made the sound, ending with a throaty gurgle. The owl refused to return the cry.

The woods were silent until the first squeak of cricket, followed by young frogs in the creek below and the rising drone of cicadas. He inhaled the heavy scent of summer earth, a loamy musk that settled over him like a caul. He was home.

Abigail sat in the swing at the end of the porch. He hadn't heard her leave the house. He joined her and the chain creaked as their knees touched. In the dim light from the house, he could see the silhouette of her powerful chin. It was like a handle for her head. He wondered if she appreciated any of his features as much as he enjoyed that chin.

"Virge." Her voice was low and calm.

He didn't answer.

"Your mom told me about Troy coming up here."

"Don't say nothing to nobody."

"You don't have to tell me," she said. "All this is a hard one on your mom."

"I know it."

"And for you, too, Virge."

Starlight slipped between tree limbs and glowed across the yard. Abigail had a quality that always made him feel less of a man, and he suddenly knew what it was. Abigail was happy, and he resented it. He felt as if they were in seventh grade again, trying to outmaneuver each other for the one thing they both wanted—a kiss. When it finally happened he pressed his lips so hard against hers that he mashed his nose and couldn't breathe. She whispered for him to open his mouth, and he realized that she knew more than he did.

"Troy coming up here was wrong," she said.

"Well, it wasn't right."

"That's the same thing."

"Not exactly."

"I don't want to fight with you, Virgil."

"I know you don't. This whole thing has got me messed up. Right and wrong are gone. Nobody cares about that anymore, not even the sheriff."

"You do," Abigail said. "I know you do."

"It'd be easier if I didn't. People might leave me alone."

"Is that what you want?"

"I don't mean you."

They didn't speak for a few minutes. The swinging chain made a steady rasp. A dog barked over the hill, its cry rising up the hollow and fading along the ridge.

"I have some good news, anyway," Abigail said.

"That'd be a switch."

"I got a promotion and a raise."

Virgil didn't know what to say. She already drew a bigger paycheck than he did.

"Well," she said. "Aren't you going to ask me how much?"

"How much?"

"Enough to get into a house with some land. We could use your money for fixing up."

"Fixing what up?"

"You know, box in a porch if we needed extra bedrooms or something."

Virgil wondered what the cutoff age was to join the army. He knew a lot of boys who had gone years ago but he couldn't see the point if there wasn't a war.

"It's just something to think on," she said. "I thought maybe it'd be better than this other."

"I'm about run out of thinking."

"I understand. I know how that is. I got the same way up in Ohio. You hit a certain place and there's nothing left but doing."

"I ain't there yet. I'm more in between."

"I want you to know something, Virgil. You have to hear me on this. Whichever way you go, I'm with you. I'm there. You do whatever you need to do—for yourself. Don't matter to me. I'm on your side."

Virgil nodded.

"I got to get on down the road," she said. "Tell your mom I said good night."

She rose awkwardly from the swing, setting it in sideways motion. She leaned to kiss him and left. The big engine spewed exhaust that stayed in the air after her red taillights vanished among the trees.

She wasn't against it, which meant she was for it. Abigail was trying to play cagey, but tonight was the first time she'd been direct about children. Perhaps she was trying to snare him when he was preoccupied with other matters—murder or marry, like a judge who tells a drunk to do the time or take the cure. He wondered if she would continue to love him if he became a killer; it wasn't as if he could quit and change back, like giving up liquor.

A half moon hung low above the hills, its light washing away the surrounding stars. The hills were black and the woods were blacker and the hollow below was blackest of all. Virgil had always been able to see well at night. It was more recognition than actual sight, the ability to know forms by their silhouette. Most people treated night the same as day only with less light, which was a mistake. The secret to darkness was not to blunder about, but to look carefully at what was there.

Marlon came onto the porch, trailed by Sara's voice saying, "Shut that door behind you tight."

Moths the size of a man's hand battered the screen. Marlon lit a cigarette, handling the matches in a deft fashion. Both men were quiet. Marlon cast a field about him that made people uneasy, but Virgil was accustomed to it.

"Sara send you out here?" Virgil said.

"Yep."

"They tell you about Troy?"

"He's so crooked he screws his britches on."

"Whole thing's about eat my head up, Marl."

A soft rain spattered the tree leaves and moved across the night. The evening air became damp.

"Some rain," Virgil said. "We could use a gully washer."

"Way them women talk we can always use more of something."

"Full of plans, ain't they."

"For other people," Marlon said. "They'll lay their ears back like a cat eating, and knock you down with talk. A man can't pay that much mind. It's like weeding a garden to me."

"How's that?"

"Just pick what to listen at."

"Wish I could, Marl. That's a gift."

"Not really."

"I'm stuck with hearing all of it."

"Make your head go crazy that way."

"I ain't that far from it. You know what I'd really like, I'd like to be left alone."

"Get that long enough and you'll not like it."

"Maybe so. Is there anything you'd like, Marlon?"

"Learn to weld."

"Weld?"

"Open me up a muffler shop."

Virgil nodded, wishing he was as clearheaded and free of guile as his brother-in-law. Marlon was loyal and hardworking, and there was no higher compliment in the county.

"Let me ask you something," Marlon said. "Ever notice how an oak'll hold on to a fall leaf through winter?"

"Now that you say it, yes."

"That old tree not wanting to turn loose of a dead leaf. Something to think on, Virge."

Marlon went in the house and a few minutes later came out with Sara. They said good night and got into Marlon's truck, sitting very close on the bench seat. In the brief flash of the domelight, they looked as they had five years ago, leaving on a date. They were a little bigger now, including the truck.

Moonglow lay over the darkened land. Virgil recalled evenings he'd stood with Boyd on the porch, trying to watch darkness arrive. Boyd had thought that each molecule of air became darker and, like watching snow accumulate, you could witness the actual blackening of the sky.

Virgil could not leave without telling his mother good night, but if he sat outside long enough, she would go to bed and he'd be free to go. She came to the door. Interior light spread her shadow across the porch, diffused by the screen. Her hair was pulled to the back of her head in a bun the color of ash. Virgil knew that she would wait there until she was invited out. He'd seen it with his father many times.

"Come on out, Mom."

"Well, if you're wanting company."

"Always yours."

"I ain't a-caring, then."

She stepped onto the porch and quickly pulled the door shut. She sat in her chair, picked up the fly swatter that lay beside it, and placed it in her lap.

"I shouldn't ort to have set," she said. "I don't know how I'll get up."

"I'll start to get worried the day I find you sleeping there in the morning."

"You remember the time Sara's first cat got up in the yard oak and she started crying."

"We was all just kids," Virgil said.

"Boyd, he told her to hush up, that cat would come down and he could prove it."

"I don't remember that part."

"Oh, yes. He said you could walk these hills a hundred years and there'd be one thing you'd never find—a cat skeleton in a tree."

"That sounds like how he'd think."

A chimney swift flew in an arc away from the house. The air cooled. The night had softened, as if settling into itself until dawn.

"You know your daddy weren't no coward."

"No."

"It took more spine to go under them hills than it ever did to stand up to a bully. They ain't a miner who ain't brave."

"I know."

"Boyd never understood that. He seen your daddy take mouth off other men and walk away cold. Boyd thought your daddy less for it. It hurt your daddy, but it hurt Boyd more."

"It would."

"You're a cross between both."

"I always thought I was more like Daddy."

"No. Boyd's temper is worse, but you got more anger in you. My fault I reckon."

"No sense worrying about it now, Mom."

"Maybe not. All depends on what use a body's got for packing anger around."

"Not too much, I don't reckon."

"At the right time it can be handy as a pocket on a shirt."

"It never was for Boyd."

"I ain't talking about him."

Virgil suddenly knew what she meant. The steady creaking of the swing's chains stopped. He stared into the night. It seemed to him as if his body were a shell that his mind had fled, and he was observing the proceedings from some distance. Two people sat on a porch. Their world was not vast.

"Marlon is a good boy," his mother said, "but a blind man can see through him. A part of me always wished Sara had married Troy. Tonight was the first I ever was glad of her not. You understand why, don't you."

"I might." Virgil had hopes one way, but the biggest part of him had fears the other. "I don't know."

"After Troy come up here the way he done, it would look pretty bad later if he was married in."

The roof of Virgil's mouth was dry and he was breathing through his mouth, trying to take deep drinks of the night. There was a certain point at the bottom of his lungs that needed oxygen. He stood, and when the swing bumped the back of his knees, he nearly fell. He began to tremble. He steadied himself against a porch strut and stepped off the porch. His mother was a dark lump in the shadow of the porch.

The moon was gone and clouds blocked the stars. He walked into the darkness. The road made a sharp climbing curve to his trailer at the end of the ridge, surrounded by trees. He sat on the bottom step. He was cold but the air was warm. His clothes wrapped his body, and skin was just a bag that stretched to hold different sizes of people. Inside they were the same bunch of bones.

4

Divorce Court sat beside Clay Creek in the widest hollow of the county. A network of gravel lanes held a hundred identical trailers that Rocksalt Community College rented to older students, many of them divorced. Virgil and the garbage crew had worked hard all morning. Gravel dust rose in their wake and settled over every surface like hoarfrost. Mist trailed above the creek that bordered the road.

Beyond Divorce Court, separated by a few trees and a rail fence, was the old drive-in movie lot. During its final summer of operation, the owner had showed X-rated movies. Cars jammed the lot. Everyone had come to see naked flesh twenty-five feet high gyrating among the dark hills. The first week, four cars ran off the road as they drove by. There were nine wrecks the following week, including two preachers and a nun from the new hospital. The movie got held over, and was known as the nun-wrecker. X-rated movies were eventually banned and the movie screen poked like a giant tombstone between the hills.

Taylor stopped working to dig through an immense pile of boxes. He found a pair of boots, a box of shotgun shells, and a metal water pipe. From a cardboard box, he pulled a gun cleaning kit.

"Brand new," he said. "Never used."

"Somebody must be moving on," Rundell said.

"I believe so."

Taylor held a plastic picture frame made to look like wood. The glass was broken. Behind it was a picture of a man and a woman. The photographer had used a special effect to nestle the couple's faces inside a long-stemmed glass with a rose at its base. The man's picture was slashed. Taylor studied the woman in the photograph.

"My opinion," Taylor said, "some old boy just got his ass throwed out."

"It's our stuff now," Dewey said.

"That ain't all that's up for taking." Taylor used his fingers to comb his hair. He read the address off the side of the trailer. "Twelve Two-W. I'm getting me some strange."

He carried what he'd culled from the garbage to the truck cab and slid it behind the seat. Virgil steered to an overhang of silver maples that turned their soft-bellied leaves to the breeze. The trees seemed dusted by snow. With the truck engine off, the silence was a weight pressing against Virgil. He'd felt it before, a heaviness as if he were compressed in deep water. The summer air produced a sodden force that cloaked sound and motion. You could yell and the moisture trapped your voice and held it tight.

The men carried their lunches to shade along the creek. Taylor didn't eat, preferring his thermos of spiked coffee, cigarettes, and amphetamines.

"Say, Rundell," Taylor said. "You been underly?"

"No, I feel fine."

"Looks like you got the furniture disease." Taylor tapped Rundell's big belly. "Your chest done fell into your drawers."

Rundell knocked Taylor's hand away and rubbed his gut. His flannel shirt was thin and faded as an old snake skin. Taylor laughed until the sound turned to a rasp. He cleared his lungs and spat a hocker the size of a pawpaw. He found his cigarette where he'd dropped it.

"A good cough is like running a snake down a drain, ain't it," he said. "Sure makes a cigarette taste right."

He dipped his hands in the creek and scrubbed his fingers and face. He broke several twigs from a sassafras tree, peeled the bark, and rubbed the inner meat over his teeth and gums. He combed his hair without removing his hat.

"I'm heading on over to Twelve Two-W," Taylor said. "That woman's a-setting there waiting on me to come take a bite out of her."

"Best tuck your shirt in," Rundell said.

Taylor obeyed. He was very thin.

"By God, you look like a Christmas turkey," Rundell said. "Plumb full of shit."

"She loves me, boys. I can't help it."

The men watched Taylor saunter into the shimmering noon sun. Tendrils of willow swayed behind him like curtains. Virgil opened his dinner sack. Every morning he stopped by his mother's house for a brown bag containing a sandwich, apple, and chips. She'd fixed him carry-lunches since he was six years old and walked to school with his brother and dog. Virgil went along with it now although he'd explained to her that it was no longer necessary to mark a V on the paper bag in crayon.

"What you got?" Dewey asked him.

"Pickle loaf and government cheese. Want some apple?"

Dewey ate his lunch from an old bread sack. It was the same food every day—leftover breakfast of sausage and biscuit. White grease on the sausage patty made it smooth as wax. Virgil passed the apple to Dewey, who dug his thumbs on either side of the stem, and split it down the middle. He gave the larger piece to Virgil. Rundell ate soupbeans and fatback from a thermos, with a chunk of cornbread.

The muddy creek's bank was strewn with plastic milk jugs and bread sacks.

"Creek's got a bankful," Rundell said.

"Don't it," Dewey said.

"You know that water runs into the ocean."

"I don't reckon."

"Sure as Carter makes little liver pills."

"You ain't telling me there's an ocean close."

"It don't have to be close, Dew. This runs into the Blue Lick River which feeds into the Ohio, and that goes into the Mississippi, and you know where that goes, don't you."

"Goes to Mississippi."

"Well, yeah. But after there, that water runs into the Gulf of Mexico."

"I don't know," Dewey said. "I never heard of no Mexican Ocean."

"It ain't a ocean. It's a gulf."

"Now, no, Rundell. Mexico is a country, ain't it, Virge?"

"Right."

"See there," Dewey said. "No sense in a man who don't know Mexico's a country getting briggety over creek water."

After lunch, Virgil lay beside the creek, listening to it splash against rocks. His father had grown up in an ancient log cabin that was still standing two counties over. It was on a farm that had been willed to another family branch as a means of punishing Virgil's grandfather for slights so trivial that no one recalled them. Virgil had long wanted to buy the cabin. He would dismantle it and move it to a spot beside Clay Creek. He'd rent a minidozer and carve a road that wound through the woods. Virgil had been saving money for five years. He had never told anyone his plans.

"Here he comes back, by God," Rundell said.

Virgil opened his eyes, blinking at the abrupt light. Taylor slung aside willow branches and kicked at a rock.

"Look at him," Rundell said. "Hey, Taylor, ain't you done a little early?"

"She's a goddam prick-tease if ever I saw one," Taylor said. "Wasn't wearing enough clothes to wad a shotgun and stood there like a pullet with her lungs hanging out. I should have slapped the taste out of her mouth."

"Got him a way with women," Rundell said, "don't he?"

"My opinion, she's a damn lebanese."

"Then what was all that man's junk doing laying outside her trailer home?"

"She just don't know it," Taylor said. "Worse kind of lebanese there is. Only knows what she don't want."

"And what she don't want," Virgil said, "is you."

"The worst I ever got was better than any you ever had," Taylor said.

Virgil didn't answer. Taylor talked five quarts to the gallon, but he never fought.

"What you ort to get is some rest," Rundell said.

"I got eternity for that," Taylor said. "Biggest thing I'm afraid of is getting old and regretty. I got me a uncle that way. Sumbitch just sets. Wouldn't hit a lick at a snake. All he talks about is what he never done. About like Virgil's going to be one day."

"I do what I want," Virgil said. As soon as he spoke, he wished he hadn't.

"It's what you don't do that you regret. And they ain't a man of us that don't know what you ain't doing."

"What?" Dewey said. "What don't we not know?"

"That Virge here's letting that boy who killed his brother walk around."

Virgil's insides felt hollowed out.

"The way you act," Taylor said, "they could start picking off the rest of your family. Was me, I'd do some waylaying."

"It ain't you," Virgil said.

"They're lucky it ain't," Taylor said. "Only one thing to think of a man lets his own brother rot without doing nothing. He's chicken, ain't he, Dewey."

"Yellow stripey."

"Cluck," Taylor said. "Cluckety-cluck."

Virgil stood slowly. He was trembling, and sweat rushed down his body. His entire world had shrunk to a narrow cylinder of vision that ended at Taylor. He moved toward Taylor, who took two steps back.

Rundell rose swiftly from the grassy bank.

"Taylor's a damn fool and you know it," Rundell said to Virgil. "Ain't worth the powder it'd take to blow his brains out."

Virgil slowly sidestepped him. Taylor backed away until he was against the trunk of a locust. He arched his back from the sharp thorns that carried its seed. Virgil stopped with his shirt an inch from Taylor's narrow chest. He was eye to eye with the locust thorns above Taylor's head. Birds ate insects that were blown onto the spikes, and after a fierce storm, he'd seen spindled birds eaten by a raccoon. If a wind came big enough to drive the coon into the barbs, he supposed a man would eat the coon. He wondered what animal would eat a man who got hung on the barbs, and the answer surged forward: a man would eat him.

He leaned his face to Taylor's until their noses touched. When he spoke, his lips brushed Taylor's mouth.

"I ain't that hungry yet."

He moved away from Taylor and down the slight slope and stepped into the creek. Water spiders scuttled from his shadow. Crawdads jerked backwards as if yanked by a string. The hollow opened and the creek became shallow, marked by ripples and tiny dams of trash. He walked steadily, his legs wet to mid-thigh. He climbed the bank through a high patch of ragwort. Riled bees flew tight arcs of warning before returning to their work. A frog hopped into the water and Virgil sat on a rock where the frog had been. A ladybug landed on his leg. The air was heavy with the musk of life.

He began to relax in the one place where he felt safe. He'd spent half his childhood in the woods, much of that time with Boyd. Among the oak and maple, pine and hickory, he had a sense of belonging that had always eluded him in the company of people. He tossed a rock into the creek. As a kid he'd supposed that all objects were sentient and had envied rocks their perfect existence. Nothing was expected of them. He and Boyd had spent hours discussing the imagined opinions of a tree, the road, or a cloud. Did a shovel enjoy digging? Did coal mind being burnt? Would a chunk of ash rather be a baseball bat or an ax handle?

The sound of the creek steadied Virgil's thoughts. He remembered Boyd as a child climbing a tree and leaping to a sapling, which bent with his weight and eased him to the earth. Virgil climbed the tree. He stood on the limb for a long time, afraid to jump. Finally he'd climbed to the ground and headed home.

Now a red squirrel watched him from a log gone to peat, then fled through swaying fronds of cinnamon fern. Virgil began walking the creek bank. The air cooled as the hollow narrowed. He reached a split in the creek and took the smaller fork, a trickle that led into darker woods. Trees were huge and ancient, the land being too severe for logging. Birdsong rose and fell around him. The dense canopy allowed sun in a flowing mosaic of darkness and light. The creek ended at a rock wall green with moss and Virgil climbed the hill, following a crescent of pine.

The slope was steep and he moved in a crouch, his body close to the earth, limbs spread like a spider. At the spine of the hill he rested. Though he'd never been here before, he knew where he was. Town lay one direction and the rest of the world the other. He walked four miles along the ridge top before the last of the anger left him.

The smell of wood smoke drew him to a thin column of gray rising from a house. The back door was painted green to ward off witches. He circled the house to approach it from the front and a dog ran at him, barking. A board path was embedded in the yellow clay dirt. There was no grass. The topsoil had been scratched away by chickens, leaving veins of clay that ran between exposed tree roots. Tarpaper covered the house and an oak shoot poked from the roof. Green moss clung like velvet beneath the eaves.

A woman sat on the porch with a pistol in her lap. She stripped the ribs from a wide leaf of tobacco and pushed it in her mouth. Near her chair was a bucket and dipper.

"Where'd you up from?" she said.

"Ridgeline."

"Fall off a train?"

"Walked from town."

"You ain't from there."

"No."

"Who's your people?"

"Caudill."

"Which bunch?"

"Biggest is the yellow-headed bunch. We ain't the holler Caudills, if that's what you want to know. We might be kin five or six grandmaws back, but I don't claim it. My mother was a Cabe."

"I've knowed many a Cabe."

Her slight nod sent a ripple through the wattles of flesh below her chin.

"Could I might have a little water?" Virgil said.

"Drink all ye want." She pushed the bucket to the edge of the porch with her foot. "You'll have to open your shirtfront when you do it."

Virgil unbuttoned his shirt. The dipper was stobbed in three places by whittled pegs. He eased it into the water to avoid bugs that floated on the surface. The woman leaned forward to study his torso as he drank.

"I suspicioned you for a haunt walking out of the woods that way, but you ain't one I don't reckon. Water drains right out of a haunt."

"It does."

"Did you not know that?"

Virgil shook his head.

"They're awful bad to be dodgy, a haunt is. They stick like bark to a tree. Got to be nice by it, get that haunt so it forgets what it is. Then you catch it in a dry gourd. Wax gourd's best. A gourd goes to rattling, it's the haunt trying to out. See there."

She pointed across the earth, the gesture setting to motion the hammocks of flesh below her arm. Four gourds dangled like skulls from a coffee tree. They were small and blanched by weather. Beyond them stood the dark woods.

"You're the first man ever to come up here a-wanting water," she said.

"I had in mind something else."

"Did you." She placed her hand on the pistol. "And what was that?"

"Whisky."

"Whisky's against the law."

"I'm Boyd's brother, Virgil."

The woman lifted her hand from the gun. Her toothless grin was a stretched knothole.

"That damn Boyd was a case," she said. "I heard he's gone under."

Virgil nodded.

"I'll miss him," she said. "Now, Little Boyd, what do you want and how much? I got brown liquor and white."

"Half-pint of ever what he drank."

"I stocked Maker's Mark for him. Never sold it to nobody else. You sure you don't want more?"

"No."

"No you ain't sure, or no you don't want no more."

"One's good."

"It wasn't nothing for your brother to come up here four times a night. I'd leave bottles hid for him in a paper poke. He'd stick money in the poke and go on. That way I'd get me some sleep."

She stepped inside and Virgil wondered where the pistol went. He hadn't seen it disappear. She came from the house carrying three half-pints of bourbon. Red wax covered their lids. She leaned on the porch rail and passed them over, her shoulders humped around her zinc-colored head, making it look small. She waved away his offered money.

"That ain't something you have to do," Virgil said.

"Hush up and take it."

Virgil slipped two bottles in his jacket pocket and opened the third.

"Whoa now, Little Boyd," she said. "I only got one rule—no drinking on the property. That was my daddy's law and his daddy's before that."

"This place was always your all's?"

"No, my daddy, he was from down to Bell County. Kept a still under the house with the chimney running up through the floor and into the flue. That house set right on the state line. If the Tennessee law come on him, he'd just go over to the Kentucky room. And if the Kentucky law got after him, why he'd step into the Tennessee side. They got in cahoots on him once, and that's when he come up here."

The folds of her dress sagged heavily below her right hip. There was a hole in the fabric surrounded by a dark burn and Virgil realized where the pistol was hidden.

"By God, I'm going to break Daddy's rule," she said. "Just talking about that son of a bitch makes me want to."

She went in the house and came back with a jar of white liquor.

"Here's to Boyd," she said. "The whole county's lucky he never got religion. Take a month of Sundays to get him saved."

She drank half the jar off while Virgil took a small sip. She wiped her mouth and spat off the porch.

"Boyd was different," she said. "You couldn't tell if it was something missing or extra. He scared people, but there wasn't no man more loved on this creek. That's what got him killed, my opinion. Men wanted to be his buddy and women wanted him their way. He was like a new paint job on a car—you just had to run a screwdriver over it. People wanted him dead and didn't even know it till he was. He never followed a rule one."

She took a long drink from the jar. The liquor didn't seem to affect her. Brush rattled behind Virgil and he spun, expecting to see a haunt funneling from one of the gourds. A tall man with a big head stepped from the woods. A cap clamped long black hair from his eyes. Most of his teeth were gone. A blacksnake twined his arm like a vine.

"Hidy," he said to Virgil. "I'm Ospie Brownlow's first boy, Ospie Brownlow." He grinned at the woman. "Moses got a rabbit, Mommy. He done it slicker'n owl grease."

"Give him here."

He proffered the snake and it moved from his arm to hers, briefly encircling them in a dark nexus before it dropped to her lap. Its lower jaw hung slack, still unhinged from swallowing its prey.

The woman found a lump the size of a softball several inches behind its head. She placed both feet on the tail, wrapped her hands around its body behind the lump, and squeezed. When she'd gained some slack, she brought her lower hand behind the lump and squeezed again. The snake lunged at her but its lower jaw was useless. Sweat gleamed along her brow and slid down her softly whiskered jaw. She held the snake upright in her lap, its head knobbing the end. Slowly her hands moved up, forcing the lump through the snake's gullet. She closed her eyes, jaw tight, chin tipped back. In a powerful motion, she jerked from the snake a pale clot of fur that thumped to the floor.

The woman was breathing fast and heavy. Her arms hung at her sides, legs splayed wide. The rabbit lay in a crushed heap, bits of bone splitting the reddened fur. It was flat as a mitten.

"Take and wash that good," she said to Ospie. "Then skin it out. Ain't nothing wrong with the meat."

He picked up the dead rabbit casually, as though it was something misplaced, and walked around the house.

"I purely do like rabbit," she said. "Ospie, he ain't safe with a gun and I can't see good to shoot except up close. Could use a man to hunt if they was one wanted to."

The blacksnake slithered to the edge of the porch and dropped to the ground. Virgil drank from the bottle, letting the quick burn quell the nausea that churned his guts. Many people kept a blacksnake to hold down rats in a barn, but he'd never heard of one that provided meat.

"Your brother brought me game," the woman said. "Fetched Ospie some boots once, too."

She motioned for Virgil to come close to the porch. She leaned over the bowed rail and lowered her voice. A gray film covered her eyes, thicker on one than the other.

"I never told the sheriff nothing," she said. "He came sniffing around after Boyd got killed. Wanted to know if he bought off me, who he come with, and whatnot. I know who killed Boyd, but I never said a word. Ain't aiming to get in your way."

Virgil turned away, wanting the safety of the woods.

"Hey, Little Boyd," the woman called. "You're doing the right thing by laying back. Let that boy think he's safe, then pick your time. I never liked a Rodale, their family tree don't fork."

He left the road for a faint game trail into the woods. The liquor made his throat ache. The foliage in the hollow was thick and green, marking water, and he moved down the slope to a creek that swarmed with gnats. Toadstools broke to white chunks like cake beneath his boots. The hills lost their tight slant, opening into softwood glades glowing from the horizontal light of afternoon.

Virgil sat and drank. The creek ran wide and slow. He thought about leaving but didn't know where to go. So many people from the hills had headed north for work that a Pittsburgh neighborhood was called "Pennsyl-tucky." He had cousins there. He drank some whisky. He'd never been a big drinker, and he suddenly knew why people liked it. Liquor made you feel better, but first you had to feel pretty bad and Virgil never really had. He'd liked himself and the world he lived in. He wondered what Boyd had felt so bad about to drink as much as he did.

He took another drink and stood and nearly fell. Half the whisky was gone. He felt as if it were sloshing in his head. He capped the bottle and walked. The hills cast a heavy shadow, and he wanted out of the hollow by dusk. If he didn't make the road, he needed to be on a ridge at least, where enough spare light still burned in the sky. Memory trickled through his mind like an underground stream against a limestone bed, finding its way through tiny cracks—Boyd asking if Virgil wanted a Hertz doughnut, then hitting him in the arm and saying, "Hurts, don't it"; Boyd reading the Bible for the good parts in Ezekiel where Aholibah was condemned for harlotry she'd learned from the Egyptians; Boyd teaching him to play poker with a greasy deck of cards.

Virgil stopped for another drink and dropped the lid to the whisky. When he stooped for it, he lost his balance and fell to the damp earth. He rolled on his back and stared at the section of sky visible between the hills. Treetops swayed as if clawing at the stars.

He closed his eyes and felt dizzy and opened them. The dark had come fast, like floodwater that flowed over the land. He stood and began moving with the precise steps of a drunk. Lightning bugs flicked yellow spots through the trees. Dead leaves clung to the mud on his clothes. He was near a road. He heard the rattle of an engine not hitting all its cylinders and recognized it as a car driven by a man from work and knew he could have gotten a ride. The moon's light moved through the night.

He slipped to his knees as he climbed the bank and wondered why blacktop looked pale at night. He didn't care which way a car came, he'd go with whoever stopped and get out where they were going. Boyd had done that twenty years ago. Virgil was getting a late start at everything. He wished a helicopter would pick him up and drop him somewhere.

Virgil leaned against a sycamore. The desert was too hot, the North was too cold, cities were too big, and the Midwest was too flat. He chuckled. He couldn't even decide which way to go on The

Road, let alone the whole country. It didn't matter. Nothing did. He felt fine. He finished the bottle and opened another. He should have gotten drunk and thought about things sooner. It occurred to him that if he was going to leave, he might as well go ahead and kill Rodale first.

5

Car lights came around the curve and Virgil stuck his thumb out, squinting against the harsh flare of light. A pickup braked to a stop, and the driver leaned his head out the window.

"Can you drink a cold one?" he said.

"Yeah," Virgil said.

"Get in, then."

Virgil climbed inside the cab. A bedsheet covered the seat, the corners tucked beneath the springs. The driver wasn't wearing a shirt. He handed Virgil a can of beer.

"You're the first damn hitchhiker ever I did see."

"First time I done it," Virgil said.

"By God, my brother-in-law hitched four miles to the store, and like to never heard the end of it from the family."

"How come?"

"They took it as him putting a stranger ahead of kin."

"Well."

"Hatingest folks in all creation. Ain't two good ones to the whole bunch. That's why I'm celebrating."

He mashed the accelerator and left twin streaks of rubber on the road. The rear fishtailed before slowing at Pig Berry curve. Beer spilled on Virgil's clothes.

"You best watch," Virgil said. "The law sets up here a lot."

"A man wants to drive fast, it's his business. What's your name anyhow."

"Virgil Caudill."

"They's gobs of you all, ain't they."

"Around here there is."

"I'm Arlow Atkins. From Pick County. Ain't got a smoke, do you?"

"Not on me," Virgil said. "What are we celebrating?"

"I quit my wife tonight."

"For good?"

"I hope to God for good. Know what she done this time?"

"No."

"Cut the fingertips out of my gloves. Left them laying in a pile like deer sign by the couch."

"What over?"

"Porch steps."

"Were you supposed to fix them?"

"No," Arlow said. "I gave them away."

"Gave away the porch steps?"

"They was concrete block, stacked. First my brother needed one, then my cousin, and my nephew. Didn't take too long before they was gone."

"A man can always get block."

"That's what I told my wife. She said yes, but did everybody have to get them off us."

They crossed the creek and entered a hard curve. Car parts lay scattered down the creek from previous wrecks. The truck tires skipped but held to the blacktop, and they were out of the curve and hurtling down a straight stretch. Arlow tossed his empty can out the window.

"Reach me another," he said to Virgil. "And take one for your ownself."

"Where you headed anyhow?"

"Just running the roads. You got anywhere to be?"

Virgil shook his head. He pulled an unopened half-pint from his pocket.

"You don't care to take a drink of whisky, do you?"

"By God," Arlow said. "I knowed they was a reason I stopped for you. I guess you'll light up one of them left-handed cigarettes next."

"I don't reckon."

Virgil drank the neck and shoulders out of the bottle and passed it to Arlow. The outside air was black. Boyd had lived like this all his life and for the first time Virgil understood how a man could get in the habit. It was fun and there was a sense of freedom and risk, the anticipation of an unknown outcome.

Arlow swerved to avoid a raccoon crossing the road. "Ever think how a coon is close to human?" he said. "They got hands and they wash everything they eat first."

"It ain't something I ever worried much over."

"You think a coon or possum eats more?"

"A coon my opinion."

"Possum."

"A coon's belly is bigger," Virgil said. "You can tell by looking."

"Ever see in a possum's mouth?"

"I'm proud to say I ain't."

"Well, you ort to. They got about a hundred teeth."

"They don't done it."

"Damn straight," Arlow said. "One was to bite you, you'd know it. A possum will flat pour the teeth to you."

"That don't mean its belly holds more. They's many a coon the size of a dog."

"Any more of that whisky left?"

Virgil handed him the bottle. Arlow took a drink while simultaneously downshifting for a curve, flicking a cigarette out the window, and adjusting the beer between his thighs. Virgil drank some beer and felt like spitting. They were past the turnoff to his house, near the county line.

"How do you know so much on possum teeth?" he said.

"Took me a good long gander at one stuffed."

"A trophy possum. There's something I'd like to see."

Arlow stomped the brake pedal and the tires squealed. Virgil lost his beer. His forearms hit the dashboard and he could feel debris from under the seat bounce against his boots. The truck stopped sideways in the road. Arlow was standing on the brake pedal, his body arched over the steering wheel.

"That makes my pecker hard," Arlow said. "Don't it you?"

He spun the car around and headed the way they'd come.

"We ain't going to town, are we," Virgil said.

"I thought you wanted to see a stuffed possum."

"Where's it at?"

"Third hollow past the next wide place. We'll go see old man Morgan. You know him?"

"I've heard tell."

They turned onto a dirt road that forked several times and narrowed to one lane with weeds growing in the middle. Tree limbs laced overhead, blotting stars and moon. There was no ditch. The wooded hills slanted into the sky on both sides of the road. Arlow pumped the clutch for traction.

"Got to keep her in Granny gear," he said.

The hollow tightened until the road became a path and the rear tires spun. Arlow cut the engine and honked the horn twice, the sound hanging in the darkness. They left the truck and walked the path. Branches snagged their clothes. The hum of locust filled the air, rising and falling at different intervals, surrounding them but always at a distance. The path opened into a clearing where the dark shape of a house sat among white oaks. A glow of light came from a window.

"Hey, Morgan," Arlow yelled. "It's Catfish Atkins' boy, Arlow. I got a buddy here, but I'm coming up by myself." He turned to Virgil and spoke in a normal voice. "Stay here a minute. He's bad to be squirrelly."

He crossed the glade and yelled again before stepping on the porch and into the house. Virgil didn't feel drunk but knew he was.

The whisky kept him awake and gave his mind a clarity that he enjoyed.

Arlow yelled through the night and Virgil walked up the slope. The back of the house was tucked tight to the hillside while the front porch was supported by stacked rock. Virgil climbed uneven steps to the porch. The door hung at a tilt from a broken hinge. An old man sat by a cold woodstove. He held a knife in one hand and a small piece of wood in the other. Crescents of shaved wood covered his lap.

"Hidy, by God," he said. "Whose boy are you?"

"Darly Caudill's second boy, Virgil."

"Best tell me your papaw, then. They's more Caudills than dogs in these parts."

"Zale."

"Did he marry Augselle Sparks from up on Clay Creek?"

"Yup."

"Shoot, I know your whole line. Set yourself down. I been low in my gears and can't get up. I heard you'uns coming a mile away. Sound moves up here like a tunnel. This holler's so narrow I got to break day with a hammer."

Virgil sat on an ancient crate turned black from handling. Arlow turned a metal kitchen chair backwards so that his forearms rested on its laddered back. The man's knife blade flashed like a bird's beak in a corn crib. His face was brown and there were bugs in his hair.

When he finished working, he stropped his knife on a boot heel and put it away. He held a piece of wood that was two inches long and a half inch wide, the long end tapered like the bill of a duck. The other end was fat and blunt, with a notch to one side. It resembled the triggering device to a homemade rabbit trap. He passed it to Virgil.

"I'll give you it if you can call it true," Morgan said.

"Some kind of hook."

"No."

"Whistle."

"Ain't got no blower to her."

No matter how Virgil turned the wood, it looked like a piece of scrap that somebody had whittled to pass the time.

"It ain't nothing," he said.

"Sure it is. Let me see your belt a minute."

Virgil removed his belt and passed it to Morgan, who slipped the belt's edge into the notch on the piece of wood. He placed the flat end of the wood on the tip of his forefinger. He didn't hold the wood, but let it extend from his hand like a claw. It should have fallen to the earth, yet it remained in space, the leather curling like a locust seed-pod. He lifted the belt from the notch and the little piece of wood dropped to the ground.

"What is it?" Virgil said.

"Belt balancer."

"What's it do?"

"Balances belts."

"How's it work?"

"Just like that. You keep it."

Virgil slipped the piece of wood in his pocket and ran his belt through the loops. His mouth was dry.

"Tell me something that ain't true," Morgan said. "I'd whole lot rather a man lie to me than tell the truth. Know why?"

Virgil shook his head.

"Makes a man feel good to lie."

"Well," Virgil said.

"Ain't everybody who can help a man feel good about hisself. So let me hear a lie."

"I ain't drunk," Virgil said.

The old man leaned back and laughed. Virgil offered the half-pint.

"Ain't much of a drinker, are ye. Still yet got the lid."

He unscrewed the lid and tossed it on the floor.

"Never did like brown. Ain't got the kick of white. Old boy I used to know ran liquor that you'd better be standing on level ground to drink."

He tipped his head and trickled the liquor in his mouth. His eyes were closed. He didn't swallow for nearly a minute. His Adam's apple worked and he opened his eyes.

"Boys," he said. "I used to have blue eyes and a red dick. Now I got red eyes and a blue dick."

Morgan passed the bottle to Virgil and placed his hands on the chair arms as if they were tools stored on a shelf. His ears and nose were long. Behind him, a plank bookshelf held several tiny pieces of carved wood.

"How come you never went to bigger whittling?" Virgil said.

"Ain't got the learning. I know a half-inch and a quarter, but not no more. Got to eyeball it after that."

"Nothing to it," Virgil said. "Just keep cutting each measure in half. Split a quarter and you got eighths. Half that is sixteenths."

Morgan's shoulders rose and fell.

"Can't get her," he said. "Just can't."

"Where's old Duke at?" Arlow said.

"Got murdered," Morgan said.

"Why that dog wouldn't bite a biscuit. Who'd kill it?"

"Red Stumper done it."

"You aim to do anything?"

"Kill his dog back, I reckon."

"He ain't got one," Arlow said.

"What kind of man don't keep a dog?"

"Kind that shoots them, I guess."

"What's he got? Rooster? Billy goat?"

"Nothing. He lives alone."

Virgil drank from the bottle. He wasn't afraid to kill Rodale, he was afraid of where it might lead. The trouble might run for years and would cease to be specific. The meanest men in both families would continue shooting simply out of habit.

Morgan and Arlow were talking about what kind of winter was ahead and how to read the signs. Boyd never predicted, but accepted each day's fate. If it rained a week straight, he'd say the water made all the colors brighter. If there was no sun, he'd talk about how much further you could see without the glare. Winter was a good time to learn how the land was made. Virgil wondered what his brother would say about being dead.

"Well," Boyd might say, "a man ain't got to worry with warm clothes, eating meals, or getting sleep. Being dead's freer than when I was living."

"It ain't doing me any goddam good," Virgil said.

"What," Arlow said.

Virgil blinked at Arlow and Morgan, who were looking at him as if waiting. The room seemed to close in on him.

"Nothing," Virgil said. "Just talking to myself."

"Makes good sense to me," Morgan said.

Virgil stood, swaying slightly.

"We ort to let Morgan go to bed."

"No need to rush off," Morgan said.

"Where's that possum at?" Arlow said. "Me and him's got a bet on its teeth. You didn't eat that, did you."

"I've ate my share, boys. Time was, these hills was hunted so bad folks raised possum for meat. I've eat owl once and grateful for it."

"Owl?"

"Ain't supposed to, you know."

"Why's that?"

"On account of it eating meat. Same with cat or man. They ain't fit."

"Owl gets pretty good sized, don't it."

"Ain't hardly no meat to it. Biggest part of them is head and the rest voice. Kindly greasy, like a coon. A one of you boys ever eat lobster?"

Arlow and Virgil shook their heads.

"Me neither, but I seen pictures. They're pretty much a crawdad growed to the size of a squirrel and covered over with a shell. By God, it was one hungry son of a bitch who thought to eat that goddam thing. And after all the work put into it, they ain't no more meat than a baby rabbit. Well, owl's about the same. I drawed the line at dog. Guess I got to know too many. Squirrel's my best."

"Why's that?" Arlow said.

"Quick and easy, I reckon."

"Over in England," Virgil said, "they don't eat squirrel."

"Why's that?"

"They say a squirrel's kin to a rat."

"Well," Morgan said, "it might have some rat to it. It gets around like a rat, and it sure as hell chews stuff up like a rat. But I'd say it's fourth or fifth cousin. About like them Rodales."

Morgan was staring hard at Virgil, his eyes narrowed to folded slits. Virgil didn't move.

"Ain't nothing wrong with getting shut of a aggravation like that. Best way is to kill it off leaf, limb, and root. But you got to be ready for the work, same as that boy who ate the first lobster. They ain't no easy to it. More than that, you got to be ready for afterwards. That's the hard part."

"What are you talking about?" Arlow said. "Killing rats is easy as rolling off a whore." He repeated himself and laughed again until the sound sputtered out. The silence confused him and he finished his beer. "Where'd you say that possum was?"

Morgan tipped his head to indicate the rear of the house. Arlow stepped into the darkness, cursing as he bumped walls.

Virgil felt as if a hole had opened in his mind and he wasn't sure if stuff was leaking out or coming in. He felt sober. The old man kept his vision locked on Virgil's face. It was the first time anyone had mentioned Boyd to him without sympathy or expectation. Morgan's tone had been practical, as if discussing the best way to keep deer out of a garden.

Arlow staggered through the narrow house carrying a stuffed possum with its mouth open in a snarl. Its feet were nailed to a board.

"See there," Arlow said. "Bet my thumb there's more than a hundred teeth in its mouth."

"I'll not take that bet."

"Arlie-boy," Morgan said. "That's your possum now. You can have it."

"Now, no. You can't give a thing like this up. Ain't too many, my opinion. Might be worth something."

"Take and put it in the truck, Arlie-boy. Then you set and wait for your buddy here. He'll be down directly."

"They ain't nothing I've got to give you back."

"You give me plenty, you just don't know it. Now hush and go. Wait on Caudill, here."

"Thank you. I mean it. Thank you."

Arlow cradled the possum to his chest as if it were a sack of eggs and went outside. The call of a bobwhite came through the door. Virgil felt nervous alone with Morgan.

"I'm fixing to tell you something I ain't told a soul in nigh forty years," Morgan said.

He closed his eyes and began to talk, slowly at first, as if he were a man who'd just learned how to use his voice.

"Used to, they made firebrick from the clay herebouts. Brickyard's been shut down a long time but my daddy worked at it. They was a union war. Not like in the coal fields, but over who was going to run things—the AFL or the CIO. They're joined up now. Back then they was enemies.

"My daddy, he was on the CIO side. He'd moved here for work and his buddies had went CIO. They had themselves a gunfight at Hay's Crossing. Two AFLs was pinned down by more CIOs than you could count. They was all young and it was big fun, shooting all day and pissing on the gun barrels to keep them cool. One boy got sent home for food, ammo, and whisky. Daddy said it was the prettiest day in a month.

"Long on to dark, one AFL boy tore the bottom off his T-shirt and stuck it on a stick. Hollered that he was give out on fighting. The CIOs could have the union. He just wanted to go home and eat his supper. Well, nobody shot or said nothing. He come out of the brush scratched up and waving that flag, and got shot twice and went down like a stuck hog. As forehanded a man ever walked these hillsides. He lived but limped.

"My daddy, he got the blame on account of not having no kin living here. That way it was just him and not a whole gang to fight. It was best for everybody but us. Daddy saw he didn't have no choice, and let it stick, but he told me he never done it.

"Somebody bushwhacked Daddy walking to work. Shot him right square in the same leg as the AFL boy. Now they both limped. Folks said you could see one coming and you'd not know which it was till he was full on you. Things got back to peaceable after that. It was the AFL boy's father who done the shooting and everybody knowed it, even Daddy, but he let it go. He got religion. They was too many to go up against anyhow. Daddy said it was the price of moving into a place where you didn't know nobody. Said he had a good job and his family was happy. It was just me. They'd tried to have more kids but something was seized up in Mommy's forks.

"Daddy, he took me out to the woods and learned me how to shoot pistol, riflegun, and scattergun. Daddy said he didn't ever want me to be crippled up. Said a crippled man wasn't worth the extra dirt his leg dragged. Said it wasn't religion that kept him from getting that bunch back, it was being a coward. Not even Mommy knowed that.

"Then he'd beat me with the stick he walked with, tear me up one side and down the other. If I was to try and run, he'd laugh and say nobody ran from a gimp but a chicken. Said he was beating me so I'd not be yellow like him. Said he'd quit the day I just stood there and let him do it. He'd know I was brave.

"Then a bad thing happened, the worst thing. He got blood poison and the doctor cut his leg off. Took four men to hold him, but it was too late. That poison was in him like a snake. He died.

"Well, I practiced shooting every day for nigh a year. Then I had me a growth spurt. I was sixteen and ort to have been sniffing girls out, but I never. Nobody had ever liked us. I didn't have nary a friend and Mommy stayed at the house. They hated us for not leaving. We reminded them of what they were—a whole creek full of liars.

"I didn't know that then. All I knew was what it felt like to grow up a stranger. I decided to give them a reason to hate me and do what Daddy should have done. He never had the chance to see how brave his beating made me.

"I worked it all out in my head. If I was to go on a shooting spree, they'd damn sure know it was me, and they'd get me. What I done was not do a damn thing different. I went to school. I chopped wood and hauled water for Mommy. I worked in the garden and every now and again I killed me a man. Nobody knew who it was. They was all scared and they took to suspicioning each other, the same way I'd lived my whole life. They laid the blame off on first one then the other. About the time they was ready to shoot somebody, I'd kill another man and the whole thing would start again. By God, I was proud. I ain't no more, but I was swelled up then like a poisoned pup. It was the first time I ever felt like I belonged there.

"They was one last man I wanted took care of and then I set down in this holler. They ain't exactly big gobs of people know I'm over in here. Your brother was one. He was like a son to me. But he don't know what I told you.

"I know what you're thinking on doing and I know why. You'd best be stout is all I can say. The doing ain't easy, but it's the living after that's hard. I've set here and studied on it plenty. They's better ways to live a life than always on lookout."

Morgan lifted his concealed right arm and placed the barrel of a revolver against Virgil's forehead. The motion was smooth and very fast, the metal cold against Virgil's skin. Virgil stopped breathing. He wanted to swallow but was afraid his face would move and Morgan would fire.

"The thing about killing," Morgan said, "it makes you worry about getting killed. Just remember, there'll be somebody to track you down. You'll have to kill again and it don't get no easier. You just get better at it."

He lowered his arm and tucked the pistol from sight, moving with the cunning of an animal. Morgan's face glistened from water that had leaked from his eyes. It ran into the creases of his face like rain hitting gullies on a hillside.

Virgil moved to the door and breathed the sweet air of the woods, listening to the silence. The hills surrounded him like a box. The sky was a black slab etched with stars. He wondered how many shallow graves lay in the earth nearby.

The path curved into the woods and he stopped to let his eyes work out where he was. The light from Morgan's house was gone. He followed the darker color of the path and slowed when moonglow glinted off the truck. Arlow's head was tipped against the door, his eyes closed. Air whistled from his mouth. The stuffed possum stood on the seat beside him.

Virgil pushed him across the seat and backed to the fork, where he turned around. Morgan's story had worn him to a nubbin. The whisky was coming on him like a landslide and he wanted to go home. His trailer was eight miles away by the woods, twenty by road. The bottle held three fingers of whisky and he drank half, feeling it revive him. Dust blew in the windows and settled on his eyebrows. He turned from the hollow onto The Road and the warm night air rushed against his face. He remembered Boyd's first car wreck, when he was fourteen. He'd run an old Dodge into the creek. "That damn car," he told their father, "it just laid down on me." It became a family joke—if you tripped and fell, it wasn't your fault, your boots just laid down on you.

At his trailer, Virgil dragged Arlow onto the couch that spanned the narrow wall. He left the possum in the truck. He went out the back door and sat on a log and looked into the woods. He finished the last of the bourbon. He had no idea what he wanted to do, but he was pretty sure what he didn't want to do. If he could pile that up on one side of his mind, he could sniff out whatever was left over.

He flung the empty bottle up the hill. Everything came back to killing Rodale and that made him sick. He didn't even hunt. What he wanted was his father's cabin and to be left alone. He'd marry Abigail and have a mess of kids and get his name on a shirt.

He stretched on his back in the dirt and looked at the sky. The moon was gone. Its absence made more stars visible, as if they'd come from hiding. When he was a kid, Boyd told him that stars were holes in the land's roof and the moon was the gap where an old stove flue had poked through. Clouds were shingles that got blown around. A rainbow was an exposed rafter.

6

Virgil opened his eyes to a monstrous thirst. He could not bear the light. He closed his lids and let time move around him.

Something jabbed his leg. A man was kicking him and he thought it was his brother waking him for school.

"You hurt?" the kicking man said.

Virgil's slow awareness that he wasn't dreaming sent a sliver of fear along his spine. Knots of memory exploded in his head. He was unable to move his arm. He looked at the shirtless man, who continued to kick him.

"Don't," Virgil said.

"What happened to you?"

"Nothing. Just sleeping."

"This your place?"

"Yeah."

"Sure you ain't hurt now."

"Can't move my arm."

"Hell, you're jammed up against the woodpile." The man extended a hand. "Here."

Virgil took it and the man pulled until Virgil was able to sit. His head spun with such pain that it felt detached from his body, and he wondered if he'd been struck in the face. He looked at the man and remembered his name.

"I feel rode hard and put up wet," Arlow said. "We didn't have a wreck or nothing, did we?"

"I don't think so."

"Good. Did I drive?"

"No."

"Good. One more pop and I lose my license."

Sunlight slid through the tangled tree limbs overhead. The scent of honeysuckle came on a breeze. Virgil knew he needed to get up, but wasn't sure he could make it. He felt poisoned and beat up. He began the slow operation of standing, trying to keep his head level. His body swayed and he wanted to hold something for balance, but there was only Arlow.

"A short beer would fix us right up," Arlow said.

"I ain't drinking no more."

Virgil clung to the doorjamb as he entered the trailer, ashamed of the weakness in his limbs. He filled a glass with water and drank.

"I'm going to lay down," he said.

"How do I get out of here?"

"They's not but one road off this hill."

"We'll see ya, buddy. Old Morgan's a case, ain't he."

The memory of Morgan's story flared in Virgil's head like a blowtorch. He gripped the sink and stared at the faucet.

"Goddam son of a bitch!" Arlow yelled from outside. "There's a fucking possum in my truck! You got ary a gun?"

Virgil nodded but an eruption of pain stopped the motion. It hurt to move his eyes.

"Rifle's no good this close," Arlow said. "I might could use some help if you're able."

Virgil moved to the door and looked at the three steps with dread. Arlow had his hand on the truck door handle. In one quick motion he jerked the door open, slipped and fell, and began scooting backwards. He circled the truck and looked at the immobile animal.

"Sick, ain't it," he said. "Might be rabies. Good thing I seen it. Jeezum Crow, it could have got me."

"It ain't real," Virgil said.

"Damn sure is."

"It's dead, Arlow." Virgil began to laugh and tried to stop because it made his head hurt. "It's stuffed."

Arlow leaned to study the possum through the safety of the windshield.

"By God if it ain't," he said. "Now where the hell did that nasty thing come from?"

"Morgan."

"Ain't nobody else fool enough to stuff a damn possum." He opened the passenger door and kicked it across the bench seat and out the driver's side. "There, by God. It's yours now." He laughed, then turned his head and retched a stream into the dirt. He wiped his mouth with the back of his hand.

"About time," he said. "I been waiting on that all morning. You ort to, too."

He got in the truck and slammed the doors and started the engine. He leaned out his window. "Keep your ass wiped," he said. Rock and dirt flew from his rear tires as he drove down the road, honking the horn. The possum lay on its side in the yard. A blue fly veered past it to Arlow's vomit soaking into the earth.

Virgil took four aspirin and stumbled to his room and lay on his bed. He wondered if it was possible to die from a hangover.

When he awoke he felt better but not much. The smell of alcohol rose from his skin. He stepped into the shower and hunched beneath the hot water spraying the back of his neck. As soon as he left the bathroom he felt worse. He returned to the shower's comfort until the water turned cold.

He drank coffee on the trailer steps, staring at the stuffed possum. It didn't know it was dead. Only the living cared, but the way Virgil felt, he didn't care enough. Knots of grass made green patches in the sloped yard's clay dirt. The sun hung above the western hills. He hoped no one came visiting because he was embarrassed to be seen. He stepped into the woods.

Two cardinals flashed low through the brush, and Virgil turned his head to watch, scraping his face on a tree limb. He preferred its sharp pain to the dull thud inside his head. He circled a blackberry patch and went downslope to a low ridge. He was sweating inside his clothes. The effort to negotiate the woods made him forget how bad he felt, but he could feel the liquor tearing at him. His eyes were dry and heavy. His head hurt.

He reached a low ridge, very narrow with no trees. On the ground lay a variety of feathers. Pale bones poked from the leaves. Beneath an evergreen was a gray owl pellet the size of a crow's egg. Virgil was in a hunting zone. It was an ideal place for an owl to kill whatever animal came along.

The shadows opened to light and he headed for it, moving through a wall of pine that covered him with the smell of sap. The heavy woods ended at the ridgeline that marked the boundary of what everyone called "company land." It was owned by the mineral company that had left holes in the hills forty years before. The land was routinely logged. Younger men had begun growing marijuana on it. Virgil remembered having come here years back with Boyd, hunting a Christmas tree for their grade school. They had shared a pair of gloves, one apiece, each keeping the bared hand in a pocket. Boyd used a shotgun to blast the tree down. They dragged it to their school and walked home through the early darkness. Wind blew cold along the ridge. High hills ringed the gray sky, treetops aiming at the stars. Like many mountain families, they had an artificial tree, a sign of town sophistication. Boyd said people who lived in cities preferred real trees.

Now Virgil was squinting down the hill, seeking evidence of

the tree they'd taken twenty years back. The crimson light of afternoon sliced into the eastern hillside, moving slowly along the ridge. When the sun reached the top, it would be full dark in the hollow, like the bottom of a well. Climbing the hill gained an extra hour of daylight.

At the top, the land opened from its steep-walled maze to the Blizzard Cemetery. Virgil and Boyd had come to the graveyard as kids to smoke cigars, then cigarettes, and eventually dope. They'd dared each other into the graveyard. Boyd had gone first. He always did—first down a snowy slope on a car hood, first to get thrown from an unbroken pony, first to ride a mini-bike up a homemade ramp. Now he was first dead.

Virgil crossed the road in the immense silence of the hilltop and climbed the fence into the cemetery. Gnawed acorns lay beneath the oaks. He hadn't been back since the funeral but he walked straight to the grave, approaching from an angle so he wouldn't have to read the name on the stone. The earth was still slightly humped. Wired to the marker was a bouquet of plastic flowers that Boyd would have hated. Beside it was their father's grave.

A steady breeze crossed the top of the hill. Hickory limbs scraped each other, a sound that made Virgil edgy. He refused to turn and look. Nothing was there but rock, dirt, and trees, with boxed bones below the surface. He stood beside the grave. Etched into the rock was his brother's name. It occurred to Virgil that carving the names of the dead was a strange job.

He'd only cried once, after seeing the expression on his mother's face at losing a son. His tears had been for her. Now, six months later, Virgil could feel his own grief rising through him.

"Fuck you," he said. "You son of a bitch. Look at you now. Goddam fucking dead. Fuck you, Boyd. Fuck you."

The words clogged his throat until he couldn't speak. His shoulders rose and fell. Somewhere deep inside was the instinct to shut it off, not so much like turning a faucet but more like doubling a hose to choke his sorrow. When the sounds coming out of him ran down, Virgil stood and began kicking the granite headstone. He kicked until his foot hurt. Steel-toed boots were better for the job and he laughed at himself for thinking that way. Boyd had always made fun of the practical turn to Virgil's mind. His face was cold from tears. He began to walk.

At the top of the hill were the oldest graves, surrounded by white oaks. Dry leaves crackled beneath his boots. The gravestones were standing at a tilt and grown with moss, the earth sunk before them. One had been broken and repaired. Lines of rust ran down the stone from the bolts that held it together. The grass was very green and Virgil didn't like to think why. A flicker flew by, cutting scallops in the air. Dusk was coming on. Virgil wished he was the one who'd died. If he had, Boyd would already be locked up for having killed Rodale. He wouldn't have let six months go by.

A young maple grew in a corner, out of place among the old hardwoods. In the shade beneath it was a plain marker. The dates were seven years apart, a child. Virgil stared at the small grave for a long time. He didn't recognize the name, and he wondered if the parents still lived in the county. He felt another layer of sadness, not for himself, but for them. Their boy was taken away and there was nothing they could do. It was worse than his situation.

Virgil began to cry again. He dropped to his knees and let all the tears he'd ever forbidden move through him and out of him and into the earth. He cried until he gagged and his body wanted to retch. He squelched that urge, then let that happen, too. It smelled of coffee and whisky. He continued to gag until bile filled his mouth and ran over his chin. He lay on the soft ground and pressed his head to the earth and struggled to control his breathing. There was nothing else in him to come out.

He lay there a long time and slowly realized that he'd been asleep. He was cold. The sun was sliding behind the western hills, sending a red fan of light across the ridge. The liquid scent of pine carried across the road. He rubbed his eyes and looked at the marker above the child's grave.

In the dim light he could just make out the name carved into the headstone.

JOSEPH TILLER

He stared at it for a long time. The faint glimmer of an idea began at the border of his mind, then raced over him like heat, followed by an exhilarated terror. He felt something shift within him, an alignment of body and mind. The idea was both terrible and great, and he shivered at its enormity.

7

The following day Virgil called in sick for the rest of the week. Lying was easier than he expected because people wanted to believe what they were told. At the post office, he caught a ride to town and retrieved his car. He bought a U.S. atlas and spent the rest of the day in his trailer studying maps. Lexington was a hundred miles away, a place he'd never been.

He wrote down everything he could think of about his idea until he'd covered several pages with scrawled notes. Slowly he began forming a plan. He hadn't applied himself with such diligence since college and he liked it. He was good at it. He felt as if he were assembling a jigsaw puzzle and making the pieces as well. The biggest problem was money. He wasn't sure how people went about getting it, aside from incremental raises in pay.

He rose early and drove to Frankfort. The governor's mansion was very big and Virgil figured he must have a good-sized family. In front of the capitol was a large floral clock that lent a lovely scent to the air. Its hands were longer than he was tall, and he wondered how many people actually visited the clock to check the time.

Main Street held a few businesses that were competing with a new mall. In a secondhand store he bought a typewriter. Several black people were in the store and he tried not to stare, never having seen any before. He wanted to move near for a better look, but was afraid to, and didn't know why. They ignored him and he wondered if it was deliberate. He decided not, since they probably saw plenty of white people.

He received directions to the Bureau of Records and walked up its granite steps, wondering how many men were employed merely to clear them of snow in winter. Beyond glass doors a sign warned of video surveillance. He turned around and went down the steps to his car.

He drove east, working on the problem in his head. He couldn't get a post office box in another name without identification, but he couldn't get the identification without a post office box. It reminded him of looking for work as a kid. He was caught in a similar crossfire between experience and a job, unable to get one without the other. The solution then had been to lie, telling the boss that he'd painted houses with his uncle the year before. Virgil was hired, and spent the first month hoping nobody noticed that he barely knew which end of the brush to hold.

An abrupt thought caused him to swerve into the breakdown lane. He steered back to the road. In Lexington he bought a city map and studied it in a diner. The waitress gave him directions to the police station. New Circle Road wrapped the city like a lasso and he missed his exit and became lost in a maze of streets. Two hours later, he arrived at police headquarters, a mile from the diner.

He sat in the car for a long time, working out all the details in his head. Horns honked around him. Automobile exhaust mixed with the heat and the general smell of a city—many humans compressed into a small space. There were no trees on the street. He tucked his wallet in the glovebox and left the car. It was the first time he'd locked a vehicle in his life.

The air inside the police station smelled of sweat and cigarette smoke, cut with industrial cleaning fluid. There was a gauntlet of two benches filled with a variety of people. At the end of the tiled lane was a window behind which sat an old man in uniform. Virgil approached slowly. He was sweating.

The old cop looked at him. Unsure of procedure, Virgil stayed quiet.

"What?" the cop said.

"My wallet," Virgil said.

"Your wallet."

"It was stolen."

The cop shuffled through papers for the correct form.

"Okay. Stolen wallet. Name?"

"What?"

"Name. What's your name?"

"Joe Tiller," Virgil whispered.

"What?"

"Joe Tiller."

"Address?"

"Five-twenty South Avenue."

"Go on."

"What?" Virgil said.

"What town?"

"Here."

"Phone?"

"No phone."

"Description of the wallet."

"Brown."

"Tri-fold or bi-fold."

"Regular, you know."

"Okay, bi-fold. Contents?"

"Forty dollars. Some pictures. All my ID."

"Type of ID?"

"Driver's license, birth certificate, Social Security card."

"Okay. If we hear anything, we'll mail you a card."

"What about until then?"

"Search the area where it was stolen. Look in garbage cans and dumpsters. They usually get rid of it fast and keep the money."

"No, I mean, for ID."

"That's not a police matter."

"What do I do?"

"You'll have to apply for new."

"Can you give me something that says my wallet was stolen?"

"I can give you a copy of this form. It'll be a few minutes. Take a seat."

Virgil found a place on the bench. It was nicked and greasy, carved by pocketknives. Two children sat on the dirty floor in front of their mother. She was wearing large sunglasses, and beneath them Virgil could see the swellings on her face. She kept one arm stiff to her body. People dozed against the wall. Others stared at the floor or at the space in front of them.

Boyd had always said that the best lie was to tell the truth in a way that made the listener believe it was false. Next was to keep your lies very close to reality. Virgil was veering far from either course and it worried him. He'd never been in a police station and thought it would be nicer. He expected a squad of policemen to arrest him at any moment. They knew he was lying. They'd searched his car and found his wallet. He became aware of a yelling voice, and people were looking his way. The old cop was staring at him. He stood in a panic, ready to run.

"Mr. Tiller," the old cop called. "Mr. Tiller."

Virgil crossed the room and the cop handed him a photocopy of the police report. Outside he leaned against a light pole and forced himself to breathe slowly. Lying was easy. Finding his car took half an hour. In the woods he could locate a tree he'd touched years ago, but in Lexington he was immediately lost. He'd seen deer stumble across a road at night, stunned by car headlights, and he felt the same sense of bewilderment.

He was hungry, but he had one more stop. He climbed another set of steps and waited in line at the post office. The male clerks wore ties, and he chuckled at the thought of Zephaniah in one. He prepared in his mind what he was going to say.

"I'm sorry," the man behind the counter said. "You must have two forms of ID to rent a box."

"My wallet got stolen," Virgil said. "I have a check from my old job coming, and I got to have somewhere for them to send it."

"Use a friend's address."

"Don't know nobody."

"How about where you're staying, then."

"Ain't got a place yet. That's just it. I can't get one until I get the check, and I can't get the check until I get a mailing address."

"Well, buddy, you're in a hole of water got no deep to it." He lowered his voice. Virgil recognized an accent from the eastern end of the state. "Was me, I'd go to one of them mail services."

"Mail service?"

"Yeah, they got them now. It's like a post office but it's private."

Virgil found a listing in the phone book and drove to the storefront business. He told the clerk about the check from his last job and offered six months' advance rent on a mailbox. The man gave him a set of keys, thin metal slivers that would open his future.

"Thank you, Mr. Tiller," he said as Virgil left.

He drove home along the interstate, remembering its construction when he was a child. It had employed many men, but when the site surpassed a commuting distance of three hours, men who'd worked a decade were suddenly jobless. Their children were half-raised, their homes partially paid off. The federal government had followed the mineral companies in creating a boom-or-bust economy with a disposable workforce.

The road east went through the lovely rolling land of Lexington's horse farms. Wind rippled the bluegrass as if it were the sea. There was a villa that resembled something from Mexico, and farther along, an actual stone castle. The land began its hilly ascent in Montgomery County, where the Pottsdale Escarpment jutted from the earth, marking the geological boundary of the Appalachians. Beyond that lay the disorganized terrain that was Virgil's country.

Night had come to the hills by the time he reached Rocksalt. Its few traffic lights blinked yellow. There would never be a New Circle Road here because the hills pressed too close, leaving room for only three streets that crossed town. The night air was sweet and rich. Stars spread like dust above the treeline. He drove up the dirt road of his home hill.

Virgil wrote a letter requesting a copy of the birth certificate for

Joe Tiller. He typed it, using the mailbox in Lexington as a return address. If he dropped it into a public mailbox in town, it would get trucked to Lexington and postmarked there. When he finished, he burned the handwritten original outside. A glowing wafer of ash wafted into the night sky.

He went to bed but couldn't sleep. Everything was much bigger than he was and he'd barely begun. He was impressed by his undertaking until he considered the reason. He lay grimly immobile for a long time while his mind continued to work. He wasn't sure how to shut it off. That posed a fresh problem and he chuckled at the absurdity of applying his mind to the problem of turning off his mind. It was like asking a lawyer to sue himself, or a killer to kill himself.

Through the small bedroom window he saw the moon and he remembered a song his mother sang to him about the moon seeing him through the old oak tree. He wished he were there. He wished he could live on the moon in his father's old log cabin. It had holes in the walls the diameter of a rifle barrel, bored in strategic locations during the Civil War. Once inside, he could live until his water and ammo ran out. He'd heard that a man could live on bananas and milk. He'd need a cow and a banana tree. And a ton of ammunition.

8

July went by in a blur of heat. Virgil moved through the month with ease, maintaining a smooth distance from his family and the men at work. Taylor was nervous around him the first few days, but Virgil bore him no ill will.

On a scorching Saturday, he drove to Lexington and parked near the mailbox rental business. He waited until the lobby was empty and walked in swiftly. The door opened behind him and he knew with absolute certainty that a policeman had entered to arrest him. A woman checked her mail and left. He opened the drawer and withdrew the official envelope that lay inside. His hands were trembling as he sat in the car with the birth certificate of Joseph Edward Tiller.

Virgil stared at the paper until the words blended together. He folded the document four times and slipped it in his sock. He pulled onto New Circle Road and got off at a mall that included a hotel and a large bookstore. Virgil had never been in a mall. It seemed like a world turned inside out. The outer walls had store names and a locked door, while the windows faced the interior. Large trees grew indoors. The air was bad and there was no sunlight. A large platform held a map and Virgil considered it strange that a map was necessary for the indoors. He couldn't imagine a worse place to spend time.

At a department store, he bought a duffel bag and a wallet. He went into a restaurant with tables that held napkins in metal rings. The room was empty of people. A woman in a short dress walked toward him.

"Just one?" she said.

Virgil nodded and she led him to the only dirty table in the room. He hadn't been to a restaurant of this caliber and he wondered if all the other tables were reserved. After a few minutes, the woman returned. She told him the specials and asked if he had any questions.

"Is there a big crowd coming?" he said.

"No. Lunch rush is over."

"Working with a short crew today, are you?"

The woman shook her head in a brisk fashion that made her earrings sway. Her face bore an expression of distaste.

"Then how come you put me at a dirty table?"

Her vision flicked rapidly over his clothes.

"Would you like another?" she said.

"Yes."

She turned away and Virgil knew that he was to follow her. She stopped at a fresh table, its turquoise linen spotless, a flower placed in a slender glass. The woman was waiting for Virgil to sit, and he understood that she disapproved of how he dressed. He walked away, wishing he could leave tracks of mud.

He left the mall and searched for his car in the immense lot. Regardless of the birth certificate and the wallets and all his plans, a stranger had recognized him for what he was. He'd like to see how that woman would fare in the woods. He sat in the car, becoming more and more angry until he realized with devastating intensity that he was also mad at himself. The woman's disdain for him had made him crave her. He was angry with his own desire.

At the far end of the parking lot was a phone booth from which he stole the Lexington phone book. He was becoming everything he had been raised against—a thief, a liar, ashamed of his background.

He drove to the Social Security Administration. After a long wait he sat beside a cluttered desk across from a woman who appeared sad.

"Need me a Social Security card, I reckon," he said.

"A replacement?"

"No. Just a card. You know, for work."

"A new card?"

"Yes, ma'am."

"You've never applied for a card before?"

"No, ma'am. Nobody in my family ever did."

"I see. And you're from?"

"Pick County."

"I see."

Her expression was the same as the woman's in the restaurant. He decided to use it to his advantage, like finding enemy ammunition that fit your weapon.

"Have you held a job before?" she said.

"No, ma'am. I mean, I ain't lazy. I've worked plenty, but on our own land. Then Daddy died and we everyone had to hunt work. I got on at one of them horse farms you'uns got here. Stable hand. They said they couldn't pay me less'n I had me a Social Security card."

"All right," she said. "You fill this out and we can get started."

She passed him a pen and a clipboard with a form. He held them without moving, the way he'd seen illiterate men at the post office act.

"You must fill that out," she said.

"They never said nothing about that at the farm."

"It's necessary for government records."

Virgil arranged a smile that he hoped appeared fake. He was almost beginning to enjoy this. The woman spoke softly.

"Do you need me to write this for you?"

Virgil passed her the clipboard. He stared at his lap, trying to seem embarrassed. He was elated. Now there'd be no record of his handwriting on file.

"You do have a birth certificate," she said.

Virgil crossed his leg. He retrieved the document from his sock and unfolded it and offered it to her. She didn't take it, but waited until he placed the paper on her desk. Virgil hoped that she'd remember this behavior instead of his face. He supplied her with the address for the mailbox in Lexington and left.

In the morning he crawled under his trailer and disconnected a heat duct that led to a large vent in the kitchen floor. The air was cool and slightly damp near the earth. He squirmed to daylight, cut scrap plywood to fit the measurements, and crawled below the trailer again. He nailed the new piece of plywood to the joists below the vent, making a shelf. He hunched on his knees, working over his head. Each strike of the hammer shook the trailer and dropped dust into his eyes. He finished and replaced the tin siding that served as a hatch. Inside the trailer, he placed the wallet and birth certificate in the duffel bag, lifted the vent cover, and set the bag on the shelf. The cover fit snugly back in place. From the proper angle, a flash of the gray canvas was visible through the grate, but he had few guests and no one would be looking close.

August began with unusual rains that made the air sodden and thick. Day-old trash smelled as if it had moldered in the heat for a week. Virgil's new distance protected him from the bickering that resulted from laboring in the humidity. At night he opened his trailer to the outside world and hung wet towels over the windows and doorways. Insects treated his house as part of their domain. One morning he woke to find a raccoon on his kitchen table.

In the Lexington mailbox, he found a Social Security card for Joe Tiller. He watched in astonishment as he participated in the events he'd set in motion, bringing about a situation from which he could not easily escape. He advertised his truck for sale, and by the end of the week he'd accepted a reasonable offer. He bought a cheap car he despised, but he was a few thousand dollars ahead. He kept the money in the duffel bag. He began to grow a beard.

In Lexington he took the written exam for obtaining a driver's license in the name of Joe Tiller. He'd considered a number of plausible stories as to why he didn't have one—service in Africa as a missionary; an army license overseas that got revoked; being recently released from prison. He discarded each as being too cumbersome.

Claiming to be from Pick County was enough. Nothing was expected of such people, and they could submit no surprises.

His work buddies regarded his change of cars as a sign of impending marriage, and Virgil encouraged the rumor by not denying it. It was an ideal cover that explained his preoccupied silence. He avoided his family, except for short visits to his mother late at night. They talked of mundane events.

From a pay phone in Rocksalt, Virgil arranged with a driver's training company to use a vehicle for his road test. The following morning he shaved his beard but left a mustache. He drove to Lexington very early. At dawn the city was quiet and empty, and he could see it as a field of cement, patched with sections of grass, bordered by the buildings where people lived and worked. He could almost imagine living there if no one was around.

The driving instructor was younger than Virgil expected, a man with a ponytail and an earring. Virgil wondered if he was funny-turned. The man accompanied him to a parking lot where a state trooper sat in the passenger seat and adjusted his gunbelt. Virgil held the steering wheel tightly.

"First license?" the cop said.

Virgil nodded.

"Pick County, huh? I used to know some Atkinses over in there."

"They's two or three bunches."

"I knew the rough ones. I used to operate out of that post in Rocksalt."

"You did."

"What'd you do, lose your license and forget to reapply?"

"No. Never had much call to leave the holler. My brother did most of the driving. Then Daddy died and things just generally went to hell."

The cop gave instructions. Virgil drove into the street and stopped at the appropriate distance from the stop sign. He made a right turn, a left turn, and parallel-parked. They returned to the lot and the cop completed the form.

"You did good," he said.

He signed the form and handed a copy to Virgil.

"Carry this until you get your license."

Virgil nodded.

"You know, one of my first investigations had some Tillers in it," the cop said.

Sweat began forming on Virgil's forehead. He didn't want to bring it to the trooper's attention by wiping it off.

"A kid's death," he said. "They gave it to me because I was a rookie. Routine accident report. Any kin to you?"

Virgil swallowed in order to speak.

"Cousin," he said.

"I always wondered what happened to the parents. It graveled them up pretty hard."

"They moved."

"Look, I don't mean to bring it up again. They were nice people's all."

Virgil grunted.

"Back then," the cop said, "I never thought I'd wind up giving driver's tests. Things change. Yessir, a man can't tell where he's headed, can he?"

Virgil shook his head. The cop left the car and the driving instructor got in.

"Congratulations," he said. "Man, you look nervous. Don't worry, I've seen people wet their pants."

"You drive," Virgil said.

"No problem, man. We can do a doobie if you want."

"A doobie?"

"Yeah, man, you know."

He made a subtle motion with his hand to his mouth and Virgil realized that he'd been right, the man was funny-turned. It bothered him that the guy thought he was, too.

The Department of Motor Vehicles was the final step. The woman behind the counter fed the name Joe Tiller to a computer and linked it to the new Social Security number, which became the driver's license number. Virgil knew nothing about computers, but he didn't trust them. He thought of his grandfather's immense suspicion of electricity and hoped that he wasn't being as hard-headed as the old man. His grandfather wouldn't allow a clock in his house and had never owned a driver's license.

The camera operator told him to stand at a line painted on the floor with his back touching a gray backdrop fastened to the wall. In a rush of fear, he wondered what the camera would see. The man waited with an expression of bored patience as Virgil moved cautiously into position. He'd never taken a stand on anything and now that he had, he understood that it was a terrible stand. He felt like a train shunted to a private track, hurtling toward a dead end.

The bright lights flashed twice and he sat in a hard plastic chair to wait. He remembered his father teaching him to drive fifteen years ago. He had set Virgil loose in the cemetery at the top of the hill and said not to worry, that if he wrecked, he couldn't kill anybody.

"Tiller," the woman called.

Virgil received a piece of thin plastic that contained his photograph beside the name Joe Tiller. The mustache was a stripe across the middle of his face that made his head look wide. It was all that separated him from the new name. He hid the license in his trunk and drove home, proud that a lowly Blizzard boy like himself could pull this off. He wished he could tell someone. He recalled his mother quoting the Bible: "Pride goeth before a fall." The snake's punishment for the Fall was condemnation to a life of crawling on its belly. He wondered what sort of animal it had been before.

At home, he carefully shaved his mustache. The face on the license belonged to no one.

Two weeks later he took another Friday off, acceptable behavior at the maintenance department of Rocksalt Community College. Most work crews quit unofficially at noon on Friday anyhow. If a man was willing to forgo a day's pay, no one cared if he missed work. Virgil rose at dawn, filled a wallet with his new identification, and placed it in the trunk with the cash he'd made from selling his truck. He spread a map over the hood of the car and traced his route with a finger. Getting to Cincinnati was easy—drive to Lexington and make a right.

The night before, he'd stayed awake late working out the day's plan. Now he was filling in the blanks, the way a child stayed within the lines of a coloring book. Virgil Caudill was the inventor and Joe Tiller was the outcome, while he, whoever he was, was merely a facilitator.

Virgil crossed the Ohio River with caution, unsure if he should drive fast to get off the bridge sooner or go slow to prevent undue vibration of its struts. The water was dark and muddy. He was amazed by its width. He stopped at a gas station in Ohio and asked the attendant for directions to the airport. The attendant wore a narrow beard that surrounded his mouth like a stain. A single tattoo of a dark blue rectangle covered his entire forearm. Virgil tried not to look at it.

"Go over the bridge and hang a right," the man said. "It'll take you in."

"No, I mean the Cincinnati airport."

"Like I said."

"I just came over that bridge."

"Well, you went too far."

"Too far for what?" Virgil said.

"You want the airport?"

"Yup."

"Go over the bridge and hang a right."

"I already did."

"No, man. The Cincinnati airport's in Kentucky."

"That don't make much sense."

"A lot don't. I tell you something else, too. Louisville Sluggers are made in Indiana."

"Anything else?"

"Man o'War never ran a race in Kentucky."

"He didn't."

"There's tons of weird shit like that. This country ain't been right since Elvis joined the army."

Virgil left and recrossed the river. There was another bridge in view and two more around a bend. It seemed like a waste to have so many bridges over the same stretch of water. He followed signs to the airport. A plane went past his windshield as if suspended on wires.

He switched wallets, put the money in his pocket, and entered the terminal, curious as to why the doors were so tall. A man gave him a card that said he was deaf and mute and wanted money. Virgil looked at the man, thinking that such a malady was handy in a place as noisy as an airport. The man took the card back.

Virgil bought a newspaper and scanned the automobile ads. When he found one in his price range, he called for directions, walked to a taxi service, and asked for a ride to a town called Rabbit Hash. Having never ridden in a cab, Virgil hesitated at the door.

"Get in the front," the driver said. "This ain't no limo."

Virgil climbed into the car.

"Just get out of the can?" the driver said.

"What?"

"Only guys I seen traveling light as you were convicts coming home."

"Not me."

"Hey, nothing personal. Just that you don't look like a business traveler."

"I got business in Rabbit Hash." Virgil handed him the address. "See a man about a car there."

They passed a hitchhiker leaning against his pack.

"Ever do that?" the driver said.

"Once."

"It ain't a good habit. I got picked up by a dude in a station wagon, man. Made me sit in the back seat. After a while I noticed my shoes were wet. Battery acid. Dude had about a hundred batteries in the back, leaking all over hell. He asked me if I knew any dirty jokes. I told a couple and the dude never laughed. All I could see were his eyes in the rearview mirror. They were bad-looking, man, like burn holes in leather. All of a sudden he pulled over and told me to get out. Last thing he said to me was, 'Anybody knows jokes that good deserves to live.' Two weeks later he was on TV getting arrested down in Missouri. He'd killed four hitchhikers. That's when I started driving a cab. I ain't been out of radio contact with the world since."

Virgil nodded. The more he saw of the world outside of the hills, the less he desired contact.

They left the highway for neighborhoods that reminded him of Lexington, and he wondered if all cities were laid out in blocks. At home the roads ran beside creeks, while foot paths followed game trails. Without animals or water, the cities had no underlying sense of organization.

They reached the address, the last house on a dead-end street that butted against a chain-link fence. Virgil left the car and knocked on the door. A man wearing a Hawaiian shirt opened it. His hair was long and gray, and his face looked unable to produce a beard. Virgil had no idea how old the man was.

"The car," Virgil said. "I called about the car."

The man looked at the cab and his eyebrows rose.

"My brother-in-law," Virgil said. "It's his day off."

The man gestured with his thumb toward the rear of the house. "Key's in it."

Virgil walked around the house and found a plain two-door Chevrolet with a stick shift. All four corners were dented. The side mirror was gone. The driver's seat was sprung and an S-hook held the glove compartment closed. The ashtray and radio were missing.

He had to lift the door to close it. There was no lock. He turned the key and was astounded at the engine's power and its steady rumble. He backed out of the drive and circled the block. The cab driver met him on the street and opened the hood.

"Rebuilt V-8 three-ninety-six," the driver said. "What the fuck kind of car is this?"

"I don't know."

"Hell, this baby could run a stock car. How much is he wanting?"

Virgil told him the price and the cab driver whistled.

"It's the real deal," he said. "Best make sure it ain't warm."

"Warm?"

"Stolen or wanted or something."

Virgil went back to the house. The gray-haired man sat on an ancient rusty glider. He spat a brown line of tobacco off the porch.

"She'll run," the man said. "Pull a hill in the winter. Haul block up a creek bed."

"Tires are slick."

"It's got a spare."

"Have to light a candle to see if the headlights are burning."

"Loose wire's all."

"Generator, I'd say," Virgil said. "Man'd have to put an awful lot of work against it being much count."

"Sure be something when it was done."

"How come you're wanting to sell it?"

"Raise money for my boy," the man said. "It's his car."

"Why ain't he selling it his ownself?"

"They got him locked up."

"Not for stealing cars, do they."

"Hell, no," the man said. His voice was indignant. "I didn't raise no thief. They got him on drugs, what else. That's what they're after all the boys for these days. Every time you turn around there's some politician saying he's sorry for being a drunk, and my boy's in jail. Let me ask you something—how come being hooked on whisky's a disease and smoking pot's a crime?"

"I don't know."

"Insurance companies."

"How's that?"

"If you make being drunk a disease, insurance will pay for treatment."

"I never thought about it that way."

"Not everybody does."

"How bad you want to sell that car?"

"Bad enough."

Virgil removed some money and counted it into his palm, offering half the asking price. The gray-haired man narrowed his eyes at the cash.

"You take this and we're done," Virgil said. "No more phone calls. No more talking to people who just want to dicker and ain't got no money. Here's the money and there's the car."

The man hesitated and Virgil knew he was trying to calculate how much more he could get by holding out. Virgil turned to leave.

"Well, buddy," he said. "It was good meeting you."

"Wait," the man said.

Virgil knew he could have offered less. The man signed the title, transferring ownership of the car to Joe Tiller.

"Remember," the man said. "Drunks kill people. Potheads don't."

Virgil followed the cab to Erlanger where a garage gave the car a tune-up and fluid change. The mechanic told him it should go three thousand miles before needing attention. Virgil drove to the airport, parked in the long-term lot, and walked to his other car. He put the new title and leftover money in the trunk and headed for Lexington. The sun lay to the west, the whole of the continent sprawling beside him.

In Lexington he returned to the Department of Motor Vehicles.

There was a long line at the registration window, and he wondered how people could work inside all day, dealing with strangers in a world of numbers. Virgil could never do it although he knew that many people felt the same about running a garbage route. He registered the car and bought a license plate. There was an insurance company nearby and he arranged for minimum coverage.

He was becoming comfortable with negotiating New Circle Road—go slow, read the signs, and be prepared to backtrack. It was much like following game in the woods. By the time he got home the light was fading behind him. The hills were dark humps in the dusk. Virgil put the plate, title, registration, insurance, and leftover cash in the duffel bag beneath the floorboards. The evening air held the edge of a chill that marked summer's demise. He felt sad that he'd miss the bulk of autumn, his favorite season.

A dog's bark carried along the ridge, followed by another. Virgil recognized them by their cries, knew their habits and who owned them. They were sounds of comfort, the same as freight trains that rumbled the tracks at the bottom of the hill. He wanted to hear them for the next few days, smell pine, walk in glistening dew that made his legs damp. His body sagged beneath the weight of impending loss. He went inside and lay in bed. Sleep took him as if he'd drowned.

He rose at dawn. The rising lilt of birdsong surrounded the trailer and seemed to press against its walls. Virgil spread a mound of coffee grounds in an old handkerchief, twisted it into a tight ball, and dropped the knot into a cup. He poured boiling water in the cup and carried it outside. The morning sun bestowed a sweet light upon the hills. He wrapped a few of Boyd's old weapons in a feedsack, put it in the trunk of his car, and drove to town.

Mist rose like smoke from the creek. In Rocksalt a patrol car waited at a light and Virgil had a quick panic but continued through town to the interstate. As he accelerated up the ramp, he felt as if he were leaving a creek for a river of tar and cement. He wondered if the government had foreseen the results of building the four-laner. The road provided escape, but nothing of merit had been brought in yet.

He exited at Mount Sterling and drank coffee in a diner. Montgomery County had legal bars, lots of money, and a new jail. Virgil recalled the time Boyd had gotten arrested on a drunk charge in Rocksalt. It was late Friday night and the jail was full. The cop phoned the Mount Sterling police. By the time they arrived, Boyd was sober and the Montgomery County jail was full. The jailer kept him in his office until his shift ended, then took him home and locked Boyd in his son's old room. In the morning Boyd woke to the smell of sizzling bacon. The jailer released him, gave him a clean towel, waited outside the bathroom until Boyd finished, and escorted him to the kitchen. After breakfast the jailer and his wife drove Boyd back to his mother's house, and stayed for supper. Boyd liked to say that the only better jailing he ever did was with a boy who'd smuggled dope into the cell.

Virgil finished his coffee and found a gun store. He carried his bundle inside, where a large man stood behind a glass display case. His shoulders lay across his body like a bench. Behind him was a poster that said "American by Birth, Kentuckian by the Grace of God."

The man jerked his chin to acknowledge Virgil. Razor burns marred his jaw. His right hand was out of sight and Virgil knew it held a pistol.

"He'p ye?" he said.

Virgil unwrapped the burlap feedsack to display two shotguns and an old semi-automatic .22 from Sears, Roebuck. He opened the breech of each weapon. The man inspected them slowly, working the action, squinting along the sights. His face showed no sign of his appraisal.

"You sure they're yours?" he said.

Virgil nodded.

"I ain't going to have the law in here looking to confiscate them, am I."

"I can't speak for the law," Virgil said. "But those are my guns."

The man kept his stare fastened to Virgil. His eyes were pale blue and separated by a space the width of three fingers.

"Sale or trade?" the man said.

"Little bit of both."

"What are you wanting?"

"Depends on what they're worth to you."

"Well, that .22 ain't worth more'n a few bucks."

Virgil began wrapping the weapons in burlap. The man placed his empty right hand on the counter.

"I might could use them other two," he said. "What are ye hunting?"

"Pistol."

The man moved to a case full of handguns. Virgil inspected a .45 automatic, a .357, and a nickel-plated .38. He bypassed an expensive Glock 9mm and returned to the .45. It was heavy but attractive, with handcrafted wooden grips. As he hefted it, he casually asked how much his own weapons were worth. The man named a high price, and Virgil knew it was relative to the cost of the pistol he was holding. He set it down and asked for a cheaper .22 revolver. The man's lips tightened. Boyd would have liked to play against him in a poker game.

"If we swap straight up," the man said, "we'll just keep Uncle Sam out of it. No Brady, no tax. Nothing."

Virgil traded for a box of cartridges, drove home, and cleaned the pistol. The sharp scent of gun oil filled the trailer's kitchen. He reassembled the pistol and ate a sandwich of baloney on white bread. Everything was in place, there was nothing left to do. He wore a jacket so he could carry the pistol and ammunition in a pocket and entered the woods behind his trailer.

A chunk of cloud came over the hill and through the sky. He moved downslope, grabbing saplings to slow his pace. The woods held full summer's green and he crossed a dry rain branch and began to climb. The western sun had made tree leaves crinkle and drop. Virgil felt as if he'd moved from summer to autumn simply by crossing a creek. He walked deep into the mineral company's land. No one would bother him there, and he'd not have to worry about trespassing. Company land was handy to have around. He wondered if city people had the same attitude toward a park.

He loaded the pistol and began firing. He was concerned with smooth action rather than accuracy, and after sixty rounds he felt satisfied. It was very loud. The problem with gunfire was that it sounded like gunfire. Many people recognized the differing sounds of pistol, shotgun, and rifle, and some could name caliber. Virgil let the revolver cool before slipping it in his pocket. He had never seen a silencer except on television, and he no more understood how one worked than he did an aspirin.

He returned to his trailer and watched dusk arrive. He wished his brother were alive to give him counsel. He'd be jealous that Virgil got to have the fun of revenge. It was a task more suited to Boyd.

9

After work the next day, Virgil cashed his paycheck and closed out his bank account in Rocksalt, asking for the cash in hundreds. The teller had been skinny and old when he was a kid and now she looked the same. She never gossiped or misspoke.

"How's your mother?" she said.

"Pretty fair."

"And your sister?"

"Not much changes with her."

"More kids?"

"Says she's done."

"How about Abigail?"

"Got herself a promotion."

"I heard that."

She counted a few thousand dollars onto the counter and slid it into an envelope.

"Here you are, Virgil," she said. She smiled without showing her teeth, a sly expression that drained twenty years from her face. She winked. "Hope you young people luck."

Virgil was astonished at the wink. She'd heard that he and Abigail were getting married. The story had probably gotten back to Abigail by now and he felt bad that he'd not seen her in a while.

He strolled the familiar sidewalk of Main Street, passing people whose faces he recognized—as Boyd put it, men he'd howdied but never shook. Teenage boys outside the pool hall stood very close to each other. As they got older, they would move farther apart. Old men in front of the courthouse owned a segment of space that surrounded them like a web. He tried to think of the changes since he was a kid coming to town once a week for groceries with his mother. The drugstore had moved across the street. A new theater had been built, its carpeted floor providing enough static electricity to create fingertip shocks. The small stores were still operated by the same families. There was absolutely nothing to miss.

At a realtor's office, he transferred ownership of his land and trailer to Sara. He explained that it was a surprise gift, and the realtor promised to keep the transaction a secret.

He drove to his sister's house at the head of Bobcat Hollow. The dirt road crossed the creek several times, and in spring the two mixed freely. At the top of the ridge, trees glowed with autumn colors, but near the creek, the leaves were still green. Two dogs loped around the house and barked. A young billy goat with one horn stared at him through a fence, the only penned animal on the place. Sara stood in the garden behind the house. Her legs were spread as she bent from the waist among the furrows. A lard bucket filled with stove ash sat beside her.

"Lord love a duck," she said. "Look what the dogs drug in. Will miracles never stop?"

She stood straight and rubbed her lower back.

"You know, Virge, sometimes I'd rather sort cats than hunker in the dirt all day."

"Best wear welding gloves for that chore."

"They's some to cut the claws off a cat. Did you know it?"

"It's untelling what people will do to an animal."

"I've seen them treated better than kids."

"How's yours?"

"Susie wants to wear lipstick and Jeannie wants to play basketball. Them boys fight bad as roosters."

"Ary a one here?"

"They're in the holler somewhere."

Sara walked primly between the furrows to the porch. She settled into a metal glider with rust spots showing through white paint. Virgil sat in a chair he recognized from his mother's house. It fit the contours of his body like an old coat.

"Wondered what happened to this chair," he said.

"You came around more, you'd know."

"That's sort of why I came by today."

"I kindly had the idea you had something to announce." Sara's grin was sly. "I know you."

"Do you, Sara? I don't feel like the person everybody thinks I am."

"Abigail knows you good enough."

The glider creaked in a steady rhythm that reminded him of bedsprings while making love. One side of the hollow was in shadow. By morning, there would be frost on the dark side of the hill.

"Turning off cold overnight," he said.

"Reckon you came to talk about weather."

"Look, Sara, I know I don't visit enough to suit you. And I got no excuse for it. I envy what you and Marlon have. This is a good place for you all, a peaceful pocket."

"You could have it, too, little brother."

"Maybe, maybe not. That ain't what I'm here over, either. The thing I'm trying to say, what I want you to know. It's just that. Well."

He suddenly recognized the safety of living in a hollow, the security of flanking hills with one route in. There could be no surprises here. Everything came at you straight on. You gave up sunlight but you were shielded from rain, wind, and ambush.

"I know we didn't always get along, Sara. And I know you think I never liked Marlon, but that's not true. I wish. I hope. Well, what I'm trying to say. Sara, I'm glad you're my sister."

"I love you, Virgil. You're a good brother."

Virgil wished everything could be that simple for him. He was unable to say those words, let alone reduce the complexities of family to such acceptance. What he was planning had everything to do with family but nothing to do with love. He stood. He wished she would stand so he could hug her. He faltered slightly as if tired. He wanted to leave before the kids arrived.

"You tell Marlon what I said. Hug your babies for me. Keep them warm. Tell them the truth about me, hear."

"Why, Virgie, the way you talk, anybody'd think you were fixing to elope on us."

He opened his mouth to speak, but closed it.

"You don't have to tell me nothing," Sara said.

"Keep in mind you said that," he said. "Don't you ever forget what you just said."

The glider swayed. As he walked away he knew that he'd never be here again, a thought that was a bludgeon. He backed the car in a half-circle, honked twice, and headed out of the hollow. He wanted to memorize every piece of it, the old fence post covered with vine, a willow that dangled its fronds in the creek. He reached The Road, grateful not to have encountered Marlon or the kids on his way out. Bobcat Hollow stretched toward darkness in his rearview mirror, just another dirt road that followed a creek into the hills. It was behind him now and always would be.

He sat on his trailer steps and listened to the sounds of evening in the woods, the rustle of animals, the call of owl and bobwhite. A strip of scarlet lined the horizon. He was perceiving the world with greater appreciation, like someone who'd nearly died. He lay awake a long time, running through his plans.

In the morning he drove to work for the last time. At the end of the shift, the sound of the time clock hitting his card was a familiar comfort. He lifted the card and dropped it in the hole again. He punched the clock several times until someone yelled behind him, and Virgil placed his card in the rack and joined the flow of men moving down the hall, through the door, and into the sunshine. His car sat between white stripes with the others in the lot. He belonged.

He stopped walking and the men moved around him like water parting for a snag. The old ones plodded to their cars while the young men flicked one another's caps to the ground. The air held an autumn snap. The sky was crisp and clean. This was the time to lay in wood for winter and turn the earth with fall plowing. It was the season to hunt.

He waited for Rundell by his car. The two of them leaned against the hood.

"I know I ain't been much good here lately," Virgil said.

"You work."

"It ain't like it was."

"Live long enough, Virge, you find out nothing ever is."

"You're a good man, Rundell. Best boss I ever had."

Rundell was quiet.

"I've learned a lot off you."

Rundell nodded.

"I'm fixing to make some changes, Rundell."

"Change is good for a man."

"I don't see no way around it."

"You won't be so alone either," Rundell said. "Best thing about it for me was kids. Now I got grandbabies."

"That ain't exactly it."

"I ain't saying she's pregnant."

"You don't understand, Rundell."

"Work buddies see each other different from family and regular friends."

"Maybe so."

"You're a good man, Virge. You ain't afraid of work and you ain't mean. Ever what's eating at you will go away. Just start eating it back."

"Might be that don't do no good."

"Then go on a diet."

Rundell laughed, the lines of his face etched hard but gentle. Virgil reached in his pocket for a small knife.

"Here," he said.

"That's your knife."

"No it ain't, it's yours. No sense in me walking around with another man's knife in my pocket. Take it, now. Go on and take it."

Rundell accepted the knife. He opened the blade, spat on his forearm, and shaved a patch of hair to test its sharpness.

"Good steel," he said.

Virgil walked quickly away and drove out of the lot. He was giving away all his goals at once—his father's cabin, a life with Abigail, becoming a crew boss. There was little to life but work and family, and he was throwing them over the hill. He cut down a side street and parked beside Abigail's car. Virgil climbed the stairs to her apartment door and she let him in.

"Hidy," she said. "I thought you died in a wreck."

"Ab."

He stepped into the room, slightly dismayed as always by the furniture. Abigail had received a touch of sophistication in Ohio, and every surface was made of chipboard covered by woodgrain vinyl that glowed with a perpetual shine.

"Sit down, Virgil. You look peaked."

"I'm all right."

She brought him a bottle of Ale 8, Kentucky's native soft drink, with a distribution limited to one end of the county. The dark green bottle chilled his hand. He took many small sips because he didn't know what to say. He admired her chin.

"You looking at my chin again?" she said.

"Reckon."

"That's why I put up with you, Virgil. You're the only man to think it makes me special."

"When we were kids, you were pretty much all chin."

"And you were one solid cowlick."

Abigail laughed, a familiar sound, and he wondered if everyone's laughter stayed the same, like a fingerprint. He suddenly realized that he'd not considered the leaving of fingerprints. The only gloves he owned were heavy work gloves, not suited to handling a pistol. He wasn't sure if it was a necessary concern since there'd be little question as to who he was. He supposed a man could wrap rubber bands around the joints of his fingers and use a razor blade to carve new prints.

He realized that Abigail had been talking and was now waiting for a response. He felt as he had in grade school when a teacher called on him and he hadn't been paying attention.

"What," he said.

"Now I know what folks are talking about," she said. "I heard you were out of it half the time. Somebody said you were smoking pot, but I said no."

"Not hardly."

"Virgil the hophead." Abigail laughed. "No, it just don't fit."

"People talk, Ab. I know what they been saying, too. I hope you don't let it get to you too bad."

"I don't listen at it much."

"There's something I want to tell."

Her eyebrows rose and Virgil recognized her listening face. When she became truly interested, a vertical line formed between her eyes. He hadn't planned on the visit, let alone what he would say.

"Ab," he said. "Ab."

She nodded. Late afternoon sun refracted through the window, soaking her face and hair with light.

"Ab. I know I've not been close lately. I mean, sort of distant."

He glanced at her and she nodded.

"So what I want to tell you is that it's going to get worse. A lot worse."

He shuffled his feet, wishing he smoked so he could spend a good two minutes lighting a cigarette.

"Now, Ab. You know how I feel about you, and us and all. That's what you've got to remember. Always know that. But I want you to promise me something."

She was very still, as if poised to leap.

"Ab, if anything ever happens, don't you wait around. There's plenty of men in this county to treat you right. You know what I'm saying."

She shook her head tightly. Her fingers were gripping the chair arm. Virgil became aware of a terrible tension in the room and he didn't know what to do.

"Now, Ab, I ain't saying I don't, that I don't want us to be, you know, together. I just want you to know that if something ever happens to me, you'll go on. You know?"

"Are you trying to tell me something?"

"No. I mean yes. What I said."

"Who is she?"

"What?"

"Don't get cute, Virgil Caudill. I don't see you for weeks and your family don't see you either. Then you come up here and tell me to go find a new man. I ain't stupid. It's that little bitch who works in the office at maintenance."

"Who? No."

"Don't say it ain't. I know where she lives, down on Lower Lick Fork, off the interstate. I heard you been driving out that way couple times a week."

Virgil shook his head. He couldn't believe how fast this had gone bad. Abigail's face was red. Her voice had risen steadily, controlled and hard, fury at its edges.

"Don't you sit and shake your head, Virgil Caudill. I won't be treated this way. I ain't your whore to let go of when you're done."

"I know you ain't, Ab."

"Listen at him. He knows I ain't no whore. Thank you. You're pretty nice for a son of a bitch."

"Abigail, it ain't any of this."

"No? Then what? What is it?"

"It's me. That's all."

"That's all," she yelled. "There ain't no that's all to it. I'm part of it, if you didn't know."

"I know."

"Then tell me what's going on."

"Nothing. I mean, I can't."

"Which is it? Nothing or you can't?"

"Both."

"Bullshit! It can't be both. Don't lie, Virgil. You never lied to me, so don't start now. Just tell me."

"There's nothing to tell."

"You know how many people have asked me when the wedding date was? Do you know what it's like to answer those questions when I haven't seen you in a month?"

"I'm sorry, Ab. People do me the same way. They ain't got no life of their own so they want to mess with yours."

"I have a life, Virgil. It's a pretty good one, and you're in it, right? Tell me I'm in your life."

"Ain't me being part of yours enough?"

"Tell me I'm in yours."

"Not just now."

"Get out!"

"But there's nobody else."

"Go on and get!"

"Just remember that I came over here, Ab. You're my best friend. I wish. I . . . I."

Virgil rose and walked awkwardly to the door and stopped. He loved her as much as ever, but he didn't feel it now. He couldn't.

"Get out!" she said.

She was beginning to sob and he knew that she wanted privacy, that for him to see her cry would be another wound. He went out.

"Who are you?" she screamed from the door. "I don't know you anymore. Who are you!"

He descended the steps in a daze. The door muffled her voice, but he knew that she would run through the apartment, slam her bedroom door, and cry on the bed. He sat in the car, feeling terrible.

At his trailer he undressed and lay in bed, unable to sleep. All of his planning ended at Rodale. Afterwards he'd drive to Cincinnati, but he wasn't sure whether to take the interstates or the old state roads. They all ran the same direction, roughly parallel to each other. He could make better time on the interstates, but he'd be more visible, easier to trap. The state roads were private, and offered many routes of escape if he was chased. He was reminded of a question he and Boyd had often asked as children—during a slight rain, did you run to get out of it sooner and risk hitting more raindrops?

He began to worry about the noise that his pistol would make. He wondered if Rodale had a dog. He wondered if he would be able to do it. Sleep was far away. Boyd had always told him that instead of counting sheep, he should talk to the shepherd. Virgil tried but the man transformed to his brother and then to his father. This was not the night for them. He was in it alone.

10

Virgil woke about light. He glanced at the clock and remembered that he wasn't going to work. His limbs tingled as if touched by electricity. He dressed and carried his coffee outside, aware of each movement. He savored the sunlight. The softwood leaves had begun to tighten, their edges shifting color. A cold snap would turn the leaves, and a hard rain would knock half down. Only the oaks were still green. They were the last to shed in fall and the last to flower in spring, as if holding back to make sure of each season's arrival.

After cleaning the small trailer, Virgil shut off the water at the well, flushed the toilet, and ran all the faucets until the lines were empty. He crawled under the trailer with a hacksaw and sliced through the lowest point of the drainpipes. The remaining water spilled to the ground. He watched it soak into the earth, realizing that he would never get town water. He wished he could remain there forever, safe and hidden in the darkness.

He crawled out and poured antifreeze into the drains. The trailer was ready for winter. He unplugged the refrigerator and emptied the food into a sack for his mother. From the floor vent he removed the duffel bag that held his new identification, keys to the car at the Cincinnati airport, and the banded piles of money. He put it and a blanket in the trunk of his car.

As he walked through the tiny confines one last time, he was transfixed by the frozen snarl of the stuffed possum. He'd heard that they didn't play dead, but actually fainted from fear. He placed it in the front seat.

His mother's grass was high again and he decided to cut it. Sara had taken her to town. He was grateful for the time alone at home. The lawnmower engine had a new muffler, and he realized that Marlon had replaced the old one. As he mowed, Virgil wondered vaguely how a muffler could suck up sound. The red leaves of poplar had been the first to drop, and the blades shredded them like a spray of blood.

The work emptied his mind, and an idea leaped into the blank space. He shut off the mower, removed the muffler, carried it into the shed, and fastened it between the jaws of an ancient vise. He retrieved the pistol from the car and selected a drill bit that matched the caliber of the gun. Very carefully, he drilled a hole through the length of the muffler. He changed the drill bit to a sanding head and ran it through the hole until most of the burrs were gone.

After a search of the dim shed, he found a screwdriver with a tiny blade and removed the pistol's front sight. He wrapped the barrel with electrician's tape to act as a bushing. He slipped the muffler over the end of the barrel and used a metal hose clamp to hold it in place. He stared at the pistol, unable to figure out a way to ensure accuracy. A pile of wooden dowels lay in the shed. He wiped them clean and tried several until he found one that was identical to the caliber of the pistol. He slipped it down the muffler and into the barrel to align the muffler's hole with the bore of the pistol. He tightened the hose clamp and removed the dowel.

Outside he loaded the pistol. His mother was still gone and he fired into the freshly mown grass. The sound was more altered than silenced, having lost the sharpness of a pistol shot. He fired several more times. It was loud, but no one could identify the sound as gunfire.

His mother would return soon, and he wanted to avoid his sister. Dust rose from his boots as he left. Ten thousand times he'd walked this route. He knew every tree along the way, recognized the bend of bough, each new scale of bark. He entered the woods as if stepping into a house he was ready to abandon, seeing everything for the last time. Sunlight dappled the forest floor. He followed a game trail to Shawnee Rock. Gray moss furred the north face. He sat within its shadow, remembering that the area was haunted. He'd never seen a spirit and didn't know anyone who had.

He hoped for guidance, but none came. He was just a man alone in the woods. When he spoke, the sound hung in the air.

"So long, Boyd."

He lay on his side with his back against the base of the rock. He closed his eyes. Sleep came on him like a layer of loam.

He woke to late afternoon's red light cutting through the trees. He thought he should have dreamed something profound, but there was only the awareness of being cold and stiff. He walked to his mother's house. She stood in the kitchen, puzzled by the groceries he'd brought from his trailer.

"Fridge broke," he said.

She began putting items away with smooth, practiced motions. He'd always found it easy to lie to her because she preferred to embrace falsehoods rather than accept unpleasant facts. A path worn in the linoleum led from sink to refrigerator to stove. Her face had aged. Virgil was overwhelmed by sympathy and love. She was going to suffer more, and for the first time since he'd embarked on his plan, he felt regret. His departure would mean the loss of another man in her life. She'd be down to a son-in-law.

Virgil moved to her and hugged her tight. He felt her strength passing into him as it had during bad times as a child, and he was astounded once more that he had come from her body. He was leaving forever and he wondered if she would forgive him.

His mother returned his hug with great ferocity. As he relaxed, she did, too, following their familiar cues. They released each other. A pearl of water lay on her cheek. He wiped it with his thumb, a gesture he recognized as hers, one of many he carried.

"How's Sara?" he said.

"Doing good. Said you stopped over for a visit. Said you're full of plans."

"Well."

"Reckon we'll all know soon enough."

Her hair contained more gray than dark, a change he hadn't noticed before.

"You got anything needs done?"

She thought for a moment, cocking her head. The familiarity of the trait startled him. It was as if he was seeing her again after twenty years away.

"No," she said. "I'm pretty much caught up. Plenty of wood. Chimney flue's open. Gutters are clean."

"Marlon's been helping. Sara's lucky there."

"We all are, Virge."

"I just thought you might need something."

"Having you here is enough."

Virgil was trying to memorize her hands and the play of light on her face. She was wearing her Rocksalt clothes, which were slightly garish and tacky. She looked exactly like what she was—a country woman dressed for town. He supposed all people resembled what they were. He would have to change his style of clothing.

They prepared supper together, his mother tolerating his assistance though he knew she preferred to work alone, a family trait. The sunshine fell abruptly away and a chill slid through the room. He performed his tasks with care, hoarding each gesture for future memory.

They ate in the comfort of silence at the table he'd sat before all his life. They washed dishes together. Afterwards they sat in the living room before the blank television.

"What," his mother said to him.

"Nothing."

"You got something in your craw, Virge. I know the signs."

"Just felt like seeing you."

"What brought that on?"

"I don't know, Mom."

"You sure?"

"No reason."

"You never done nothing without a reason your whole life."

"Reckon I'm changing."

"You're an educated hillbilly," his mother said. "The best of two worlds."

"Or maybe the worst."

"Now you're talking out of your books."

"Not with you, I ain't."

"I'm proud of you, son."

Virgil turned on the television. His mother possessed a surprising amount of information on the private lives of the actors. She knew more about them than she did about Virgil. At nine o'clock she said good night. Virgil rose from the chair by the couch, his father's chair, then Boyd's, soon to be Marlon's.

"Mom."

"Yes."

"I, uh."

"I love you, Virge."

"Me, too."

She left the room and Virgil felt pummeled by loss. He left the TV on so she'd think he was still watching. In the bathroom he found an unopened bottle of Valium that the doctor had given her after Boyd's death. He ground a few of the blue pills to dust and mixed it with raw hamburger.

The autumn air carried a chill that focused his mind. Stars glinted in the black sky. His brain worked better in cold weather and he decided to go somewhere that offered a long winter.

He drove off the hill, and on impulse he stopped at the post office. The flag was gone, rolled up on its pole and lying in the building, but Zephaniah would still be there. He lived in the rear of the old company store. He'd long ago trained the community not to bother him over postal matters in his off hours. Virgil went to the back and knocked. Zephaniah was wearing slippers that made him walk differently. He looked older than at work. Virgil sat on the couch. The last time he'd been inside was as a child when he and Boyd had asked for water in summer.

A black-and-white photograph of a man and woman hung inside an embossed frame. The woman was pretty. The glass was rippled.

"That you?" Virgil said.

"And Pearl," Zephaniah said. "She died."

Virgil had assumed that Zeph had always been alone. The thought of him as a young man in love was disconcerting.

Zephaniah placed his feet on a stool made of six large juice cans covered with red cloth. He leaned back in his chair. His glasses were missing an arm and hung askew on his face. Light from the kitchen spread into the room. Virgil tried to think of something to say. He tipped his head against the back of the couch and stared at the ceiling. The corner was dark. A strip of wallpaper hung like a dog's tongue. Virgil closed his eyes. The scent of kerosene lingered in the room from many winters' worth of heat.

He opened his eyes and was briefly unsure of his surroundings. Dusk had turned to night. Zephaniah sat in his chair, his fingers folded toward themselves as if fused together. Virgil moved to the door. The outside air was black.

"Good-bye," he said.

Zephaniah nodded once.

Virgil stepped into darkness. As he closed the door he watched the interior light condense to a strip that ran across the yard and vanished.

He sat in his car a long time, his mind moving in a dozen directions. He was dismayed that, having lived in one place all his life, he had so few people to tell good-bye.

He drove east and turned left at the fork instead of toward home. He followed an overgrown dirt road through the creek and up the hill. It was the remnant of an old logging trail that met a fire road at the top of the ridge. Virgil stopped and left the car. From the trunk he removed the paper bag that contained the hamburger and the pistol. White tree stumps rose like teeth on the trail. The moon lay on its back.

Virgil moved along the treeline that seamed the ridge. At its edge, he crouched in the brush and looked down at the small house where

Billy Rodale lived. Starlight illuminated old tires lying on the low-pitched roof. They held the tar paper against the wind that gusted off the ridge. Rodale's car sat close enough to the house that a driver could step onto the porch.

He watched for a long time as the woods settled into their overnight silence, broken by an owl's cry or the movement of a forager in the brush. Virgil was hot and cold at once, as if suffering from fever. He felt his heart working hard. He slipped his right hand inside the front of his pants to keep his trigger finger warm.

He could walk away.

He could return to his car, drive home, and go to work tomorrow.

He stood and stretched. The sky was black. He loaded the pistol and began descending a steep hill, holding the pistol awkwardly against his chest. When he heard the first rattle of the dog's chain, he threw the paper bag toward the doghouse. The dog barked several times, a sound that hushed the woods and drew a sweat from Virgil's forehead. He could hear the rustle of paper as the dog began eating the hamburger, and he hoped it wouldn't die. The shiny muffler gleamed in the moonlight, a ridiculous-looking weapon.

He waited a long time before tossing a rock at the doghouse. It bounced twice. There was no response and Virgil threw another rock. The night stayed quiet. He eased from the woods to the open space of the yard. He ducked beneath the window of an add-on bathroom, remembering that he and Boyd had come here as kids to watch its construction.

At the corner of the house he stopped. The urge to flee nearly overwhelmed him. He endured a trembling spell. When it ended, he stepped onto the porch and a board creaked. He walked on the sides of his feet to the door. He drew back the hammer on the revolver, a click that roared in the quiet, and turned the doorknob as gently as possible. His knuckles brushed the faceplate as he pushed the door open. Dim light shot across the floor in front of him. He stepped in fast, facing the kitchen. The door to his left was the bathroom he'd passed outside, and he moved the opposite way to the front room. He froze at a low steady sound and the flicker of movement. A wave of sweat drenched him. He remembered to breathe. There was a dull gleam mixed with the sound and Virgil realized that a television set was turned on, and the station had gone off the air. Facing the screen was a couch on which Billy Rodale lay asleep. He was breathing from his open mouth, a sound that droned through the room.

Virgil felt his entire being turn inside out. The sodden smell of dirty dishes, stale beer, and unchanged clothes hung in the air. He felt each particle of air that touched his body. He could hear the man's breath twined with the hum of the TV and the sound of his own rushing blood. Virgil was aware of tremendous power. Rodale was small and pathetic. He was beneath pity. He was an animal in a dank lair, the runt of an abandoned litter. He should have been drowned at birth.

Virgil stood still until he felt in full command of his faculties. He had a sense of being part of all life. He moved a small step forward, his vision held to Rodale's face, the pistol before him. It weighed nothing, like holding a twig. Rodale's face was pulling the gun barrel across the room, which in turn pulled Virgil's hand, his arm, and his body. He stepped into the TV's glow, blocking its eerie light.

Rodale's eyes opened. He stared without moving. He compressed his lips but didn't speak. He closed his eyes and opened them and they appeared to age as if a disease had attacked. His entire body seemed to retreat into itself, a drawing in, as if to present a smaller target.

Virgil wanted Rodale to talk or move, give him a final reason to fire. Every molecule of his body was at war with itself. He had the sensation that the pistol was part of his body, that the bullets it contained were made from his marrow.

The television flickered.

Rodale glanced at the change in light and Virgil squeezed the trigger. Rodale's head bounced against the cushions. A hole appeared in his face and Virgil continued to fire the pistol until the room filled with the smell of cordite and the hammer was clicking against an empty chamber. The couch glistened with fresh blood. Rodale's legs were twitching and part of his face was gone.

Virgil didn't move for a long time. He lowered the gun and moved to turn off the television. In its brief flare of light, the bits of bone and bloody flesh that remained of Rodale's face burned into his mind. The air became very dark. Silence entered the room like a force, a void that lacked Rodale's breathing.

Virgil stumbled from the house. He gulped the night air like a drowning man who'd resurfaced, then vomited with great force. It hit the road hard enough to raise dust. The smell rose to his face. He turned to the dark hills that were no longer his.

Slowly and with great effort, he entered the woods and climbed the hill. His car was where he'd parked it. The trees were the same. Nothing had changed.

11

He drove down the rough road to the blacktop and headed for town, forcing himself to maintain a slow speed. Rushing air rinsed his face. At a railroad crossing he threw the pistol into a hole of water, remembering that he and Boyd had swum there naked as boys. He banished his brother from his mind. The debt was now discharged. He was free.

He followed a state road bearing west, his mind a house he'd battened down for a storm. He could not risk thought. A shower slapped through the trees and was gone. After three hours of winding roads, he parked in the airport's long-term lot and shifted his gear to the other car—blanket, jacket, possum. A domed garbage can gleamed like the top of a skull. He pushed the metal flap open and hesitated, not wanting to discard his wallet so easily. A car entered the lot and he released the old leather.

He continued north. Stars spattered the night like flung paint. Huge trucks sailed past as if they were ships leaving a wake that rocked his car. He was tired. He felt as if the car were standing still and the road unfurled before him. Near the Wabash River he stopped for a small room that smelled of old smoke. He slept rough, waking several times, after enduring a dream from childhood that filled him with terror. He remained in bed long after light seeped through the curtains, infusing the room with a dreary glow. He no longer had a future or a past. There was only the inescapable now.

He was astonished by the size of the Mississippi River. He left his car and walked along the bank, past beer cans and condoms lying in the weeds. His feet sank in mud. The murky surface rippled like muscle, swirling as if it contained many creeks that twined through its body. He cupped his hands to drink. It tasted bad but he didn't think a river that big could be poison. In the slanting red light of afternoon the bridge glowed as if the metal had been heated by flame. He returned to his car, placing each step with precision. He felt unbalanced walking such flat terrain, as if he might tip onto his side.

Corn in Iowa had been harvested, leaving splintered stalks rising from the earth. Pigs foraged in the fields. Barns sat very near the houses as if to conserve the energy of walking. A flock of dark birds rose from the low remnants of soy, lifting like a blanket to hide the light. Near dusk he reached the Missouri River and stopped at a scenic overlook, curious as to what constituted high elevation on such flat land. A tower rose from a parking lot. He climbed its five open flights to a platform from which he could see Nebraska, a vista that filled him with profound unease. On every horizon lay a treeline. Abruptly he didn't know where he was. He began to tremble with such force that he gripped the railing to prevent a fall.

In South Dakota his motel room matched the one in Illinois except for the carpet, which was the color of grass parched by drought. He lay unable to sleep, still feeling the rhythm of the road throbbing in his body. Fragments of Rodale's death seeped into his mind and he tried to blot them like a stain. He hoped the dog had revived.

After a few hours he woke, confused until memory bludgeoned him and he quickly rose, with no idea of where to go. The empty landscape was flat as tin. He felt like a bug exposed when someone lifted a flat rock. He drove west all day, and in the afternoon, he watched the sun begin its decline. Dusk was short. Kentucky nights began on the ground, in the hollows and the woods, moving upwards to join the sky. Here, the darkness dropped from above.

He made Wyoming by night and slept in a field. In the morning he crossed Dead Horse Creek, a bed of dry grass with no horse in sight. The land was desolate save for oil wells, their steady motion reminding him of chickens pecking for seed. The only shade was in a ditch. A pale blue line etched the horizon, jagged and white, too high for land. He expected a storm until he realized it was the Bighorn Mountains with snow lying along the upper ridges. They rose from the earth like a wall to the west.

He entered Montana through the Crow Reservation. The lack of humidity kept the air clear, making everything appear distinct regardless of distance. The land seemed oddly like a model, as if constructed on miniature scale. Clouds rose in the east while the western sky held the darkness of distant rain. He enjoyed a physical sense of insignificance. The landscape had an inviting quality, seductive but lethal.

A four-door pickup passed him, driven by a young man wearing a western hat. Heavy mudflaps covered the tires. In the rear window hung a lasso with a pair of baby shoes dangling in the center of the coil.

He slept behind a rest stop and rose with the pink dawn, surprised at the lack of grass, dew, and birdsong. The Absaroka Mountains stood in the south, hazed by distance, topped with snow. The hum of silence filled the chilly air. He continued west on I-90, passing a three-tiered stack of hay the size of a house surrounded by a split-rail fence. Though he was driving fast, several cars passed him, and he wondered about Montana's speed limit. He'd seen no signs.

The land continued to rise. He thought the hill between Bozeman and Livingston was of good heft until he began the long climb to Homestake Pass. At its crest was the Continental Divide, where flat rocks protruded vertically from the earth like plates of stone. He felt bad for the crew who'd built the road, but was deeply envious of the man who'd laid it out. It was the harshest land he'd ever seen.

He began the long descent into Butte, a town sculpted into a mountain, presided over by a giant statue of a woman. He'd left the realm of autumn colors for uniform slopes of conifer trees. The mountains became steep and the valley tight. Several times he crossed the Clark Fork River, shallowed by the season to the size of a creek. Afternoon sun gleamed on great bluffs that rose beyond the water. Logging trails laced the slopes. He arrived in Missoula at dusk, took a room, and slept fourteen hours. After a meal and a short walk, he returned to bed. The next day he slept and ate and slept again.

12

On the third day Joe Tiller rose early and walked the wide streets of Missoula, his breath visible in the cold air. Many of the low buildings were made of stone, with broad alleys and parking lots behind. There was a spacious quality to the town that was absent in Kentucky. Mist lifted from the mountains to reveal giant white letters made of concrete—an L and an M. He wondered if there were so many mountains that they were coded rather than named. A herd of elk browsed the slopes above the town.

The only open business was the Wolf, its orange sign aglow. Just inside the door was a locked cabinet containing pints of liquor to go, and a long bar where a few men waited for the first drinks of the day. A rifle collection hung from pegs high on the wall. There was no clock. Most of the clientele looked as if they had long ago abandoned a life that revolved around being anywhere at a specific time. Beside the bar, several people were eating breakfast at a low counter. A man slept at a table. A dog slept by the door.

Joe ordered breakfast. As he ate, he dropped a slice of toast, and a grizzled man beside him grinned. "They put stuff on that to make it slippery," he said. His voice held the jocular camaraderie shared by single men eating public meals alone. In that instant, Joe decided to stay in Missoula.

He looked through the local paper. Work was scarce and the classifieds had a section labeled "For Giveaway" that offered pets and furniture. The cheapest rates were sharing a house, but he knew he couldn't live with anyone. He shoved the paper away and spilled his coffee, which flowed along the counter toward the man beside him. Joe apologized and the man shrugged.

"I can't believe how much it costs to live here," Joe said.

"Movie stars," the man said. "They're ruining it for the rest of us." He gave Joe a careful look.

"Don't worry," Joe said. "I don't even like movies."

"This used to be a working man's town."

"I'm looking for work, too."

"I can't help you there, partner. This is a bad time for it. Maybe in the spring."

"Shoot, I got to find a place to live first."

"How fancy you want it?"

"Not too."

"Used to be, you could rent fishing cabins through the winter up some of these creeks. Might be cold."

"What creeks?"

"Grant Creek's out, it's full of movie stars. Rattlesnake's crammed with houses, too. Even little old Lolo Creek's got million-dollar log cabins on it now. About all that's left is Rock Creek. Best thing is to drive up there and ask around."

Joe thanked the man and left the Wolf. At a gas station he stopped behind a convoy that included a six-horse trailer and two pickups. One truck bed was filled with provisions and another held the remains of several elk. Rows of rifles blocked each rear window. The outfit reminded him of a military operation rather than a hunting party, and he thought of men at home emerging from the autumn woods with a rifle in one hand and a gutted deer slung over their shoulders.

He drove east along the river, found Rock Creek, and stopped at a bar. The female bartender told him about a cabin several miles up the road. He entered a hollow and was reminded of Kentucky—a narrow road that separated hillside from creek. The land opened to a wide bottom that offered summer campsites, RV hookups, and tipis you could sleep in for an appalling price.

Just beyond a bend, a man stood in water to his knees. He wore a short vest and rubber boots that ran past his armpits. He didn't seem to have entered the creek so much as to have grown from it. Suddenly he snapped upright and a fishing rod flashed above his head, trailing a thick luminous line. He pulled the line with his free hand and Joe shook his head at the tangled mess that would surely surround him in the water.

The narrow road twisted with the water's flow. Half the hollow lay in deep shadow cast by the mountaintop. Rock Creek glittered to Joe's right, swift and wide, broken by vacant beds of stone. A small green sign announced his passage into Granite County. The road became dirt. He followed a turnoff to a small house beside a stack of firewood bigger than the house itself. The ground was hard and tipped by frost. There had been a light dusting of snow but wind had moved it, leaving patches of white against the earth. Winter lived here while town still held autumn.

A man stepped from the woods, wearing a flannel shirt with sleeves ripped away at each elbow. He carried an ax in a casual manner. Joe was chilly in his jacket, but the man seemed impervious to weather.

"Came about the cabin," Joe said.

The man led Joe through open woods to a twin-rut road that ended at a small cabin made of log. A stove flue poked from the roof. "Door's open," the man said. His voice was low and thick, as if unaccustomed to speech.

The inside air was much cooler than outdoors. The cabin was one large room and a bath with pine walls that soaked up light. The furnishings consisted of a bed, a table, two chairs, a couch, and a bureau. There was a woodstove with a metal thermometer attached to the flue. From the window Joe could hear the rush of water over rocks. Another thermometer was visible through the glass.

Outside, the landlord removed a tube of lip balm, uncapped it, gave his mouth a coat, recapped the tube, and slid it into his pocket. He performed the entire process with one hand.

"Looks good to me," Joe said. "How warm is it?"

"It's a summer cabin, insulated with sawdust and newspaper. You'll need plenty of firewood."

"Can I get it off you?"

The man shook his head. He gave Joe a scrap of paper with a name and phone number for wood. He told him the rent.

"If I pay in advance, will you lower it?"

"Now you're talking my language," the man said. "I'm Ty Skinner."

He offered his hand and Joe hesitated before taking it. He wanted to get the words right. He should have practiced.

"I'm Joe Tiller." It sounded hollow and thin.

"Proud to know you. I'll be your neighbor, but you won't hear a sound out of me. Nearest phone's at the tavern by the interstate. You can get your mail there. It's got the only TV for miles. Only people, too."

"I'm here for peace and quiet."

"You'll fit in, then. But you got to be out by May. Rent triples for tourists."

"Tourists?"

"This is the best fly-fishing stream in the world. It's famous. Canyon fills up with boneheads all summer."

Joe understood that a canyon was the same as a hollow.

"Think I'll need snow tires?" he said.

"They just mean you travel further before you get stuck. Then you got a longer walk back."

"I never thought of it that way."

"Most of you southern boys don't."

"How'd you know that?"

"You got an accent. Don't worry, I like southerners. It's the Californians I'd like to shoot. They think blue's the same color everywhere. Out here it's not."

Joe nodded. He was confused by Ty's words, but didn't want to show any affinity to a Californian.

"Is that them standing in the water back there?"

"No," Ty said. "They're locals. Fish all winter. Best thing about Alaska was no Californians."

"You lived up there?"

"Ten years."

"Like it?"

"Fucking loved it, man."

"Then why leave?"

"Got lonely. I came down to Montana for the social life."

"I heard it's beautiful up there."

"You can't eat the scenery."

Ty looked at him briefly and walked into the woods. The tall pines took him swift as sudden dusk.

Joe went inside his house. He turned the faucets on and off and tested the shower. He plugged in the refrigerator and listened to the hum. He sat on the couch. He moved to the chair. He lay on the bed, which sagged. He opened each drawer of the bureau and lifted the windows to flush a stale smell. There was nothing on the walls. He went outside and sat on a stump. The cabin was half the size of his trailer, and the mountain rose behind it like a fortress wall. He was Joe Tiller and this was where he lived.

He returned to Missoula, where he called the wood man and arranged for a delivery the next day. The treeless mountains surrounded the town in pale green humps that seemed to be set in place rather than rising from the land. Higgins Street ended at a large red sculpture of the letter X repeated four times. Joe wondered why the town emphasized the alphabet.

The midday air warmed him. He thought vaguely of buying a calendar, but time had ceased to be important. Beside a bar was a pawnshop filled with knives, CD players, leather coats, and guns. The proprietor wore a pistol on his hip and moved with an athlete's grace. His pale eyes were flat and hard. On a glass display case was a stack of bumper stickers, each of which said FEAR THE GOVERNMENT THAT FEARS YOUR GUN.

Eventually Joe would need a weapon, but he couldn't yet bear the notion of handling a gun. Instead, he bought a snakeskin belt and a leather buckle imprinted with a royal flush in diamonds.

"I'll be back for a pistol," he said.

"You need a Montana driver's license. Plus there's a five-day wait. Government sticks its beak in all our business."

"Why's that?"

"Can't take care of its own, I guess."

"Don't make much sense."

"No. They forgot it wasn't too long back, we used guns out here for protection. I been here four generations. My grandfather killed off wolves that bothered his stock, and now they're putting wolves back and taking our guns. I'm glad he's not around to see it. Here, take this."

He handed Joe a leaflet printed on a single sheet of paper, folded in thirds. On the front panel were the words LIBERTY TEETH and a crudely drawn American flag. Joe opened the paper to a drawing of two crossed rifles and the words "A well-regulated militia being necessary to the security of a free state, the right of the people to keep and bear arms shall not be infringed—UNITED STATES CONSTITUTION."

The third panel showed a blurry picture of George Washington with a word balloon above his head: "Firearms stand next in importance to the Constitution itself. They are the American people's liberty teeth and keystone under independence."

"George Washington," Joe said. "Think he really said that?"

"He was a soldier, wasn't he?"

"Reckon so."

On the wall behind the man hung a prosthetic leg. It was old and heavy, with exposed springs and cracked leather straps. Joe figured it was an antique. It was colored to resemble flesh but had faded to the hue of a terrible burn. Joe pointed to it.

"Guess I'll know where to come if I need one."

"I thought he'd be back the next day."

"How long you had it?"

"Two years," the man said.

"He must have been hard up."

A small girl pushed the door open, carrying a man's jacket over her arm. She placed the jacket on the counter and stared at the floor. She was very thin.

"Your daddy send you in?" the man said.

She nodded.

"He in the bar next door?"

She nodded again.

"Tell him I can't take it today."

She left with the jacket. The man's expression returned to its hardened cast.

"That ain't right," Joe said. "Her coming in here that way."

"It's a free country."

Joe went outside and threaded the belt through the loops of his pants, feeling closer to belonging in the West. The sun poured heat into the town. A tall woman wearing a fur coat and high heels emerged from an espresso shop. She sat sideways in a sports car, swiveled her legs into its plush interior, and drove away. Seconds later, a young man holding a straight razor backed out of a bar, forced by an older man who gripped the kid's wrist. In a deft motion, the man disarmed the kid and sent him stumbling against a parked car. The man returned to the bar, which released a stream of laughter before the door shut again. The kid skulked away as if kicked. It occurred to Joe that a snakeskin belt didn't make him belong here at all.

At a secondhand store he bought clothes, a sleeping bag, several blankets, and kitchen supplies. Many of the customers were Indians and he was careful not to stare. They appeared sad, rather than fierce, reminding him of people from the deepest hollows in Kentucky. They dressed the same, too—quilted flannel shirts, jeans, and boots.

He stopped for groceries and drove east on the interstate, past a sawmill pumping thick smoke into the pristine air. At the mouth of Rock Creek he headed south toward the Sapphire Mountains. Half the canyon was deep in shadow.

Outfitting the cabin required less than half an hour, and he washed the kitchen supplies twice to draw out the chore. He spent several minutes arranging his pillow and sleeping bag on the bed. In the kitchenette he changed the order of food along the shelves, stacking the cans in descending order of size. He distributed the clothes among the bureau drawers. On a nail by the door he hung a heavy coat with a phony sheepskin collar. His mother had always had a junk drawer in her kitchen, and he designated one as such, except he had nothing to put in it.

He granted the possum a place of honor on top of the refrigerator.

Dust fell from its pale fur. One eye was gone. He stroked its back. The bare walls made him sad, and he went outside and sat on a stump. The enormity of the decisions he'd made crashed against him like surf.

He rose abruptly, as if motion would blot the past, and looked around for somewhere to go. The woods at home had always served as solace and he decided to see Rock Creek. A faint path wove through the cottonwood and pine. Trees grew farther apart than in Kentucky, and groundcover was thin. The creek had no bank. The land ended and the water began. Orange moss shimmered on the bark of a cottonwood, the biggest tree along the stream, and at its base was a necklace of gnaw marks left by a beaver. Joe admired the beaver's ambition, the boldness necessary to make such an attempt. He wondered if it was a bad sign to envy animals.

The water sparkled in the sun, running swift and black in the shade. The sun receded behind the mountain peak like an eye that abruptly closed and doused the canyon's light. Joe remained by the water, soothed by its motion, as darkness moved through the valley like wind. The air became cold. Stars were bright and very close. A high-pitched yip echoed through the woods, trailing away in a mournful call. It came again, rising and falling in a lilt, repeating itself, and though he'd never heard the sound before, he knew it was a coyote. When it stopped, the woods seemed more silent than before. Full night had arrived. Joe headed for the cabin, quickened by a faint fear of losing his way. He undressed and went to bed.

He woke in a fetal ball, watching his breath turn white in the glimmer of dawn. His face was cold. Inside the sleeping bag, and beneath several blankets, his body was very warm. The thermometer attached to the woodstove read thirty-eight degrees, and the outside thermometer said forty-five. Joe gathered his clothes, stepped outside, and dressed in the sun. Larch flared in lines like candles along the higher slopes.

He fixed coffee and sat on the stump. A magpie's black-and-white wings made a pattern that reminded him of rowing rather than flight. He washed his cup, then washed all the dishes he'd bought the previous day. He made his bed. He adjusted the possum. He felt the urge to tidy the cabin but there was nothing out of place. He sat on the stump and tried not to think of Rodale. His mind skipped to Abigail, then to his mother, Sara, Marlon, and Rundell Day. He didn't want to think about them.

He went in the house and stood before the bathroom mirror, which framed his face in metal strips.

"Hi, I'm Joe Tiller," he said.

He shrugged. It didn't sound right.

"Name's Joe," he said. "Joe Tiller."

"Nice to meet you. They call me Joe."

"I'm Joe. Joe Tiller."

"Just call me Joe."

He looked over the cramped room, the narrow shower, the single nail for his towel. Sheetrock tape showed through the plaster where the corners met.

"I'm Joe Tiller," he said, "and this is where I live."

He walked around the cabin, checking sightlines. Anyone could easily see inside. He'd have to keep the curtains closed. Under the porch he found a shovel with a split handle. The land glowed beneath a clean sky. He ate lunch. He wished he smoked for something to do.

A man arrived in the afternoon with two cords of firewood. His dump truck held dents on every surface, including the roof, as if it had been batted about by a giant bear. The side mirrors were fixed in place with wire. A small boy sat in the passenger seat. The man eased to the ground, talking before he got the door shut. An eye was gone and the skin sagged over the hole like a slack drape.

"You're lucky," he said. "I had wood left over. Not much call for a load this size. Demand's went down in Missoula since that new law."

"Which one was that?"

"It won't let them burn wood half the winter."

Joe laughed.

"I'm serious as a heart attack," the man said. "New houses can't put a woodstove in. They got an anonymous phone line to report your neighbor for heating his house with wood. About like a tip line for poaching."

"What for?"

"Damn air's no good. The same air stays in the valley till spring. Everybody just breathes each other's old breath, about like being in the joint. I was at Deer Lodge for thirty-two months and ten days. You ever do any time?"

"No," Joe said. "Why?"

"You got a look is all. I seen it before. Down the road from Deer Lodge is the old territorial prison from a hundred years ago. You know it's a tourist place now. People pay good money to go in there."

"I can't see that."

"Tell you something else I don't get is being a guard. Every damn one was a registered son of a bitch. They spent all day in the same place as me, only difference was they went home to eat and sleep."

"Maybe get a little fresh air."

"Not if they lived in Missoula. Some days you're supposed to stay indoors."

"How do you know when?"

"It's in the paper."

"Well," Joe said.

"Indians wouldn't camp there in the old days. The fire smoke didn't go nowhere. Then the white man came along and built a town."

The man was becoming agitated. Joe jerked his head to indicate the child in the truck.

"Looks like you got you a helper."

"My boy," the man said.

"Family business?"

"Dad owns the land we log."

"Must be nice to work together like that."

"Right now I live half a mile from my folks," the man said. "Sometimes I wish it was more like five or six."

Joe paid in cash and the truck bed rose on its hydraulic stem, dumping the wood. The man drove in little jerks to dislodge the last of the load, leaving deep grooves in the grass. He circled the cabin and Joe waited for him to return and stack the wood. The sound of the truck's engine faded through the woods and after a while he realized that the man was not coming back. Joe studied the wood, dismayed to find it was all the same—thin pine. There were no big chunks of hardwood for overnight, no hot-burning ash to take the morning chill off the house. The timber business was better in Montana than Kentucky. The wood cost more and weighed less, and the customer stacked it himself.

Inside, he stroked the possum's back, wondering if they lived in the West. He wished he'd asked Morgan what had possessed him to stuff the ugliest animal in the woods. The cabin was dark. The walls seemed to be closing in on Joe like a cardboard box that was slowly being crushed. He hurried to his car and drove to town. Mountains ringed Missoula like the sloping sides of a giant bowl. A layer of gray clouds made a lid that clamped in car exhaust and chimney smoke. His eyes stung. His throat hurt.

At the Department of Motor Vehicles he took a written test for switching to a Montana driver's license. The majority of the people in line were newcomers from California who wore western shirts with button-down collars. Joe passed the test but decided to grow a beard before the photograph. He wanted the picture to look nothing like his face at home.

At the edge of town he stopped beside the mountain where he'd seen the herd of elk. He followed their trail as it wound through the saddle of a gap, then left it for the summit. Hard snow lay like web in the crevice of shade made by rock. At the top he rested, his breath gusting in the chilly air. Sweat cooled inside his clothes. He'd penetrated the haze that draped the town, as if he'd risen above a high-water mark left by flood. The air was clean, the light pure. Missoula sat below the surface like a city beneath the sea.

Joe lay on his back and remembered a boy he'd grown up with who couldn't wait to leave the hills. He'd gone to Detroit and worked in the auto plants for ten years, and finally returned. He bought an old house on his home hill and put a mail-order skylight in the roof. Neighbors came to see it, astounded at the thought of someone cutting a hole in his own roof. After nine months the man left again, as if being gone had poisoned him for living in the hills.

Joe began walking down the mountain. Two hawks spiraled a thermal, rising in a column to the darker blue above. He wondered if he'd ever love this land strongly enough to be ruined by living away from it. Montana was similar to Kentucky except the mountains were higher and there was no oak. At home the poor people lived in the hills and the rich people lived in town. Here it was the other way around.

On his way out of town, he stopped at a used-car lot. He looked at a four-door pickup with twin tires in the rear and heavy bumpers. Another truck had aluminum siding over a plywood topper with a chimney flue protruding from its pitched roof. He bypassed the late-model cars for an old Jeep Wagoneer. It reminded him of a station wagon crossed with a truck, jacked high all around. The locking front hubs were alien to Joe, but it was the kind of vehicle a man wearing a snakeskin belt might drive. He traded for it, paying a little boot.

He drove home and sat on his stump. A zigzag shadow cast by the mountain split the canyon. The land was as alien to him as the inside of his cabin. The air turned gray, then black. The coyote called. Snow began to fall.

He had food but wasn't hungry. He had a Jeep but nowhere to go. He had a new name and no one to call him.

13

November descended over the valley with a harsh freeze. Every morning Joe woke to a dead fire and the desire to stay in bed. Scales of frost covered the interior windows. The stovepipe made an angle that should have been an elbow but more closely resembled a dog's hind leg. Smoke leaked around loose rivets at each joint. He opened the door of the cabin and wondered if cold air entered or warm air left.

After a month of evenings alone, Joe drove to Missoula at dusk, where people in light jackets walked on clear sidewalks. The inversion that held bad air close to the earth also kept the temperature high.

He parked beside a sculpture of a mountain lion that resembled a giant pile of cement manure and walked around the corner to the Wolf. He stepped aside for an elderly man who staggered toward the door, holding each stool for balance. An Indian woman slept at the bar, wearing a faded jacket bearing the name of a tavern. Beside her slumped a skinny cowboy with a dog at his feet. The back of the cowboy's neck was scarred. His huge ears had several holes in them, and Joe realized they'd been hit with a load of small buckshot.

"Dad was in a rocky place," the man was saying to the bartender. "He jumped from one rock to another. The rock went. Killed him. Big rock. They'll kill you."

A raspy voice announced Keno numbers through a speaker that hissed and crackled like a green wood fire. The smell of spilt beer, fried food, and cigarettes clung to the room. Computerized slot machines jingled and hummed, occasionally emitting the electronic music that serenaded a winner. The players stared at the screens as if hypnotized. Beyond them hung a tarp that served as entrance to a strip club. An extremely fat biker checked IDs at the door. Crude tattoos covered his hands.

Joe walked past the tarp to the last chamber of the Wolf's warrens—the poker room. It had its own mini-bar and bathroom. A TV was mounted on the wall, tuned to a channel of perpetual sports and no sound. Ribbons of smoke twined overhead. Two players wore sunglasses and headphones, and Joe wondered if blotting the senses aided gambling or was the ultimate goal. Above the cashier's cage hung a hand-printed sign that said, "Not even Mom gets credit."

The cardroom manager limped to a chalkboard on the wall.

"You're first up," he said. "What's your name?"

"Joe."

He wrote Joe's name on the board. The dealer wore a multicolored hat shaped like a bottle cap that looked like it clamped to his head. A ponytail hung down his back. He waved a bill and asked for twenty hard, thirty soft and the manager carried the bill to the cage for chips and change. Joe sat on a stool and opened a gambling magazine. He enjoyed seeing his name on the board and having people know it referred to him.

The Wolf's primary game was Texas Hold'em, played at ten-dollar limit. The dealer placed five community cards in the center of the table, to which each player added his two hole cards to make a standard poker hand. There were four betting rounds. Hold'em moved faster than most other games and could seat many players. Joe studied the competition as the dealer shuffled. There were a couple of rocks who only bet on winning hands, possessors of enormous patience. A woman sat at the table with her top two buttons loose. She flirted openly. Joe recognized her as a very good player, made better by men's underestimation of her. If she was in a pot, Joe decided that he would simply fold.

Hanging from the walls were portraits in oil and Joe recognized one of the players, who was eating biscuits and gravy and using hand signals to indicate his action. He was tall and lean, with a drooping black mustache. His hands were big enough to conceal ten chips, which made it impossible to gauge his bet. A wall of chips was stacked in front of him.

The game continued with a steady rhythm of cards and chips, the passing of the button that marked the player's force bet. After half an hour, a player pushed his chair from the table and stood. His face held no expression as he slipped on his jacket and turned away empty-handed. He headed for the strip club, as if the sight of nude flesh in dim light would compensate for bad cards in harsh light. Joe pretended to read the magazine. He was waiting for the manager to call his name because he wanted to develop the habit of responding to it.

"Seat open, Joe," the man said.

Joe moved to the low table covered by scarred green felt and laid his money down. He belonged. After a few hands, it became apparent that everyone was after the endless cash supply of a man with powerful forearms and large fingers that covered his cards like piled lumber. He drank steadily, bet each hand, and didn't seem to mind losing. When it was his blind bet, a new dealer asked if he was taking points.

"What for?" the player said.

"Tournament. That's how you qualify."

"When is it?"

"Saturday."

"I'll be in Hawaii."

"Think of me," the dealer said.

"I will. I just got back from Alaska. Six months on a boat. I never want to see snow again."

No face registered the news, but everyone knew that the man from Alaska had ended the fishing season with a wad of cash. With a mark like him at the table, the game became a contest to see who got more of his money. Players only left if they got broke and were unable to borrow a stake.

Two hours later, the fisherman departed cheerfully after dumping six hundred dollars into the game, the price of reassuring himself that strangers liked him. Joe had captured seventy dollars and considered cashing out. Instead, he loosened his play and chased poor hands. Within thirty minutes, he'd lost his winnings and was making a rebuy. He concentrated on getting even.

After an hour of folding bad cards, he won three pots in a row. He tipped the dealer and stacked his chips. He was on a rush and could feel the luck surrounding him. Other players sensed his power and threw away cards they'd normally play. He won two small pots simply by raising in good position. He was playing well because he truly didn't care if he won or lost. He understood why Boyd had been such a consistent winner.

The dealer gave him pocket kings and he raised the limit before the flop. Four players called. The dealer flopped three cards simultaneously, a nine of hearts and an ace, deuce of clubs. Everyone checked to Joe and he bet out. Two players called and he put one on a club flush draw, the other on a pair of aces. The dealer burned a card and turned a king. With three kings, Joe checked, setting a trap. There was a bet and he raised, and a player re-raised. The third man called the bet and Joe considered folding. Three kings was a good hand but the action suggested higher cards against him. Joe made the final raise.

The river card was a nine of clubs. That gave the board two nines and three clubs with an ace and a king. Joe had a full house, kings over, against a certain flush and an unknown hand. He bet the limit, found a raise, and re-raised. The player raised back. Joe pushed the remainder of his stack to the middle, and the other two players called.

"Let's see what we got," the dealer said.

Joe hesitated before displaying his hand, in order not to appear overeager for the pot. He showed his cards and prepared an expression of sheepish good humor, as if he felt bad for possessing a hand of such strength. One player flashed his club flush and threw it in the muck. The other man flipped two aces, giving him a higher full house than Joe's. The dealer paused so everyone could see the outcome, then shoved the chips to the winner. Joe pushed his chair from the table. He had a headache and an urge for candy.

"Drawing dead, wasn't I," he said.

He walked through the cafe in a loser's daze, reliving the hand. It made a good bad-beat story, but everyone had them, and no one wanted to hear another.

The bars had closed and people were staggering into the cafe. A trio of bleary-eyed students bumped against him and continued without apology. Joe stepped aside as a biker escorted one of the strippers to her car. In the bright fluorescence, she looked tired and lost. A young woman sat before a slot machine, pushing buttons in a daze. A scar cut her eyebrow in half. At her feet slept a baby in a car seat.

A waitress stood beside a table of fraternity cowboys from the university. She raised her voice and called to the cook behind the counter.

"He needs them," she yelled. "We got one who needs them!"

The cook grinned at the waitress, who was grinning at her customers. Everyone seemed to be grinning but Joe, who was envious of a kid so much at home here that he could order brains and eggs for breakfast.

Outside, falling snow blurred the air. The lights of the city were softly diffused, casting a glow over the silent streets. Joe drove home, parked, and stepped into the harsh wind that sliced through his pants and numbed his legs. He recalled making a windbreak for his trailer at home. He had planted hybrid poplars that were guaranteed to grow six feet per year, the result of a special root grafted to each stem. He felt similar to those trees. Just as their alien roots had grown into the earth, he needed a past that led here.

In the cabin he built a fire as his father had taught him, tightly rolled paper on the bottom, kindling with air channels, two small logs over that, and a big log in the back. Making a fire was one of the few endeavors that he enjoyed. He went outside and stacked wood on his right arm against his chest. The smell of smoke hung in the air, held to the earth by snow. He remembered Boyd's contempt for people who lived in a hollow rather than on a ridge. "House in a hollow makes weather follow," he'd often said. Now Joe had become a lowly hollow-dweller, even though the hollow was fairly wide. This much open space in Kentucky would be the site of a town.

Light leaked through wall cracks like grain from a slashed feed sack. There were hills and trees and a creek, but none of it was his. He thought of his father's log cabin and knew he'd never live in it. It was the only thing he'd ever truly wanted. He wanted to cry, but it was a distant sensation, like the first urges of hunger.

He packed the stove, knowing that the wood would burn to ash by morning. He slid into his sleeping bag. The bare walls seemed to contract and expand like a lung. He wanted some pictures and a radio. He wanted something to read.

In the morning, fog lay across the mountain peaks as if the trees were wrapped in gauze. He drove to Missoula. The Wolf's bar was already lined with drinkers and he vowed to stay out. He searched the junk shops until he found a clock-radio, a deck of cards, and a toaster. The book selection was mainly romance with a few cookbooks. Deep in a corner, beneath a brittle canvas tent, he discovered a milk crate filled with paperback westerns, a thick history of railroads, a computer guide, and an economics textbook. While carrying the crate through the store's narrow aisles, his elbow brushed a pile of tri-folded pamphlets to the floor.

At the top of each in big letters were the words LIBERTY TEETH. Below was a quote from James Madison: "Americans have the right and advantage of being armed—unlike the citizens of other countries whose governments are afraid to trust people with arms." At the bottom of the page was the phrase MONTANA FOR FREE AMERICANS ONLY.

Joe stacked the pamphlets on the counter, confused by their purpose. Kentucky was a gun culture, but he'd already seen more weapons in Montana than at home. It seemed odd for people here to be concerned about having enough guns, like a wheat farmer who worried about running out of seed.

He paid and walked to his Jeep. West of town he parked at a tire store, surprised by the line of people. There were three clerks, two men and a woman, and when it was Joe's turn, the woman stepped forward. Her snap-front shirt was embroidered with roses.

"Busy, ain't it," he said.

"Weather does that."

"Weather?"

"It's snowing up high. Road to Lolo was a mess this morning. I passed two pileups on the way in."

"Not too bad now, is it."

"I'm not driving to work now, either."

"I guess not," Joe said. "I need four new tires."

"Who doesn't." She laughed. "What are you driving?"

Joe gestured through the plate-glass window. He wasn't sure what to call it—a Jeep or a Wagoneer, a car or a truck.

"That blue rig?" she said.

"Yup."

"Will you be driving snow, gumbo, or highway?"

"I'm not exactly sure what gumbo is."

"If you don't know, you aren't driving it. Snow or highway?"

"Just regular road, I reckon."

She came around the counter and rolled two tires off a rack. He admired the ease with which she handled the heavy rims. He had never bought new tires before and she patiently explained variations in width, tread, and grip. After twenty minutes, he bought a set and waited in a small room while the mechanics switched the tires. Three other men were there.

"Snowing up high," Joe said. "That Lolo road was a mess this morning."

No one looked at him.

"Good for the tire business, I guess," he said.

The man sitting directly across from Joe lowered his head in a single slow nod and looked away. In Kentucky the men would be hunched forward, discussing weather, dogs, and tobacco prices. These men maintained a studied effort to occupy their own space.

When a mechanic drove the Wagoneer to the lot, Joe returned to the office and settled his bill. A burly man in a short-brimmed pearl Stetson was talking to the same woman who'd helped Joe. The man became confused by the variety of options. It seemed to annoy him that a woman knew more than he did about truck tires. He raised his voice and spoke slowly to her, the same way people in Lexington had spoken to Virgil when they thought he was a dumb hillbilly.

The woman stepped backward and began to nod. A male clerk took over and the woman began anew with an Indian couple. They listened carefully and asked many of the same questions as Joe.

He paid cash and received his change. The woman in line behind him was nearly fifty, but was dressed like a college student. She reminded Joe of a woman from the hollows at home who'd moved to town and married a doctor.

"I feel sorry for that gal," she said. "Don't you?"

"Who," Joe said.

"Her." She gestured to the saleswoman talking to the Indian couple about tires. "It's just a shame she has to spend her time educating those people."

The man behind the counter gave Joe a receipt.

"They're from deep on the Rez," he said. "Probably the first time they bought new tires in their life."

"I don't guess they'll pay with a credit card," she said.

"We got all kinds of payment plans," the clerk said. He tapped the bald spot on the back of his head. "See that? It's from the tipi flap hitting the back of my head sneaking in and out at night."

Joe looked from one to the other, unsure of what to say. They had taken him for a Montanan and he was pleased until he realized that their mistake was based on his skin. As he left, the saleswoman began to raise her voice and speak slowly to the Indians.

He drove to his cabin and spent the afternoon watching squirrels work like ants, dragging pine cones the size of their bodies to hideouts in the woods. Instead of dusk, the light simply ceased. He built a fire and stood in the middle of the room with a blanket over his shoulders. The radio emitted fuzzy static across the dial. He wished he could get religion. People at home took it up when they drank too much, got old, or were hunting a spouse, but Joe figured God wasn't ready to hear from a murderer so soon. When the stovepipe glowed he lay on the couch. He nodded to the stuffed possum and closed his eyes. Sleep came easily, the sweetest of escapes.

The cold woke him at dawn. The plank floor chilled his feet through wool socks. In his long johns, Joe stepped to the porch for more wood and was transfixed by the sound of many geese. They flew overhead in long ragged lines, their cries braiding in a harmony that surrounded him like wind. As they followed the valley south, the air slowly stilled until silence returned. Stray light haloed the mountain peaks.

He made a fire, and when the stove was hot enough he boiled water for coffee. The radio still didn't work. He started reading a paperback western but it opened with a man alone in a cabin, and he set the book aside. He wished he had photographs for his walls. Already the memory of his mother's face was fading in his mind. He'd spent much of his life outside, and he wasn't sure if walls kept him in, or the world out. People covered them with things, and he wondered if it was to hide what walls were—obstacles to light.

In the bathroom mirror he tried to find a sign of himself. The features were familiar. He had his father's jaw and cowlick, but the face was no one he knew. A beard was growing. The deep-set eyes were the same, pale and squinty.

He went outside and sat on the stump. Mist turned the trees from green to gray. The most light was near the water, and the sound of Rock Creek carried easily over the snow. He rose and struggled through heavy brush to the water's edge. At a sharp curve in the creek's path he watched the water come out of a turn, race past him, and plunge into the next bend. It moved much faster than the Blackfoot or the Clark Fork River, and was at certain points wider than either one. He couldn't figure the difference between a creek and a river in Montana.

Motion in the landscape made him still, and he breathed through his mouth to reduce sound. Brush shook across the creek two hundred yards upwind of where he sat. A large white shape emerged tentatively from the woods of a narrow draw. Joe thought it was a deer covered with snow until he saw the short neck and the dark horns that curled from the heavy head. The ram stepped into the clearing and drank from the creek. Its fur was thick and shaggy. As abruptly as it appeared, the bighorn vanished into the woods. Joe watched until the brush stopped moving.

Beyond the water, green moss glittered on the granite bluffs. Joe spoke for the first time all day.

"My name is Joe Tiller and this is where I live."

He repeated himself over and over. His voice mixed with the hum of the creek, and his words swept into the woods. When his throat ached from the cold he returned to the cabin and went to bed. The weight of blankets pressed against him as if nailing his body in place. He stared at the pine ceiling varnished to a gloss that caught light in the burrs of its knots.

This was not his world.

14

The first snow never left, but stayed in great drifts that completely obscured the rear of Joe's cabin. Montanans, he noticed, never referred to snow as snow, but called it weather, as if the term made the season easier to endure. He wondered what they called spring rain.

Without a work schedule, Joe's body found its own rhythm. He rested when tired and ate when hungry, adopting the simple cycle of an animal. He spent part of each day restacking the firewood, building columns and filling between them with smaller logs. He read the history of railroads and wondered what became of all the Chinese who'd done the work. The books on computers and economics he used for kindling, a page at a time.

A pine knot made a dull explosion in the stove and Joe went outside to gather more wood. It was the most sun in a week and he felt grateful. The brightest light shimmered ahead of him and he trudged through a knee-deep drift to face the sun. A gust blew snow from the boughs of an ancient pine. His face warmed. He closed his eyes. For a moment he forgot himself and wondered how his mother was. Boyd had taken care of her as best he could, a responsibility that Joe had inherited. Marlon would take the role now. She was probably deciding if the giant candy canes made of cardboard would last another Christmas. Joe's mind moved like lightning to chop that thought short. He opened his eyes. Trees along the peaks were glowing silhouettes.

When his beard was full, he went to town for his driver's license. The clerk asked for his address.

"I'm in a fishing cabin on Rock Creek," Joe said.

"Rural route?"

"I don't know."

"Mailbox number?"

"It's just temporary," Joe said. "I get mail at a bar."

"We'll make it general delivery, Rock Creek," the man said. "Social Security number? Or do you want your own?"

"My own what?"

"A different number?"

"That'd be fine."

"I figured so," the man said. "It takes a little longer."

Joe wondered if Montanans had a special respect for privacy, or if everyone outside of Kentucky did. He stood awkwardly before the gray background and waited for the camera's flash, another act that would sever him from home. The state was supplying him with proof of who he wasn't. The clerk made two photographs and gave Joe the spare. He sat in the waiting area and studied the tiny picture, confused by its resemblance to his brother. Joe didn't think he looked like Boyd in the flesh, but the picture did. He stared at it for a long time, trying to understand the difference.

The clerk shook Joe's shoulder.

"Hey, Mr. Tiller. You all right?"

Joe blinked at the man.

"I called you three times," the man said. "Here's your new license."

Joe slipped it in his pocket and left. Outside, he stared at the mountains around the town—his town now, his land and sky. He removed the Kentucky license from his wallet. The picture didn't look like anyone now. He bent it in half and dropped it down a sewer grate.

He drove through Missoula, trying to understand why people lived in such a tight cluster. He supposed they had more friends than he did, but town only made him lonely. Driving offered comfort, the motion itself a form of solace, and when he reached his cabin, he didn't want to go in. It was a pathetic-looking little shack, cold and dark, like old man Morgan's house.

Stricken with panic, he turned away and ran, lifting his legs high of the weedy snow. His breath blew hard. He was the only color in a land of black and white. His foot slipped and he fell and his head bounced against a snow-covered rock. He rolled on his back, waiting for his vision to clear. A silken sky stretched between the mountains, the blue of water overhead. He felt as if he were lying on a beach looking out to sea.

He'd heard that freezing to death was the easiest way to die. You were supposed to get warm after a while and slide into sleep. The snow would cover him like a quilt. He'd never awaken in a strange place again. When he realized where his mind had taken him, he was overwhelmed with terror. He stood and began moving. With no one to turn to, he had to be careful not to turn on himself.

He returned to his Jeep and drove out of the canyon. Spruce boughs drooped beneath the weight of snow. The creek was frozen along the bank, forming a white border for its flow. He met a car and the driver lifted a forefinger in what passed for a wave. Joe was still a stranger, but his vehicle was known.

He stopped at the bar by the interstate and parked beside three cars, one bearing a Buffalo Bills bumper sticker. As he stepped inside the saloon, his head grazed a gigantic moose head hanging from the wall. Below it was a cigarette machine. He sat at the bar, a long slab with high stools placed on a floor covered with peanut shells and sawdust. Slot machines lined the wall. A machine gun was fastened above the bar with Christmas lights hanging from its front sight. Two men shot pool in the back.

The bartender had a stalwart cant to her posture as if she was prepared to withstand rough weather and rougher men. Joe ordered juice, and while she filled a glass, he studied three large squares of posterboard that hung behind the bar. A list of names was crudely printed on each.

"That's who's barred," the bartender said. She pointed to each list in turn. "Barred for a week, barred for a month, and barred for life."

"What'd they do?" Joe said.

"The first list is for fighting and the second is for coming in with a weapon."

"What's the third?"

"Using the weapon."

She was looking Joe in the eye, a female version of many Montana men, thick-shouldered with no neck, big hands, and a determined attitude—not someone to get riled. The fact of her gender made her more intimidating than the men. She strode away and Joe watched her hips inside her jeans.

The opening door flashed a line of light across the floor as an old man entered. He walked in a peculiar flat-footed way, exerting motion from the hips down, while his face and shoulders remained still. Joe wondered if his gait was the result of hours on horseback or a lifetime of walking in high-heeled boots.

The man sat at the other end of the bar.

"Ugliest bartender in the West," he said.

"Red beer, Coop?" she said.

He swiveled to look at Joe. "One for him, too."

The bartender half-filled two glasses with tomato juice and poured beer on that. She brought one to Joe. The man lifted his glass in a toast and Joe sipped the drink. It tasted like watered tomato juice with beer's tang behind it. He joined the old man.

"Hate to drink alone," Coop said. "Even if I can't really drink."

"No?"

"Red beer's like sending a boy to do a man's job."

"How come you can't drink?"

"Had me a heart attack. Blew the bottom tip right spang off. Doc said it was like an engine threw a rod from running out of oil."

"That's rough."

"Not so bad. They tell me if I eat an egg, not to eat the yolk. About like having a screw without a kiss. Now that's what you call rough."

He was wearing a baseball cap with a Buffalo Bills emblem.

"From the East?" Joe said.

"Hell, no. Never been there."

"Reckon you just like football," Joe said.

"Professional sports is the fourth worst thing ever happened to this country."

"It is."

"Television's third."

"I don't have one."

"Maybe there's hope for you yet."

"What's the others?" Joe said.

"The second's both parents having to work just to get by."

"How about number one?"

"You're not ready for that yet."

A fine network of lines crossed Coop's hands like cracks in an old plate. Each heavy finger held a large gold ring.

"That's not for show, partner," Coop said. "And not for fighting either. That's gold. This hand is worth more than a credit card. Paper money used to be good for gold, but not since the thirties. Now plastic stands for cash. You know most of the money in the world don't exist?"

"I didn't know that."

"Don't exist at all. All money is blood money, but only gold is real. That's why there's sawdust on the floor."

"I don't get you."

"In the old days, people bought drinks with gold dust. At the end of the night, the owner swept the sawdust and sifted it for gold dust. Gold's not much count. Bends too easy and won't hold an edge. But you can trust it for value."

He tilted on the stool to pull a gold coin from his pocket and passed it to Joe. It was very heavy.

"Fifty years ago," Coop said, "twenty of those would buy a new car. It's the same now. Twenty still gets a car. That don't work with cash."

Joe placed the coin on the bar, wishing he had one. He'd never owned a new car and couldn't recall anyone who had. He'd always heard that two years old was the best buy. He wondered how many gold coins that would take.

The two pool players joined them from the back. One was a wiry kid who moved in reckless jerks as if attacking the air that surrounded his body. The other man looked a few years older than Joe and also wore a Bills cap.

"Found a friend, Coop?" he said.

"Just a beer buddy."

"Coop don't get a chance to talk much," the man said.

"He was doing all right," Joe said.

"Usually does. Was he going on about gold?"

Coop's chin rose and his eyes closed down as if they had flaps.

"Damn straight," he said. "There's a trillion dollars on paper in the world, but only a billion cash. That's a tiny percent. It's not money anymore, it's data."

"I know it," the man said.

"This kid don't. I'm just trying to educate him. Doing a damn fine job until we got interrupted."

"Aw now, Coop," the man said. "Let's all have a beer." He made a gesture to the bartender, then offered his hand to Joe. "I'm Owen. Coop here is my granddaddy. This is my little brother Johnny. You don't live around here, do you."

"Got a cabin up Rock Creek."

"You rent it off Ty Skinner?"

Joe nodded.

"Is it warm enough?"

Joe shrugged. He didn't want to complain about the cold, or the cabin, especially since the men knew Ty. No one spoke. Joe had the feeling he'd stepped into a brier patch. He thought of Boyd's ability to make conversation with anyone, by continuing to talk until someone responded. He'd heard men discuss sports for hours, a habit he'd never understood.

"I guess you all must be big Bills fans," he said.

The men didn't answer, which confused him because of the hats.

"I like baseball, myself," Joe said. "It's the only sport left where anybody can play. Size don't matter."

"It ain't about football," Johnny said.

Owen gave his brother a hard-eyed stare, then turned back to Joe. Owen was a big man and Joe didn't want a problem. He sipped the red beer.

"You must like it private up there," Owen said.

"I do," Joe said. "Usually I go to town when I get jumpy, but tonight I came in here."

"Town?" Coop's voice held a tone of disgust.

"Yeah. Plenty to see." Joe glanced at Owen. "Less trouble, too."

"There's no trouble," Owen said. "We just don't want anybody taking advantage of Coop. Don't take much for that coin to disappear."

Joe stood.

"Thanks for the beer," he said to Coop.

"Don't let Owen run you off," Coop said. "It's just his way."

"Maybe so. But it ain't mine."

Joe left, and as the door swung closed behind him, he heard Owen's voice quiet the old man's complaint. Silence hung like a weight in the clear night sky. The Big Dipper aimed its bottom lip north while Orion struggled over the mountain. The parking lot spread into the dusk beneath a marble moon.

Joe's eyes in the Jeep's mirror seemed sad. He inspected his new license in the dim shine of the dome light. The eyes were too small to see. He drove to the door of the tavern and rolled his window down.

"I'm Joe Tiller," he yelled. "I live here, too."

He drove to town very fast, overtaking every vehicle on the road. Snowflakes the size of quarters vanished against the windshield. He passed through Hellgate Canyon, a narrow entrance to the flat basin of town. Missoula was brightly lit, thick with Friday night traffic. Ranch kids in pickups cruised down Higgins, circled the 4-X sculpture, and drove back through town. The snow was gone and the air was warm. Bare mountains surrounded the town, dark hulks that blocked the sky and held in weather. The gritty air clung to his face.

He entered a bar with no sign. The front half was crowded with old hippies and bikers, Indians, cowboys, and Vietnam veterans. Regulars received every third drink free, signaled by the bartender rapping her knuckles against the wooden bar. On the walls hung framed photographs.

The rear of the tavern held a throng of university students. Many of them carried backpacks with plastic mugs fastened to them by a mountain climber's carabiner. Some wore shorts with long johns that ran into heavy boots. Hair was either very long or very short.

Joe's rough appearance made people think he was a local, but the crowd only increased his sense of isolation. He wasn't sure how to act. Men at home usually drank outside, separate from women. In Montana bars, it seemed as if everyone yelled to be heard above everyone yelling. He ordered a red beer, a drink no one at home would touch, but holding it made him feel as if he belonged.

A man behind him shouted to a woman.

"I'm from California but I've been here six years."

"I'm a native of right here," she said.

"All your life?"

"Not yet."

"How long you lived here?"

"Till now."

"Yeah, right," the Californian said. "More power to you." He turned to Joe. "I'm from California but I been here six years. Where you from?"

"Mississippi," Joe said.

"The river or the state?"

"What?"

"You know, like how people always say about New York. The city or the state?"

"Yeah," Joe said. "Sure, I know."

A woman at the bar laughed, spit flying from her mouth. She wore a leather vest and held a cigarette beside her mouth. Her eye was freshly blacked and swollen. Two men squared off by the cigarette machine and backed up like roosters. One shouted "Happy birthday," and they ran toward each other, heads bent low, arms at their sides. Their heads butted and they bounced apart, grinning madly.

A short, broad man carried a tumbler of Scotch with no ice. He was battered as an old ship, still intact and making headway, people trailing behind him as if drawn by his wake. His voice was a rapid growling rasp. "The shit you see when you don't have an automatic weapon."

Joe turned back to the Californian, but he was gone and another man had filled the space.

"Order me a tequila if she looks at you," he said.

"Okay," Joe said. "Where're you from?"

"Albania, but I been here twelve years."

Everyone tried to compete for a Montana pedigree. It began with old families and worked its way down to the recent arrivals. The longer you'd been in the state, the more deserving you were of living there. Each group of newcomers resented the next and everyone conveniently left the Indians out of the equation. It seemed to Joe that people forgot Americans were allowed to live anywhere in the country, including Montana.

Two men pushed past him and ordered shots of whisky.

"Did you see her eye?" one said.

"I've seen better heads on beer."

The woman with the black eye lurched off her stool. She grabbed the man's left hand and pointed to his wedding ring.

"I call that a no-pest strip," she said. "So you can shut your goddam hole."

She dropped his hand and veered toward Joe.

"I'm from the South," he said, "but I been here a month."

"Anaconda," the woman said, "but don't hold that against me."

A young woman with long brown hair walked through the bar. She was tall and attractive, and held a basket of roses for sale. A man in a crumpled western hat bought three and handed them at random to nearby women. The seller continued to stand there, and someone nudged the man and told him she was waiting for a tip.

"I'll give you a tip," he said. "Stay out of Butte."

Everyone laughed and he bought more flowers. The wide-shouldered man Joe had seen earlier ordered a round of drinks for a dozen people. He handed Joe a full shot glass.

"Thanks," Joe said. He pointed to the photographs on the walls, several of which had gold stars affixed to a corner. "Who're they?"

"Patrons," the man said.

"What's the stars for?"

"They died."

The man lifted his glass in a silent toast to the dead. Joe drained the small glass, wincing at the taste.

"You from here?"

"El Paso," the man said. "How about you?"

"Ken—" Joe began, then stopped. He forced himself to shrug. "Around," he said.

The man nodded as if the answer was common. Joe pushed his way to the door, stepping over the legs of a man sitting on the floor. He was furious with himself. Outside a dog was chained to a rack of bicycles. Two pickups raced down the street, driven by teenagers in western hats, and Joe thought of Boyd drag-racing his big Chevelle on the straight stretch of road below their hill. He stopped and looked into the shadowy reflection of a store window. Fuck you, Boyd, he thought.

He walked until he felt calmer, passing new stores with pastel awnings and coffee places that didn't serve a straight cup of coffee. A shiny shop was devoted to upscale bathroom gear. Coming toward him at a rapid pace was an Indian man wearing an army jacket. Beneath his arm was a stuffed teddy bear. His eyes looked as lost as Joe felt.

The bright orange sign of the Wolf protruded at an angle from the building's corner, but Joe continued past the front door and down an alley. Like a porno shop or a speakeasy, the Wolf had a side entrance for the poker players. A seat was open and the dealer gave Joe a hand before he sat down. Joe raised without looking at his cards, and the dealer held the flop until Joe threw money on the table. Someone bet. Joe raised as he removed his coat. The dealer burned a card and turned one face up and Joe raised the bet again. He made the final bet before the river card, and three players called. Joe flipped his cards. He had a pair of tens and there was one on the board.

"Three tens," the dealer said. "Takes the pot."

He pulled the chips in a heap and used one arm to sweep them to Joe.

"You should cash out," a player said. "Quit while you're ahead."

Joe laughed. At the table's end was a man dozing between hands, his shirt risen high to expose his belly. One of the dancers played cards while waiting to go onstage in the next room. A young kid sat at the mini-bar, asking people to lend him a gambling stake. The green felt of the low table was smooth, and the chair molded to Joe's body. He felt good.

He settled into the intricate web of the game. Players came and left, tapping out, buying in, complaining about the dealer, demanding a new deck, filling the air with smoke, and covering the table with fine ash. Joe's stack of chips continued to grow. He played as if under a hypnotic spell, adding chips to the pot with a flick of his wrist, playing as Boyd had taught him. He was hitting overpairs and big kickers on every flop. His good hands received callers. If a flush bet out, he'd last-card a boat. When facing a full house, he'd hit quads on the river. He flopped sets again and again, slow-playing until the turn, then hammering the bet. The cards were running over him and he was running over the game.

At one in the morning the game broke. They were down to three players and the dealer's rake was pounding them with chip removal. Joe cashed out with seven hundred dollars. He was tense and hungry but didn't know what to eat.

He stepped into the dim confines of the strip club and was blasted by the sound of music, the smell of sweat and beer. Two bikers shot pool. A woman in boots strolled a small stage with a slick floor and a mirrored wall. Off-duty dancers carried drinks on small trays. He'd never been in a strip club before.

The dancer squatted before a cowboy who held a rolled dollar bill between his teeth. She removed his hat, leaned close to his face, pressed her breasts together and used them to take the dollar. She backstepped quickly, her face angry. "Fucking asshole," she said. "Don't lick."

She moved down the line like a nurse ministering to patients. No one touched her. She laughed with a few men, and gave the older ones special attention. Joe pulled a five-dollar bill from his pocket. When she squatted before him, he wanted to ask her name and how she wound up with the occupation. Perfume surrounded her like a cocoon. He looked in her eyes and gave her the five.

"Here you go," he said. "Thanks."

"Back at you," she said.

She leaned to kiss his cheek and he smelled her hair and lipstick. Sweat glistened on her breasts as they pressed against him. He reached for her without thinking, but she was gone, had pulled back as if anticipating his movement. Joe watched her walk away. He felt as if she were twitching her hips for him alone.

The man on the stool beside him elbowed Joe. "Wish I had that swing on my back porch."

The lights were dim, the music loud. The woman prowled the tiny stage until a man waved a dollar and she leaned over him, bending from the waist with her back to Joe. He had never seen a woman stand in such a way and he felt a tingling below his belly, the first desire in months. Her legs were strong, the muscles of her thighs taut. Joe imagined standing behind her. He wondered when she got off work, and if she had a boyfriend.

A woman tapped him on the shoulder. She was wearing a halter top and denim shorts cut high above each hip. She asked if he wanted a drink. He nodded, unable to speak. He felt like he had as a child when he came off a ride at the county fair, overwhelmed by sensation, wanting more.

"What can I get you?" the waitress said.

He continued to nod and she turned away. The dancer was kicking crumpled dollar bills toward the rear of the stage. The music ended. Another dancer stood in the wings, holding a cassette tape, waiting her turn. She removed gum from her mouth and pressed it against the rung of a chair.

Joe waited for the dancer to come out of the dressing room, and after a few minutes she joined the bikers playing pool. Joe watched, feeling as rejected and ignored as he had in high school. He left the bar and hurried through the diner to the street.

Just outside the door, two men struggled on the pavement. A short guy clung to the other man's long hair, beating at his face. The tall man rolled on his back to pin the short one beneath him. A city patrol car arrived and two cops approached the fighters.

"Get him off me," the tall guy said.

"It looks like you're on him," the cop said. He bent over the men. "Come on, Jim Buck, turn loose of his hair."

The two men rose and stared at each other while the cops stood between them. The car's toplights flashed red and blue across the concrete.

"Jim Buck, you start walking south," the cop said. "And you, what's your name?"

"Nick."

"He come up and grab your hair from behind?"

"How'd you know?"

The cop shrugged. "He's from Bozeman. Got a car?"

"Around back."

"Go on home."

"I just got here."

"You got an ear problem?"

"I'm going, I'm going. It just don't seem right."

"Stay away from here tonight."

Joe headed for his cabin. At the edge of town, the red sign of a motel was partially lit by flickering neon. Joe impulsively pulled into the lot. A bleary-eyed desk clerk gave him a key. In the room was a single bed and a television. Joe lay on the bed. The ugliest picture he'd ever seen was fastened to the wall by six screws. A phone sat on a table and he felt an intense urge to call Abigail. He couldn't remember if the time in Kentucky was earlier or later than Montana.

He woke fully dressed on top of the bedspread. Sunlight filtered through the curtains as he removed his clothes and went back to sleep. In the afternoon he took a long bath. Winning money at poker had given him the first good feeling in months and he strolled downtown. A faint snow made the buildings indistinct, as if seen through silk. The money felt free to him, come from nowhere, and he wanted to buy something before it wound up transformed to a stack of chips in someone else's pile.

The courthouse reminded him of the one in Rocksalt. It was built of stone and occupied an entire block, with a statue of a soldier charging across the wide lawn. Across the street was a bail bondsman and a lawyer's office. It occurred to Joe that Montana made life handy for criminals.

He found a pawnshop with rows of leather jackets and stereo equipment, a motorcycle, and a pinball machine. The young proprietor wore a heavy mustache that ran to his jawline. Joe inspected several pistols and asked for a .32 caliber that would fit in a coat pocket. The man gave him a form to fill out.

"Costs fifteen dollars to run the Brady check," he said. "Come back in five days."

Joe didn't want to put his new name into the federal system. A driver's license was risk enough.

"It ain't the money," Joe said, "but I don't come to town that often. I'd just as soon get everything taken care of at once."

"I understand, but I can't."

"What about if you just sell it to me personally?"

"Wish I could, partner. All these guns are catalogued already and I have to account for them."

"Ain't they nothing I can do?"

"Use the paper," the man said.

"What do you mean?"

"Take a look at the classified ads in the newspaper. Hell, it's like a black market."

"How about ammo?"

"Don't worry, they'll have that, too."

Joe bought a gun cleaning kit, and inquired about gold coins.

"What weight?" the man said.

"How's it come?"

"Ounce, half-ounce, and a quarter."

"Ounce I guess."

"Eagle or Maple Leaf?" the man said.

"Shoot, I don't know."

"Eagle is American. It's ten-percent copper alloy but the value's the same. Canadian Maple Leaf is solid gold."

"What do most people get?"

"You know how it is around here. Folks mainly go for American. Had some Krugerrands out of South Africa but some man bought them all. Came in wearing full fatigues and carrying a Glock. Paid in hundreds."

"Reckon I'll take the Eagle."

The man stepped into the back room. Stacked on the counter were new Liberty Teeth pamphlets. The front held a quote from Thomas Jefferson: "No free man shall ever be debarred the use of arms." Inside was a drawing of a scaffold with a man hanging from the noose. Pinned to his shirt was a note that said RACE TRAITOR. A fire burned below his dangling feet. At the bottom were the words MONTANA FOR AMERICANS ONLY.

The man returned with a gold coin in a small plastic bag. It was very heavy. One side bore a raised image of an eagle bringing a sprig to its young in a nest. Below it were the words ONE OZ. FINE GOLD—50 DOLLARS.

"Fifty bucks," Joe said. "I'll take half a dozen."

"I guess you would. We go by spot price in the newspaper, plus twenty dollars."

"Then what's the fifty on it mean?"

"Original mold." The man shrugged. "They never changed it. I don't know why."

The price of the coin was very high, but Joe bought it anyway and slipped it in his pocket. He tapped the pile of pamphlets.

"What are these all about? I keep seeing them."

"Some friend of the owner drops them off. I threw out two bunches and got in trouble over it."

"What's a race traitor?"

"Hell if I know. I can't keep up with that bunch. One week it's Indians, next week it's taxes." The man shook his head. "They started out being over gun control and I was all for it. The government wanted us to hold a guy's gun for three days when he took it out of hock, but that didn't work out. Pawnshops put up a stink all over the country. Now they got the sheriff's office doing extra work, running background checks. Some of them are so busy with paperwork, they can't get out and do no sheriffing."

"Do these pamphlets help?"

"Hell, no. They piss a lot of people off, including me. But it ain't my store. If it was, I'd get rid of the damn guns and deal in video games. Biggest turnover we got. You don't want to look at a setup, do you?"

"I don't have a TV."

"No problem, partner. We'll fix you right up."

Joe shook his head and left. Though it was late afternoon, he ate breakfast at a diner and read a newspaper. For the first time in months, he took an interest in events of the world. There was an article about Christmas spending having risen since last year. He checked the paper's date and was astounded to learn that it was January thirteenth. The holidays had come and gone without his notice. He thought of his mother and was stricken by the knowledge that she'd stayed near the phone in case he called.

From a pay phone he called a number in the paper that advertised guns for sale. The voice on the other end was curt, stressing that he only had legal weapons. Joe told him he wanted a small-caliber pistol and arranged to meet the man in the parking lot of a tavern. Outside, a thick snow fell. Neon bar signs tinged the air with gleaming shades of red. Joe drove to the lot and waited. Half an hour later, a small white car parked next to the Jeep. Joe opened the passenger door and sat inside.

The driver was in his forties, with long hair and a black Stetson. He wore a light denim jacket and beneath it Joe could see the web harness of a shoulder holster. The man didn't talk as he opened a duffel bag and handed Joe one pistol at a time until he chose a .32 caliber. Joe asked for a box of ammunition and the man nodded. When Joe asked how much, the man held up two fingers.

"Two hundred?" Joe said.

The man nodded.

"That's too much."

The man shrugged and held out his hand for the pistol. Joe counted the money into the man's palm. The silence made him nervous. He slipped the gun in his pocket and opened the car door. The man touched his arm. Joe stiffened, a quick surge of fear rushing through him. He turned warily and the man handed him the box of ammunition. Joe left the car.

Snow made a screen that blocked the street. He locked the front hubs into four-wheel drive and crossed the Clark Fork in snow too thick to see the guardrails. His headlights reflected off the wall of snow and shined back through the windshield. He passed two car wrecks, one deserted, the other attended by police and ambulance. He suddenly had no idea how far he'd traveled or how much time had passed since he'd left town. No one knew where he was. He held the steering wheel tightly, afraid of losing his balance and falling from the seat. He wanted to pull over and wait until daylight, wait until spring.

Lights flashed in his rearview mirror and he steered to the edge of the road as a small pickup passed him very fast. Joe drove through the whirl of snow left by the truck's passage, deciding that the driver must be a local. He wondered if he'd ever be able to rush into the slippery darkness with such confidence.

He stopped at the tavern by Rock Creek, hoping to show off

his gold piece, but it was empty. The bartender sat at the bar with a glass and a bottle of liquor. A situation comedy flickered on a small television.

"I don't know why I watch this shit," she said.

"Nothing else to do."

"You can watch with me, if you like. Everything's on the house tonight."

She offered Joe a glass of whisky. As she leaned forward, he saw a flash of delicate black lace inside her shirt. He took a quick sip, which burned his throat and brought on the memory of driving county roads with Arlow. That night seemed like a decade back.

The bartender was still leaning and he didn't want to look at her because he knew he'd see her bra again. A Liberty Teeth pamphlet lay on the bar. He held it up.

"You believe this stuff?"

"Hell, no," she said. "That crap's nothing but a bunch of crap. Some of these round-asses think they're better than the rest of us. They blame everybody else for their sorry selfs."

"Then why keep these things here?"

"People just drop them off, same as lost-dog flyers or church bake sales."

"Is it the Ku Klux Klan, or what?"

"Are they the ones who wear sheets?"

Joe nodded.

"Not them, then. Nobody around here can spare the bedding."

She finished her drink and poured another, her long hair trailing the bar.

"Who is it then," Joe said.

"Could be you best not ask," she said. "Could be that's just the kind of thing you don't want to know. Now sit here and let's watch some TV."

Joe stayed where he was. He sipped the whisky, and the burn ran from his throat to his chest and spread along his limbs.

"Tell you what," she said. "I'll fix you something special. Ever hear of a mat drink?"

"No."

She swayed to her feet and grabbed the stool. She sucked on her cigarette as if it would make her sober and pointed to the other side of the bar.

"You take that rubber mat and drain off all the spills into a glass, then drink it."

"This is fine," Joe said.

He touched the glass to his mouth as she sat down.

"Come on over here," she said. "What's the matter, you don't like TV?"

"Not really."

"My God in heaven. Why the hell not?"

Joe watched the television screen for a minute. At the next joke, the actress paused for the laugh track to begin.

"Right there's why," he said. "That's not real people laughing. I mean it's real, but it's on a tape. They just turn it on and off."

"It's a comedy is why."

"It doesn't need us," Joe said. "The damn thing laughs at itself."

"You sure think different from the rest of these cowboys around here." She pointed at the liquor shelf. "Sure you can't find nothing you want?"

What he wanted was her, but he was afraid, and the fear bothered him, even as it increased his desire.

"Where you from?" he said.

"Up on the Hi-Line. Daddy moved us to Missoula when I was twelve. How about you?"

"I got a place on Rock Creek."

"Not one of those tipis, is it?"

"I don't reckon."

"Aw, shucks," she said. "I was hoping you might need you a tipi creeper sometime."

She finished her drink and looked at him, her gaze moving from his face to his boots and back to his face.

"I was ready to close up when you came in," she said. "This snow holds business down and the road's too bad for me to get home. I usually just stay over. Got a bed in the back."

"Guess I'll be going then."

"Have another drink," she said.

"That's all right."

"There's plenty of it, and more to come."

"I probably ort to leave."

"Maybe the roads are too bad for you to make it," she said, as she stood. "Wouldn't want you to wreck on us."

"I'll be careful."

"I like careful men," she said, and moved close to him.

"I do my best."

"Me, too," she said. "Why don't you stay and find out what my best is."

She leaned forward and kissed him, bumping against his body. Her lips tasted like whisky and smelled of smoke. Joe returned her kiss and she pushed against him, her arms hanging slack at her waist. She stumbled, nearly pulling him to the floor. Joe maneuvered her to lean against the bar. He gripped her arms and kissed her hard, feeling the desire rising in him until the fear surpassed it. He leaned away, abruptly angry. He hurried across the room, hearing her laugh as he went out the door.

He drove through the Valley of the Moon, veering around boulders that had fallen into the road. The creek was dull black at the bottom of a steep drop and he wondered how many collisions had happened here. He felt an urge to stand on the gas pedal, yank the wheel, and plunge down the bank into the water. He slowed to make sure he wouldn't do it.

At his cabin he parked out of the wind and left the truck. The snow fell in a steady rush, a blanket that never stopped. He stood in the darkness and let it settle on his head, making epaulets along his shoulders. He felt ashamed for not staying with the bartender, and wondered if there was something wrong with him. Perhaps he'd spent so much time alone that he'd been ruined for company. He thought about Abigail. Leaving the tavern was not related to her and it had nothing to do with the bartender either. He'd left because he couldn't be with a woman until he was sure of who he was. Virgil Caudill was gone and there was no grave, no marker, no place for sorrow and rage. He had simply ceased to exist.

His mind ran through the events in Kentucky. There'd be no question as to who had killed Rodale, but the official interest would go only as far as it had when Boyd died. The police would take a report and little else. The sheriff wouldn't do anything. Joe hadn't told anyone where he was going because he hadn't known himself, and he hadn't contacted anyone at home. He'd gotten rid of the gun. He'd paid for everything with cash so paper wouldn't follow him. The only improvement he could see was to have spared Rodale.

He went inside and studied the mirror. Facing him was long hair and a long beard, but it was still Virgil. He wondered who had killed Billy Rodale—Virgil or Joe.

He built a fire and went to bed. Everything he owned had once belonged to other people. Another man's foot had stretched the leather of his boots. His sleeping bag conformed to the shape of someone else's body. Even his name had come from the grave. He looked at his hands and wondered if he would recognize them on another man, or loose in a bin at a junk store.

15

Darkness and snow formed the borders of Joe's life. He ceased to shave or bathe. He began a dozen books but never read past the first chapter. Many days he stayed in bed. One side of the canyon was always shade, with the sun arriving at midmorning and leaving by midafternoon. Great snow drifts muffled the land. At night the snowlight glowed.

As a child he had watched his father chop wood for the fire each day. He and his brother gathered kindling in a box. He remembered his father saying that wood made you warm twice—first when you split it and second in the fire. Now Joe split wood until his ax was dull and he had enough kindling to last for years. He reorganized the woodpile to make a separate place for the kindling, arranged according to size, then changed his mind and restacked it again.

He spent hours listening to static on the radio, turning the dial slowly to catch each tenth of every number. Occasionally he'd hear a scrap of music, the distant echo of a voice. When he tried to imagine what might be coming over the airwaves, his mind always returned to the advertising jingles of his childhood. He sang one again and again:

There is a reason why
everybody wants to buy
at Glasser Supply
in Rocksalt—
McCulloch Chainsaw!

This was followed by the sound of a chainsaw's whine, which Joe duplicated with his voice. He walked around the house as if holding a chainsaw, cutting the walls and destroying the furniture. He pretended to lop the possum's head off, then felt guilty and apologized. The possum continued its blank-eyed stare. Joe combed its tawny fur with his fingers.

"Wouldn't it be something," he said, "if there was a million dollars stuffed inside you. Even a thousand dollars. But don't you worry, I won't cut you open. Not on your life. I'll never hurt you. Never."

A crackling sound outside stopped him. He walked slowly to his bureau for his pistol and eased the safety off. He peered out each window but saw only snow, sky, and the dark wall of trees. His heart was beating fast. He heard the sound again. It came from the front of the cabin. He jerked the door open and stayed behind it, peeking through the crack between door and jamb. The sound came again. Very quickly, he stepped around the door, leading with the pistol. A squirrel stood immobile on the woodpile. It stared at Joe for a long time before biting into a pine cone.

Joe's hands were trembling, and sweat soaked into his long underwear. He turned from the door, placed the gun on the refrigerator, and kicked the stove until its door caved in. He flipped the kitchen table on its side. He hurled his few dishes across the room, and knocked his canned goods to the floor. He emptied the drawers and ran through the house with a saucepan, beating the walls and doors. He threw his sleeping bag to the floor and stomped it until he tripped himself. In the bathroom, he stared at the mirror briefly before smashing his forehead against it. When he pulled his head away, a shard fell to the sink.

He ran outside without his coat and kept running to stay warm. His breath turned to ice on his beard. He leaned against a tree and heard his ragged breathing, his lungs aching in the cold. He followed coyote tracks along the frozen lane of a gully that fed Rock Creek. Twice his foot broke through the ice. The coyote had its own troubles, visible in the occasional wild scrapes and slides in the snow. There was a sudden spotting of estrus, and Joe recalled Rodale's dark blood glistening in the night.

The tracks veered left and Joe rested beneath a tall pine. Brown needles covered the ground like sand. None of the pine trees in Kentucky were this big. He had no purpose in the woods, served no function. The coyote hunted game while deer ate bark. Geese had a flock. The ram he'd seen had a mate somewhere on the mountain. He was sick of himself. Terror rippled through him. For the first time in his life, his thoughts scared him. He could not be alone any longer.

He circled his cabin through the open woods and headed for Ty's house. Juniper trees rose from a talus slope patched with snow. Ty's pickup truck was parked a foot from his door, and Joe knocked but there was no answer. He knocked again, banging until his knuckles were raw. Ty stepped around the corner of the cabin holding a rifle.

"You all right?" he said.

"I don't know." Joe shivered in the wind. "Maybe not."

"Let me let you in."

Ty opened the door and motioned Joe to a couch. The coffee table was strewn with parts of a dismantled pistol. A gun cleaning kit lay open, its rods and patches neatly ordered. Ty placed his rifle on a wall rack that held four other weapons.

"Been hunting?" Joe said.

"No. I don't get many visitors."

"You must be getting jumpy as me."

"It's February," Ty said. "Cabin fever sets in hard. The Crow people have a tradition of not gossiping after the first snow."

"Why's that?"

"Too easy to hurt people's feelings and get somebody killed before the thaw."

"Well, I didn't come over to gossip."

"Would you like tea?" Ty said. "I have chamomile. The Etruscans used it for snakebite."

"Sure."

The cabin was bigger than Joe's, lined with the same pine panels. The stove was new and the room was very warm. Beside an easy chair was a bag containing two long needles and several skeins of yarn. A shortwave radio sat on the other side. A pair of half-rim reading glasses lay on a small table. Scattered about the room were several books, which Joe inspected while he waited. There were treatises on philosophy, history, and religion, manuals for converting semi-automatic weapons to full auto, and several accounts of armed battle, from the Peloponnesian War to the most recent American conflicts. Four different Bibles were stacked beside the knitting bag.

The walls held contour maps of Rock Creek and the Bitterroot Valley to the west. Joe found the place where they were joined by Skalkaho Pass. Another map traced Rock Creek to its headwaters. In a corner there was a vise and a grinding wheel bolted to a heavy, homemade table. Pieces of metal lay along the surfaces. The cabin smelled of gun oil and cinnamon.

Ty came into the room carrying mugs with spoons protruding like chimneys for the rising steam. He sat in the easy chair with a directional lamp behind him. He was chubbier than Joe remembered. They sipped their tea in silence. It tasted odd, like clay dirt, but the heat calmed Joe.

"Nice place," Joe said. "You knit?"

"Something I learned in Alaska. You got to have a lot of home projects in winter. How do you think the Swiss got so good at making watches? I've tried it all—beadwork, leatherwork, knife-making, even candle-making. You need something that doesn't take up much space and won't accumulate. What do you do in your place?"

"Nothing really. Walk. Chop wood. Been playing poker in town some. I sleep a lot."

"Yeah, most people do. They eat, get fat, get depressed, and eat more. Then before you know it they're killing their wife and kids. Drinking's no good either, but a lot pass the winter that way."

"I've seen a bunch of drunks, all right."

"Try Alaska. People go up there for work, but the best way to get rich in Alaska is to open a saloon. I guess I been stuck in here awhile, the way I'm talking. You don't notice it until somebody visits, do you?"

"I don't know. I haven't had a visitor. You're the only person I know."

"It takes a while. People like to see if you'll last more than one winter. Go two years and you'll be all right. What do you make of Montana so far?"

"Long winter."

"People spend half their life fighting weather. In Alaska it's more like three-quarters."

"I don't much care for fighting." Joe gestured to the weapons around the room. "You look like you might."

"Not me. I just tinker till spring. I don't even hunt. Me, I'm what they call a gun enthusiast."

Ty lifted the teabag with his spoon, wrapped the string around the bag, and used it to squeeze the remaining tea into the mug. There was a delicacy to the act that amused Joe.

"Look," Ty said. "I know how it is to come here and not know anybody. Same thing happened to me. Hell, I'm from the Bronx."

"Where's that at?"

"New York City, man."

"Never been there."

"You wouldn't like it. Surprising how many New Yorkers live in Montana. Thing about the West, anybody can come out here and fit in, because there's not much to fit in with. Leave people alone and they won't bother you. Same as New York."

"Where I'm from's like that, too."

"Used to be that way all over the country. Now people are scared, and the laws don't have anything to do with crime anymore."

"Like the new gun laws."

"You got it, brother. Most gun owners are men over thirty. They have a family and they start thinking about how to protect it. That's only natural."

"I know many a woman who can shoot pretty good."

"That's true, in the South and the West especially. You see, in the city a gun is a threat, but in the country it's a tool for defense. Back east, they don't want their criminals to have guns, so they take everyone else's."

"Because they got more crime?"

"Tons more. The cities are packed with homeless people, drugs, and crime. D.C.'s a war zone and nobody does anything. Those people pay taxes and don't even have a senator or a governor. We fought a war to end that and we're doing the same thing in our own capital."

"I never been to Washington, either."

"You wouldn't like it. People blame guns for crime, but you take away guns and you'd still have the crime."

"Why can't they stop it?"

"Politics, my friend, nothing but. Politicians want votes, so they ban guns and put more cops on the street. Prison is a growth industry right now. We've got more prisons than all the other countries combined. We're the freest country in history and we lock up the most people."

"You know a lot about it, Ty."

"Everybody should. Our government is robbing us of rights every day."

"Like what?"

"Let's see." Ty set his mug aside and idly fingered the pile of yarn by his chair. He squinted out the window. "You flown in an airplane lately?"

"No," Joe said. "I've never been on one."

"You wouldn't like it. You have to show a picture ID to get on a plane. That means a driver's license. You got one, right?"

"Sure."

"It's got your Social Security number on it, right?"

"I asked for a separate number."

"Good for you. Most people don't have that much sense. To fly in an airplane, you got to show it to some flunky. It has nothing to do with driving. It's a passport for domestic travel. You think that's right?"

"I never thought about it."

"Exactly. Most people don't. The same thing happened in Germany during the twenties—they disarmed the citizens and made them carry identification papers. And the citizens let it happen. The poor bastards just stood by and watched. That's what's happening here, my friend. Right now in America."

"We're turning into Nazis?"

"Not literally, no. But the same things are happening here that preceded the rise of the Third Reich. The country's broke. There's no jobs and people don't trust the government. The Feds are cracking down on the people. They take away their weapons and their rights and lock them up."

Joe sipped his tea. In Kentucky, people considered all politicians to be crooked. At work he'd heard plenty of men complain about the government, but it was usually the county or the state. You either liked the current politicians or you didn't, and it often depended on the condition of the road by your house. Many people in the hills didn't have a driver's license, but the reasons were practical rather than political—they couldn't be bothered to go into town for something they didn't use that often.

"Shouldn't people carry ID in case they get hurt or something?" Joe said.

"Yes, and always wear underwear in case you go to the hospital. A driver's license has your picture and your number on it. That makes it nothing but a citizen ID card that lets some folks drive. You already have to show it to rent a video."

"I don't rent videos."

"Good. The states are worse than the Feds. In Wisconsin you can lose your driver's license if you don't pay library fines, or don't shovel snow off your sidewalk."

"Bullshit."

"Those laws are on the books, Joe. Oregon has a hundred offenses where they suspend your license, but only fifty that have to do with driving. And Kentucky takes away a teenager's license if they miss school nine times. It's not about driving anymore."

Joe stood and walked to the window. The sky was silver with snow. He didn't want Ty to see his face at the mention of Kentucky. Winters at home were short. Snow came in great storms that turned the woods to chandeliers of light and melted in a week. The temperature rarely dropped below twenty and you didn't need hobbies that lasted until spring. Joe wanted to know why Ty had come to Montana, but didn't want to risk having to answer the same question.

"You got a checkerboard?" Joe said.

"No."

"Deck of cards?"

"No."

"Maybe you can teach me how to knit, then."

"It's tougher than it looks," Ty said.

"I never had a hobby that was doing something."

"What do you mean?"

"I collected stuff."

"Sure," Ty said. "Old money, comic books."

"Where I'm from, there's no new money. I collected what I could find—rocks, bark, feathers."

"Makes it tough in the winter, huh. A lot of people, they tie flies till spring."

"I always went to work," Joe said. "When I was a kid we rode sleds and had snowball fights."

"Where was that?"

"Texas."

"You don't talk like a Texan."

"I can't help it."

"I guess you're from north Texas."

"Maybe."

"Up where they get a lot of snow."

Joe looked into his mug. Silt swirled at the bottom and he set it on the table. He felt uncomfortable that Ty knew he was lying, but he wasn't ready to leave.

"It's not a law to carry ID, is it?" Joe said.

"Not yet, my friend. But last year over four thousand new laws were passed."

"That's a lot."

"Yep, and most are about controlling people."

"Like what?"

"The seat-belt law," Ty said.

"That ain't new."

"No, but it's the best example of a bad law."

"Why? What's wrong with it?"

"Everything. Only a moron doesn't wear a seat belt, but being a moron shouldn't be illegal."

"I know some people glad of that."

"You're missing the point. It's the same with the motorcycle helmet law. Congress is wasting taxpayers' money to legislate common sense."

"A lot of folks don't have it."

"That's right. Our country is the only one that makes it against the law to be stupid. Is that free?"

"Don't reckon."

"You're not from a city, are you?"

Joe shrugged.

"Don't worry," Ty said, "I'm not trying to get personal. But the government is naming every little dirt road in the country. No more addresses like Rural Route 4, Box 60-A. Now every dead-end road gets its own private name."

"Yeah, I know. It's so an ambulance can get there in an emergency."

"That's what they're telling you, Joe. But ambulance drivers know their territory. They don't need a street sign at every podunk crossroad. The reason for naming roads is to provide the government with a list of every house in the country, where it is, and who lives in it. That and the national identity card give them a precise record of exactly who lives exactly where. It's all about privacy, Joe. There is no privacy anymore. And without privacy, there's no freedom."

Joe didn't consider the government an enemy. It was more of an entity to manipulate if you wanted fresh gravel on your road, or a family member out of jail. People at home didn't worry about the government, they ignored it. Men hunted out of season to feed their children. Families made moonshine for export, and when demand changed they grew marijuana. Laws didn't have much bearing in the hills, especially when the sheriff was an elected official.

"I got to go," Joe said. "Getting late."

"Glad you came over. You'll have to excuse me for talking so much, but we all get lonely."

"Think this snow will pass?"

"Tomorrow it'll be deep and still."

"What do you mean?"

"Deep as your ass and still snowing." Ty laughed. "That's what they say in Alaska."

"Thanks for the tea."

"You bet. Remember, spring will come. The main thing is to get through winter without parking one in the brain pan."

The trees were black against the snow, becoming pale shades of gray farther up the mountain. Clouds opened in cracks that striped the slopes with sunlight, filling the valley with a liquid shine. Sight-lines spread in all directions and snowflakes fell to the ground as if towed by thread. Joe wondered how scientists knew there were no two alike.

Inside his cabin he built a fire and cleaned the mess. It seemed as if someone else had wrecked the place a long time ago. He'd come to Montana to cut himself off from people, but that was impossible for him. He was a small-town person who'd been happiest at work. Ty was right, he had to get through winter. He had food, shelter, and a sleeping bag. When spring arrived, he needed to find a job and a community.

He patted the possum on the head. He decided to bury it at the first thaw.

16

In March the winter began easing away. Icicles clinging to the slopes ran their water over rock. At night they formed again, making the cliffs appear to bear long talons. Frosty ground thawed to mud. Snowmelt flowed down the mountains to fill Rock Creek. Joe used the old shovel to clear a path to his Jeep.

Montana had none of the pastel budding of eastern woods, no brilliant slashes of forsythia or blossoming fruit trees. Instead there was a quickening to the air, the stirring of life. An enormous energy soared among the mountains. The land appeared fuller, as if each tree held a slight swelling. When the first rain came Joe stood on his porch inhaling deeply, craving the moist air in his lungs. Water encased each surface with a bright prism, transforming the bleakness of winter into living earth. Snow had left the woods.

In April the ice went out of Rock Creek in great crashes that echoed through the valley. Floating chunks scraped the bank, and the stream ran with quiet ferocity. A layer of light lay over the land. Joe slipped the .32 in his jacket pocket, loaded the stuffed possum into his Wagoneer, and threw the old shovel in the back. Its broken handle had been repaired with short nails and frayed tape.

He drove several miles south on the dirt road, turned right, and began climbing Skalkaho Pass. He parked at a wide spot. The air was cold and fresh. He carried the possum and shovel into the woods. The deer trails still held ice, frozen arcs that veered through the woods, bearing the delicate imprint of tracks. Boulders were covered with a velour of moss.

The woods were quiet, as if the animals had fled before his approach. Pine boughs brushed him. He held the possum under his arm and descended to a shallow basin of pink mountain heath that was surrounded by rock bluffs. He moved through a chamber of light and stone, and climbed to a narrow ridge that held no trees. The spot was ideal. He began to dig. The loose soil kept sliding back into the hole. He hit rock just below the surface and realized that there was not enough topsoil for his plan. He placed the stuffed possum in the hole but its head and back protruded above the ground.

He pried large rocks from the earth and stacked them around the possum. The shovel handle broke free of the blade. He ranged farther along the ridge, gathering rocks and mounding them until he had a cairn. When the possum was completely covered, Joe rested. He pulled a nail from the splintered end of the shovel handle, held the blade in his lap, and stared at the blank metal. He wanted to write everything, but it was a mistake to write his name. He scratched his initials into the old metal. He worked the nail back and forth until the letters were etched deep—V.C.

He placed the shovel blade on top of the cairn and sat crosslegged before it. He was beyond praying, although he wished he wasn't. He spoke for the first time in several days. "Good-bye, Virgil. Now you got a grave and I got somewhere to come to."

He felt as if he should say more, but he couldn't think of anything.

He lay on his back and stared at the sky. Heaven was up there. It was very blue. His fingers ached from labor. He closed his eyes.

He awoke chilly, the mound of rock before him like a shrine. He rose and walked away, carrying the shovel handle over his shoulder. As he descended the ridge, he smelled sage, a scent that had become familiar. He recognized the contour of the mountain range across the canyon. A speck in the sky became a hawk. He reached the bottom of the slope, where the land opened into a basin of buffalo grass and chickweed. The cry of a bird carried through the air, and he stopped moving to listen. He couldn't name the bird, but he knew its cry. It was a Montana sound, as was the rustle of pine needles in the wind behind him. He began crossing a meadow of budding heath. A coyote ran straight away from him, its tail streaming like a banner, and he wondered if it was the same one he'd tracked in winter. There was a sharp crack and his left leg went out from under him.

He was lying on his back, but it seemed impossible that he could fall from a standing position. His leg began to hurt and he touched it and found blood. He figured he'd walked into a bear trap. The pain grew, occupying his entire consciousness, and when it receded he understood that he'd gotten himself into a bad spot. Night would soon arrive. He knew he could not walk.

Brush scuffed behind him. "You stay lay there," a voice said. "We'll just wait, you son of a bitch."

Joe didn't move. He wondered how crazy the man was, and what he was waiting for. The weight of the little .32 towed Joe's jacket pocket to the side and he hoped the man didn't notice. Grass pricked the back of his neck. It felt rougher than grass at home, but he banished that thought; he was home. This was where he lived. Now this was where he'd die.

Clouds moved like tumbleweeds across the sky. He flexed his leg muscle and the pain raced through him like electricity. He closed his eyes. Hurried bootsteps pounded the earth. A man knelt beside him.

"You bad hurt?"

"Leg," Joe said.

Two more men stepped into view. Joe recognized Owen from the tavern, Coop's grandson. Beside him, with an expression of triumph on his face, stood Owen's brother Johnny. He wore camouflage and held a small pistol. Joe couldn't believe that in a state this big, he'd been shot by someone he'd met.

"I'm going to lift your leg," the stranger said to Joe. "It might hurt, but I have to see where the bullet came out."

The man probed the wound and a jolt of pain ran from Joe's leg to his brain.

"We're fucked twice and lucky once," the man said. "Once by Johnny shooting him, and second by no exit wound. Bullet's still in his leg."

"What's the lucky part?" Owen said.

"Missed the artery."

"Knocked him down with one shot," Johnny said.

"You shouldn't have shot him," the man said.

"I thought he had a rifle, Frank."

"Great," Owen said. "You used his name."

"It's not a rifle," Frank said. "It's a fucking tool handle."

"He's probably a Fed," Johnny said.

"That's even more reason not to shoot him," Frank said.

"Listen, Johnny," Owen said. "You can't just go around shooting people on account of who you think they are."

"You don't want to wind up like me," Frank said.

Joe chuckled. They were discussing his fate and he'd just buried himself. He didn't care what happened.

"All right," Frank said. "We got to get him off the mountain and into a hospital."

"No," Joe said.

"What?"

"No hospital."

Owen leaned close to Joe. "You got a bullet in you. Do you understand that?"

Joe nodded.

"We have to take you to the hospital."

"No hospital."

"You got a job?"

Joe shook his head.

"They'll take care of you for free, then. Don't worry about the money."

"That ain't it," Joe said.

"This might work out," Frank said. "If he don't want a hospital, he probably won't want the law either."

"That right?" Owen said to Joe.

Joe nodded.

"That don't leave a lot of outs."

"One in his head'll fix him," Johnny said.

"Don't say another damn word," Owen said.

"What about Rodney?" Frank said.

"What about him," Owen said.

"He's got tools and medicine. He can dig a bullet out."

"His wife won't like it."

"It's not something she has to know."

"Rodney's a damn horse doc!" Johnny said.

"I thought I told you not to talk," Owen said.

"Well, he is."

"Give me your gun."

Johnny handed him the pistol butt-first. Owen checked the safety and released the cylinder. He removed the remaining bullets and handed his brother the gun.

"Shit fire," Johnny said. "I can't do nothing with this."

"That's the idea, buckethead."

Frank opened his pocketknife and cut Joe's pants from the cuff to the wound. The fabric fell to the earth, heavy with blood.

"Leg's not broke at least. Blood's trying to clot already so we'll help it along. Johnny, take off your jacket and give me your shirt."

"Why me?"

"Listen, Johnny. You're not catching on here. You just shot a man armed with a shovel handle. You'd best help us out of this tangle before it takes a bad turn."

Johnny removed his jacket and flannel shirt and passed Frank his T-shirt. It was white, with the emblem of the Buffalo Bills on it. Frank sliced it into strips, made a compress bandage, and tied it tightly to Joe's leg.

"You'll have to walk a ways," he said. "We got a rig parked on a fire road over there."

Joe thought of the soldiers casting lots for Jesus' robe and wondered if the robe cared who won. He'd probably feel better if Johnny went ahead and shot him in the head.

Owen and Frank squatted behind Joe, gripped his shoulders, and lifted. His leg fired a shot of pain up his body that exploded in his head. He leaned between the two men until he was able to put his weight on the good leg. Frank and Owen moved across the grassy basin with Joe swaying between them, swinging his good leg forward and back. The other one hung straight down, streaked with blood. He watched his boot pass large rocks rolled from their sockets in the earth.

"Bear sign," he muttered.

"Don't worry," Owen said. "We got Johnny."

"He'll shoot or talk him to death," Frank said. "How's the leg?"

"Shot."

They circled the basin's rim to a faint trail up the slope. Frank and Owen laced their arms behind Joe's back and tucked their hands in his armpits, making a sling. They moved uphill slowly, all three grunting when Joe leaned his full weight on them to bring his good leg forward. He felt oddly close to them.

They reached a rise and stepped through a dense stand of fir. The boughs tore at Joe's face. They stood on a rough dirt road beside a truck that appeared to be outfitted for everything but the sea. There was a winch on each bumper. The tires were jacked high for two feet of clearance. The bed was covered with tin that rose to a peaked roof, and the exterior carried drums of water and gasoline lashed to eye-bolts. Every surface was painted flat shades of green and black.

Owen opened the rear and folded down two metal steps. He climbed inside. Joe sat on the steps and leaned backwards. Frank lifted his legs as Owen dragged him inside. Joe's pants were red and wet, the wound having bled through the T-shirt. He lay on a thin mattress.

Beside him were shelves of canned food, cookware, rope, weapons, and tools. A propane lantern hung from the ceiling. Several metal ammo boxes sat in a row. It was a Conestoga wagon crossed with a tank. Frank opened an elaborate first-aid kit and passed Joe four aspirin and water. He removed the makeshift bandage, squeezed ointment onto the wound, and applied a sanitary bandage.

"You're doing good," Frank said.

"Truck's high enough, ain't it."

"That Owen, he likes to ride over a dogfight and not hit the dogs."

A hatch opened between the cab and the rear of the truck. Owen spoke through the gap.

"You all right?" he said.

"Good to go," Frank said.

"It'll be rough the first quarter mile."

"He's already over the rough part."

"Maybe," Owen said. "I'd like it better if that bullet had gone on out."

"My fault."

Owen closed the hatch and put the truck in gear.

"It ain't your fault," Joe said.

"Yes it is. I was in a bar once and two bikers got in an argument. One pulled a .25 and emptied the clip. The other guy was wearing a leather jacket and it stopped every bullet. Took six rounds. That's why I gave Johnny a .25, and that's why the bullet stayed in your leg. It ain't much of a weapon. My fault."

"Next time give him a pellet gun."

"There won't be a next time."

"I ain't saying nothing against him, but maybe he's a guy who wants a next time."

"No, Johnny doesn't think that way. He lives right now all the time."

The big engine rumbled, and the truck jerked forward. Joe clenched his teeth at the vibration. His leg bounced jolts of pain along his body. The lantern swayed above his head.

"Johnny's not somebody you need to worry about," Frank said. "He's just Johnny. Kind of twitchy and kind of mouthy. But I'm sorry you got hit."

"What was I, trespassing or something?"

"Not exactly. It's federal land."

"Then we all own it."

"That's how I look at it," Frank said.

"Land's land."

"You pay taxes and the government still tells you what you can and can't do on your own spread."

"I don't own nothing," Joe said.

"That's one way."

"What's another?"

"Were you in the service?"

Joe didn't answer, although without the distraction of talk, his leg hurt more. He felt weak. He realized that he might die, and was surprised that he didn't want that. Getting shot on the mountain was one thing, but bleeding to death in a truck was another.

"How far's the vet?" he said.

"Not far."

"Tell Johnny I don't hold it against him."

"You can tell him."

"I mean if I don't get a chance to."

"You'll come out of this," Frank said. "You got the right spirit. I seen it in Asia—the right and the wrong. It's all in your attitude toward Mr. Death."

"Fuck him."

"Exactly," Frank said. "You got it."

"I'm starting to get light-headed."

"You lost blood."

"It hurts some, too."

"Fucking Johnny."

"It don't matter."

The truck hit a pothole, and Joe's leg lashed him with pain.

"What were you doing up there?" Frank said.

"Trying to dig. The shovel broke."

"It would against that rock."

"It ain't even my shovel."

"You got bigger worries than that."

"I guess."

"This vet we're taking you to, he mostly works on horses. You know what they do to a horse in your shape."

"Well, don't let Johnny do it. He might miss."

"What's your name?"

"Joe."

"You talk pretty big for a man with a bullet in him, Joe."

"I deserve it."

"You got something against your leg?"

"That ain't what I meant."

"Then what?"

"Nothing. Just that I was due for a bullet. You think Johnny was aiming for my leg?"

"No telling."

"I heard about a blind man back home left a bar with his girlfriend. Somebody tried to rob him in the parking lot. He pulled a pistol and started firing. Shot the robber. Shot his girlfriend. Shot himself in the foot."

Frank laughed. "Where'd this happen?"

Joe didn't answer. He was from Montana now. He had a private graveyard and he was building history. For the first time in six months, he didn't feel alone.

The truck left the fire road for gravel. The rattle of objects dulled to a steady murmur of metal and wood. Joe closed his eyes. He heard Frank's voice moving through the dimness in the truck.

"Breathe in long and slow," he said. "Take it deep in your body. Send the clean air to your leg. Now breathe out slowly. Take the bad air out. Bring the good air back. Long breaths slow."

The truck was rolling on blacktop now, and Joe was getting cold. He wanted to sleep. The truck jolted to a stop and Owen opened the rear door. Light spread through the interior, washing shadows, glinting on metal. Briefly, Joe thought he was in Kentucky, camping with Boyd. He lifted his head and saw his leg glistening in the sun. It hurt. He lay back.

Owen brought a tall man who looked inside and shook his head.

"Not in the office," he said. "The old lady's in there. Go around to the barn and I'll bring a bag. This is fucked, by the way."

"I know it," Frank said. "But it's where we're at right now."

Owen and Frank helped Joe outside. He was very weak. His leg felt like a heavy weight. They walked him across a barn's dirt floor and laid him on a makeshift examining table. The tall man entered, carrying a satchel. He snipped away the bandages on Joe's leg, administered a local anesthetic, and cleaned the wound. He checked Joe's temperature and listened to his chest.

"He's lost plenty of blood," he said. "But it looks worse than it is. He's not in shock yet."

"What about the bullet?" Frank said.

"I'll have to probe but it's close to the bone, I can tell you that right now."

The tall man leaned to Joe's face.

"I'm Rodney," he said. "What's your name?"

"Joe Tiller. This is where I live."

"Sure, Joe. I'm going to look inside the wound. It's going to hurt, but not much. Mainly you'll feel the instruments. If it hurts too bad, we'll give you more anesthetic."

Joe felt the instrument pushing his flesh, and bursts of pain that were dull and distant. He smelled hay and horse manure, a comforting scent. The rafters overhead were bare.

"Hell's fire," Rodney said, stepping away from Joe.

"What," Owen said.

"The bullet's right against the bone."

"So."

"I can't get it out."

"You have to."

"I've done what I can," Rodney said. "He's stable. There's no danger of infection for twelve hours. It needs to be X-rayed and removed at the hospital."

"He doesn't want to go."

"He doesn't, or you don't want him to."

"Both."

Rodney switched his attention to Joe.

"Joe, this bullet's hung up in there, and I'm not able to get it out."

Joe remained silent.

"Do you hear what I'm saying," Rodney said.

"Help me sit," Joe said.

Rodney lifted him into a sitting position. Joe slipped his hand into his coat pocket. The small .32 was cold to his touch. He swiveled his body until he was able to dangle his bad leg off the table. It didn't hurt so bad. He pulled the pistol from his pocket and everyone became still. He gestured to Rodney.

"Back away a little."

Rodney moved to the wall. He was calm and slow, and Joe knew that he was probably very good with animals. He waved the gun at the knot of men.

"Son of a bitch," Owen said. "At least now we know he ain't no Fed."

"What do you mean?" Johnny said.

"Look at that little gun," Owen said. "Our sister carries a bigger one than that."

"You can't shoot us all before we get you," Frank said.

"Hush now," Joe said.

He was having trouble thinking clearly. Owen and Frank were the chief threats. He aimed the pistol at Johnny.

"Owen, you and Frank get out of here."

"He's bluffing," Owen said.

"I don't think so," Frank said. "Me and him had quite the talk in back. He don't much give a shit right now. I don't blame you either, Joe. Tell me what you want."

"I want you two out. Then Rodney. Then Johnny."

Owen moved sideways to the doorway and stepped through it. Frank followed him.

"Stay where I can see you," Joe said. "Now you, Rodney."

Rodney slowly joined the men in the barn. Johnny's forehead was wet with sweat. His camouflage pants quivered at the knees.

"I'm not going to shoot you," Joe said. "Just back on out there with them."

Johnny didn't move. His eyes were wide and his face was very white. He moved his mouth but couldn't talk.

"Help him, Rodney," Joe said. "But do it easy."

Rodney took Johnny's arm in a gentle grasp and tugged him backwards.

"Everything's got to go real slow," Joe said.

Owen glanced at a pitchfork and Joe shook his head.

"No," Joe said. "It's not what you think. I can't go to a hospital. None of us want the law involved. I'm sorry about scaring your brother."

Joe gathered a deep breath. He lowered the pistol to his bad leg and pressed the barrel into the wound. It felt the same as when Rodney had probed. He held the gun at an angle that matched the entry channel. He caught a sweet scent on the breeze and wondered what grass the horses had been eating.

"Rodney," Joe said. "I have to trust you to help me afterwards."

He took another breath. He began a long slow exhalation, and at the end, just as he'd been taught by his father, he slowly squeezed the trigger. There was a terrible roar in the small space. He felt as if someone had struck his leg with a crowbar. He was briefly aware of falling from the table when his perception grew dark at the edges and closed in on itself.

17

He felt nothing. His mind and body were gone, leaving only the faintest sense of space and time. A light was a speck in the vast darkness. Joe willed himself toward it. The light became bright and turned into a rectangle, its edges shimmering. He strained to see it and as weakness took him, he understood that it was a window holding sunlight within its frame.

Later he became aware of a coolness on his face, of someone near him. His leg hurt. He was thirsty.

Joe's eyes were open and he was staring at a plaster ceiling that had cracked into a network of fine lines. A bare bulb dangled from a ceramic fixture. It was not the ceiling of the cabin. He shifted his weight and an eruption of pain jolted his leg and he remembered with an exhausting suddenness the events on the side of the mountain.

Through the window and many miles away, the sky held crescents of cloud like spilt ashes. A cow scratched its throat on a fence post and Joe wondered if his leg was still attached to his body. When he leaned forward an unthinkable pain took his breath. Sweat spread a sheen across his face. He lay back panting, his body weak.

A woman blocked light as she entered the room.

"Lay still," she said. "You got healing up to do yet."

She tugged the blankets to his chin and blotted the perspiration from his forehead. Her touch was firm, the fingers tight with muscle. She held a glass of water to his lips.

"You'd best not move your leg at all."

He was silent, watching her face. It was very smooth, with large eyes and thick black hair. She was close to his age. Fatigue settled over him.

The next time he woke, he felt stronger. The room was small, with the lowest ceiling he'd ever seen. The window ran from the floor to the ceiling, and as he looked through the glass, a bull trotted by, its gait as buoyant as that of a deer. A flock of starlings landed among the boughs of a cottonwood. He heard children laughing. Wind moved the high grass like the surface of a lake. His leg ached and he was relieved to see its outline below the blanket.

Joe could recall nothing after the truck ride off the mountain. Something prowled the edges of his mind but he couldn't capture it. The woman entered the room and he feigned sleep until actual slumber came.

Each time he woke he was stronger and more hungry. On a bedside table were a clock, toothbrush, water pitcher, and glass. Two bedpans sat on the floor and he was embarrassed by the sight. He wondered if he could walk, a thought that drenched him with fear.

The room seemed to belong to a young boy. Rough planks mounted on the wall held the bounty of the woods—skulls of raccoon, fox, bird, and deer. There was a beaver skull bigger than his clasped hands, its incisors the dark gold of feed corn. Beside severed bird claws lay what appeared to be the scalp of a great horned owl and next to that, a roundish skull with huge eye sockets. The walls were festooned with feathers he didn't recognize. The pelt of a coyote hung beside an enormous wing. A snakeskin was pinned to the window frame.

Beside him the digital clock flicked a minute. He didn't like such a clock, which seemed to hold time in place. A clock with a face and two hands lent a sense of time's movement, its immensity, and Joe wondered if he was old-fashioned. Maybe people had felt the same resistance when timepieces became portable enough to carry on their person. He had no idea how many days he'd been in bed.

He woke later to a presence in the room and slowly recognized Ty sitting in a chair. Joe tried to speak but the words emerged slow and garbled as if he were hearing his voice underwater. Sleep overcame him. When he woke again, Ty was gone and the woman was back. She wore boots, a denim workshirt, and heavy wool pants with red suspenders. Against the low ceiling, she seemed very tall.

"You look better," she said. "Hungry?"

Joe nodded.

"About time."

She left, the heels of her boots heavy on the slat floor. She closed the door and Joe noticed that it had no interior knob. He stared through the window. Above the ridge was the biggest cloud he'd ever seen. It was like a gunship moored in the sky, its lower half dark gray, its wispy tips a glare of white. The woman returned with a plate of cold meat. His jaw ached from the abrupt salivation but after six bites his appetite was sated and he was tired again. As sleep pulled him, the woman wiped grease from his lips.

When he woke, he heard the sound of children's voices rising in laughter, turning to tears. The woman was changing the bandage on his leg. It throbbed at her touch. The entry wound was healing into a slight depression, but the other side of his leg was still a mess.

"Not as bad as it looks," the woman said. "I've seen legs worse that a bull walked on."

"Who are you?" he asked. His voice sounded rusty at the edges, a neglected tool.

"I'm Botree."

"How long have I been here?"

"Ten days."

He frowned in surprise.

"You're on drugs," she said. "They make you sleep and lose track of time."

"What kind?"

She plucked a small bottle from one of the shelves. Three more sat beside it.

"Butorphanol," she read aloud.

"Never heard of it."

"Knocks a horse out easy."

"I could have swore I heard kids."

"You did."

"Was Ty here?"

She nodded.

"Am I a prisoner?"

"No."

"Then why's there no doorknob?"

Botree pointed to a screwdriver on a string that was tied to a nail beside the door.

"That'll get you out. Been there twenty years."

"What is this place?"

"My room when I was a girl," she said. "Like it?"

Joe closed his eyes. His leg stirred him with pain and he swallowed the pills by the table. He didn't know if weeks or hours had passed when the low voices of men woke him.

"This whole damn setup could cost my license."

"Nobody knows nothing on it."

"Johnny talks a blue streak."

"He won't."

"He might brag it up, Owen."

Joe opened his eyes. Two men stood just outside the door, talking quietly.

"There's other things to worry on right now," Owen said.

"Like me getting used as a medic for your games."

"These aren't games and you damn well know it."

"You got your first casualty, a goddam innocent victim."

"We don't know anything about him."

"Took three men to bring down one in the timber."

"Rodney, we all appreciate you taking care of him."

"Yeah, and I'll appreciate you paying off my school loans if I lose my license over treating a man ought to see a real doctor."

"You're a real doc."

"We're talking about a man might not walk again," Rodney said.

Joe pushed himself up on his elbow.

"I'll walk," he said.

The men stepped into the room and Rodney's gaze calmed the flare of anger that had driven Joe to speak. Owen emptied a sack onto the bedside table. Joe recognized his toothbrush and personal items, including his cash, the gold piece, and the belt balancer Morgan had given him. He wondered about his pistol.

"Got this stuff off Ty Skinner. Travel light, don't you."

"I get it," Joe said. "You shoot a man, take his stuff, and evict him all at once."

"That's not how it is."

"I guess it'd be a whole lot easier if I went ahead and died."

"I don't know how easy it'd be," Owen said. "But things would sure be on the simple side. Rodney here'd sleep better, and I'd get to keep your money."

Joe began to laugh. The two men joined him, awkwardly at first but relaxing into the shared need for release. Joe realized that laughing with these men was what Boyd would have done.

Rodney sat on a chair beside the bed and lifted the blanket to expose Joe's leg. Owen left the room. Rodney removed the bandage and cleaned the wounds, his touch gentle, his expression tightly focused. Joe flinched at the rivets of pain that cleared his head and watered his eyes. He stared at the yellowed skull of a deer and repeated in his mind the phrase "Not me, not me." The pain subsided and he relaxed. Sweat slid into his eyes. He was more fully alert than he had been since the barn.

"Well," he said to Rodney.

"It's bad."

"Tell me all of it."

"The first bullet lodged against the lower femur near the knee. Your little surgery drove that bullet out pretty good. Problem is, the second bullet fragmented. I picked pieces out all night. You cracked the bone, but that's pretty much healed already. There's nerve damage but I don't know how much. Worse is you nicked the patella and severed the medial collateral ligament."

"What's all that add up to?"

"Know how a knee works?"

"No," Joe said.

"It's where your leg bones meet. Ligament holds them in place. There's a big one on top that covers your kneecap, two in between the bones, and two more on the side. You cut the side one in half."

"What's a ligament?"

"It's like a short piece of rubber stapled to the bones. The rubber gives when you walk but it always snaps the bone back in place."

"So what's that mean?"

"Bottom part of your leg won't always stay where it's supposed to."

"Because the rubber piece is cut in half," Joe said.

"You got it."

"How can I make it stronger?"

"You can't. You can strengthen the leg and let muscle protect it, but the ligament will always be weak. A sharp pivot and it'll go out on you."

"Anything else?"

"Your meniscus is probably tore up, but I can't tell how bad without X-rays."

"What's a meniscus?"

"It separates your bones. Sort of like a rubber gasket. What it does is keep your leg bones from banging against each other when you walk."

"So now they'll rub."

"Not too bad, but yes."

"Anything else?"

"I don't know," Rodney said. "The whole knee is a bad design for the weight it has to carry."

"You mean I got hurt because of a bad design?"

"No. It was the bullets that did the hurting. The way the knee is built is pretty much proof that we used to walk on all fours. Another million years and our knees won't be so vulnerable."

"How do you fix it?"

"Used to, a surgeon cut off the extra tissue, trimmed the ends, overlapped them, and sewed the whole rig back together. I don't know what they do now. Knee surgery is the only branch of medicine where they use power tools. They can restring a knee like a tennis racket."

"Can you do that?"

"No."

Joe moved his gaze to the light fixture on the ceiling. He felt something shift within him, a settling of some depth, and he realized that he'd aged. Just as children endured growth spurts, aging happened in short bursts, and he'd moved one step closer to the dull white skulls on the shelves above his head.

"What's that stuff I'm on?" he said.

"Started you with an opiate-base, then tapered you off into Percodan, now just Darvon."

"Is that animal dope?"

"The first one was, but it's the same routine for humans. Begin with morphine, then back you down."

"I'd like to quit them every one."

"That's up to you and the pain. I'll leave some ibuprofen. You might take the Darvon at night to sleep."

"Is that the best?"

"No," Rodney said. "The best painkiller is heroin, but it's against the law to give it to someone who's dying, no matter how bad it hurts."

"Why's that?"

"The government's afraid they might get addicted."

Rodney gathered his tools. He wadded the old dressing and stuffed it into a plastic bag.

"Any more questions?"

"Just one. Why'd Johnny shoot me?"

Rodney stood and Joe noticed straw adhering to the bottom of his jeans. There was an expression of resignation on his face.

"Now you know why I like working with animals," he said. "They don't talk."

After Rodney left, Joe felt better, but he was exhausted. He'd forgotten to ask about walking. He shifted his body and the pain made him gasp. He reached for the Darvon, changed his mind, opened the bottle of ibuprofen, and swallowed four pills. He was furious with himself on every front. He shouldn't have shot himself. He shouldn't have buried the possum. He shouldn't have come to Montana. He closed his eyes. He'd brought it all on himself, and he hated himself for it.

His leg hurt but the fatigue was stronger. As sleep took him he realized that he didn't blame Johnny, and he wondered why.

He awoke to a different presence in the room and blinked several times to shed the haze of sleep. Sunshine poured through the window, edging everything with a rim of light. Two small boys stood just inside the door, their faces solemn. Joe waited for them to disappear into the light of reality until he understood that they were actual children.

"Hidy," he said.

"It's my brother's birthday," the older boy said. "He's three."

"Happy birthday," Joe said.

"He gets presents."

Joe closed his eyes but a shadowed after-image of the boys remained outlined against the glowing light inside his head. He thought of Sara's children and how he'd failed to tell them good-bye. A sudden sadness pressed him to the bed. His limbs felt heavy and thick. He opened his eyes and regarded the younger boy. His hips were as broad as his shoulders, but he had no neck. His head rested directly on his body as if bolted to his shoulders.

"I have something for you," Joe said. He held his cupped hands in the air. "It's just what you need."

The older boy stepped forward.

"No," Joe said. "It's for the birthday boy."

"What is it?"

"I can only tell him."

The older boy coaxed the young one closer to the bed. Joe extended his arms and opened his hands in a quick motion toward the boy's head.

"That was a neck," Joe said. "Now you have a neck."

The boy covered his throat with a hand.

"I got a neck," he said. "For my birthday. A neck."

"Now get out of here," Joe said.

The boys ran from the room. Joe's leg ached. It had been hurting all along but he'd forgotten about it in their presence. A quick anger overwhelmed him and he wondered if he was mad at the boys for returning his pain.

Through the window, the shadow of the roof pointed at the seam of sky along the ridge. Much of Montana was vacant—the land, the streets, the riverbeds. The sky was often bereft of cloud. Perhaps it was natural that he'd stayed here. There was less need to fill the emptiness in him when he was surrounded by an equal amount of empty space. The anger shifted to a profound despair. His leg hurt and he couldn't walk. He wanted to lie in his childhood bed, tended by his mother. At birth his grandmother had given him a stuffed bear that he'd slept with for many years. He missed it as much as all of Kentucky.

He slept. Three times the pain woke him in the night and he ate ibuprofen, determined to wean himself from the heavier medication. In the morning Botree changed the dressing and brought him food. He ate slowly, careful not to spill anything among the sheets. His leg hurt worse than it had in days and he wondered how much time had passed.

She pulled a chair near the bed and smiled for the first time, a breaking of light that was just as swiftly gone.

"A neck," she said.

"I didn't mean it to be an insult."

"It's already his favorite present. His brother wants one now. A bigger one."

"Of course."

As she looked at him, Joe was abruptly embarrassed at his weakened state, his dependence, the nakedness she had seen. He wished he was still taking painkillers.

"How long you all planning on keeping me here?" he said. "What are you anyhow, drug dealers?"

"What," Botree said. "Who?"

"The whole bunch of you."

"No. We're not drug dealers."

"Well, you're damn sure something fishy. Shooting a man for no reason, then keeping him knocked out on animal dope."

"You're a hair on the fishy side yourself," she said. "No mailing address. Carrying a pistol. Few thousand in cash. Burying a stuffed animal."

"Nothing wrong with any of that."

"Nothing wrong with going to a hospital, either."

"My business. What'd Johnny shoot me for, anyhow?"

"I guess that's his business," Botree said. "Why'd you shoot your leg?"

"I don't rightly know."

"There's plenty of people out here who've killed themselves. But you're the first dumb enough to try it in the knee."

"I guess I thought shooting would knock out the bullet that was already in me, like driving two pool balls into a pocket at once. I didn't think the second bullet would bust up like it did."

"You didn't think at all," Botree said. "About like every man on this land."

Joe's anger flared, then faded as quickly as it came. He couldn't recall ever having been so volatile and wondered if the medication was responsible. The pain in his leg was part of his being and he tried to accept it. Another part of him, deep at cellular level, craved the sweet release of narcotics. Getting mad temporarily alleviated the need.

"Is this your house?" Joe said.

"No. It's Coop's."

"Who all lives here?"

"Me and the kids, and Coop, Owen, and Johnny."

"So they're your brothers."

"I'm in the middle. Owen's oldest, Johnny's the baby."

"He's not a baby."

"Johnny doesn't feel too good about what happened."

"I don't either."

"He wants to come and see you."

"Why's that?" Joe said. "To finish the job?"

"Talking to you would make him feel better."

"I know he's your brother and all, but how he feels ain't exactly high on my list right now."

"What is?"

"Walking," he said.

Botree rose from the chair. At the door she turned, a grin lurking in the lines of her mouth.

"A neck," she said, shaking her head. "A neck."

Joe didn't want her to leave.

"Your kids?" he said.

"Yes. You have any?"

"No, but I like them. What's their names?"

"Dallas and Abilene."

Joe lifted his eyebrows.

"It's where their fathers are from," Botree said. "I lived in Texas for a while. Long story."

"They're good boys."

"It's nice you think so. Their uncles are hard on them, and Coop doesn't have much use for kids."

"I never understood people like that."

"I do," she said. "People who don't like kids don't like people."

"Yeah, so."

"And if you don't like people, you generally don't like yourself."

"How about if you like animals?"

"I guess there's hope," Botree said.

"My daddy always said animals and kids were a lot alike."

"That sounds like something a man would say."

She left the room, easing the door shut, and Joe stared at the ceiling. The dull pain was deep in his leg like the ache of a mountain after the coal was removed. He ate four more ibuprophen. His father had died in a bed at home and Joe decided that tomorrow he would rise.

In the morning he asked Botree to stay after she'd changed the dressing on his leg. The wound was healing gradually, like earth settling on a fresh grave. Both legs had withered from disuse. He carefully pivoted his hips to move his bad leg to the edge of the bed. Bending the knee produced an enormous pain. Breath blew from his mouth in a harsh gust and he squeezed the mattress until his hands hurt. He refused to look at Botree. He sat until his breathing was normal. Slowly he stood on his good leg, using the bed for balance, and prepared for what scared him the most—taking a step.

He tested the weight on his bad leg. It didn't hurt as much as he'd anticipated. Encouraged, he moved his bad leg forward slightly, one hand placed against the wall. He stared at the six inches he intended to walk. He stepped forward and his bad leg buckled and he fell against the wall. When the pain subsided, he leaned backwards until he found the edge of the bed, and lowered himself to sit. Hours seemed to have passed, but he knew the entire action had taken a few seconds. Sweat trickled down his back.

He began the slow process of lifting his bad leg, leaning backwards, scooting sideways on the bed, and swinging both legs to the mattress. Botree moved to help but he waved her away. He lay on his back panting like an animal.

"You did good," she said.

He nodded.

"You'll walk," she said. "I know you will."

After she left he took more ibuprofen and slept. When he woke, the pain was worse and the wounds were seeping. He called to Botree, who changed the dressing.

"I hate you having to do this," he said.

"It doesn't bother me."

"I don't like needing help."

"Nobody does."

"Or owing anybody, either."

"You don't owe me nothing, mister," she said. "I'm just paying off people who helped me already."

From outside the door came the sound of running feet, and the children raced into the room. They wore small cowboy boots. Dallas spoke while Abilene stared at Joe.

"What's the difference between a lake and a creek?"

"A creek moves," Botree said, "and a lake doesn't."

"No, Mommy," Dallas said. "A lake moves. Just real slow. Only people who move slow can see it."

Joe chuckled and Botree gave him a quick smile.

"I guess I could see it, then," Joe said. "Nobody moves slower than me."

Abilene whispered in his brother's ear. Dallas looked at Joe.

"My brother wants to know if you're going to die there."

"Dallas!" Botree said. "That's no way to talk."

"It wasn't me, it was him. He said it."

"No," Joe said. "I ain't dying here. But I was wondering if you can tell me what kind of skulls these are."

The children remained with him the rest of the afternoon. Dallas identified all the bones and feathers of the room, and labeled the variety of cattle outside his window. Abilene occupied a three-year-old's world that was wholly his. At six, Dallas was twice his brother's age. They'd never be as far apart as they were now, and Joe tried to explain this to Botree when she brought him a plate of supper.

"Maybe that's why you got a way with kids," she said. "How you think's not like most."

"Most people don't think."

"I know. I been around them all my life."

"Well, maybe I think too much."

"There's something you think too much about."

"What's that?"

"I don't know," she said. "But it's there."

Joe turned away too fast, driving a pain into his leg like a knife between the bones. When he turned back to her, she was looking out the window, allowing him the space to recover. He wondered if that distance was her own style, or the way Montanans were.

The next day she brought him a set of aluminum crutches and accompanied him outside. He felt the strain in his triceps and his wrists. The wing nut for the adjustable handhold caught his pants pocket and ripped the fabric, tumbling him against the wall. He asked Botree for something to cover the wing nut and she brought him a roll of black electrical tape. As he bound the metal, he recalled winding the same material around the barrel of the pistol he'd used on Rodale. It seemed like years ago.

He hobbled down a long narrow hall to a large room with a fireplace and high ceilings. Beyond it was a kitchen and another long room that contained a table and chairs. The house was the longest Joe had ever been inside, very different from the cramped houses of Kentucky. Botree guided him through a utility room, where a washer and dryer stood beside a freezer, a row of hooks, and a large wash basin. They went outside through a side door. A breeze cooled Joe's face, the first fresh air he'd felt in weeks. The light burnished the metal roof of an outbuilding, causing him to look away. They circled the house. He took small steps with the crutches, glad for the hardness of the earth. At home, the tips would have sunk deep into the soil.

They slowly climbed the slope to the top of the rise. Botree moved with surprising grace over the rough ground, her boots finding purchase where there appeared to be none. Joe followed on cow trails worn smooth by thousands of hooves. The country was hard, its beauty grim. He crested the hill and looked across a vast green valley specked with cattle. A band of water wound through the bottomland, marked by the rich green of cottonwood trees. Dark clouds dropped lines of rain to the north while sun in the south glared off the river and made the land glow.

Joe leaned on the crutches to rest, his armpits raw.

"What is this place," he said.

"The Bitterroot Valley."

"Nice country."

"That mountain over there was named for my great-great-grandfather, one of the first to homestead here."

"When was that?"

"Nineteen-twelve. I'm fifth-generation Montana. Not too many of us."

"Counting your kids, you all go through folks pretty quick."

"People in my family either die off or run off."

"Your dad one of them?"

"He died after Mom run off. Coop was drinking hard. Owen left and I went down to Texas for three years. It wasn't easy around here for Johnny."

"Don't reckon."

"He's scared of you," Botree said. "He thinks you might want to get him back."

Joe shifted his weight to look her in the face. Her eyes were neither hard nor soft, but regarded him with patience. She gave nothing away.

"I'm not mad at Johnny over it," he said. "He didn't know me so it wasn't anything against me personal."

She nodded.

"It was a mistake or you all wouldn't have kept me alive."

"There's some who think that was the mistake."

"Who?"

"Just people."

"What people?"

Botree adjusted her hat until its brim jutted from her forehead in a straight line. The action served to enclose her in a private space.

Joe backtracked rapidly through events, trying to learn what made him a threat. The only reason they'd want him dead was if he'd stumbled across something valuable. At home that meant coming too close to someone's whisky still or pot field. Here, the ground was too rocky for marijuana, and liquor was legal everywhere.

"Up there in those woods," he said. "I got too close to something, didn't I? What was it, a gold mine? Or maybe you're a bunch of gun runners. What is it, Botree? I know it's something because Owen and Frank didn't want me to go to a hospital."

She turned her head to gaze across the valley. A rainbow formed beside the mountains as the dark cloud moved south, firing lines of lightning toward the water.

"Don't getting shot give me a right to know?" Joe said.

"A right?" Botree said. "What do you know about rights? We got ten in the Constitution, and none of them cover somebody else's business. I wouldn't get into rights if I were you."

"Well, I'll be goddamned," Joe said.

"You don't have to cuss at me."

"I ain't," Joe said. "I'm cussing in general. I never cussed a person in my life. I just want to know what's going on."

"You got your secrets, too."

"There's a difference."

"There always is when it comes to someone else."

"I got shot over your secrets."

"The fact is, Joe, they ain't mine to tell."

"Who, then?"

"Damn near anybody else. Owen, Johnny, Coop. Take your pick."

"How about Frank?"

"Him, too."

"Who is he, anyhow? How come he don't come around?"

"He plays a lone hand."

"Everybody out here does."

"It's the way we are, Joe. That's what all the old pioneers came out here for. The mountain men first. It's a way of being free."

"Free?" Joe was astonished. "Freedom ain't silence, freedom's being able to talk. You all don't say nothing."

"It's not either one," Botree said. "It's just doing what you want to do and not hurting nobody."

"Well, I sure got hurt."

"I know it. We all know it. That's why we took you in."

"Hell's fire, the way you talk, I ain't no more than a stray dog."

Botree smiled briefly.

"In that case," she said, "it's a good thing I like animals."

Joe stretched on his back. Sun followed the rain cloud along the valley, peeling shadows from the mountaintops as if lifting dark scalps. His face warmed. A hovering hawk was a smudge in the sky. His leg throbbed from the climb, but it was the pain of exertion rather than damage.

He picked pebbles from the rubber tread of each crutch, thinking that the crutch had not progressed in a hundred years. Someone could make a lot of money with a new design. He remembered Boyd's ideas for inventions—a razor with a narrow blade for men with acne; hand tools with a retractable cord that fastened to your clothes. His greatest idea was a tire-changing tool that used the car engine to remove lug nuts.

Joe pulled his good leg beneath him and rose unsteadily, using the crutches to push himself upright. Botree didn't offer any help. She showed neither pity nor sadness for him, only a kind of dispassionate concern, similar to how he'd felt about Rodale's dog. He looked at her narrow back curved inside the man's wool jacket. Her hair flowed over the collar. She was lovely.

"Botree."

His voice was gentle and she turned to him. Her dark eyes were soft, her lips slightly parted. He wanted to say more but couldn't. He felt like a child. He craved her touch, her smell. He turned and began his tedious descent.

Last year's dead grass swayed above the fresh green tufts. Pasture fence surrounded the house while pronghorn grazed with the cattle on the upper slopes. Botree's children waited at the bottom of the hill. Abilene was eating a spider in a casual fashion, as if raised to it. His brother watched without judgment.

"When we're all dead," Dallas said to Joe, "will there be dinosaurs?"

"Yes," Joe said.

Dallas nodded slowly, as if the expected confirmation lent credence to a grand theory. Joe waited for him to continue, but the boy was distracted by the glitter of a button on the ground. Joe leaned against the fence. Botree joined him. Sunshine glowed through dandelions gone to seed.

Joe felt a contentment the likes of which he'd not experienced in nearly a year. He no longer missed Boyd and he didn't feel homesick. What he missed was Virgil. He felt like a man who'd abandoned his religion without having found a replacement. The laughter of the children drifted in the still air. He glanced at Botree and away. The sky was a plank of blue between the far peaks.

18

During the next several days, Joe refused narcotics and endured the gnawing pangs of withdrawal. His appetite returned. Botree continued to care for him as she might an animal—providing regular food, kind words, the occasional gentle touch. Joe was bothered by his dependence, although he was glad of the attention. Every morning Abilene asked which was Joe's bad leg and began pounding the other one.

Owen brought a checkers set to Joe's room and beat him easily. Coop came by once, standing rigid and awkward in the presence of a damaged man. Joe never saw Johnny, an omission for which he wasn't sure if he felt gratitude or disappointment. Rodney visited, smelling of horse and dog, carrying a six-foot length of rubber sliced from an innertube. He looped it through the handle of a window, tied the ends together, and showed Joe how to exercise his leg. He hooked his ankle into the loop and strained against the rubber, then shifted position and demonstrated how to strengthen the muscles of the thigh and hamstrings.

Each day Joe spent two hours exercising. He used a sock filled with number-four shot as an ankle weight and performed a variety of leg lifts. His knee felt stronger, but he despised the tedium of routine and wondered what bodybuilders thought about during a workout. He discarded the crutches for a cane.

Owen came to his room one afternoon while Joe was icing his knee. There was a change in his demeanor, a remoteness that Joe had come to think of as the Montana distance.

"There's something we got to do," Owen said. "I'll be waiting in the mud room."

"We going somewhere?"

"Not far."

"Do I need anything?"

Owen shook his head and left. Joe maneuvered himself into a pair of jeans and hobbled out of the room. Owen led him to an old pickup that Botree called the ranch rig. It bore no license plate, and the dashboard was covered with paper and tools. The cab needed hosing out as much as the bed.

Owen drove the dirt road past the old bunkhouse to a barn. The scent of sage drifted along the fence. Several vehicles that Joe did not recognize were parked on the barren earth. Owen left the truck and motioned Joe inside the barn. Two pairs of ancient chaps hung on the wall, one as stiff-legged as tin pipes, the other a rotted set of woolies. He was enjoying the smell of hay and manure until he saw a man with a military rifle in the shadows.

Owen led him into an old tack room that still smelled of leather. Several men were inside, including Coop and Frank. The men were dark from sun and carried pistols on their hips. Their faces were serious, their eyes hard. Several wore Bills hats.

Frank gave a curt nod and gestured to a stool. Joe sat, his leg stretched in front of him. He propped the cane across his lap like a rifle.

"How's your wheel?" Frank said.

"My what?"

"Your leg."

"Coming along," Joe said. "Stiff in the morning."

Coop spat through a gap in the boards. "I used to wake up that way in my younger days," he said.

The men ducked their heads and a couple chuckled. Light glowed from a dusty window with tape that covered cracks in the glass.

"Boys," Frank said. "This is Joe Tiller in the flesh. He had the bad luck to lean against a bullet going past." He spoke now to Joe. "These gentlemen have some concerns, and we're hoping you might clear the air."

"I'll do what I can," Joe said. "But I don't know what it is you want."

"What were you doing on that mountain?"

"Burying a possum."

"Why?"

"It just came on me to do it."

"Why there?"

"No reason," Joe said. "Highest point that was close to my cabin mainly."

A man wearing military trousers spoke.

"It's not that close," he said. "You had to travel a ways."

"It was easier to get up in the mountains there than right beside the cabin. Plus there was a road."

The man lifted his hat to rub his head. A white scar ran across his scalp and ended at his ear, the top half of which was missing. Joe wondered why he didn't grow his hair long to cover it. The man's voice was low and slow.

"You ever in the service?"

"No," Joe said. "Were you?"

The man's face hardened like wet clay in the sun. Instead of answering, he looked at Owen, who spoke.

"It's what you wrote on the shovel blade is why he wants to know."

"I don't get it," Joe said.

"V.C.," Owen said. "That's short for Viet Cong."

"It's nothing like that," Joe said.

"Then what was it?"

There was a rustling overhead and Joe watched a swallow leave a mud nest built against a rafter. Joe spoke calmly, without rancor or challenge.

"I can't tell you," he said.

"Why not?" Owen said.

"It don't have a thing to do with anybody here."

"Then tell us."

"Sorry." Joe shook his head. "It's personal."

"We have to get personal," Frank said.

"What are you going to do?" Joe said. "Shoot me if I don't talk?"

He tried a quick grin that faded when none of the men showed any response. He could have been talking to the land itself. The faint scent of straw and oats threaded the air. Owen's voice was gentle, as if speaking to family.

"Where you from?"

"West Virginia," Joe said.

"Why'd you come this way?"

"Just took a notion."

"You on the dodge from the law?"

"Why would you ask me that?"

"We need to know who you are. You just sort of leaked out of the landscape on us."

"I'm Joe Tiller," he said. "What else is there to know?"

Frank looked at each man in the barn before returning to Joe. His face held a sad expression, nearly apologetic, but his voice was firm. He reminded Joe of Rundell reluctantly preparing the crew to work.

"There's eighteen people named Joe Tiller in the United States," Frank said.

He unfolded a piece of paper and glanced at it.

"Two are women. Four are black. One's a priest, two are in prison, and one's a state representative. Two are in old folks' homes. Three are dead. That leaves three more unaccounted for."

Joe tried to keep the fear from spreading across his face. His fingers hurt from squeezing the cane.

"One of those three is you," Frank said. His voice softened. "The problem is, you don't seem to exist."

"I don't know what you mean," Joe said. "I'm as real as any of you boys here."

"You don't have any credit cards," Frank said.

"I'm a cash man."

"You've never been married."

"Came awful close once."

Joe had the feeling that he was being judged, but he didn't know how. He couldn't defend himself until he learned in what manner he'd offended these men.

"You've never had health or life insurance," Frank continued. "You never served in any branch of the military. You never held a government job. You don't vote. You don't have a passport. You don't have any kids. You never owned a hunting license, a fishing license, or a boat license. You're not a pilot, doctor, or lawyer. You never got a driving ticket or had a wreck. You've never been arrested. You didn't go to college. You never won big on the lottery."

His voice was low and steady in the tiny room, a continuous pressure. The rest of the men were staring at Joe.

"You don't own land," Frank said. "Or a house or a business. You don't have a bank account. You never borrowed any money. No state has ever held money in escrow for you. You never filed for bankruptcy. You don't own any stocks. You've never been sued and you never received a summons. You've never been to court, jail, or prison. You don't belong to a union. You haven't received food stamps, welfare, or workers' comp. You never inherited any money or land. You never even had a phone."

Frank stopped talking. No one spoke for a long time. Joe was scared to hear what else they knew, but needed to know.

"Is that it?" he said.

Frank regarded him for a moment.

"You don't pay federal taxes," he said.

Another man spoke. He was short and stubby with a gut that tipped his oval belt buckle to aim at his boots.

"Don't get us wrong. We respect these things."

A few of the men nodded.

"It's the way the country was meant to be," said a man, "according to the Bill of Rights."

"There's two reasons for you not to have any trail," Frank said. "You're a government spy or you're a fugitive."

Joe waited. To deny either was to acknowledge the other, and he couldn't think of a third option.

"Nothing makes you look spooky," Owen said. "The question is who you are and what you're running from."

"Way I see it," Joe said, "the real question is who you think you are."

"This isn't the best time to go on the prod," the short man said.

"I'm lamed up from a bullet and you threaten me," Joe said. "You got me outnumbered in a barn. You got a piece of paper telling who I ain't and what I never done. That don't mean nothing. If somebody'll give me a lift, I'll head right back to Rock Creek."

"We can't do that," the short man said.

"Why the hell not?"

"We don't want folks to know Johnny shot you. We can't risk you bugling on us."

"I understand that," Joe said. "I give you my word I won't. That's all I got left to give. You done took my leg, my cabin, and my gun."

He used the cane to push himself to his feet. The tall man with the severed ear stepped in front of the door. He moved casually, but Joe understood that he would not be allowed to leave. He gestured to the sheet of paper Frank held.

"Where'd all that stuff come from anyhow?"

"It's public information," Frank said. "A man can get it and not even leave the house. All you need's a modem and a computer. There's more than nine hundred government data banks that cover every inch of us. Lucky you don't use credit cards, they leave a trail wide as a cow path."

"Now that you mention it," Joe said, "I can see how lucky I am."

"Either lucky or smart," Owen said. "The two partnered up's tough to get around."

"I never made no claim to be smart," Joe said. "And so far it looks like my luck sprung a leak. All you know is who I ain't. And all

I know is you got a fancy computer and a brother who likes to shoot people."

"It's your story," Coop said. "You can make it as big as you want."

Joe turned to face the old man. Dribbled snuff stained the white whiskers of his chin.

"You don't want to hear my story," Joe said.

"There's one thing we left out," Frank said.

"It don't matter to me."

"I expect it might," Frank said. "Your Social Security card is a recent issue out of Kentucky."

A quick fear in Joe's chest spread through his body and seeped along his limbs. He locked his good knee and pressed the tip of the cane hard against the earth.

"Must be one of them other Tillers," he said.

"It's your number, Joe."

"How do you know? It's not on anything I've got."

"It's in the computer files," Frank said. "I ran your Montana driver's license and it popped up in the data bank."

"These days," Owen said, "a newborn baby gets a Social Security number at the hospital. You can't deduct a kid off your taxes without one. That's how the government tricks you into marking your children for life."

"Ain't supposed to be that way," Coop said. "When they voted in Social Security, they said they wouldn't use the number for identification."

"That's right," Frank said. "You only have to give it to an employer."

Joe shrugged. His knee was throbbing as he lowered himself to the stool.

"It ain't a question of who I am," Joe said. "It's who I was. You have to understand that what's behind me stays there. I ain't talking about that, not now and not ever."

"Where are you from?" Owen said.

"Like I said, West Virginia."

"What about your Social Security number?"

"Who says it's out of Kentucky?"

"The number does," Frank said. "Each state's got its own code and your first three numbers are 406. That means it's a Kentucky issue."

"Kentucky's handy to West Virginia," Joe said. "Cross the river and you're there. It's the same mountains and the same people, like Idaho and Montana."

"Idaho people aren't like us," Coop said. "They're barely civilized."

"That's how it is with Kentucky and West Virginia," Joe said. "I came west to get away from that. Nobody but you all know I'm here. And Ty."

"Did you know him before?" Frank said.

"Before what?"

"Before renting that cabin."

"No. Heard about it at the Wolf and tracked him down."

"That damn Ty's too easy to find," Owen said.

"Ty's not important right now," Frank said. "We have this pilgrim."

Joe wondered what Ty had to do with any of this.

"I'm no pilgrim," Joe said. "I'm a prisoner of war with no war."

"Oh, there's a war all right."

"Who with?"

"You're a little ahead of us in action," Frank said, "but your thinking is lagging."

"It must be," Joe said, "since I don't know what you're talking about."

"If we could find this much out about you, think what the government can. Your mistake was having a driver's license at all."

"Maybe so," Joe said. "But you have to have one."

"I don't," Frank said. "None of us do."

Joe glanced around the dim room. He was stunned that they could so easily dismiss something he'd worked hard to acquire.

"We don't have bank accounts, either," Frank said. "And we don't pay taxes."

"Why not?"

"We don't recognize the authority of the federal government over private citizens."

"I don't understand exactly."

"It's simple, Joe. We aren't afraid to defend our freedom. Right now, the biggest threat is from the government. Washington doesn't want patriots, it wants sheep. The people of this country are mind-numb from the media. All they want is comfort."

Frank stepped forward and spread his arms to include everyone in the room. He looked at each man, speaking slowly.

"And now our freedom is up for sale. The Second Amendment's long gone. They're taking guns left and right. The Fourth is unreasonable search and seizure, and that's blown out of the water, too. If you don't look right, the cops will shake you down.

"The Sixth Amendment protects private property from government seizure, but cops can confiscate cash from someone accused of a crime. People are in jail just for having money on them. I believe in law and order, Joe. I believe in democracy and freedom. But I don't trust the government and I'm afraid of the police. I won't support a country that cares so little for its people."

Frank stopped talking abruptly. Joe was entranced by the man's charisma, which surpassed that of the best preachers he had heard at home. The room was quiet, and he realized that Frank was waiting for a response.

"This is new to me," Joe said.

"We've gone off the grid," Frank said. "That's why we're interested in you. You went one step further than us. You came back on the grid as someone else. The government can't control you because they don't know who you are or where you are. I admire that."

"We all do," Owen said. "You're the first outsider we've taken in."

"There'll be more," Frank said. "People know what's happening here. They've always come west for freedom, same as you, Joe. To start again. To be free."

Frank leaned toward Joe, an expression of understanding on his face.

"That's why I came," Joe said, his voice a whisper.

"You left home in such a hurry," Coop said, "you forgot to take the right name with you."

The men laughed. Joe became aware of a new ease in the barn, as if he'd passed muster, although he wasn't sure how.

"Gentlemen," Frank said. "I'm satisfied. If anyone isn't, now's the time to talk."

Everyone was silent except the man with the damaged ear.

"I dug that possum up," he said. "I cut it open and rooted around in there. That's the second time it got itself skinned. If you're anything but what Frank says, I'll do the same to you."

He lifted his chin to Frank, who nodded once in dismissal, and the man left the barn. One by one, the rest moved outside, squinting against the light.

Botree was a silhouette the size of Joe's thumb at the top of the ridge. Behind her the mountains were glazed by sun, stretching in a lavender line. Joe leaned against the fence, feeling grateful for the vast space after the confines of the barn. Owen joined him on one side and Coop the other, each propping a boot on the fence in the exact same way.

"You bushwhacked them boys," Coop said. "There's a couple who thought you might be all hock and no spit."

"It don't matter to me what they think."

"That's to your credit," Owen said.

Sun warmed Joe's face. The sky was blue as water and so close that he felt as if he could drink it.

"I like how it stays light till late," he said.

"Guess you believe in daylight saving time," Coop said.

"Never knew it was something you believed in," Joe said. "Like Santa Claus or flying saucers."

"Then you're letting Congress tell you what time it is. To hell with the moon and the earth's rotation and all that. I don't recognize the authority of Congress over time."

"Time don't have anything to do with us or Congress," Joe said. "A wristwatch is the same as handcuffs."

"You're coming along," Owen said. "Most of us don't wear watches."

He adjusted his hat in the same manner as his sister, and Coop spat tobacco to the rocky dirt. He rested while standing, like a workhorse that lifted a leg. The sound of a truck engine filled the air, and was joined by another. Wind carried the scent of exhaust. The passing vehicles raised a quill of dust that settled to the ground like frost. Joe watched them leave. At the corner of the barn Johnny stood by a truck.

"Now that you know I ain't no spy," Joe said, "he can go ahead and finish the job."

"That boy ain't been worth two sticks since shooting you," Coop said.

"I don't care."

"If I were you, I wouldn't either," Owen said. "But we're stuck with him and you both."

"Look," Coop said. "Johnny wants to say something to you. We'd appreciate if you'd let him. It might help us get some work out of him."

Johnny wore new jeans and a pink shirt with red piping, and crescent pockets. He stood mute and sad, and Joe realized that he had dressed for the occasion. Joe limped across the dusty land. When Johnny saw him coming, he flicked the cigarette away, spat between his teeth, smoothed his shirt, and tugged his pants. The cigarette butt trailed a line of smoke.

"Pick that up," Joe said.

Johnny moved quickly, as if grateful for release. He mashed the paper and tobacco into the earth and scuffed it in a circle until there was nothing but dirt. He kept his head down. Joe leaned across the truck hood, to take weight off his leg. He rubbed the back of his neck, a gesture he recognized as having belonged to Boyd. Johnny kicked dust and looked at Joe and away. He tried to speak but no words came. He tried again.

"What happened," he said, "you know, in the woods."

Joe sensed that to look at Johnny or even nod would make him stop talking.

"That day," Johnny said, "when you got shot." He stared at the ground as if he'd never seen it before. "It was my gun. Me that, you know, did it. I didn't mean to exactly. Everybody says you're all right." His voice tapered to a ragged whisper. "Anyhow, I'm sorry."

There was not much Joe could say and he wanted to be sure Johnny got everything out. Johnny pressed his head against the fence rail, speaking to the dirt.

"I feel real bad about it. That's why I never came to see you or nothing. It's not like I go around shooting people. I'm not that way."

He gathered breath and straightened his body.

"I know there's nothing I can do to make up for it," he said. "But if you want, you can shoot me back."

From the pocket of his jacket he withdrew a pistol and proffered it butt-first. Joe took it as casually as borrowing a pencil. It was a .22

revolver with wooden grips and a long barrel, more of a target pistol than anything else. Oil glistened along the moving parts.

"Just the leg," Johnny said. "So's to square things out."

His mouth was tight and a strip of sweat clung to his forehead.

Joe held the gun loosely, its weight comfortable in his hand. He released the cylinder, swung it open, and dumped the bullets to the dirt. They made six tiny pocks in the dust like the heavy drops of rain in advance of a storm. An expression of disappointment entered Johnny's eyes. Joe returned the empty gun.

"Owen know you got this?" Joe said.

"No. I mean yes, but he don't know nothing about this."

"I had a brother used to hunt squirrels with a pistol. He'd aim with his eyes instead of the gunsight. The whole idea was to put a bullet in the tree bark so close to the squirrel's head that it died from shock. He called it barking a squirrel."

"Not much meat to a squirrel."

"Hunting that way gave him a challenge. He said any damn fool could kill a deer with a rifle and a scope."

"Hard part's getting a deer home," Johnny said. "Last time Owen got one, he had to quarter it and make four trips out, mostly at night. He never went again."

"Somebody should tell him to hunt close to the house."

"Nobody tells him nothing. Not even Coop."

"How about you?"

"Everybody tells me what to do."

"They tell you to talk with me?"

"That was my idea," Johnny said. "I was kind of hoping you'd shoot just now. I know it don't make much sense."

"I might be just the man to understand that."

"How's that?"

"It didn't bother me too much you putting one in my leg."

"No?"

"It's not that I liked it," Joe said. "But more a case of not minding. I guess part of me thought I deserved it."

"Same here."

"You don't, Johnny. You were just doing your job out there, weren't you."

"Yeah."

"A leg shot ain't that bad."

"Wasn't like that, Joe. You don't care for me calling you Joe, do you?"

"No. What do you mean?"

"It wasn't your leg I was aiming for."

"Just a warning shot that got lucky?"

"No." Johnny's voice was forlorn. "I was aiming spang at the middle of your chest, but I got scared at the last and dropped the barrel."

Joe held the cane tightly in both hands, glad he'd unloaded the pistol. Johnny bunched his mouth like pulling a drawstring bag tight. He wiped his chin with the back of his hand. His voice was hoarse.

"Owen don't know about that," Johnny said. "He'd think I was yellow."

The anger went out of Joe like a dumped sack.

"Anybody can shoot somebody," he said. "It takes a lot more guts to hand a man a loaded gun."

"You ever kill anybody?"

Joe looked upslope. A steady wind bowed the cheatgrass in a gentle curve, aiming its spikelets east.

"Not me," he said. "But I used to know somebody who did. It didn't do him a damn bit of good."

"What was it, an accident?"

"No more accident than you tracking me."

Four cows crested the ridge and descended along a path cut into the earth. The last cow's swollen udder swung like a bell beneath her legs. Johnny squeezed his thumb to the side of his hand, forcing a huge lump of flesh to rise.

"Feel that," he said.

"What is it?"

"My milking muscle. Go ahead, feel it."

Joe tapped on the tight skin. The muscle beneath was hard as clay.

"See that cow," Johnny said. "Only one we never got rid of. She's my favorite."

"How come?"

"Got the softest tits I ever touched."

The cow's back ran straight as a rope from neck to rump. Manure clung to its tail. Joe felt a terrible sympathy for this boy.

"Johnny," he said. "I forgive you. You'll never understand it, but I appreciate what you done. I think you're as brimful of courage as an egg is of meat."

Johnny looked quickly away. He tugged his hat and stared at the sky. There was no sound of bird, animal, or wind. Bullets lay at his feet.

"Joe," he said. "You want to go to town?"

They took the ranch rig. The Bitterroot River flashed silver panes of light beside the road. The mountains were blue, their peaks still topped by snow. Johnny drove with his palm on the bottom of the steering wheel and his other arm out the window.

"How come you to shoot me anyhow?" Joe said.

"You were too damn close to Frank's place."

"I guess so," Joe said. He wasn't sure what Johnny meant. "How close?"

"Mile, maybe two."

"What were you all doing?"

"Me and Owen brought in supplies. We do that every month. Food, water, and propane mostly. Fresh batteries for his CB and shortwave. We're the only ones who know where he's hiding out. Us and Ty."

"Ty Skinner?"

"Sure. They post me on sentry when they work their plans out. That's what I was doing when you came along."

"Working plans out with Ty?"

"He'd already left. He's not part of it, you know."

"I didn't think he was," Joe said. "But I don't know what it is he does do."

"He's the gun man." Johnny turned in the seat. "But don't let on I told you, okay?"

Joe nodded.

"He's got the nicest guns I ever saw."

Dimming strips of crimson lay in the western sky. The mountains became deep blue, then gray, and finally black. Johnny flicked on his headlights. In Missoula they stopped at a three-way intersection near the fairgrounds, where traffic was backed up in all directions.

"Malfunction Junction," Johnny said.

"How come everybody wears those Buffalo Bills hats all the time?"

Johnny shrugged. "It's just a sign."

"Of what?"

"That we believe in the Bill of Rights."

"I got another question."

"Fire away."

"What are those damn letters on the hillsides for?"

"High school kids do it. The L is for Loyola. Then a bunch of dumb college kids put the M up. They started out rock but now they're concrete."

"Where do you want to go?" Joe said.

"Heck, it's town. We can go anywhere."

"Name a place."

"I don't like college bars or music bars except on country nights. And I don't like sports bars or old men bars, either."

"That leaves plenty. This place is full of bars, ain't it."

"Ever been to the Wolf?"

"Once or twice."

Johnny drove into the clear streets of Missoula's old downtown and parked in front of the Wolf. A line of drinkers sat at the bar's end, their backs turned to the world. Hard men and women sat at tables beneath the garish fluorescent light. The poker room held three players waiting to start a game. Joe followed Johnny to the strip club, where the doorman let them in free. The lights were dim and the walls held many mirrors that reflected shadows. Slot machines stood beside the restroom doors. Johnny sat at the table farthest from the stage and Joe was amused by his shyness. They ordered beer while watching a woman remove her shirt. She walked with her shoulders arched back and her chin high, kicking her legs forward as if in a marching band. Just above her G-string was the faint scar of a cesarean section.

After a few minutes, another stripper approached their table. She wore knee boots, a short skirt, and a leather vest. Her left eyebrow was split by a scar and Joe wanted to touch it. He felt very warm. The woman smiled at Joe and sat on Johnny's lap. She held his head in both her hands and kissed him, pressing him against the wall. Joe had never seen a dancer do any more than accept a kiss on the cheek. He hoped she'd kiss him next.

The woman pulled away from Johnny, who shouted above the music.

"This is Sally," he said. "Sally, this is Joe. He's sort of a friend of the family."

"Uh-oh," she said. "I don't like the sound of that."

"He's not like the rest," Johnny said. "He knows my sister."

"Nice to meet you," Joe shouted.

She smiled, her teeth bright in the dusky light. Her black hair was long and straight. Makeup lay on her face like enamel. Joe wondered if Johnny's family knew where he spent his time.

During a lull between songs, she spoke.

"I sunbathed in my yard today," she said. "The baby sat in a box and watched."

"Anybody else?"

"No way, honey. But you know I have to get a tan all over."

"You could go to one of those tanning beds."

"I hate those things," she said. "They're like a microwave."

"Anybody can see you in the backyard."

"You got it backwards, Johnny. Anybody can see me in here."

"That's different."

"I think you're jealous is what I think." She turned to Joe. "Do you think he's jealous?"

Joe shrugged and faced the stage. The dancer was completely nude and working for the dollars that customers flourished in the air. Two young men sat immobile, as she quickly rid them of a pile of money beside their beers. The music ended and the dancer left the stage.

In the sudden silence, poolballs cracked against each other across the room.

"I can't stay now," Johnny said. "I came with Joe so I have to go back with him, too."

"He's sweet," she said. She wiggled on his lap. "Let's talk about the first thing that pops up."

A woman tapped Sally on the shoulder. Sally kissed Johnny,

walked backstage, and emerged into the light. She moved with a confident grace that Joe hadn't noticed at the table. She smirked while prancing, as if flaunting the power granted by the men.

"Come on," Johnny said. "I hate to see her dance. I mean, I like seeing her dance. It's the guys who watch I can't stand seeing."

Outside the night spread like black oil, shiny stars glowing low in the sky. The mountains were dark hulks on the horizon.

"She's a nice girl," Joe said.

"I like her, you know. I really like her."

He glanced at Joe.

"I don't just see her here. We have dates. Her kid's great, she's just ten months, but she knows who I am. She can say my name, Joe. She knows me."

He stopped talking and Joe looked away to grant him the privacy of emotion. Joe took the keys and started the truck, letting the big engine warm itself.

"Is she yours?" Joe said. "The baby?"

Johnny nodded.

"Is that why you never told the family?"

"No."

"Because of her job?"

"That's not it. Sally makes good money and they treat the dancers better than you'd think."

"Does it bother you what she does?"

"Sometimes," Johnny said, "but that's not it, either."

"What, then?"

"She's an Indian. Salish-Kootenai."

"That doesn't matter."

"Around here it sure does."

Johnny slumped in the seat. Joe wondered if Botree would mind that he went to a strip club with her brother. He jerked his head as if to sling the thought from his mind, and tried to think of Abigail, a wedge he could slip into the gap. Abruptly he knew that he had never loved her. At the fore of his feelings lay sympathy. They'd been together because the community had expected it. He suddenly understood that he'd spent his life following patterns that were designed by other people.

He felt the faint glimmerings of actual freedom, a sensation that scared him. At a red light he looked through the front window of a tavern. There was another bar across the street. Town was where people went when they didn't have anywhere else to go. They drank and loved and fought, and Joe wished he could be one of them, but knew he never would. He was tired of trying to be like everyone else.

19

By June the days were long slabs of sun. Weather moved down the valley like water in a ditch. Joe limped around the house without his cane, saving it for outdoor walks on rough ground. He tied a leather strip to its handle and carried it slung over his back like a carbine. He no longer wore a bandage on his knee.

Botree offered to take him fishing. They rose early and drove the mud-spattered ranch rig to a dirt road heading south. Owen and Johnny watched the boys. An overnight snow lay like shredded lace against the red rock slopes.

"I can't believe it snowed in summer," Joe said.

"When I was a girl, it snowed in July."

"At least August's safe."

"Coop said they got snowbound in August when he was a kid. They wore long underwear all year long."

"Must be hard on kids in winter."

"Winter's hard on everything."

"I mean school," Joe said. "I had to walk up and down a hill every day for twelve years."

"I don't see having that problem."

"The school bus come all the way out to the ranch?"

"No," Botree said. "I'll be home schooling."

"What's that?"

"Teaching them at home. They're already off to a good start. Dallas knows the alphabet and can count to a hundred."

"You won't send those boys to school?"

Botree shook her head.

"Don't the state get on you?"

"Not here," she said. "A lot of people do it. You'd be surprised."

"How come?"

"Freedom to learn, Joe. School doesn't have anything to do with learning anymore."

"It doesn't?"

"You take a puppy and you train it for a month. Then you put it on a bus full of other puppies. When it comes back home it starts shitting in the house again."

"You lost me already."

"Schools aren't educating kids, Joe. They're raising them. That's my job."

"Teaching is the school's job. Teachers go to college for it. They're trained, like any work."

"Trained to make kids shut up and sit down," Botree said. "They have class until the bell rings, then it's time to stop. That doesn't have anything to do with learning."

"Keeping your kids out of school doesn't sound that great to me."

"If I sent them, it would make me a hypocrite."

"How's that?"

"It's supported by taxes, which I don't believe in paying."

"This is a state road," Joe said. "Does driving it make you a hypocrite, too?"

Botree swerved to avoid a rough spot. "Tax money working hard there."

"I tell you what," Joe said. "It's pretty easy not to believe in something. Do you have a driver's license?"

"No."

"How about a telephone?"

"No."

"Reckon your kids don't believe in brushing their teeth or taking baths."

"You leave them out of this."

Along the river, rock bluffs glinted orange and green, laced with crevices like dark veins. Botree stopped for gas. The attendant wore a cap emblazoned with the emblem of the Buffalo Bills and carried a pistol on his hip. Leaning behind the counter was a military rifle gleaming with oil. Botree paid and left.

"It's still the Wild West out here, ain't it?" Joe said.

"Not really. All those guys were from the East—Buffalo Bill, Wild Bill Hickok, Doc Holliday, Wyatt Earp. Billy the Kid was from New York. Families back East sent their crazy sons out here. That lawless time only lasted about twenty years."

"Still pretty wild to me."

"Only for somebody like Johnny. He believes that Code of the West stuff. It's a big crock, but you can't tell any of them."

"Them?"

"All the young boys," Botree said. "The worst is when they start trying to be outlaws because they think outlaws are cool. They can't rob trains or rustle cattle anymore, so the only thing left is moving drugs."

"You know a lot about it."

"Don't take much to know. Over half the people locked up are in for drugs, including Dallas's daddy. That leaves the real outlaws free."

"If a drug dealer ain't an outlaw, what is?"

"Killer. Rapist. Robber. People who like to hurt people."

"Are you saying they don't lock them up?"

"I'm saying half of them go free because the cells are already filled with guys who picked the wrong drug."

"Well, what's the right drug?"

"Alcohol, or cigarettes."

"Look, Botree. The way you talk and all, I guess it makes me think you might be a dope addict or something."

The truck weaved from her laughter. She lifted her foot from the accelerator and straightened the wheel, still laughing.

"No," she said. "I don't even smoke or drink."

"Then what's this all about?"

"Making something illegal doesn't stop people from doing it, it just turns them into criminals. Laws should protect us from bad people. Nothing else. If they protect us from ourselves, they hurt freedom."

Joe was astonished not only by Botree's words but also by her vehemence. He had never spoken with such conviction about anything, not even his work or family. What she said made a certain sense but he couldn't put the bootlegger at home in the same category as a town drug dealer.

"All I know," Joe said, "you all sure got a funny way of being free. Don't pay taxes or get a driver's license. Coop don't believe in daylight saving time, and you don't believe in schools. What's Owen against?"

"Gun laws, mainly."

"So's that guy at the gas station. That looked like some kind of machine gun he had."

"No, it was an AR-15."

"Reckon you're a gun expert, too."

"It's made by Colt. The civilian model of an M-16. The only difference is it doesn't have the full-auto lever. Takes the same ammunition as an M-16."

"And what's that?"

"Two twenty-three caliber in a thirty-round magazine."

She rounded a curve and the river valley opened before them like a fan. An eagle dove at an osprey that carried a fish. The osprey dropped the fish and the eagle caught it in midair and glided to a bare tree limb.

"What's so special about Frank's place?" Joe said.

"Who told you about that?"

"Your brother."

"If it was Owen, you'd know what was special. So it must have been Johnny and he let something slip."

"You know your brothers all right."

"If this has to stand between us, there's nothing we can do. I can't tell you about Frank."

"Can't or won't."

"It's all the same, Joe."

"Why?"

"Because I won't have a hand in it, that's why. Ask Owen. Coop'll run on till you don't know what he's talking about, and no telling what Johnny might say."

"What do you say?"

"I have a few things to say, but not yet."

"When, then?"

"Depends on you."

"Now you're talking just like the rest of your family, out of the side of your mouth. I'm tired of that, Botree. I don't mean to fight, I just want straight talk."

"I never met a man yet who didn't like to fight. They like to tell me what to wear, what to do, where to go, and what to say."

The low sound of distant thunder drifted over the river. Snow made a white skullcap on each mountain peak.

"You all know a lot about me," Joe said.

"Right," she said. "That business at the barn."

"Did I pass?"

"It's not that way."

"And this is my reward?"

"You got it backward, Joe. Just like every man I ever met. This isn't your reward, mister. This is a damn date."

She pressed the accelerator. Tools and supplies banged in the back and Joe thought of Taylor driving the trash truck, careening through campus. Dewey and Rundell followed in his thoughts. He quickly blocked them off as if building a wall, but Marlon, Sara, and his mother rushed over it. Each attempt to keep someone out brought a new person in. When Abigail appeared, everyone left, and he knew that he'd been trying to prevent her memory all along.

He studied Botree's hands in the glow of morning light. Her fingers were long and slim. She pulled onto a narrow lane and parked beneath a cottonwood near the river, and left the truck without speaking. Joe followed, his leg stiff from the ride. She assembled a flyrod, tied a fly to the transparent leader at the end of the yellow line, and demonstrated the three-stroke motion for casting. She gave him a pair of heavy black glasses like safety goggles. She stepped into the river as though it was grass.

Joe stood on a shoal and watched her work. Her posture changed, gaining fluidity and grace as if the act of fishing lent a greater purpose to life. She began walking upstream, weaving an S with the line in the air to keep it ready to cast. The swift whisper of the leader hummed about her shoulders. She jerked her head rapidly to maintain a constant surveillance of the water. She twitched the rod to place the lure beneath an overhang near the bank.

"There's one over there," she said.

"One what?"

"Fish."

"Where?"

"By the log."

The glasses reduced glare, but Joe was unable to see the fish, the lure, or the log. He walked downstream and prepared to cast. He moved his arm rapidly between the clock positions of ten and two, letting out line on each forestroke. It required both hands, but he couldn't control the motion of the line. He made his initial cast, snapping his wrist and aiming with his hand. The line shot straight forward, then dropped over his shoulder and doubled behind him. He began reeling. The line zipped past him. He turned away from the river and faced the treeline. His lure was deeply tangled in a bush. He spent the next half hour retrieving his line while Botree caught three fish, gleefully holding each aloft for him to see.

He made a few casts that successfully landed in water, but was never able to see the fly, or a fish taking it. He went farther downstream and his bad leg sank in wet sand to his knee. He set the flyrod aside. Each time he dug with his hands, the sand flowed back into the hole. He had a moment of fear, which was quickly replaced by a determination not to ask Botree for help. He wiggled back and forth as if his leg were a posthole digger and he was trying to widen the hole. His leg rose slowly from the earth. When he regained his footing, the rod had floated away. The leader was wrapped around his other leg and the tiny hook was embedded in his pants. He began hauling in the line, hand over hand. He tried to coil it but soon gave up and let it surround him like a net. By the time he had reeled in his rod, his clothes were wet and cold.

Joe sat on a piece of driftwood beside a head-high stand of cane, watching Botree. She moved in an arcane dance of water and woman, fish and sky, her shadow flowing over the surface of the stream. She tracked fish like a bounty hunter, choosing the particular trout she wanted to stalk.

She waded to shore, casting as she moved, and joined him on the rocky bank.

"How'd you do?" she said.

"No luck."

"I saw you catch your rod. They're not that easy to land."

"The bush was easier."

She abruptly grabbed Joe and yanked him into the water. After three steps he tried to jerk away from her, but his leg buckled and he dropped to one knee in the swift water. He clenched his teeth as the cold water surged past his waist. The river strained at his legs as if a thousand tiny hands were pulling him downstream. He pushed her away from him and nearly fell.

"What are you doing?" he yelled.

"Look." She pointed toward the bank.

A few yards behind where he'd been standing, a female moose left the brush and entered the river. Just beyond it came her calf, stumbling over the slick rocks that lined the riverbed.

"They're damn near blind," she said. "Lucky for us. She'd have killed you in two passes."

"Because of the little one?"

"Yeah, they're worse than bears that way. And faster."

"Pretty tough mama."

"They have to be out here."

Joe watched the moose vanish in the brush. Botree helped him walk and for a short while they stood together, her hand around his waist. The wet clothes outlined her hips. The sun was hot and the river was cold. Botree jerked her rod upright, and Joe realized that she'd never given up her vigil of the water. The line pulled taut. She held the rod over her head, lowered it, and began reeling rapidly, the line spewing a crescent of water. The fish leaped from the water in a silvery arc. She handed the rod to Joe. He instantly felt the pull of the fish, as if the stream were a muscle of the earth. The fish changed directions and yanked his arm like a powerful dog reaching the end of its leash. He was no longer aware of Botree or the cold, the sky or the land. He'd entered the realm of the fish. It pulled one way and then the other, showing itself in a brief flash of silver.

The rod bowed nearly double and he heard Botree yelling for him to let out more line. The workings of the reel were incomprehensible to him, and he passed the rod to her. It was like releasing a wire that pulsed with electricity.

Botree waded toward the bank and brought the fish into her hands. It was long as Joe's forearm and thicker, a gray sinew with fins.

"Westslope cutthroat," Botree said. "A ready biter. Prettiest fish that swims around here."

"I'd hate to see an ugly one."

"I played this fish too long. It's not doing too good."

"What do you mean?"

"Not supposed to tire it out."

"What's it do, mess up the taste?"

She turned the fish upside down in the water and worked the hook, but it was embedded very deep. She cut the leader near the trout's mouth, leaving the hook protruding through its body. She righted the fish, aimed its head upstream, and gently moved it back and forth. When the gills began moving, she released the trout. It twitched its tail and vanished into deeper water.

"What did you do that for?" Joe said.

"It was wore out."

"I was going to eat that thing."

"Not that one, you weren't."

"Meat's no good?"

"Meat's great. Just you can't keep them because it's protected. Catch and release is the only good law the government's got."

"You mean you get yourself wet and cold and don't even eat lunch out of it?"

"Oh, we'll eat lunch, Joe. I got sandwiches in the truck."

"What about the hook?"

"It'll rust out."

"This ain't fishing."

"What do you mean?"

"You wear the fish down, leave the hook in its mouth, and nurse it back to health. Then you turn it loose."

"That's right," Botree said. "About like we've done with you."

Wind fluttered the surface of the river, making it glitter like fire. Water drained from the folds of Joe's clothes.

"You saying nobody'd care if I took off?" he said.

"The kids would care."

"Anyone else?"

"Coop and them don't, if that's what you mean."

"I don't know what I mean."

"When you figure it out," she said, "you tell me."

"I guess I was wondering about you."

"I don't know, Joe. Not yet I don't."

"When you figure that out," he said, "you tell me."

The river eddied around their bodies, and Botree extended her hand, the skin red from cold. They shook hands as if to seal a bet. Her eyes were dark and large. He tensed his arm and tugged as gently as possible and felt an answering pull. He leaned forward and the water rose along his chest. He could see it darken her shirt as she moved toward him. Their heads brushed. She was smelling him with quick intakes of air. He pressed his forehead to hers and rolled his face across her face. Their lips moved over each other but they didn't kiss, as if the skin of their faces needed to become familiar first. They leaned together like birds in wind. The river spread around them. Joe tightened his hand around hers.

"I don't much care for catch and release," he said.

Botree eased his hand away until he was holding water.

"There's no catch," she said.

They ate sandwiches on a log by the truck. His leg felt strong. The horizontal lines of Montana landscape lay before them—a stripe of blue water, the narrow brightness of a rock shore, a long chunk of green forest, the jagged gray mountains and a strip of blue sky. The only vertical lines were cottonwood trunks near the water, like bars to a prison of light and space.

"You're sure good at fishing," Joe said.

"Not much else to do around here."

"I never seen anybody run around like that and catch so many."

"You want shallow water," Botree said. "The fish have less room and they become predictable. Like people in town."

"Did you ever fish the other way?"

"I tried lake fishing, sure. You sit and wait for the fish to come to you. I like to go where the fish are. It's easier with a raft."

"It might be drier."

"Just quicker. A raft gets you from place to place."

"So rafting is for work. What's Montana fun?"

"Break horses."

She smiled easily, the sunlight glowing in her hair. Behind her the sky was thick and blue.

"You know," Joe said. "I been here awhile now, on my own up Rock Creek, and with you all. I spent some time in town, too. But I always feel like I'm over my head. Like I'm in another country. It's been that way since I got here."

"What are you running from, Joe?"

He looked at her and away. A single cloud moved a patch of darkness along the valley floor.

"I know it's something, Joe. Everyone does. They asked me to spy on you but I wouldn't do it. So I'm asking now for myself only."

"Why?"

"Once in Texas I opened the door and found a woman with three kids on my porch. Three of the prettiest little babies you ever saw. They looked familiar, but I couldn't figure out why. I knew I didn't know them. And she just stood there, staring at me. Then she started crying. I thought she was crazy. I asked her what was the matter, and she said she was crying for me. Me, I said, why for me? Because you don't know, she said. Don't know what, I said. Then she cried more and said, I'm sorry to have to tell you. What, I said. I was getting mad.

"She touched Abilene, and right then I knew why her kids were so familiar. They looked like Abilene's daddy. We stood there staring and damned if he didn't come home. When he saw us, he drove right on without even stopping. I never saw him again.

"I don't want that happening again, Joe. I couldn't stand myself if it did."

"I've never been married and I don't have any kids."

"There was a time when the only thing that kept me alive was knowing my kids needed me."

"Good thing you had them."

"Yeah, but it was having them that made me not want to live."

"I don't think I understand exactly."

"A woman alone with kids is hard is all."

"I didn't leave no wife and kids behind."

"It better be that way."

"It is. There's something, all right, but not that."

She looked at him for a long time. He felt as if she were gauging him, or maybe gauging herself. She had made mistakes. She was making one with him. He was stunned to realize that he loved her.

"How do you know when to move?" he said.

"Back home from Texas?"

"No, not that. Botree, it don't matter to me what you did down there. I don't judge a past. All we've got's now."

"Then what are you talking about?"

"Fishing. I seen you going back and forth from place to place."

"There's something they call the twenty-minute theory. When a fish is caught, all the trout leave that part of the water. Twenty minutes later, they come back."

"Maybe it's the other way around."

"How's that again?"

"Maybe the trout know a human will move on within twenty minutes of catching a fish."

"Maybe," she said. "Some men move on sooner than that."

"I got nowhere to go, Botree. This is where I went to."

"It's going to take me a while to get used to a man who talks like you."

"I didn't used to be this way," he said.

Rising, she offered a hand, but he pretended not to see it. He wanted to touch her again, but it was more important to work his leg. It had begun to stiffen. He followed her through the brush to the truck, with the cane slung across his back, determined not to use it. He remembered how Boyd had quit smoking by keeping a cigarette in his shirt pocket until it crumbled to dust.

Botree drove uphill along a dirt road and slowed for a switchback carved into the mountain. Small stones thrown by the tires dropped over the steep edge and bounced down the slope. She steered with both hands, her head hunched between her shoulders, intent on the narrow road. The trees became smaller, Douglas fir and hemlock, and the ground held little grass. The road ended at a small plateau and Botree left the truck.

Joe followed her along a path that climbed at a gentle angle. Moss campion spread like a carpet along the rocky earth. After half a mile, Joe smelled rotten eggs. Botree stopped amid steam rising from a pool of water. She sat on the warm stone beside the water.

"Animals sleep here in the winter," she said.

"What is it?" he said.

"Hot springs. This is a safe one. Some are real hot. The old mountain men who found them thought they were passages to Hell."

"I never seen one before."

"There's a lot of them around if you know where to go. One at Lolo feeds a swimming pool."

"Can you drink it?"

"No, I just thought it might be good for your knee."

She leaned back on her elbows and stretched her legs. The jeans were taut to her skin. The spring sunlight gave her hair a red cast, her face a golden warmth. Her eyelids drooped. Joe walked to the edge of the rock and followed an animal trail that led higher up the mountain. He bent forward from the waist to keep his weight spread among his limbs. He remembered climbing a sheer rock cliff above the railroad tracks with Boyd as a kid. They'd spent an hour walking the tracks, searching for a loose railroad spike to use as a climbing tool. Boyd had always gained the summit first. He waved his arms over his head and bellowed his triumph and threw his railroad spike high in the air.

Joe reached a narrow flat space and rested against the side of the mountain. Orange moss on the rock was the color of salamanders in Kentucky. Beads of snow filled the creases of his jacket. Across the valley the sun gleamed like oil on the rock slopes. He wondered at what point in the air the snow melted.

Below and to the west four horsemen were climbing a narrow path. With a rifle he could pick them off easily, vulnerable only from the air. The timber was dense enough that he could elude a helicopter if he slept by day.

Botree's dark head was a speck in the center of the pool. Steam rose around it like dust. He stood and yelled, waving the cane about his head. The sound of his voice echoed back and dissipated into the air. He yelled the way Boyd used to yell, and without forethought he tossed the cane down the mountain. It vanished among the treetops.

Joe left the ledge carefully to prevent rocks from falling into the water below. Descending the mountain was harder than climbing, something he'd forgotten. It occurred to him that wisdom was simply remembering what you already knew.

The air warmed. The snow was gone from his clothes and his hair lay wet against his head. When he stepped from the woods, he saw Botree's boots and clothing stacked on the rock. She lay in the pool to her neck, drops of water glistening in her hair. Joe undressed, flinging his clothes in sweeping gestures until he was clad only in T-shirt and shorts. He felt shy, even though Botree had seen him nude many times. She averted her head as he entered the pool. It was shallow and very warm, and the bottom was soft. A spatter of raindrops struck the surface like sparks.

She was reclining below the surface and he lowered himself until they faced each other. Heat surrounded his body. Steam rose from the rain, hiding the trees beyond the pool. He placed his hands on her ankles and held them there. The warm water relaxed his muscles and he slid his hands slowly along her legs. Their heads were very close. She was breathing through her mouth. Her collar bones held tiny circles of water and she arched her back gently until her breasts rose like islands. The rain was turning to snow. He eased forward, feeling her hands move over his hips. She shifted underwater and he felt himself brush against the soft apex of her thighs. They looked at each other, their faces very near. Her eyes were dark and scared. He waited for them to soften. Their lips brushed. She tugged his hips and he slid deeper into the warmth of water. They pressed themselves together and stayed that way a long time, holding each other in the hot water while snow cooled his back. He moved his hands to her face, the water the thinnest of skin between them. He began to move, watching her eyes.

The water rippled in rings around them. It lapped the rock shore like surf, as if a storm was coming from far at sea. Mist rose in swirls blown by wind. The water pounded the stone, turning it dark in great splashes that hissed and ran with steam. Their bodies slowed the motion of the pool. The water hushed its splash. They lay still, their skin red from heat, taking air in panting gulps. Twilight moved through the trees. The air cooled as day faded behind the western hills. Night came down the slope and melded the water with the shadows of the firs.

They lay on their backs in the heat. The sky was rich with darkness and stars. Snow landed on their faces, melted into the waters of the pool. She stirred against him.

"We have to go."

They dressed quickly and went down the mountain cold and wet, giggling like children. They huddled in the truck while its engine heated the cab. The windshield clouded from within and they rubbed it with their hands, making peepholes to the sky. The stars gleamed close. The truck smelled of minerals and flesh.

20

The woods of Idaho caught fire late in June. Smoke lay in ribbons along the horizon, transforming dusk to a garish display of color. Joe had never seen so much smoke. Kentucky woods were moist and shady, and the occasional blaze was easily controlled. Here, the fires lasted for weeks.

He and Botree attended a Fourth of July picnic at a meadow along the Bitterroot River. Clouds moved like surf across the sky. Abilene and Dallas joined other children. Women clustered around a young mother and her infant beneath a cottonwood. Owen talked with a group of men Joe recognized as the ones who'd questioned him in the barn. Near the river, Coop played a game of horseshoes, his pitched shoes arcing once, sunlight flashing on the iron.

Joe felt as if he was passing for a local in a foreign country, with Botree as his camouflage. He stayed near her, shaking hands and being polite, much like a church social at home. He recognized a few people, including the gas station attendant and the man who'd sold him wood last autumn.

Men and women tended to separate, except for the teenagers, who roamed in a pack. They were dressed in high-fashion ranch clothes—crisp jeans, shiny belt buckles, new hats and boots. Each boy's back pocket held the round imprint made by a tin of snuff. A young girl bent from the waist and bit the leather Wrangler patch loose from a boy's pants. She scampered away, giggling.

Botree laughed at Joe's startled expression.

"That means they're going steady," she said. "It tells everybody else that boy's taken."

"What's the next step?"

"Wearing shirts that match."

"Shoot, my clothes don't even match each other."

"You know what impressed me most at their age?"

"What?"

"When the boy made his dog sit in the back."

"All this is a new one on me," he said. "Do I have to watch the back of my britches around you?"

"No, I'm over my buckle-chasing days," Botree said. "I knew one gal used to custom-order her belt. Instead of her name on the back, she'd put her phone number."

"Where's she at now?"

"Got six kids and a ranch by Great Falls. Goes to town once a month if the weather holds."

"Sounds rough."

"Around here," Botree said, "that's the top of the line. Only thing lonelier than a ranch is not having a man with you on it."

Dallas and Abilene ran down a slope, their faces flushed.

"Know what," Dallas said. "I climbed a tree. From the top I could see past the world."

"Know what?" Abilene said. "Me, too."

They ran away.

"Where's Johnny?" Joe said.

"Probably up by the trucks with his buddies," she said. "They think nobody knows they've got half-pints in their boots."

"I figured there'd be more people drinking. Beer, at least."

"Not with the families around like this. That's why the young bucks go off on their own. You want some?"

"Not really."

"Don't stay dry on my account," Botree said. "Once in a while won't hurt. You should see me on tequila."

"I never drank it."

"More like it drinks you. The best in Texas had a worm in the bottom."

"What for?"

"I don't know. But that worm kicked worse than a mustang in a tin barn."

Several hundred yards away, children were playing in a grove of aspen. Joe could see each leaf clearly. He enjoyed Montana's dry climate, the light and space that offered a solace he'd never found at home.

Botree touched his arm. "I've got to take a look at Gailie's new baby."

Joe watched her walk through wild grasses, moving over the earth in her heeled boots. He climbed the slight rise to the parked trucks silhouetted against the sky. The last one had its tailgate dropped. Johnny and two young men sat on its edge, passing a half-pint of whisky. Johnny offered the bottle to Joe.

"Take a slug of redeye," he said.

"Ain't bourbon, is it?" Joe said.

"Some blend," one of the men said. "We been drinking Canadian whisky since Prohibition."

"What are you all chasing it with?" Joe said.

"Cigarettes and spit."

Joe lifted the bottle and let the liquor slide into his mouth. The burn spread along his limbs. He spat and took another drink.

"Damn, boys," he said. "That stuff works like gravy on Sunday." He passed the bottle to the nearest man. "I'm Joe."

"Kip," the man said. He wore a white Stetson with a pale gray band. He gave the whisky to the other man.

"Here, Z-man," Kip said.

Z-man took the bottle. A wispy mustache grew above his mouth. "Two bubbler," he said.

He finished the whisky in two swallows, which forced a pair of bubbles to the surface. He jerked the empty bottle from his mouth and blinked rapidly.

"That's got a whang I like," he said.

"Where's the other bottle," Johnny said. "Joe's got to catch up."

"That's all right," Joe said. "You all are too far ahead."

"I just started," Kip said. "Z-man's out front a mile. He couldn't hit the ground with his hat."

"I could with yours," Z-man said.

"Don't mess with my hat," Kip said.

"Why not?"

"I'll kick your ass so hard you'll have to take off your shirt to shit."

Z-man began to giggle. He pulled his shirttail free of his jeans, held it away from his body, and leaned backwards. He lost his balance and stumbled against the truck.

"God doggit," he said. "I didn't even see him hit me."

Johnny uncapped a fresh bottle and gave it to Joe.

"Don't pay them any mind," Johnny said. "They been that way all their lives."

"What are they," Joe said. "Kin?"

"Brothers."

Joe passed the bottle back to Johnny, who capped it. Sunlight flared off the truck's chrome bumper. Joe squinted. He felt great. The river glowed in the western light.

"Johnny," he said. "You're lucky to have these boys for friends."

Johnny ducked his head and stared at the dirt.

"Give me that damn bottle," Z-man said, "before he gets blubbery and starts kissing."

Johnny tossed him the half-pint. After finishing it, they went downslope. Joe walked carefully so no one would know he was a little drunk.

"Hey," he said to Johnny. "Maybe we can take Botree and the kids to town one day."

"Botree doesn't go to town, Joe."

"Why not?"

"Said she got enough of it down in Texas."

"Enough of town? I don't get it."

"There's people in Missoula she don't want to run into."

"Who?"

"Hell, I don't know. She was pretty wild for a while."

"What do you mean, wild?"

"You know what I mean," Johnny said. "The kind of wild a woman can get."

Joe circled the group to Botree standing near the river. The mountains were violet in the afternoon sun. Botree sniffed the air, her nose wrinkling.

"Your breath would crack a mirror," she said. "You found Johnny's bottle, didn't you?"

"Well," Joe said. "I got a little primed."

"For what?"

"Ever what comes down the pike."

"We better get you some food before you chase the wrong calico."

"Not me. I'm in good shape right where I'm at."

Botree smiled, her eyes soft. Joe brushed her lips with his. A golden light suffused the air. The smell of barbecued chicken blended with wildflowers.

"We used to meet like this every weekend," Botree said. "We'd talk in the day and sing at night."

"You sound like you miss it."

"I do."

"But not now."

"Things changed," Botree said. "There used to be more of us. We met for holidays, birthdays, people's anniversaries. We played softball and went swimming. But when Frank stopped organizing it, everybody just quit. Yes, I miss it. We all do. I wish it could be like before."

"I know that feeling," Joe said.

"Sometimes I get afraid of what we're turning into."

"What do you mean?"

"We used to be really part of each other. Now, I don't know. I don't see anybody but other people in the Bills. We always talk about the same things."

"What's that?"

"How bad things are."

"Well, things are pretty bad, aren't they?"

"We used to talk about how we were going to make things better. For the country and for ourselves. I don't hear that anymore."

"You can always leave."

"I did, Joe. I went down to Texas and it was like another world. I didn't fit in. This is what I came back to."

"It sure is pretty country."

"We don't see it the same as an outsider," Botree said. "Everything you think is pretty is a piece of bad history to us. The beautiful cutbank is where a cowboy went over and broke his leg. That stand of cottonwood is where we found a whole string of cows dead from lightning. Ranchers spend more time looking at the sky than the land, worrying about weather."

"You ain't a rancher."

"No, but we used to be. Coop leases range land. He had to sell off a piece to pay the bank a few years ago."

"That's tough."

"It about broke him. You wouldn't believe what this land is worth, Joe. He gets calls every month. There's one guy in California wants to move here and raise llamas."

"For what, the fur?"

"Who knows? We're all that's left of a ranch family, and Owen's give out on the work. It's all Johnny can do to mend fence. We'd have to sell land to buy cattle, then rent our own grazing back."

"That's no good."

"Not much to raise my boys into."

The sound of ringing metal carried across the meadow. An older man stood beside the table of food. He dangled a horseshoe on a string and beat it rapidly with another horseshoe. He stopped, and as the sound echoed along the valley, he shouted:

Beans in the pan
Coffee in the pot
Come on and get some
Eat it while it's hot.

Across the meadow, people began moving toward the food. Two women headed for the trees to bring the children.

"Is beans the main dish?" Joe said.

"No," Botree said, "that's what he always hollers. He was a cowboy in the Depression. Him and Coop lived on son-of-a-bitch stew one winter, and beans the rest of the year. It was the hardest time of their lives, but to hear them tell it, the happiest."

Joe thought of Morgan's claim to have eaten owl during the Depression. His mother had never spoken of that time, which meant she preferred not to remember it. He knew people at home had lived on wild greens that grew in their yards.

They joined the line of people moving toward the food. Botree fixed plates for the boys and led them to a quilt with other children. Frank walked slowly to the tables, shaking hands and chatting on his way. He stopped opposite Joe, who was spooning salad onto a paper plate. Behind Frank and to his left stood a man wearing fatigues with a rifle slung over his shoulder. Joe recognized him as the man with the damaged ear.

"Hello, Joe," Frank said. "Good to see you on your hind legs again."

"Thanks," Joe said. "How you been getting on?"

"Fine, just fine. The battle never stops, does it?"

"I guess not."

"People are impressed by you, Joe. Nothing but good to say, nothing but good. When I first met you, I thought, here's a man who knows his own way. Could have been better circumstances, huh?"

He focused his entire being on Joe, prepared to smile or become serious. Joe had seen a preacher act the same way toward a man whose soul he was bent on saving.

Joe smiled at Botree. "There's harder ways to meet folks."

"But you just can't think of them right now," Frank said.

He laughed, joined immediately by several others. The man with the rifle remained impassive, as if mirth was beneath him. Frank spread his arms in a gesture that included the meadow, the river, and all the people.

"Isn't this grand," he said. "The Fourth of July. It makes me feel like I'm not alone in this world to see so many good people together, bound to each other for a common good."

"And what is that?" Joe said.

The crowd became very quiet.

"What?" Frank said.

"The common good," Joe said. He could feel the whisky in him. "What exactly is it?"

"Why, Joe," Frank said. His voice held the fluid tone of a man who was running for office. "We're all here for the same reason—to protect freedom. You're the first in a long line of patriots who are coming to join us."

He swiveled his head to the crowd, spreading his arms to take in the entire meadow.

"All across the country, people are getting fed up with crime, drugs, and poor schools. They're fed up with a court that lets murderers go. They're fed up with a government that passes useless mandates. They know what America should be, and who it is for.

"I love Independence Day, Joe. Democracy is a wonderful invention. And like all good things, it's got to be taken out and oiled once in a while. Right now, our country is an old machine that's showing wear, and our government is a lousy mechanic. It cannot simultaneously drive the car and keep the engine running. That's why 'We the people' are the first three words of the Constitution. And we the people must band together to make sure it protects us. I love America. I want to keep this country what it was meant to be—free."

Frank moved to a slight rise and raised his hands. The sun was bright behind him.

"You know," he said, "the act of breaking bread is a mark of peace the world over. Has been since the beginning of time. I've often wondered what Adam and Eve's first meal was. They were truly in paradise—no mud people or government to bother them."

Joe grinned to himself, thinking that God's ban on eating the apple was like a useless federal mandate. He wondered what mud people were.

"This is a splendid sight," Frank said. "It does me good to see honest, hardworking people gathered by the water. I especially like seeing the children—all the small white faces of the future. This country is great because of God-fearing people who know right from wrong. Our families settled this land. Our grandparents fought for it, and our parents worked it."

He stopped talking, his voice echoing off the river.

"I know I need to hush before I bore everybody by exercising my freedom of speech too much."

He let the laughter subside before he continued in a gentle voice.

"Let's have a moment to enjoy our right to worship with a silent prayer of thanks."

He bowed his head and people looked down. In the brief silence came the shrill cry of a sandpiper across the river. Joe watched the crowd. He felt as he had when attending church at home—glad to be part of the group, though possessing less faith than most. One by one, people finished and lifted their heads.

Frank said a few good-byes and left, accompanied by the man with half an ear. Joe sat beside Botree and ate chicken and potato salad. Men encouraged people to sample their wives' dishes, while women complimented each other. Botree rose to serve her children dessert.

Owen squatted beside Joe. "Got a minute?" he said.

Joe stood awkwardly, favoring his bad leg, which had stiffened. He and Owen joined Coop beside a rotting aspen log felled by a beaver. The river moved like a silver ribbon that frayed into small side channels. Behind them, people were working fast to clean the area before the coming dark. Three men were preparing a fireworks display beside the river. Dusk transformed the mountains into an unfurled bolt of crushed velvet.

"We're willing to move out of the house," Owen said, "so you and Botree can live in it with the kids."

"What?"

"Make things easier on everybody all around. We'll put up at the old bunkhouse. Johnny, too. That way you two can test the waters."

"I ain't making a deal for her," Joe said. "What kind of people are you? Swapping her off like that."

"She knows about it," Owen said.

"I don't believe it."

"I did me some cowboying when I was coming up," Coop said. "And one time we found a brush fire. Wind was blowing hard and there wasn't no water for fifty miles. What we done was shoot a big steer. We skinned out half of it and tied ropes to a front leg and a back leg. Two riders dragged the skinned-out side across the fire line, turned around and dragged it back. It was like taking a rag to dust. After a while the fire was out.

"My granddaughter is like that wildfire, son. She's had some boys to run a bloody carcass over her a few times, and she's been smashed down pretty hard. Most of the fire got beat out of her. But you're the first man that's blowed on her spark in a long while."

Folds of darkness covered the mountains. Joe worked his mind one direction and another, as if he were bewildered in the woods and had found a path that he didn't fully trust. At any moment it might turn to a rabbit trail ending in briers.

"Look," Joe said, "I like Botree fine. She's smart and she's kind, and that's more than most people. But this other, how you're talking, it's kind of a long way past where we're at right now."

"That comes fast," Owen said. "Hell, that's the easy part. Right, Coop?"

"I don't know," Coop said. "Been so long since I was with a gal, I forget if you get on from the right or the left."

His laughter trickled to a phlegmy gasp and he spat lines of snuff to the earth.

"I ain't agreeing to nothing till I talk to her," Joe said. "You all got a way of answering some questions to death, and letting others rot on the vine."

"What do you want to know?" Owen said.

"What's Frank hiding from?"

"Nope."

"Just like that."

"Yep."

"For as much space as there is around here," Joe said, "you all got me codlocked pretty tight."

"That's Montana all right," Coop said. "More cows and less butter, more rivers and less water, and you can see farther and see less than anywhere else."

They heard the whine of a car driven too fast for the dirt road, its headlights shining on people carrying bundles of food. The car stopped beside the parked trucks. The driver sounded the horn in a steady rhythm of three long notes followed by three short. Joe followed Owen and Coop swiftly up the slope.

"Somebody dead?" Coop said.

"No," said a man.

"What then?" Owen said.

"It's Lucy," the driver said. "She's in jail."

"Where?" Owen said.

"Missoula."

"What charge?"

"No driver's license. No registration."

"How'd they get her?"

"Busted taillight."

"Those bastards," a man said. "She's sixty-two years old."

"Never did a mean thing in her life," said another.

"All right," Owen said. "Let's ease down a notch. What's the bail?"

"Five thousand," said the driver.

He stepped away to confer with a few men as dusk moved down the slopes. Cigarettes glowed among the men. Owen returned to the group.

"They're just messing with us," he said. "I want everybody to bring some money to Coop's tonight. Don't worry, you'll get it back. Lucy won't turn outlaw on us."

Families hurried to cars and trucks, speaking in low tones. Joe found Botree with the kids in her pickup.

"Just drive around," she said, "until the boys go to sleep."

"I'm not sleepy," Dallas said.

Joe headed toward the ranch. Night flowed down the valley. Abilene slept, sucking on a finger, his head in his mother's lap. Soon, Dallas was asleep.

"What about this Lucy business?" Joe said.

"I've known her all my life. Everybody has. She's a good woman. Her husband died and she lost her spread. Taxes just ate her up. She doesn't belong in jail."

Joe thought of his mother and wondered if the people of Blizzard would band together on her behalf. Five thousand dollars was a lot of money in the hills. Entire families lived on less per year.

"What are mud people?" he said.

"Anybody who's not white."

"Frank sounds like he doesn't like them much."

"What's to like?" Botree said.

"People are people, aren't they?"

"As long as they stay with their own."

He'd never heard talk such as Botree's before. The closest was gossip against certain families at home, usually the ones in the deepest hollows or out the farthest ridges, families such as his.

"That's prejudice, Botree."

"No, it's not. Frank might be that way, but I'm not. There was plenty of Mexicans down in Texas."

"You get to know any?"

"You sound just like Coop. That's the first thing he wanted to know when I came back. If you're worried about my kids, I can swear that their fathers are a hundred percent white."

"That's not what I mean. How can you talk that way and say you're not prejudiced."

"I'm not."

"What about Indians?"

"I grew up around them. I know what they're like."

"What are they like?"

"They just want to take. They can't help it because that's all they know. They've had everything in the world given to them, free land on the Rez, free food, even free houses. They won't work. All they do is drink."

"All of them?"

"Not every single one, no. But they're the exception. The rest just want to live off the white man."

"So you don't like Indians."

"I didn't say that. I like Indians fine. I like them best when they stay on the Rez."

Joe accelerated and the truck weaved. He realized he was too angry to drive. He parked under a cottonwood and stepped to the road. A shooting star cut briefly through the sky and was gone before he could focus on its passage. Botree left the cab, her face pale in the moonlight.

"Where I grew up," Joe said, "there wasn't nothing but poor white people out in the county. We had the bootlegger, poker games, and shootings. When we went to town, people didn't like us because of that, and they treated us bad. I knew it when I was a kid. It was little stuff, but it was there. Like at the grocery store, the bag-up boy helped everybody get groceries in the car but my mother. Later I got a job on a trash truck. People in town looked down on me because of it."

"That would never happen here," Botree said.

"No? What about a dishwasher or a poker dealer? What about a stripper?"

She turned away to stare toward the mountains, where sky and earth blended in the night. She leaned against the bumper, her arms folded across her chest.

"I know a little something about that," she said. "A long time ago I used to dance at the Wolf. I saved some money but afterwards I couldn't get work anywhere in town."

"That's what I mean."

"Then I went down to Texas and got pregnant. People treated me like I had a disease. Like I was nothing, because I wasn't married."

Ursa Major sprawled in the night sky. The air chilled Joe's arms.

"Johnny has a girlfriend," Joe said. "She's a dancer at the Wolf."

Botree stood without moving, a shadow in the moonlight.

"They have a ten-month-old girl."

"Oh, Johnny," she said. "Oh, no."

"There's another thing," he said. "The reason he never said nothing about it."

She cocked her head, waiting.

"She's an Indian."

Botree was quiet for a long time. Stars shimmered in the sky like water on paint. Wind rustled the tree boughs. Botree lifted her hair free of the jacket collar.

"What a damn shame," she said. "A half-breed'll have it tough."

"She's half your family, too."

"I don't know how much help that is. Look at how the rest of us turned out."

Joe touched her hand. She trembled and was still.

A dull thump came from inside the truck and Dallas peered through the windshield. Botree and Joe climbed in the cab. A quarter moon lay above the silhouetted mountain peaks.

"The moon's broke," Dallas said.

Joe and Botree laughed. As Joe drove, he explained the lunar cycle.

"The moon gets cut in half every month?" Dallas said.

"Sort of, yes."

"And that gets cut in half."

"Right."

"So a full moon is when it gets all its pieces back."

Within a few minutes, Dallas was asleep again. Joe turned onto the ranch road and slowed the truck as he spoke.

"I had a little talk with Coop and Owen. They offered to move into the old bunkhouse. You know anything about that?"

"Yes."

"I told them I had to talk to you first."

"I appreciate that. They don't want to be in the way."

"Are they?"

"Not to me," Botree said. "But they're my family. They're trying to help how they can."

"Help what?"

"If you want to leave, say so. Your leg is fine. There's no need in you staying anymore unless it's something you want to do."

"Do you want me to?"

"Yes," she said, "that's what I'd like."

Joe reached across the children and covered her hand with his. He wanted to remain in the cab of the truck forever, driving dirt roads in the night. The dog star glowed. The Milky Way lay like a sleeve of lace among the stars.

21

Botree carried Abilene through the mud room and down the long hall, while Joe followed with Dallas. They placed the boys in bed and watched as they rolled toward the middle of the mattress, their heads bowed to each other. Abilene placed a hand on his brother's arm.

"They're good little boys," Joe whispered.

"They fight some."

"But they stick up for each other."

"Like dogs in a pack."

Botree left, but Joe stayed for a long time, thinking of the room he'd shared with his brother, its slant ceiling and cold corners. The attic had offered them a privacy denied the rest of the family. During summer the room was very hot. Dallas rolled over and his arm brushed Abilene, who stirred before sucking his finger.

In the living room, men and women from the picnic stood about, holding automatic rifles as casually as garden tools. Several had holstered pistols on their hips. A few wore fatigues and combat boots, while others wore Bills hats. They reminded Joe of a Wednesday night prayer meeting except for the guns.

Coop huddled at the dining room table with three men. Beside a CB radio were stacks of money and gold coins.

"Is that to get Lucy out?" Joe said.

"Yes," Botree said.

"With gold?"

"A lot of these people here, that's all they'll keep."

"I guess they don't believe in money."

"That's right."

Joe wanted away from the group. They weren't his family or his friends. He went to his room and sat on the bed, surrounded by clean white animal skulls. He wondered why people only banded together to fight, rather than to protect. The same was true of Kentucky. Nothing pulled a family closer than a threat to one of its members, right down to second or third cousins.

From a paper sack beneath his bed, he removed some cash and his gold coin. His Jeep was in the barn. He could walk out the back door and be halfway to Missoula before anyone noticed his absence. He remembered Ty's talk of Alaska and wished his leg was strong enough to go.

He returned to the main part of the house. Coop was pouring coffee into several cups on a tray. A woman sat at the table, counting money. Joe set the pile of bills on the scarred table and used the gold coin to hold them in place. He leaned against the wall beside an ancient horse skull patched with moss.

"Thanks, Joe," Owen said. He turned to the group. "So far Frank don't know nothing. He's out of CB range until he gets to his camp. Locking up Lucy might be a trick to draw him out."

"Just what them bastards would try," a man said. "Getting to him through a woman."

"I wish to hell they'd pull me over," another man said. "It'd be the last time they'd stop an innocent citizen."

"They're going after the weak," said a man, "like a goddam wolf. Next they'll try for our kids."

The arrest had increased the Bills' sense of their own importance. Joe felt the excitement spread through the room, a tension that reminded him of the Blizzard post office on the day government checks arrived. People were enjoying themselves more than they had at the picnic.

Owen raised his hand to hush the crowd.

"What we got to do," he said, "is be more prepared for something like this. We'll keep money on hand to get the next person out quicker, and you can bet there'll be a next time. I want everybody to double-check your brake lights and turn signals. Don't give them a reason to pull you over."

"They'll use any excuse," a man said. "They're rabid dogs with no leash."

"Stay in radio contact with your neighbor," Owen said. "If you go to town, or even down the road, tell somebody. Make sure the CB in your vehicle works. Now about weapons. Their law says you can carry in plain sight, so don't conceal. Put your pistol on the dashboard or on your hip, not in gloveboxes and coat pockets. Keep the big weapons hid, especially your AR-15 and your Mini-14. We can get you back, but not your rifles."

Owen looked at the crowd. "Any questions? Anything anybody wants to say?"

People glanced at each other and away, as if no one wanted to induce another to speak. A man stepped forward. His hair was short and his bottom lip was swelled by snuff. He looked older than Coop.

"They will take your guns," he said slowly, "just like they took my ranch four years ago. They will come on your land and steal your property."

"When New York City went broke," another man said, "the banks let them slide, but not us."

"It's the Jews," said a man. "They run the banks and they're trying to run Congress."

"They want to make the white man weak so the mud people can take over."

"I'd like to say," a man said, "the law crossed the double-yellow on this one. Owen's right. We can't give them no ways to get at us. They got the law, but we got the Bill of Rights."

People nodded to each other. Joe sensed a hardening in the atmosphere, as if a collective will had begun to congeal. He realized that they talked about the same issues over and over, like someone recently saved by the church. He was both attracted and repulsed by the Bills, similar to the desire he'd felt for the drunken bartender.

Another man spoke.

"What happens if they don't cut Lucy loose?"

"They will," Owen said. "They're trapped by their own laws that way. We raised bail. They'll let her out."

"What about Frank?" someone said.

"We'll notify him as soon as Lucy's safe."

"Is there anything else needs doing tonight?" said a man.

"When Lucy gets home," Owen said, "it might be nice if someone stayed with her."

A woman stood and slipped on her coat.

"One last thing," Owen said. "The papers in Missoula and Spokane are going to get all over this, and we don't need trouble with them. Talk to reporters if you want, but don't go loco, and don't let them get anywhere near Coop."

A few men chuckled. The woman who had been counting money spoke to Owen in a low voice. He nodded and addressed the crowd.

"We got enough to bail Lucy out," Owen said.

People cheered and clapped their hands.

"All right," Owen said. "Time to go get her. We can't have any trouble, so no hotheads are going. No weapons, either. One problem. The vehicle needs to be registered to someone with a driver's license, or they'll arrest you, too. Who's got a government ID card for travel?"

He looked from person to person, his face impassive. A few shook their heads, and Joe sensed the group's frustration. Owen was staring at him. Other people noticed, and turned to him. Botree looked at the floor. Joe felt the way he had at the Wolf the night he'd gone on his poker rush. The action was his and he stepped forward, as if pulled.

"I've got a license," he said. "And my Jeep is legal."

He and Owen shared a gaze. Joe regretted having spoken.

"Any objection?" Owen said to the group.

The men and women looked at one another to reassure themselves of the decision. Botree continued to avoid Joe's eyes.

"All right," Owen said. "We're done here. Folks, you're welcome to stay, but I know you got families to get home to. Botree, we need something to put this money in."

People began moving to the door. Many looked at Joe as they left, but no one spoke. Coop joined him.

"Well, cowboy," Coop said. "Good of you to pitch in."

"You all helped me," Joe said. He was upset with himself for having volunteered.

"Now you know what we're all about," Coop said.

"Not really."

"Still got questions?"

"Just one, Coop."

"Fire away."

"How come you got a horse skull hanging in the dining room?"

"Ever eat horse?" Coop said.

"No."

"I did. That skull's to remind me to be thankful I never have to again."

Coop went to the CB base unit and adjusted the controls. The house was nearly empty. Botree set a duffel bag on the table and began placing the money inside.

"It's all or nothing," he said.

"I used to be that way."

"I didn't," Joe said. "It's new to me."

"You sure you want to do it?"

"No, but I'm going to anyhow." He shrugged. "What else am I going to do? Leave? If somebody else shoots me, I might not make it."

"You probably would," she said. "Most men I've met try to act tougher than they are. With you, it's different. You don't know how tough you really are."

"I never had to be, Botree. I always had somebody do that for me."

"Who?"

Owen came in the house and Botree gave him the duffel bag. Joe followed him outside. Stars showed in patches of night. At the barn,

Owen opened the door of a large feed room to reveal the Jeep. Joe climbed in and inhaled deeply, savoring the musty smell of its interior. He turned the key and nothing happened.

"Let me jump it," Owen said. "I'll be right back."

Wind throbbed inside the barn, a sound like crumpling tin. Joe wondered if it was too late to change his mind. Headlights flashed as Owen drove Botree's old pickup across the rutted land. He parked, fastened the cables, and after a minute the Jeep's engine started. While it idled, Owen wired a CB radio under the dashboard.

The Jeep handled rough, as if the metal had stiffened from disuse. Owen kept the duffel bag between his boots.

"What's Frank wanted on?" Joe said.

"There's a bunch of little charges," Owen said. "Refusal to register his car, obstructing justice, possession of illegal firearms. That sort of thing."

"They ain't worth hiding out over."

"No, those are all local. The one that's got him spooked is federal. Two days after the gun ban passed Congress, he sold four rifles to a man from Lolo. The rifles had bayonet mounts, and the man was an undercover agent for the ATF."

"This whole thing's over a bayonet mount?"

"You bet. The Feds tried to make a deal. Said they'd drop the charges if Frank gave them information on some other people."

"What people?"

"There's some extremists here, Joe. They don't recognize the federal government in any shape whatsoever. They believe in the supremacy of local law. They elected their own sheriff and put up reward posters for state cops, lawyers, and judges, dead or alive. They tried them in absentia. They even printed their own money."

"Did Frank give them up?"

"No. He skipped bail and went to the mountains."

"What's he do up there?"

"He writes letters to the government. A few newspapers printed some, but the Feds made them quit. Now he writes directly to the senators, congressmen, and President. He even sent letters to the governor of every state. He writes to the FBI and the CIA, and the ATF, too."

"What's in them?" Joe said. "The letters, I mean."

"His ideas mostly. The economy, freedom, politics. How he's building an army to protect us. His plans for the future. He's brilliant, Joe."

"I don't know how brilliant it is to tell the government you're building an army."

"One gun at a time, he says."

"That'll just get him in trouble."

"He's already in trouble," Owen said. "He says they'll come after him sooner or later, and if speaking his mind makes it sooner, that's fine with him."

Joe slowed for a turn, feeling the transmission strain in the lower gear. Wind carried smoke down the valley to block the moon. The last person he'd retrieved from jail had been Boyd when he'd been charged with public urination for using bushes at night. A Rocksalt lawyer had told him it would get thrown out of court but Boyd was found guilty and fined two hundred dollars. The judge had told him to stay in the hills where he belonged.

"I got to tell you something," Joe said. "I don't understand this whole mud people business. Or the Jews and banks stuff, either. I don't much care for it."

Joe sped along a straight stretch. Owen shifted toward him and took a deep breath.

"Let me put it this way," Owen said. "If a black man has pride, it's good. And if an Indian has pride, it's good. But let a white man have pride, and he's bad. Now why's that?"

"I don't know anything about it."

"What's good for the goose is good for the gander. White man's got to stick up for himself."

"Against who?"

"Everybody. Nobody's watching out for us. A white can be the best man for a job, but another man gets it because of his skin color. That's racism, Joe, pure and simple."

"Maybe so," Joe said, "but you can't fight prejudice with more prejudice."

"The races are supposed to stay separate. That's what the Tower of Babel is about. You know that story, right?"

"Sure," Joe said. "The old-time people built a big tower and God didn't like it. So he made them speak different languages."

"You know your Bible," Owen said. "And those languages are the races. God wanted them to stay apart."

"That's not what the Bible says."

"Then let's look at it another way. Who gets all the government services in this country? The cities. And you know who lives there? Mud people."

"Folks where I'm from get a lot of government help," Joe said. "And we're white."

"What kind of help?"

"Doctors, welfare, and food stamps mostly."

"Where the hell is that, a Rez?"

"No, down south. And sort of east."

The sky was black, specked with stars. The air had cooled. Autumn would soon start here, while Kentucky was still boiling with misty heat.

"Let me ask you something," Owen said. "Why are you with me right now?"

"Partly for Botree," Joe said. "Plus nobody else could help that lady get out of jail. She's the same age as my mom."

"All right," Owen said. "You got your reasons and I respect them. Maybe you'll come around to the rest of it."

"Don't count on it."

Trucks roared past the Jeep. The glow of Missoula rose in the sky ahead. Joe parked in the jail lot and Owen left the Jeep, holding the duffel bag. The CB emitted a steady hum, and Joe wished he had a regular radio that worked. The Bills reminded him of Kentuckians who remained loyal to the Confederacy, flying the Stars and Bars and swearing that the South would rise again. They forgot that Kentucky was never truly part of Dixie, and that secession had brought terrible destruction.

Owen came across the lot with a woman holding his arm and a policeman behind them. Owen helped her in the back. The cop circled the Jeep and wrote the license number on a small pad. He shined his flashlight in Joe's eyes and asked for his license and registration. He seemed disappointed that Joe was legal.

"Ma'am," Joe said. "Are you all right?"

"I'm fine, thank you," Lucy said. "The son of a bitches never laid a hand on me."

Joe glanced at Owen. "Any trouble?"

"None," Owen said. "They didn't want the gold at first, but they had no choice. Did you know you can use a credit card for bail?"

"No."

"I couldn't believe it. Makes it easier for rich folks to get out of jail."

"It's always easier for them," Lucy said from the back. "Surely you know that by now, Owie."

"Ma'am," Joe said, "would you like me to stop for anything?"

"Just take me home, please. And stop calling me ma'am. Going to jail made me feel young."

Joe drove to her house in Lolo, where a woman waited on the porch. Lucy invited them in for a sip of brandy. They declined.

"Tough, ain't she," Joe said, as they drove away.

"Women here have to be," Owen said. "Montana sent the first woman to Congress. Botree told me that."

"She's as tough as they come."

"So was our mother. Nobody else could stand up to Coop but her. When she died, the whole place just generally went to hell. Then the bank tried to foreclose, and Coop barely beat that."

"Botree said he had to sell some land."

"A lot of families did. Used to be, you could work something out with the bank but now the land's too valuable. People are pouring in. I've been all over the West and it's changing fast. A lot of little towns are ruined for good. Santa Fe and Aspen are the worst."

"Where they coming from?"

"All over. The eastern cities and California, mainly. There's not enough water and food for all these people. Hell, Montana can barely keep cattle alive."

Joe dropped Owen at the bunkhouse and headed north toward town. He wasn't ready for the ranch yet. He hadn't driven alone in months, and didn't realize how much he missed it. He wondered how many miles until Alaska.

Missoula was quiet. He passed the Wolf and a few taverns. Now that Joe was here, there was nowhere he wanted to go. He felt the same way about town that Boyd had.

He changed channels on the CB until he found the truckers' band. The occasional scraps of conversation lent him comfort as he drove to the ranch. If he'd surrendered after shooting Rodale, he'd be in prison now, but receive letters and visitors. Most importantly, he'd have a date for release. Instead, he had a landscape that beguiled him with its light and space, a community that wasn't his, and a woman in whom he could not confide. The promise of Alaska struck him as a last resort, like poison that a terminal patient keeps handy.

22

At summer's end the days stayed hot while night took a jacket. The rivers were low and many creeks had dried to long skinny threads between patches of dusty earth. A series of lightning storms ignited several fires in western Montana. Smoke flowed along the valleys like water. It flooded basins and rose as if in a dam, spilling black air into the next network of open space between the slopes. Daylight was tinted by floating ash. Sunsets gleamed like neon.

Coop, Owen, and Johnny moved into the bunkhouse, leaving Joe alone with Botree. Joe hadn't shared a bedroom with anyone except his brother, and felt awkward for a couple of weeks. He wasn't sure who was supposed to turn off the lights at night, or make the bed in the morning. He worried about the protocol of undressing and getting into bed. Botree's practical approach gradually relaxed him.

Every day after breakfast Botree gave the children school lessons, using mail-order textbooks that came with guides and schedules. Dallas was performing math problems at a third-grade level, adding and subtracting rapidly in his head. He thought it funny when Joe told him he still counted on his fingers at times. Botree used a system of phonics to help the boys learn to read.

While the children studied, Joe exercised his leg by walking a little farther each day. He followed the fence line into the woods and found a deer trail that led toward the river. His wounded leg was stronger, although pink scars surrounded his knee like ragged lace. He was slowly beginning to enjoy the open valley. With so much land in sight, there were few surprises. He could see an enemy coming from a long way off. Nothing would take him by ambush.

On an August morning, motion in the underbrush made him stop moving. A hawk stood on a log clutching a pheasant. Satisfied that Joe posed no threat, the hawk spread its wings for balance, opened the pheasant's chest, and began eating the interior. Small bones cracked and tendons popped. The bird's severed head lay in the scuffed dirt.

Botree was waiting for him by the corral when he returned. Dust covered her boots like a skin.

"Owen came by," Botree said.

"What are they living on down there?"

"MREs, mainly."

"What the heck is that?"

"Meals Ready to Eat. It's military food. Just open it up and eat."

"They're going to regret moving out."

"It's their choice," Botree said. "Owen brought your gold coin and some money. He said you can get work driving a supply truck to the firefighters. The fires are worse and they're bringing in crews from all over the country. They need lots of drivers. Pays good."

"I don't know about that."

"You said you used to work on a truck."

"They won't hire me. I don't have any references around here."

"Lucy's cousin is in charge of hiring. He wants to return the favor."

"I don't reckon it'll hurt to talk to him," he said.

The prospect of a job excited Joe more than he expected. He had always worked, beginning in grade school when he raked leaves for quarters from his mother. Later he had dug ditches, shoveled manure, and repaired fence. He enjoyed the exhaustion that followed labor, the strain in his limbs, the satisfaction of seeing the result of his work. Hauling supplies to firefighters would be similar to moving garbage—both were necessary and both offered a measure of autonomy. He hoped he wouldn't work alone.

That night he and Botree lay in the darkness of their bedroom. The house was quiet. The bright points of Orion were visible through the window.

"That guy," Joe said, "Lucy's cousin. Is he a Bill?"

"Yes."

"Are there other Bills working on the fires?"

"Quite a few."

"Doesn't working for the government make them hypocrites?"

"The government hires a bunch of different businesses. Trucking is just one. There's food and medical, too. You're getting paid by the trucking company, not the government."

"It's still federal money."

"A lot of the land that's burning is federal, too. That makes it our land. Your land."

"Then we should work for nothing, right? To protect our property."

"You're taking this whole thing a little far, Joe."

"Me? You all are walking around with enough guns to fight a war, and I'm the one who's going too far."

Botree rolled onto a propped elbow, curving the blanket with her hip.

"A lot of people depend on the fires to make a year's worth of money in four or five months. Next spring, they'll have work clearing the burn. Some of the people will be Bills."

Joe regretted having spoken. A job would allow him to buy the kids some toys. He wondered what Botree would like. She wore no jewelry and had little regard for possessions at all. He felt good about lying beside a woman and starting a new job. He leaned to kiss Botree. She kissed him back, then covered his body with hers.

In the morning, Abilene cried when he left. Aircraft droned along the valley, heavy tankers carrying fire retardant, and smaller planes with hotshot crews who parachuted into the fire. The western horizon was brown with smoke. He found Job Service in Missoula, and filled out an application. He was sent to a warehouse where a crowd waited for an interview. They were rough-looking men who appeared as ready to fight each other as the fires. Joe's name was called quickly, and several people glared at him. He entered a tiny room with a desk and stacks of paper. The interviewer had a burr haircut, steel glasses, and an eagle tattooed on his forearm.

"I already know you got a license," he said. "Can you drive a big truck?"

"Yes."

"Narrow roads, mostly dirt."

"I was raised on them."

"Start tomorrow. Be at the loading dock at seven for truck assignment."

"Thanks," Joe said.

"No," the man said. "Thank you."

Joe went to the Wolf for lunch. After eating he stepped inside the poker room. The dealer lifted his eyebrows in recognition and a few players glanced at Joe. A television flickered without sound. The woman in the chip cage was reading a magazine. There was an empty seat but he had no desire to play. Six months before, the game had offered a sense of belonging that he no longer needed.

He wished his brother could see him now, but if Boyd were alive, there would be no Joe, no life in Montana. Virgil would be foreman of the garbage crew, married to Abigail, and their kids would go to the same school he had attended. Every week the family would convene at his mother's house for Sunday dinner.

The next day, he rose at dawn. The western sky held a smoky darkness that would never fully leave the day. He ate a banana and drank a cup of coffee, the same routine he'd followed for years in Kentucky. He made a sack lunch and strolled to his Jeep. His leg felt fine.

In Missoula he parked at the warehouse and walked to the loading dock, where several men drank coffee and smoked cigarettes. A man with a clipboard stared at him.

"You Tiller?" he said.

Joe nodded.

"You got truck eleven."

He pointed to two young men sitting on a metal rail. They were skinny, their knees clearly defined within the bent legs of their jeans. They wore western hats and boots, flannel shirts and vests.

"You're stuck with Gerard and Phil for a crew," the boss said. "They'll tell you the procedure. You can't get rid of them until we get a new driver."

Joe joined them, aware that the other men were watching him.

"You Tiller?" Gerard said.

"Are you boys sober?" Joe said.

"As the dead."

"That's a damn shame. Which one of these rigs is number eleven?"

They led Joe to a three-ton truck with battered fenders. The engine started smoothly, and Joe checked the lights, blinkers, and horn. Satisfied, he climbed into the cab. Gerard directed him to a line of trucks waiting for access to equipment.

"We get new stuff in the morning," Phil said. "Comes in by plane and we haul it to the fire crews. Me and Gerard do this every year. At Christmas we fill in for the post office when they run out of trucks. Fire season's better."

"How come?" Joe said.

"Better pay, no snow, and the girls wear shorts."

"Plus the dope is better," Gerard said.

"Do me a favor," Joe said. "Don't smoke that shit in the truck."

The line of trucks moved forward, and when it was their turn, Joe backed to a set of sliding doors on the cement dock. Phil and Gerard began packing crates of supplies into the truck. Joe signed for the load and received a copy of the inventory, which included sleeping bags, purified water, shovels, freeze-dried food, and chainsaws.

They drove west of town and climbed a rough dirt road that reminded Joe of home. The air cooled as they went higher, but the sky turned dark with smoke. They reached the fire camp and passed a commissary trailer, a first-aid tent, and a mobile food court. Portable toilets made of blue plastic stood at crossroads. Parked by the edge of the woods were three bulldozers and a gigantic water truck. Antennae rose from a communications center beside a large trailer with a sign that said "Incident Command Post." Men walked rapidly about, walkie-talkies on their hips. The crackle of radios blended with the steady hum of generators.

"It's like a town up here," Joe said.

"Hell, yes," Phil said. "Got everything but girls and bars."

Joe stopped the truck for a line of exhausted men who were trudging across the road toward tents. Their clothes were dirty, their faces smeared with dirt and ash.

"Great," said Phil. "We're just in time for shift change."

"Is there a fire close?" Joe said.

"No, the helicopter drops them off. They got a landing zone down the road. A truck brings them here."

"That's the job you want," Gerard said. "Transporting a crew. Nothing to it."

At the supply area, Joe stood in the back of the truck and moved boxes to the edge, while Phil and Gerard stacked them on the ground. They finished, drove off the mountain, and ate lunch in the afternoon sun. Phil and Gerard passed a joint. Wind had temporarily cleared the smoke, and Joe lay on his back. The sky was dark blue overhead, like looking into water from the middle of a lake. He felt grateful for the patterns of work—rising early, performing a task, being an equal among men who worked. He appreciated the clear hierarchy of command and duty, the shared sense of responsibility. His presence was needed.

He returned to the ranch tired and happy. The children met him at the door, yelling his name, trying to climb his legs.

"How was it?" Botree said.

"A truck's a truck," Joe said. "I can drive anything."

"You seem different already."

"I like working. It makes me feel worth something."

Joe felt lucky but was afraid to say it and risk hexing what little he had. After supper he lay in bed and read to Dallas and Abilene. He woke disoriented, with Abilene's foot against his face, and a pile of books on his stomach. Botree was asleep. He undressed, feeling the unfamiliar sensation of peace.

For the next two weeks, Joe transported provisions to various camps in the mountains. Thousands of acres were burning daily.

Crude camps were hastily arranged, with men sleeping outside in government-issue yellow bags. Fire crews were arriving from around the country. The main camp became so vast that a plywood billboard was erected with information for the firefighters—maps to the sites, lists of crews and their home, newspaper articles from hometown papers of many states.

One morning Johnny was waiting for Joe by the Jeep. He looked tired and skinny. He asked if he could ride with Joe to work.

"How's the bunkhouse?" Joe said.

"It stinks. Cold at night and hot in the day. The pump's broke so there's no water. You wouldn't believe what Owen calls food."

"Botree told me. How's Sally?"

Johnny slumped in his seat and stared through the window for several miles. The western sky held a haze of smoke. An eagle flew along the river as if it were a road.

"I got to get out of there," Johnny said.

"How come?"

Johnny shrugged. He rolled the window down and the smell of smoke entered the cab.

"Look," Joe said. "Come back and live in the house."

"That's not it."

"Then what?"

"Can you get me on with the fires?" Johnny said.

"Driving?"

"I don't have a damn license. But I'll do anything else."

"I'll try."

"I'm not going back to the bunkhouse."

Johnny signed with a crew digging fire breaks, using a shovel twelve hours a day and sleeping at a camp in the mountains. Joe began a daylong trip to a fire camp near the Idaho border. The fires had spread to Canada and were continuing to jump east into Montana. Gerard and Phil packed socks in the cab to sell to the firefighters at a profit.

"You think that's right?" Joe said.

"Why not?" Gerard said. "That's what they need the most and the concessionaire runs out every week."

"I mean making money off it."

"You are, too," Phil said. "We all are. Those guys can afford it. They get the best wage except for pilots."

Joe recalled a government project in Kentucky known as the Happy Pappy program that was designed to employ fathers. One of the jobs was fighting forest fires. Joe knew several men who'd set fires in the woods, then waited near the government office to be hired.

"I used to know a boy back home," Joe said. "He wanted to go fishing, but didn't have no bait. Went up to his cousin's house and asked did he have any. His cousin said no, but he told him where to dig for fishing worms. That boy, he dug all day long. Worked hisself like a borrowed mule. Never did get a worm. At dark he said to hell with it and went to the house. Next day, his cousin went outside and planted a garden where he'd dug."

"Sounds like a bait fisherman," Phil said.

"I can just see you two charging him good money for digging."

"If he was a friend of yours," Gerard said, "we might give him a break."

The smoke became thicker as they neared the fire zone. By midafternoon, the air was dark as dusk. They passed a freshly bulldozed landing strip where several air tankers were being serviced, their huge tanks refilled with fire retardant. The base commander was a Blackfeet man with a powerful body. Joe knew him from other camps. He worked harder than men half his age, and never appeared to have had much sleep. He was always calm.

He dispatched two men to help Gerard and Phil unload the truck.

"Getting worse, ain't it," Joe said.

"We lost two men last night and I got four more burned in the hospital."

"How come this year is so bad?"

"You want the official answer, or mine?"

"Yours."

"Putting out too many little fires."

"What do you mean?"

"A lot of people move out here and build in the woods. They start crying when it catches on fire, and we get sent to put them out. Used to, we let those little fires burn. The brush builds up in the timber and there's more to burn when it ignites. That kept a big one like this from happening. But the new people got the money and the juice."

"That's the way it always is, ain't it."

"No real Montanan builds a fancy house in the woods. I got two men died trying to save million-dollar homes."

He turned to spit and the desiccated earth sucked the moisture like a sponge.

After three eighteen-hour days, Joe took a day off. The next morning, he and Botree drank coffee in sunlight the color of sweet corn.

"Got a visit from Owen," Botree said. "He wanted us to be ready to mobilize."

"What's that supposed to mean?"

"I don't know exactly. Frank might have to move his camp because of the fires."

"It's not my fight."

"He said he's just keeping us informed."

The boys ran around the house, their boots raising a trail of dust. Abilene grabbed Joe's leg. Dallas pushed his brother, then took Joe's hand.

"Why are mountains so close together?" Dallas said.

"That's just how they grow, I guess," Joe said.

"I know," Dallas said. "The seeds were close together when they got planted."

"That makes sense."

"And rocks are seeds."

The boys began hunting rocks to plant.

"You're good for them," Botree said.

"You know what Dallas said the other day? Said he had two heads—his forehead and his main head."

"Sounds like you."

"What do you mean?"

"There's you that's here now," Botree said. "And there's the other you that drifts away sometimes. Makes me wonder if we can ever have a normal life."

"What do you call normal?" Joe said. "Your kids don't go to school. Your neighbors think freedom of religion means picking which Christian church to go to. The main thing your family is worried about is keeping their guns, and they got enough to start a war already."

"What about me?"

"You're normal enough."

"My mother taught me to shoot and my father taught me to cook."

Joe watched the boys dig for a rock embedded in the hard dirt. Boyd had taught him more than his parents had.

Abilene was yelling for the stick Dallas was using to dig. Dallas pushed him, and Abilene hit his brother.

"You all shouldn't fight," Joe said. "Know what me and my brother did when we had to share?"

The boys shook their heads.

"We flipped for it. Got a penny?"

The boys shook their heads.

"Neither did we."

Joe stooped for a flat rock. He spat on one side and smeared it with his thumb.

"Now you have to call it in the air. Dry or wet."

He flipped the rock high. Dallas yelled "Wet," and the rock landed with the dry side up. Joe found each of them a stone and returned to Botree. She looked at him carefully.

"I didn't know you had a brother," she said.

Joe turned away. The mountains were spiked with trees that would remain green throughout the fall. He missed the brilliant foliage of home. Autumn had been Boyd's favorite season. Long after he'd quit hunting deer, he'd still tracked them every year, hoping to touch one in the woods.

23

In September the fires were deemed the worst in thirty years. Camping in parks was suspended. Missoula filled with evacuated families, off-duty firefighters, and emergency volunteers. The Red Cross set up temporary housing in school gymnasiums. Gerard and Phil were promoted to driver, and Joe worked alone. He lost weight from missing meals, and his leg ached from staying in one position while driving.

One morning Joe hauled cases of dried military food to a new base deep in the Flathead Valley. Each crate was stamped MRE. The slanting sun lit the Mission Mountains as if the rock walls held shards of glass. Deer cropped grass in a meadow of oxeye and balsam root. Joe followed a crude map to the first turn. A ladder of freshly dozed switchbacks climbed upslope to a new camp high in the mountains. From the summit, fire was visible in the west. It made arcing lines of orange along the slopes, forming a border of green trees and blackened earth. Aircraft circled overhead, carrying fire retardant and men.

A single tent stood beside a mess trailer and mini-dozer. Joe opened the truck's rear gate and waited for a crew to help him unload the crates of food. He stood in the sun, wearing a down vest over flannel shirt and long johns. He was eager for the day to end. Tomorrow was Abilene's birthday, and Joe had bought a board game that he and Boyd had played as kids.

Four young men approached the truck. Joe knew they were fresh recruits by the enthusiasm in their stride. These men hadn't learned to hoard their energy for the fire. They seemed vaguely familiar and Joe wondered if they lived in the Bitterroot.

"Shit fire and save matches," said a man. "Now we got to work."

"All right, boys," said another, "let's knock this out fast and loaf."

"Let's not and say we did."

"By God, he's so lazy he'd not hit a lick at a snake."

Joe recoiled from the raucous twang of their voices. He knew instantly where they were from. He turned to climb in the cab, but the men were upon him.

"What the hell's in this truck anyhow?"

"Ever you boys see food that looked like that?"

"I'd not eat that to save me from Horn-head's Hades."

"Nothing'll save you, son. You're plumb wicked. Satan's got a special room just waiting on you."

"By God, it'll be warmer than that damn tent. I'm sleeping in the middle tonight."

"Will you give favors?"

"What do you mean?"

"Shoot, last night Bobby here gave us a little brown-eye, didn't you, Bobby."

"Shut up, you heathen."

Joe hurried across the hard earth to the base commander, who was muttering into his radio. Joe waited until he finished. Strips of mist twined among the boughs of tamarack.

"Brought a load of food," Joe said.

"We need it. Threw twenty men in the fire last night. They'll be hungry tomorrow."

"Anything special you're needing?"

"Yeah. Rain."

Joe made his voice flat.

"Where's that new crew from?"

"Kentucky."

Joe stood without blinking for nearly a minute. The pounding of his head moved across his shoulders and down his spine. In as casual a fashion as possible, he walked to the edge of the clearing and entered the woods. He watched the men unload the truck. They worked without talking, moving as a team. When they completed the task, they squatted on their heels to rest.

Joe walked to the truck, careful to keep it between him and the crew. He climbed in the passenger side, slid across the bench seat, and started the engine. Its steady rumble calmed him. From the open window came a voice.

"Hey, buddy. You ain't got any water, do ye? Ain't a one of us had a thing to drink."

Joe passed a canteen to the man, who showed it to the crew behind him. Another man approached the truck. Joe thought he was staring, but couldn't be certain.

"Keep it," Joe said.

"Thank ye. We're kindly new here. What about blankets and such?"

"I don't know."

Joe put the truck in gear too fast and stalled the engine. He fumbled with the key. The second man joined the crew boss. He was staring at Joe and frowning. Joe eased the truck into reverse. The second man spoke.

"Hey," he said. "Hey, you."

Joe revved the engine and lifted his foot from the clutch. The truck jerked backwards in a spray of dirt. The two men cursed and jumped away as Joe spun the truck in a lumbering circle. He forced it into first gear and sped down the dirt lane.

Joe yanked the wheel into the first switchback and clipped a pine, shattering the headlight. At the bottom he veered off the road and scared an elk that plunged into cover. Joe jerked the steering wheel and bumped back into the road ruts, his head striking the roof of the cab. When he reached blacktop he pulled over, his bad leg throbbing. Nausea passed through his bowels and he leaned his head outside until the sensation passed. He tried to calm himself. The man probably wanted to know how to get cigarettes. Joe had been surprised by the number of firefighters who smoked.

He wiped his face with his sleeve and drove back to the warehouse in Missoula. He'd become lax. He should have watched the billboard at the Incident Command Post for evidence of a crew from Kentucky. He wondered if he was in danger. The best move was to quit, but he liked the job. More important, he liked himself for having a job. He thought of his father continuing to go into the mines after being diagnosed with emphysema. That decision had turned Boyd against work for life.

He parked in the lot and turned in his keys. The boss accepted Joe's resignation without comment. He drove through town to the interstate. At the last red light he headed east through Hellgate Canyon, where pioneers had suffered ambush by the hundreds.

He followed the Clark Fork's gentle meandering until it reached the juncture of Rock Creek. Traffic was slowed by campers and trucks pulling enormous trailers. An RV crept around a tight curve, the face of its driver tense. A tiny slip of the wrist and the whole contraption would plunge into the creek. Beyond the tourist lodge were fewer cars, and Joe felt as if he were going home again.

An expensive truck with Nevada plates sat before his cabin. Fishing gear lay strewn about the soft earth like a yard sale. Joe backtracked to Ty's place. No one answered his knock. A silken light sifted through the juniper boughs, imbuing the air with a golden glow. After several minutes Ty approached the Jeep from behind, holding a rifle loosely in his hands.

"Hey, brother," Ty said. "I thought you'd be gone by now. How's your leg?"

"Better. Stiffens up when I don't work it."

"That was some bad luck getting shot on Skalkaho like that."

"I reckon," Joe said.

They walked behind Ty's cabin to a redwood table turned gray from sun and snow. The steady rush of Rock Creek came across the grass.

"I hear you're a Fed after all," Ty said.

"What?"

"Got your snout in the fire trough."

"Not anymore. I just quit."

"And came here on a social call."

"Not exactly."

Ty sat with one leg extended on the picnic table. He seemed content to remain there for hours. A wren called from the woods and another answered. Joe struggled against the urge to explain his situation. He wanted to tell Ty about Boyd and Rodale, his family and the garbage crew, Abigail, and Zephaniah. He wanted to confess.

"I need a gun," he said.

"Talk to Owen."

"If I ask him for help, he might get the wrong idea."

"How's that?"

"I'm not a Bill."

"Me neither," Ty said. "I don't take sides."

"I know you sell them guns."

"In the eighteen hundreds, the French armed the Indians with rifles. The Indians lost, but at least they went down fighting. Then they got put in camps as bad as the Japanese in California."

Joe wasn't sure what Ty was talking about, but he believed him.

"Have you met Frank yet?" Ty said.

"When I got shot. And at a picnic."

"Take it from me, Frank is a frigging lunatic. In my line you meet all sorts. Sociopath, gun fag, religious nut, even environmentalists want guns these days. And sometimes you meet a genuine psychopath. Frank is special, like Custer. He can't wait to die in a blaze of glory. So watch your ass around him."

"He doesn't like anybody but white people."

"You figured that out, huh."

"I don't understand it."

"Let me tell you, brother. Hatred is the cheapest pleasure there is."

"One man blamed everything on the Jews."

"They're like a broken record. I always tell them they've got things backwards. First of all, Jesus was a Jew. And second, the Jews didn't kill him, the government did. The government bribed Judas, arrested Jesus, put him on trial, and executed him."

"I never thought about it that way."

"It's hard to argue with since they're against the whole alphabet soup."

"What's that?"

"CIA, FBI, ATF, NSA, IRS, UN, FEMA. There's tons if you buy it."

"What made them get that way?"

"The end of the Cold War."

"You lost me."

"During the fifties," Ty said, "the government wanted everybody to be afraid of the Russians. That brought on a bunker mentality which led to people stockpiling arms and food. When the Cold War ended, all that paranoia lost its enemy. The Feds filled the gap. Then what happened at Waco and Ruby Ridge proved them right."

"Proved what?"

"It proved that the government had turned on American citizens."

"You don't sound like you believe all that."

"I'm not a fanatic."

"Then why are you in it?"

"The first thing any fascist government does is disarm the people, then take away civil rights. If the Jews had guns, maybe the Holocaust wouldn't have happened. If black South Africans had been armed, there'd be no apartheid."

"You think guns keep peace?"

"Of course. That's why our country doesn't want anyone else to have nukes. Then the U.S. gets to tell the little countries how to act."

Joe was wearied by Ty's words, half of which he didn't fully understand. The rest made sense to him. The hard part was trying to separate one from the other, and he wondered if Ty himself knew the difference.

"What I miss about Alaska," Ty said, "nobody had time to worry about this kind of thing."

"Why'd you go up there anyhow?"

"Same reason you came here."

"I don't know what you're talking about."

"Don't bullshit a bullshitter," Ty said. "You're on the run from something."

"What makes you say that?"

"Show up in the fall with a bundle of cash. No friends or family around. Stay in your cabin all winter. It's the same way I hit Alaska."

"On the run?"

"Yeah. Ever hear of the Weathermen?"

"No," Joe said.

"I didn't think so. It was a political group in the sixties. I had to leave the country in a big hurry and I went to Canada and just kept on going. Alaska gets so cold that car tires turn square, but it's the most beautiful country I ever saw."

"Then why stay in Montana?"

"It's like Chicago all over again, brother. These people are as radical as the Black Panthers were. You know, a lot of people wrote them off for being racist, but they were feeding hungry children in the ghetto. Things aren't as cut and dried as everybody would like."

"What do you mean?"

"Radicals start change going. It was radicals who dressed up like Indians and threw tea in Boston Harbor. These people out here believe in a cause and I respect that."

"I can't figure what it is."

"Freedom, brother. The only cause worth fighting for."

"Freedom for what?"

"To live, man. To think. Thirty years ago, it was the Left calling for revolution. Now the hippies are the status quo, and the Right wants revolution."

"What do you want, Ty?"

"I want the same thing I wanted thirty years ago," he said. "The question is, what do you want?"

"I want a gun."

"You're in luck. Today, I got a real deal on a Chinese SKS. It's the coming weapon, my friend. So cheap it's practically disposable."

"Something I can carry, Ty."

"Big? Concealed? What?"

"I want one to keep hid, and it needs to put a man down to stay."

"Snub-nose .38. An automatic is smaller and weighs less."

"You got one?"

"Me, I take the Walther PPK, but this bunch of patriots out here will only shoot American-made, so that's all I stock. The AK-47 is the finest weapon ever made. The revolutionary's choice. That dog will hunt."

"Pistol," Joe said. "A simple goddam pistol."

Joe followed Ty to his pickup. He dropped the gate and reached inside the topper, where several dozen automatic rifles lay beneath blankets. A two-tiered row of metal boxes held ammunition. He opened a case and passed Joe a shiny pistol. Joe released the clip. It was empty.

"That do for you?" Ty said.

"Figured it would be loaded."

"What, you think I'm some kind of nut?"

Ty went inside his cabin and Joe felt as if he were watching the passage of wild weather. Ty returned with a duffel bag. Inside were four boxes of ammunition and two spare clips. Ty flicked the safety on and off, dislodged the clip, rammed it back, and showed Joe how to chamber a cartridge. He casually fired at a milk jug spindled on a sapling.

"Best target is a water balloon," he said. "Fill them until they're a little smaller than the human head. I know people in Texas who use a corpse. You get used to firing at a human, but there's two problems."

"What's that?"

"Getting hold of a corpse, and getting rid of it later."

He gave the pistol to Joe, who shot and missed the jug.

"Think of pointing your finger," Ty said. "It's pretty tricky with this short a barrel, though."

"You hit it."

"I've run thousands of rounds through every weapon you can name. Let me show you something."

He reached in his back pocket for a bandanna and wrapped one corner around the grip of the pistol. He held it tightly with his right hand, lifted the opposite corner to his mouth, and clenched it between his teeth. He used his outstretched arm to aim the pistol, pushing it from his body while holding the cloth in his mouth. He squeezed the trigger. The stick holding the milk jug toppled.

Ty spat the bandanna from his mouth.

"Get it?" he said. "You're giving yourself two points of support without a rest. Takes getting used to, but it's good for a long shot. What you want to avoid is being stuck with a long shot. This baby'll knock down anybody close. The ammo is expanding hollow point. Goes in like a marble, comes out like a softball."

He clasped the duffel bag full of shells to his chest and looked at Joe for a long time before he spoke.

"Just remember what Lincoln said. 'If you're not for us, you're against us.' One day they'll ask you that."

"What about you?"

"I don't live with them."

Joe looked into the woods. He knew a deer trail that led to water. Last year he'd watched an eagle nest in the rock bluffs that rose like a wall beyond the creek. If he'd gone to Alaska, he'd have six months of darkness to conceal him. His leg would work right, and he wouldn't need a gun.

Ty pushed the duffel bag into Joe's hands.

"Here," he said. "Get out of here."

"What do I owe you?"

"Take it, take it. It's a fire sale. You need a holster? Let me get you a holster."

Ty reached inside his truck for a small nylon holster designed to fit against your lower back. He stuffed it in the duffel bag.

"Thanks," Joe said.

"Forget it. I'm done here. It's getting too hot."

"The fires are pretty bad."

"I mean law hot."

Joe shrugged.

"Do me a favor," Ty said, "and give Owen a message. Something I don't want on the airwaves."

"All right."

"There's a lot of traffic on Skalkaho Pass."

"Probably fire crews."

"There's no fires around here, and I'm not going up there to find out who it is. My guess is the Feds. That's the back way into the Bitterroot, Joe. This whole thing is about to blow up and I'm getting out. You should, too."

"I don't know where to go."

"You could come with me."

Joe looked at Ty for a long time, flattered that someone wanted his company. Boyd would have gone, but Joe decided to stay. He'd already left a place once. Now he had people to stay for.

"Thanks, Ty," he said.

He walked swiftly to his Jeep, wanting to get away before he changed his mind. He backed out of the driveway and honked from the road. Ty lifted a clenched fist. Behind him the sun was fading in the west, striping the horizon with bands of scarlet ash.

24

Joe returned to the ranch by midafternoon. He left the pistol in his Jeep and joined Botree in the kitchen for coffee. The kids were making a map of the United States as a geography lesson.

"Get off early today?" Botree said.

"Not really. I sort of quit."

"Sort of, huh?"

"Had a problem with some guys on the crew."

She frowned out the window. Fire smoke dulled the sky to a sheen of gray.

"A job's a job," she said. "There'll be more if you want."

"It don't bother you?"

"Long as you don't hurt my kids," she said, "what you do is your business."

Botree's shirt had horses embroidered above the snap pockets. Joe felt bad for concealing the truth from her.

"I went to see Ty," he said.

"After you quit?"

"Yeah, he's leaving. He wanted me to tell Owen there's a bunch of people on Skalkaho Pass. He thinks it's trouble."

"What kind of trouble?"

"He says the Feds. I guess they're coming after Frank."

"Ty Skinner talks more than anybody I ever met."

"Maybe, but it scared him enough to where he's leaving. He said I should go, too."

"Are you?"

"Not without you."

Joe took the Jeep to the bunkhouse and Owen met him at the door, wearing camouflage pants, a sidearm, and a walkie-talkie. Behind him stood the man with half an ear, holding an automatic rifle. The central room contained a long table on which lay several topographical maps, a stack of military field manuals, and a base unit for a CB radio. Bare bulbs lit the room, leaving shadows along its edges. Beside each window was a canteen, an automatic rifle, and stacks of ammunition. Joe smelled coffee and dirty clothes.

Coop sat at the table, his skin like paper that had lain in the rain. Across from him Frank worked at a laptop computer that was connected to a telephone jack. The only sound was his rapid fingers on the keyboard, like mice running through the ductwork of a furnace.

"You look better," Owen said. "How's the leg?"

"Only hurts when I laugh."

"You're in luck, then. We're all serious here."

Frank lifted his head from the computer and blinked several times. He stared at the far wall. The skin below his eyes was dark as if he hadn't slept in days.

"Did you get fired?" he said.

"No, I quit. How'd you know?"

"It was radioed in that you left. We had three men get fired this week, including Johnny. I think they're doing it on purpose, getting rid of the Bills. I got to find out who it is."

He returned his attention to the tiny screen. The house was still cold from the night, and Joe wondered if it ever became warm.

"Why'd you quit?" Owen said.

"Had me a little run-in."

"Who with?"

"I never knew his name." Joe hoped his voice sounded casual. "Just some buckethead on a crew. Where's Johnny at?"

"In town somewhere," Owen said. "He dropped out of contact."

"What made him do that?"

"Who knows?" Owen shrugged. "He got bent out of shape one day and left."

"Who do you think fired those guys?"

"We don't know exactly. We have their names, but they might be undercover ATF. That's what Frank's working on."

"Botree wants to know if you all need anything down here."

"What I need," Owen said, "is a three-day drunk in another town."

Frank pounded the table with both hands. Rising dust shimmered in the glare of light coming through a window.

"Nothing," Frank said. "Not a damn thing. The men who fired them are both clean. Either it's coincidence or someone dropped a new set of numbers into every data bank available."

"You checked them all?" Owen said.

"The three biggest credit bureaus—Equifax, TRW, and Trans Union. That's over five hundred million files."

"They could be using a cutout," Owen said.

"They have the manpower," Frank said. "Or it could be deep cover."

"What's a cutout?" Joe said.

"A middleman," Owen said. "Somebody who doesn't know anything except his job. He takes an order from a stranger and reports to another stranger."

"That way he can't give anyone up," Frank said.

He looked hard at Joe, who felt a quick tension swell within the dim room. He remembered Ty's warning that the Bills would one day ask whose side he was on.

"Ty gave me a message for you. He's leaving. Said the traffic was bad on Skalkaho Pass."

"You sure about that?" Frank said.

"Said he thought it was the Feds."

The men glanced at one another. Frank cleared his throat and spat on the floor.

"I was right," he said. "There was a fire near my camp this week. It was in the crown and running, but it didn't look right. Too small. The wind turned and it burnt itself out. I thought it was set but I couldn't tell for sure."

"Fucking ATF," Owen said. "They infiltrated the fire crews. Easiest damn thing in the world to do. They probably set all the fires just to get at us."

"It's the government style," Frank said, his voice calm. "But more CIA than domestic. The ATF traditionally goes straight at its objective, like the FBI or the army."

He leaned back in his chair and laced his fingers behind his head, aiming his face at the ceiling. He could have been a banker explaining interest dividends.

"Maybe they got smart," he said. "Maybe they shifted tactics after Waco blew up in their face."

"Shifted how?" Owen said.

"They're treating us like a third-world country. Infiltrate and destabilize. Setting a forest fire is right up their alley."

"What's their next step?" Owen said.

"Neutralize support systems."

"Like firing those men?"

"Exactly. And anyone else who's visible—Rodney, Johnny. Next they'll disrupt communication and shut down supply routes."

"And then?"

"Attack."

"By air?" Owen said.

"No way," Frank said. "Vertical envelopment doesn't work. Six thousand choppers shot down is the lesson of Vietnam. They'll come on the ground. They'll come hard. And they'll come soon."

He turned off his laptop and began dismantling the equipment. The men were quiet. Joe watched, surprised by the effect of Ty's news. Frank stowed the computer in a small case and walked to the window. The sunlight framed his silhouette.

"Our time has come," he said. "The forces of evil are upon us. Owen, mobilize the men. Use the CB and the codes. Move all caches to Camp Megiddo—commo, weapons, food, water. We need to be done by dawn."

He bent to Coop and placed a hand on his shoulder.

"Coop, you can serve us best at the ranch house. You'll be radio liaison between Megiddo and the world. Monitor emergency channels, police band, and the Feds. Owen, you help him set it up."

Frank gazed at Joe.

"I need to talk with you."

Joe followed him into a small room containing two narrow cots. The walls were coarse, having been painted with undercoating years ago and never completed. There was no window. A layer of grime covered every surface.

"I know none of this is your lookout," Frank said. "You can leave if you want."

"I have a reason to stay."

"You're wanted by the law somewhere."

"Not exactly."

"We've been here a long time, fighting for this land. Now that we got it tamed down, the government's bringing back the wolf and the bear. My great-grandfather was killed by a grizzly and now I'm supposed to let them wander around my land."

"I can see how that would be hard."

"If a wolf takes a calf, it goes free. If a rancher shoots the wolf, he goes to jail."

"Is that what you're fighting for?"

"We're not fighting anyone, Joe. The truth is, we're waiting for someone to come fight us."

Frank stood close enough for Joe to smell him. Dandruff lay like frost along his shoulders.

"I hate to ask you for help," Frank said. "But there's two things you could do."

"No promises."

"We got to bring Johnny in. He's a loose cannon, and nobody knows it more than you. Right now, we can't afford to have him running around on his own."

"What's the other thing?"

"Coop's not doing good. He's losing weight and he's not always there, if you know what I mean."

"You want me to babysit."

"It's a noncombatant role, Joe."

"Are Botree's kids safe?"

"I think so."

"You think?"

"None of this is a hundred percent. For all I know, Ty's an informer planting disinformation. Maybe the Feds are running the same truck back and forth over Skalkaho Pass as a decoy. Maybe you're a spy. Maybe somebody got to Johnny, and that's why he left and hasn't come home. But none of that matters now."

"I'll watch out for Coop," Joe said. "But I don't have control over Johnny."

"Good man," Frank said. "Any questions?"

Joe shook his head and turned to leave. In the corner beside the door were stacks of paper bound by haystring. He slipped the top one free of its bundle. On the cover was a drawing of Montana's state borders filled with tombstones. At the bottom, flanked by swords and rifles, was a quote from Deuteronomy. "I kill and I make alive; I live forever when I whet my flashing sword." He opened it to a bull's-eye target. In the center was a picture of Uncle Sam with a Star of David on his hat. One arm was around the shoulders of an Indian and the other around a dark-skinned man.

Joe held the pamphlet away from his body like a dead snake that still scared him with its fangs.

"Where did these come from?"

"I thought you knew," Frank said. "I thought somebody told you by now."

"Told me what."

"Those are what sent me to the mountain."

"I thought you sold a rifle with a bayonet mount to an undercover guy."

"You know how many people were killed last year by a bayonet attack?"

Joe shook his head.

"None," Frank said. "But there's a warrant out on me over it."

"What's a bayonet got to do with these damn things?"

"The Feds were going to drop the charges if I rolled over on Coop and Owen. No way I could do that."

"Coop and Owen?"

"Sure, Joe. They print them and take them to town."

Joe couldn't speak. He threw the bundle onto the pile. Dust streamed away from the impact.

"Welcome to the real world," Frank said.

"That stuff's not real, it's made up. It's bad."

"This isn't about good or bad, it's about politics."

"Politics."

"You bet. You should have seen the leafleting we did in Vietnam, Iraq, and Nicaragua. It's just a tool, same as my rifle and computer."

"Those pamphlets are full of lies."

"How do you know, Joe? How do you know the Jews don't run the world banks? Are you sure there are no video cameras on interstate highways? Can you tell me that UN troops aren't building detention centers in Michigan? Answer me that. Can you for sure say no?"

"It's hard to believe, Frank."

"Of course it's hard to believe. Nobody believes what's going on until it's too late. I shed blood for this country and look what it's become—a multicultural welfare state run by FEMA and the UN. We have to stick together."

"Who?"

"You get blood in your face, right?"

"What do you mean?"

"When you blush, you turn red."

"I reckon."

"That's what makes you a white man. And white men got to protect their own because the government's busy protecting the mud people. Don't look so funny, Joe. Everybody knows you're on the run. Let he who is innocent cast the first stone."

Joe stepped away from Frank. He felt smothered, as if the force of Frank's words were a fire that had leached the oxygen from the room. He inhaled deeply but was unable to get enough air in his body.

"Let me ask you something, Joe." Frank's voice was conversational, as if they were fishing buddies. "Did you know that this country's been in a declared state of national emergency since 1933?"

Joe shook his head.

"Oh, yeah. Roosevelt did it. That's not in the pamphlets. There's a lot that's not. Do you have a dollar?"

"A dollar?"

"Yeah, a dollar bill. The fake currency that's not worth the ink it's printed with. Do you have one?"

"Yes."

"Take it out."

Joe opened his wallet and removed a dollar.

"Now look on the back. See the pyramid and the eye? Good, now below is some writing in Latin. *Novus Ordo Seclorum.* Know what that means?"

Joe shook his head.

"New World Order. This has been coming for a long time, Joe. It's not new, it's old. What's new is public knowledge and armed resistance."

He smiled and leaned close.

"I am the New World Order."

Joe stepped backwards and Frank moved with him.

"Do you have a warm coat?" Frank said.

"Not really. A jacket."

"I'm glad to hear that. In Luke it says to sell your cloak and buy a sword. I get cold in winter sometimes, but my sword keeps me warm. The problem is too many people stay warm the wrong way, know what I mean?"

Joe nodded, willing to agree with anything to leave the room.

"You're a good soldier, Joe. Now I want you to take some of those pamphlets with you up to the house. Go on and grab some. Don't be shy. Take a whole pack."

Joe crossed the room to the stacks of paper.

"Read them, Joe. Educate yourself."

Joe tried to figure a way that the pamphlets weren't as bad as he knew them to be. He told himself that having killed a man removed his right to judge.

"Take them, Joe."

Joe faced Frank. He was very scared.

"No," Joe said. "I won't. You all got some good ideas, but those things are evil."

"What do you know of evil? The Four Horsemen are riding black helicopters over Skalkaho Pass."

Joe left the room and hurried outside. The valley opened before him, calming him with its vast presence of space and light. The landscape instilled a tremendous sense of loyalty, and he understood the desire to defend it.

He drove past the ranch house and up a rough slope to a clearing that overlooked the river. Sparrow hawks glittered in the field. He wanted to give Owen enough time to set Coop up and leave before Joe returned to the ranch. His sense of disbelief settled into confusion and fury. He wondered if Botree was aware of the pamphlets, then realized that she had to know. He felt as if he'd been betrayed by everyone but Ty. The Bills had duped him all along. Maybe he really was a dumb hillbilly.

Botree met him at the door. Coop was asleep in her childhood room, surrounded by feather and bone. The radio equipment glowed on a card table beside the bed. Botree went into the living room, and the couch creaked in the dark. Light from the stars slid past the curtains.

"I saw the pamphlets," Joe said.

He sat in a rocking chair that faced the fireplace. His body was very tired. He felt overwhelmed by his feelings for Botree, undercut by loss and shame. The house hummed with quiet.

"I'm glad," she finally said.

"You knew what they were doing?"

She nodded, a shadow moving in darkness.

"Were you in on it?" he said.

"No."

"But you went along with it."

"They're my family."

"What's in those things is wrong."

"It's covered by the Bill of Rights."

"Please." Joe lifted his hand as if to ward off a blow. "I can't hear any more of that right now. The only people who get to be free are the ones who think the same way as Frank."

"I don't think that way."

"If those things aren't against the law," he said, "why did the ATF want to know who was making them?"

"Other stuff was happening all over the state. Idaho, too. People weren't paying taxes. One family killed a deputy who came to serve a foreclosure notice on a ranch. Another man went in the bank and shot the loan officer. Some people got thrown in jail for buying anti-tank weapons. The Feds were looking for anything on anybody."

"Were Coop and Owen part of that, too?"

"No, they're not bad people. You know that. Somebody could have got them saving wetlands or spiking trees, and they'd have jumped on it. They were ready for whatever came along."

"This is a whole lot different."

"I know, Joe. I came back from Texas in bad shape. I didn't know what to do."

"How'd it start?"

"Frank. Nothing but Frank. He grew up here, and joined the service. After the war, he stayed gone another twenty years. He worked for the government, you know, one of those outfits he hates now. When I got home, he was here. He was fun and he was powerful and he could talk for hours. We were a big family. Frank thought the country was in trouble and people needed to protect themselves."

"When did they start making the pamphlets?"

"Frank bought a handpress and they made flyers against the Brady Bill, and the assault-weapon ban. Then Frank gave them stuff from the Constitution and things the Founding Fathers said. When that ran out, they used quotes from the Bible. Next it was about Indians and Jews."

"Anybody but themselves."

"That's why Johnny left the bunkhouse. He came and told me they wanted him to make new pamphlets. But he wouldn't. Coop and Owen don't really believe that stuff."

"So what. They put it in the world."

"It made Frank like them, Joe. That's all any of us wanted. It was important."

"You, too?"

"All of us. You have to understand, it felt good for people to be together. It's been hard for small ranchers. All the new people moving in drove up our property taxes. They keep trying to pass bonds. They want to make Highway 93 four lanes wide now. We can't afford to live here anymore."

"That's got nothing to do with the pamphlets."

"What happened up in Idaho started it at Ruby Ridge. Then the gun laws. Frank didn't talk about anything else. No more picnics or ballgames. He bought guns and everybody else did. Then we started burying them. They're in PVC pipe all over the place, twenty-four inches below the surface. We put a decoy above them."

"What do you mean, a decoy?"

"A piece of metal. That way, when the Feds came, their metal detectors would find the decoy. They'd dig to that and go on. They wouldn't be able to get our guns later, when it happens."

"When what happens?"

"It's happening now, just like he predicted. After he sold those guns to the ATF man, people really believed him, because everything he'd been warning about started coming true. Then they killed all those kids in that church down in Waco."

Thoughts flitted through Joe's mind like blinks of light. Boyd could have lived easily among the Bills, enjoying the camaraderie of weapons, the flirtation with being a small-time outlaw. He'd have burned his driver's license and Social Security card in front of the group. Under the right circumstances, he might have helped produce the pamphlets.

"Why didn't you tell me?" Joe said.

"I was afraid."

"Of what?"

"I was afraid you'd leave me."

He went to Botree and swung her legs onto the couch and lay beside her. Their arms twined and he could feel her breathe. They held each other for a long time while outside the hillsides burned.

25

Thunder in the mountains meant the threat of lightning rather than the relief of rain. Day by day, Joe knew where the worst fires were by the hazy darkness of the sky. Communities were being evacuated near Missoula, but the ranch was safe. Coop was weak and often slept in a chair facing the CB unit. Two police scanners monitored the airwaves for official transmission. The combined sounds of the three machines reminded Joe of wind and water and rustling leaves.

The family saw no one but each other. They communicated by radio with their nearest neighbors who were in turn linked to people farther up and down the valley. The Bills were living battle-ready, alert to any change.

Botree received a message that Johnny was fine, and could be reached by radioing a man who worked at the Wolf. Late at night, Frank began broadcasting from the mountains nearby, long taunts of the government forces he felt certain were preparing to attack. As Coop listened, he drew possible routes of attack and escape on his topographical maps, blotting the soft brown and green lines with his own overlapping network of heavy black. As one map became illegible, he started another. He ate little and refused to bathe.

After a week, Joe went to the bunkhouse for dehydrated food, but it was empty of all supplies, including sheets and dishes. His boots echoed like distant gunfire. Mice had gnawed the Liberty Teeth pamphlets and Joe carried them outside. The autumn sun made his eyes hurt. He siphoned gas from his Jeep onto the pile, and lit a match. The paper ignited and coils of smoke joined the brown skies above.

Joe kicked a tower of ash, which exploded into tiny black pieces that spread rapidly through the air. He jumped into the fire and began stomping the fragments of burnt paper. Ash and smoke whirled around him. He worked in a frenzy as if trying to grind the pamphlets into the earth, but succeeded only in killing the fire. He dumped gas over the unburnt paper and lit it again.

When he returned to the house, Botree sniffed at the smell of gasoline and carbon, but said nothing. They ate and played a board game with the kids. Later, after the boys were asleep, Frank's voice crackled over the air.

"This is Camp Megiddo on the mountain with an urgent message to all patriots in Montana. We have an army to protect your family. The blue-helmets of FEMA are coming. The black helicopters are coming. The yellow-bellied bastards took your guns and now they want your land.

"When David fought Goliath, he said, 'I shall strike you down and cut your head off and leave your carcass for the birds and wild beasts.' We shall be victorious in the name of the Bill of Rights."

His voice stopped. Botree and Joe stared at each other in the sudden silence of the house.

"Do you think he's got an army?" Joe said.

"Maybe. A lot of people go along with him."

"If the government thinks so, he's in trouble."

"We all are."

They went to bed, and for a long time Joe stared at the ceiling, wondering if she was right.

The morning sky was thick with smoke. Joe missed working, and he decided to forage the nearest timber for winter firewood. He wore his pistol and carried a bungee cord for a tourniquet in case of an accident. He used the ax the way his father had taught him, letting its weight perform some of the work. The pine split easily, each chip scenting the air. He gathered kindling against his body and carried it to the pile beyond the treeline. His leg ached and he limped. A man's voice spoke from the woods.

"I see you, Virgil Caudill."

Joe stopped moving. He felt an unmistakable relief.

"Turn that wood loose," the man said.

Joe let the kindling drop.

"Set down right where you're at."

Joe eased to the earth. The hard weight of the pistol pressed his back. Brush rustled and a young man stepped from the woods, aiming a rifle at Joe. Everything about him was familiar. His features were of the same rough mold as Joe's, the Scots-Irish pioneers who'd settled the hills of eastern Kentucky. His face was too young for a beard.

"I'm Zack Stargil's boy, Orben. You killed my cousin."

His accent was a comfort. Joe felt as though he'd been temporarily deaf and had suddenly regained the ability to hear. He knew several Stargils. He recalled the man as a redheaded boy, the last of a long line of brothers. Little Stubbin, they called him.

The man spat and moved closer, squinting over the rifle sight. Joe was surprised that the gun was an old .22. He lifted his chin.

"You best speak while you still yet can," Orben said.

Joe swallowed and licked his lips.

"Go ahead," he said.

"You ain't the boss of me," Orben said. "And I ain't in no rush."

He moved sideways to the pile of wood and sat on an upturned log. He was very skinny.

"Did you talk to Billy any?" he said.

Joe shook his head.

"Just killed him in his sleep."

"He was awake," Joe said.

"Know who I am yet?"

"Little Stubbin."

"They don't call me that no more."

Joe nodded.

"My cousin seen you driving a truck here. He works for the state, fighting fires out of Menifee County."

Joe nodded.

"He didn't say nothing about you having a bad leg. What happened?"

"Bullet."

"Billy get one in you?"

"No."

"You scared, Virgil?"

"Maybe."

"Was Billy?"

"I don't know."

"Well, I ain't," Orben said. "For your information, I ain't scared one bit. You smoke?"

"No."

"Me, neither. Cigarette does."

Orben laughed and pulled a cigarette from his pocket without removing the pack. He lit it and inhaled, keeping his rifle aimed at Joe.

"I bet you never thought anybody'd find you," Orben said.

Joe shrugged.

"You were pretty smart. They was all kinds of stories. The biggest was you going to Myrtle Beach."

"I don't reckon."

"They found your car in Cincinnati and Marlon went and got it. It caught on fire one night, accidental on purpose."

"Is he okay?"

"Hell, yeah. Nobody bothered him. You can't hurt that big bastard anyway."

The sun had moved past its noon spot in the sky and smoke came filtering from the west. Conifers surrounded the men with a wall of green.

"How's Marlon doing?" Joe said.

"He opened up a muffler shop down on The Road. By God, they say he's the best in the county."

"He said he wanted to, but I never believed it."

"That son of a bitch can weld. Looks like a line of sewing thread when he's done."

"Well," Joe said. "How about Sara and the kids?"

"Same I guess. I never see her out. Them kids are fine, you know. Just growing."

"And Mom."

"She died."

"How?"

"In her sleep."

Joe stared at the dirt, his mouth clamped tight.

"I'm sorry," Orben said. "She never done nothing to nobody."

"Thanks," Joe said. "What about Abigail?"

"Took off. Some said she went with you and some said she was pregnant. I heard she went up to Detroit."

"She's got people up there."

"So do I," Orben said.

"Me, too."

They looked at each other, trapped by the intimacy of meeting in a foreign world.

"Didn't you work at that car plant in Georgetown?" Joe said.

"Damn sure did, building them little rice-burners till I couldn't take that drive no more. Hundred and fifty miles a day. I got on at Rocksalt Maintenance. Landscaping crew."

"I'll be go to hell. I used to work there. You don't know Rundell Day, do you. Boss of garbage."

"He retired. Old boy named Taylor's crew boss now."

Joe began to laugh, a harsh sound in the still air of the woods. Taylor had gotten Joe's old job, drew a salary, and wore his name on a shirt.

"Taylor was the biggest drunk on the crew," he said. "He got so drunk he'd apologize for things he never done. That old boy ran on whisky."

"Not no more. He got hisself saved now. Carries a Bible in the truck. Nobody wants to work with him the way he carries on. Only man who will is his cousin."

"Old Dewey. I bet he's the same."

"He ain't likely to change." Orben chuckled. "Was he engaged when you were there?"

"No."

"He's going with some girl from Pick County. It'd take two men and a boy to keep up with them. They're broke up one day and getting married the next."

"Pick County." Joe shook his head. "What'd he think he was doing over in there, I'd like to know."

"Getting about what he deserves."

Orben and Joe laughed together until it trickled away, leaving an awkward space of time. Orben adjusted his cap and lit another cigarette.

"Grade school's closing," Orben said.

"Ours?"

"Yeah, buddy. They're already building a new one halfway to town. Remember that bunch of trailers called Divorce Court?"

"Yeah, I used to pick their garbage up."

"Well, they're all tore out. And that's where the new school's going in."

"By the drive-in?"

"That's gone, too."

"Anything else?"

"Post office shut down. Zeph, he retired, and down it went. I always liked him."

"Me, too," Joe said. "Reckon how old he is?"

"I don't know, but he's up there. Don't he look like a turtle to you?"

"Yeah," Joe said. "I never thought about it, but he did. The way his head set on his neck. How about the bootlegger?"

"You won't believe it," Orben said. "They're trying to get bars in town now, and all the bootleggers are glommed up with the preachers to fight it. Go to church and there's a bootlegger on the front row, like a hen trying to lay a goose egg."

"You just know the bootleggers are giving them money."

"Shoot, yes. Every church in the county's got a new air conditioner and fresh gravel."

"Who they calling for to win?"

"It'll go wet if the college kids vote. The whole fight's over keeping them out."

Joe wondered if they'd build new bars, or convert stores to taverns. People who drank in cars might prefer to stay away.

"You'd not know town, Virgil. Right here lately, there's talk of building a bypass."

"A bypass of what?"

"Main Street."

"Where would it go?"

"They want it to run alongside of Main Street, back toward the creek."

"Why the hell would they do that?"

"Takes too long to get through town. Funny thing, they want to put traffic lights on the bypass. Pretty soon they'll need a bypass for the bypass."

He laughed and Joe grinned. The world had passed Rocksalt by for a hundred years, and now the town was going to make it easier.

"Town," Joe said. He shook his head. "I'd still yet rather sit in the woods any day. Even if they ain't my woods."

"Only thing Rocksalt's good for is getting out of."

Again a sense of unease entered the air between them. Wind carried the smell of juniper and spruce from deeper in the woods.

"What happened to my trailer?" Joe said.

"Marlon sold it. That's how he started his muffler shop. They say the people that bought it draws the biggest government check in Blizzard."

"They got a bunch of babies, or what?"

"No, nothing like that. There's just the two of them. It's the crazy check I reckon."

"Is there anything else gone on without me?"

"You can get Ale-8 all over the county now."

"I'd give twenty dollars for a bottle right now. You ain't got one, do you?"

"Not on me, I sure don't."

Joe's leg hurt and he shifted position to stretch it across the dirt.

Orben tensed at the movement, gripping the rifle. The woods were quiet. Sunlight spread through the tangle of pine boughs.

"Ever hear anything on old man Morgan?" Joe said.

"Don't believe I know him."

"He went deep in them woods past Sparks Branch and set down a long time back. Supposed to have killed a bunch who worked in the old clay mines."

"I heard that story. My mamaw used to tell me if I didn't act right, he'd get me. It's bullshit."

"He's real," Joe said. "He told me you'd come."

"I don't reckon."

"Not you, by name. He said if I shot Billy, there'd be somebody to come. Said they always would be. Said as soon as you kill one man, you got to kill more. Said it wasn't no easier either."

Orben watched him without moving, his hands tight on the rifle.

"You ain't talking me out of it," he said.

"I'm ready to die. Half my family's dead and I can't go home. Same thing'll happen to you. If you go back, somebody'll sneak up on you. Same as you done me."

"Damn straight, Virgil."

Orben lifted the rifle to his shoulder. It was a battered Remington, good for squirrel, rabbit, and beer cans. Ty wouldn't stock it.

Joe's voice was soft, as if speaking to himself.

"Not a day goes by that I don't wish I never done it. When I first got here I thought it was the same as Kentucky only the hills were taller. But it ain't. You're the first person in a year I talked to who knows how I was raised—start right in talking and tell everybody everything all the time. These people out here don't say much.

"It's like my world got a hole in it and all the life run out. I can't walk on land and know I've walked it a thousand times. I miss coming up the creek and seeing my home hill setting there waiting on me. I miss being in the woods bad. Hunting ginseng and mushrooms. I ain't seen a lightning bug in a year, or dew either. The colors here don't change much. The hills stay dark green, then get white in winter and back to dark. There's no songbirds or whippoorwills. I could eat a mile of soupbeans and cornbread. I miss pork something awful. I don't reckon they ever heard of a hog out here.

"I miss my family most. Mom. Sara and them. I miss Boyd, too, even dead. He didn't leave no tracks in this country. Out here the only place he's alive is inside my head.

"I miss Virgil Caudill," he said. "Who the hills made me into. This land's not mine. It's great to look at, but it's not part of me. The house I live in isn't mine. Even the kids aren't mine. Everything I've got is left over from somebody else."

Joe inhaled deeply and held the air in his lungs as long as possible. He could talk all day. Orben cleared his throat. He moved the rifle until it lay across his lap, aimed into the brush.

"I knew Boyd," Orben said. "All my buddies did. He was sure something to us. Even my mamaw liked him. She used to say the truth must be in him, because it ain't never come out yet."

He flicked the safety shut behind the trigger, a snapping sound that hung in the air. Joe realized that Orben might not shoot him and felt a dim pang of disappointment.

"I never did like Rodale," Orben said. "They was some said he got what he deserved. Said they seen it coming when he was just a tad-whacker. My great-uncle said it would have happened sooner in his day."

"Who was that?"

"Shorty Jones."

"Lives on Redbird, don't he."

"Yes," Orben said. "He raised me part way up. He don't know I left, and he don't know I took his gun. When my cousin called me, coming after you sounded like fun. I just jumped in the car and took off, but I didn't like them flat states. You can drive all day and not get nowhere. It made me nervous. Every time I stopped for gas I wanted to lay down to keep from tipping over. I don't see how people can get around on land with no hills to go by. You'd need a map just to find the store.

"By God, I was five days and three hundred dollars getting to Butte and then my car broke down. I saw the biggest mine hole in the world, I mean big, Virgil. Makes ours look puny. A rough-seeming people but they treated me good. I sold my car and took a bus to Missoula. Wrapped my rifle up in cardboard and put it over my head like it wasn't nothing."

"How'd you get down here?"

"Walked."

"All the way from town?"

"I couldn't hitchhike packing a rifle. Nights sure throw a chill." Orben gazed around the somber woods of cedar, spruce, and fir. "I don't see how you've lasted this long, Virgil."

"I didn't have much choice."

"I seen pronghorn by the road out here. Antelope, too. And elk. They got buffalo?"

"I never saw none," Joe said. "Why don't you come up to the house and get something to eat."

"I don't know about that."

"I got a sandwich right here. Baloney on light bread, and there's coffee in a thermos."

"Now, no."

"Half, then," Joe said. "It's in that poke setting on top of the woodpile."

Orben propped his rifle on a log and opened the sack. He ate most of the sandwich in three bites before offering the rest to Joe, who shook his head.

"You got to," Orben said.

He passed the food to Joe and poured coffee into the plastic lid of the thermos. He lit a cigarette.

Joe changed the position of his legs and reached behind his back. The pistol grip was cold in his hand. He began easing it free of the holster. He thought of the holes in Rodale's face, of Morgan living alone like an animal in a lair. He'd killed Rodale for his brother, but he couldn't kill for himself. He released the gun and sat straight.

"Back bothering ye?" Orben said. "I know how that is. I slept outside the last two nights. There's a knot in my hip like somebody drove a nail in."

"I got something for you," Joe said. "It's in my pocket, so don't get nervous."

"Shoot, takes more than you to make me nervous."

Joe tilted sideways and pushed his hand in his pants pocket and removed the belt balancer that Morgan had given him. It was the last thing he owned of the hills. He tossed it to Orben.

"Know what that is?"

"Belt balancer," Orben said. "Uncle Shorty made a many till his eyes went. This is a nice one. Poplar, my opinion."

He threw it in an arc that landed in Joe's lap. Joe held the piece of wood in his palm, surprised that it had returned so rapidly, like a boomerang.

"Reckon what I'll tell them in Blizzard," Orben said.

"I don't know. Maybe the truth."

"Yours or mine?" Orben said. "Damn, this coffee's good."

"Best way is not to say nothing. They'll think the worst for a while, then they'll forget about it. You can't get in no trouble that way. I used to think a good lie was close to the truth. Now I think it's not saying a word. That way they make up their own lies."

"They always said you was smart, Virgil."

Orben placed the thermos on a stump and stood. He lifted his rifle until its barrel aimed at the sky.

"See you, Virge," Orben said.

"Don't run off."

"Anybody you want me to howdy for you?"

Joe shook his head. Orben walked to the edge of the clearing. Joe slowly stood.

"Hey," Joe said.

Orben turned, his expression wary. The rifle lowered slightly. Joe wanted to memorize the way he looked, a final image of home.

"What was it Boyd did," Joe said, "that made Billy shoot him?"

"I don't know," Orben said. "I surely don't."

He stepped into the woods and disappeared among the brown trunks and drooping lower boughs of the trees.

26

An immense loneliness settled over Joe. He was both exhausted and exhilarated from the talk with Orben, as though he'd suddenly gone home for a day. The events that had transpired in his absence lay like unsorted lumber in his mind.

The sky was streaked by smoke. His eyes burned and he wondered if they needed to evacuate. The sound of aircraft echoed off the river. He walked up the slope past tumbleweed piled against the broken fence line. He had no idea how much time had passed. Orben's accent still roared in his head. He felt as if the hills of Kentucky were walking away from him.

In the house the kids were sitting on the couch. Abilene sucked his finger and held Dallas's hair, who cocked his head toward his brother's grasp.

"Coop's mad," Dallas said. "He said if we came in his room, he'd shoot us."

"Nobody's shooting anybody around here," Joe said.

Joe went to his old room, where Coop slumped over the radio like a cardplayer in an all-night game. Botree held a finger to her lips. A new map lay on the table, unmarked save for a single black circle among the whorls of elevation. Inside the circle was the letter F like a cattle brand. The CB squealed and Frank's voice crackled over the air.

"Hear this, you jackbooted thugs? Hear it?"

There was the quick noise of scraping metal and a louder sound of something ramming into place.

"That's full-auto rock and roll. Camp Megiddo is waiting. My army of patriots has fifty-caliber machine-gun emplacements. We have antitank artillery. We have surface-to-air missiles. The man who kills me is only following orders. The Bill of Rights is dead. If the government excludes itself, why must I then abide? Bless them, Father, they know not what they do."

The transmission stopped abruptly. Coop's face was slack and haggard, but his eyes gleamed.

"Does Frank really have that stuff?" Joe said.

"I don't know," Botree said.

"It might be more of his bullshit."

"Coop picked up people on the scanner. I heard it, too. You can tell it's official."

"Probably firefighters."

"It sounds like Feds," she said. "ATF or somebody. Other people in the valley heard them, too. Frank's been calling for volunteers all morning."

"I hope Johnny didn't go."

"I got word to him at the Wolf. Asked him to come home. Then he radioed in and said there was a roadblock a few miles north of the ranch. He said he was going to leave the truck and follow the river home."

Joe studied the topographical map. The black circle was ten miles from the ranch, accessible only by a narrow draw. It reminded him of

Morgan's place—one way in, one way out. Morgan had lasted forty years. With the weapons Frank claimed to have, he could repel all but the most fierce attack. The Bills would have to be overrun, bombed, or burned out.

The scanner sputtered and Coop turned slowly, his body moving like a machine that needed to be taken apart and cleaned. He squelched the noise and adjusted the scanner's controls until a different voice came.

"White Dog to Delta. What's your sitrep?"

"The approach is in our control. Repeat, the approach is in Delta control."

The voice gave way to a buzz of static. Botree was right, it sounded like a military operation rather than firefighters. Joe realized that White Dog was the command post while Delta was a ground force moving into position.

Coop leaned over the map and drew a small line with a pen. There were other marks that Joe hadn't noticed, tiny black dots that progressed up the draw. The last one was at the top of the hill near the F in a circle. Joe understood that he was seeing Frank's holdout, and the advance of the attacking force. He wondered how many people had joined Frank.

From the CB came Frank's voice again.

"Come and get it, heathens," he said. "Your day of calamity is at hand. Thomas Jefferson warned us two hundred years ago—'The strongest reason for the people to keep and bear arms is to protect themselves against tyranny in government.'"

The transmission ended, leaving a sudden silence in the tiny room. Joe hoped each side was attempting an elaborate ruse designed to make the other surrender. The attackers might have superior firepower, but the Bills knew the terrain and wouldn't be bluffed.

Coop reduced the volume on the scanner and began changing channels on the CB, revealing scraps of talk along the valley as he moved slowly down the band.

". . . won't let you drive past the Jackson place . . ."

". . . a trick, I'm telling you. They wouldn't . . ."

". . . plenty of water and ammo, what else . . ."

". . . she thinks it's Armageddon but I say the FBI . . ."

Joe felt as if the walls of the tiny room were compressing him. He left the room, feeling empty as last year's bird's nest. Missing his mother's funeral was the worst blow of all.

The sound of gunfire startled Joe, three quick shots. He thought it came from the radio until Botree ran down the hall.

"That's outside, Joe."

"Where?"

"Toward the back pasture."

"Put the kids in the tub."

"What?"

"It'll protect them."

He withdrew the .38 from the nylon holster on his belt and went to the mud room. He found a towel in a corner and wrapped one end around the pistol and placed the other in his mouth. He peered through the window. As he turned his head, the pistol moved with him like a snout. The pasture was empty. Wind cleared smoke from the air, and the sky shone like the waters of a lake. When his eyes burned, he reminded himself to blink.

The shadows of the treeline stretched along the grass of the pasture. His bad knee began to ache and he shifted his weight. He was hungry. Metallic voices issued from the radio down the hall. Joe strained to recall the gunshots, hoping to gauge their caliber, but the memory eluded him. He wondered if they had been a signal to a team that was preparing to attack the house.

Joe shook his head to concentrate on the pasture. Lines of smoke rippled along the distant peaks. A man left the woods and ran toward the house. Joe leveled the pistol sights at the man's chest. His hand swayed back and forth as the strained muscles of his arm began to quiver. He steadied the gun and inhaled. He wanted to wait until he was certain of his target. The man was close, running very fast, and Joe recognized Johnny.

Joe leaned against the wall, his legs trembling, the pistol aimed at the ceiling. Johnny slammed the door open. He was panting. Mucus ran from his nose. His shirt was gone and deep scratches covered his body. He opened his mouth, but could not talk. He began to shiver.

"It's all right," Joe yelled. "It's Johnny."

Joe led him through the house to the kitchen. Johnny held his hand on the wall as he walked, like a man with unsure legs. He was wearing an empty holster with the end tied to his thigh. Botree met them at the table and helped ease Johnny to a chair. She talked in a low murmur, more a constant soothing tone than speech. She used a wet cloth to clean blood and dirt from Johnny's wounds. His face twitched, the muscles jumping. She applied disinfectant, working down his chest, along his arms to his hands, and Joe remembered the gentle efficiency of her hands. She gave Johnny two of Joe's leftover pain pills.

She sent Joe for a blanket and he walked through the house, trying to comprehend the events of the day. Coop sat immobile as stone before the CB and scanner, flanked by shelves of skull and bone. Joe peeked in the bathroom, where Abilene slept in the tub. Beside him, Dallas was hunched over an Etch-A-Sketch, duplicating the posture of Coop and his radio. The sky through the tiny window was bright blue, as if a panel of dyed deerhide was stretched within the frame.

At the kitchen table Johnny was drinking coffee, and Joe wrapped the blanket around his shoulders. Color had returned to Johnny's face. Botree sat beside him. Joe felt as if he were watching them from a great distance. They seemed like strangers with whom he was forced to share a table at a busy diner.

"What happened?" he said.

"There's Feds all over out there," Johnny said. "They're wearing armored vests and helmets. They got M-16s, radios, and Jeeps. I mean there's an army."

"But you got past." Botree's voice was soothing and warm, as if talking to her kids. "You came home."

"We got to tell Owen. They got helicopters, Botree. Black helicopters, just like Frank said."

"We heard the shooting," Botree said. "Were they shooting at you?"

"No," Johnny said, his voice a low moan.

He looked at his injured hands, which were beginning to swell. The steady sound of static came from the door to Coop's room. A voice spoke briefly and after a few seconds, they could hear Frank's voice reciting coordinates for an airstrike, daring the Feds to attack. Joe rose and closed the curtains.

"Is someone out there?" Botree said to Johnny. "By the house?"

"No."

"Was there?"

Johnny nodded.

"Is that who shot?"

Johnny shook his head. He moved his hand to the empty holster. He looked from Botree to Joe and back to his sister. He began to talk, each word separate and precise, like a man who'd discovered the power of speech.

"Somebody was hiding in the woods," he said. "I was moving quiet like Owen taught me. I couldn't see who, but I figured it was one of those Feds. An ATF or FBI, or whoever they got out there. One of the spies they sent out. I guess he heard me because he turned around and aimed a rifle at me. I already had my gun out. I don't know how it got in my hand. I was scared, but I didn't want to do him like I done Joe. I was too scared to be yellow this time. I shot him three times. He fell down, but he wasn't a Fed. All he had was a little .22 rifle. He wasn't no older than me. Oh, Botree, what'd I do?"

His head sagged forward and his shoulders rose as he began to sob. Botree continued to stroke his hair. Joe went to the sink for water and drank several glasses in succession. He hated Orben. He hated Rodale. He hated himself.

At the table, Botree placed her hand on Johnny's arm.

"What happened to your clothes?" she said.

"I dragged him to the river and threw him in. My shirt and jacket were bloody and I threw them in, too."

"Where's your gun?"

"In the river."

The hum of voices rose and fell in Coop's room like locusts. Dallas and Abilene were yelling from the bathroom. Joe's anger lent his mind a focus that he hadn't known since leaving home.

"Listen to me," Joe said. "You did everything right. If you'd not shot, he'd have killed you. You got to look at it real hard. You're no good to any of us dead, especially your little girl."

"I'm no good, all right," Johnny said.

"That's not true," Joe said. "You were smart. You got rid of everything and came home. The family needs you."

Joe walked around the table, aware that Johnny and Botree were watching him. His knee hurt but it was a reminder that he couldn't give up. He'd gotten himself safely out of Kentucky, and now he was trapped in another battle that wasn't his.

"Johnny," he said, "I want you to lie on the couch for a while. Botree, give the kids more toys and books, whatever it takes to keep them in the tub. Tell them it's a boat or something. Do you have the key to the rifle cabinet?"

"Yes."

"I want you to open it, and check the rifles and ammunition. We've got to keep the kids away from them, but it can't be locked. Are there any illegal rifles here?"

"Not in the house," she said. "There's ten buried outside in PVC pipe."

"Nothing else?"

"No. You're not digging them up, are you?"

"I don't want anything around here that we can get put in jail over. No grenades or Mini-14s."

"There's nothing like that inside."

"Good. Use the CB to see if the roadblock is set up south of here, too."

Botree left the room and Joe helped Johnny move to the couch. Moonlight slid through the slit where the curtains met. Johnny's voice was husky from medication.

"You know what Coop did on the Fourth of July when we were kids?"

Joe shook his head.

"He put a half stick of dynamite under the anvil and blew it sky-high. I looked forward to it all winter. Then in summer I'd wait for Christmas. Coop used to climb up on the roof on Christmas Eve. He'd stomp around and yell 'Ho, ho, ho' in the middle of the night."

Johnny's chest swelled in a sigh, prolonged and weary. He closed his eyes.

"I wish that damn Frank had never come back around."

Joe tucked the blanket beneath Johnny's chin as his mother had for him. Dusk turned the sky orange with smoke as shadows joined to form the night. Botree stood beside him at a window.

"Road's blocked both ways," she said. "They're using Humvees with heavy-weapon mounts. Six people who tried to leave are in custody. The only road out of the valley is Skalkaho and there's an army guarding it."

"We'll have to wait."

"For what," Botree said.

"I wish I knew."

"Who do you think that was in the woods?"

"I don't know," Joe said. "Maybe a hunter."

They prepared a meal together and allowed the kids to eat at the table. Coop refused food, preferring the company of his glowing dials and distant voices. There were occasional bursts of communication on the scanner and CB. Every half hour, Frank recited from the Bible and the Bill of Rights. He claimed a growing army of two hundred men.

For the first time in weeks, Joe and Botree didn't talk after supper. Joe was afraid that if he started, he'd never stop. He wanted to be alone. He missed the safety of his cabin on Rock Creek.

Botree read to the boys in the tub. Joe roamed the house, checking weapons and ammunition, peering through each window. The outside air was very dark, the stars obliterated by smoke. Coop slept in his chair, his chin on his chest, his stomach against the card table. Botree was curled in a sleeping bag by the tub, her dark hair shining on the floor. Joe watched her sleep for a long time. There was nothing for Joe in Blizzard if he returned—no school, no mother, nowhere to receive mail. Home had ceased to exist except in his mind.

He made a pallet from furniture cushions by the front door and lay on his back with his pistol on one side and a rifle on the other. Perhaps Morgan's decision to remain in the hills was best, since he still had the land and occasional visitors. He had dealt with his enemies one man at a time, rather than facing an unknown army in the night.

Joe slowed his breathing and willed his mind to rest. Twice his body jerked him awake. He rolled on his side and pulled his knees toward his chest. He was very tired. The smell of smoke was in the air.

When he woke, something in the house was different. He lay immobile, his ears straining for sound. From the bathroom he could hear Botree's quiet snoring. One of the children moaned. The hissing sound of the radios flowed like water along the hall. Joe listened for a long time until he realized that the refrigerator had stopped humming. He turned on a light and nothing happened. He found a flashlight and checked the fuse box but all circuits were complete.

Careful to avoid standing in front of windows, he rummaged the mud room for candles. He lit one and placed it in the bathroom sink. The candle's glow illuminated the gentle planes of Botree's face. The children lay in the tub, curled around each other like cats. Joe remembered winter storms that blew down power lines at home, and his mother reading the Bible aloud by lantern. He double-checked his weapons. Perhaps the fires had burned a transformer.

Coop was wheezing terrible breath, a sound like an old bellows. A large flashlight sat by the radios, aimed at the ceiling. More marks were on the map, a series of black marks that moved closer to the circled F. He had switched the equipment to batteries, and voices filled the airwaves, overlapping and joining as if stitched into fabric.

A flat voice came from the scanner.

"White Dog to Delta. What's your sitrep?"

"No change. Visual confirmation of hostile position."

"Estimated number of hostiles?"

"Unknown."

The transmissions came from the mountains visible through the window, their peaks lit scarlet by the dawn. Smoke hung in lines like layers of earth in a cliff. Joe stared at the map. Botree knew the back roads and logging trails. They could take his Jeep south.

Coop moved only his arms and hands, squelching the scanner's feedback, adjusting volume and channel. Briefly, Joe imagined that Coop was controlling the events unfolding on the mountain.

Frank's voice came over the air.

"Patriots, traitors, countrymen," he said. "Greetings from the mountaintop. Camp Megiddo is warm and safe. Behold, the day cometh, that shall burn as an oven. Go to channel three."

The machine squawked and was quiet. Coop switched channels. The scanner hummed, its electronic circuits waiting to catch sound. After a minute of silence, Frank spoke once more.

"The sun is in our eyes. It's at their back and they will come. I have entered the valley of the shadow of death and fear no evil. The right of the people to keep and bear arms shall not be infringed. So be it."

The transmission stopped. The only sound was Coop's hoarse breath. Botree came into the room, her face swollen from sleep. She shivered.

"What's going on?" she said.

"It's happening," Joe said. "No power anywhere."

"We've got plenty of batteries."

"We'll need them."

"Owen stored tanks of propane in the barn and there's a generator, too. The pump's electric, but we got plenty of water cached."

She rubbed her eyes with the back of her hand, the same way as Abilene. Her face was worn but lovely. Joe wished he'd met her years ago, before her children, before Boyd's death.

The scanner emitted a squeal and settled into speech.

"White Dog to Delta. Attempt communication."

"Affirmative."

Silence rushed over the airwaves. The sky through the window was becoming pale. Joe held Botree's hand.

"Bills," Frank said. "Hold your fire and let him talk. We honor his First Amendment freedom of speech."

A man's voice entered the tiny room through both the scanner and the CB as if in stereo.

"Your position is surrounded. You cannot escape. Throw down your weapons and come out. You will not be harmed. Repeat. You will not be harmed."

The amplified tones of a bullhorn rendered the sound inhuman, the echoing metal of a talking machine. Joe watched dry stalks of curly dock sway in the wind. The flight of a magpie made a black and white blur. The children giggled from the tub.

The sound of automatic-weapon fire blasted from the CB, then stopped.

Botree closed her eyes and moved her lips in prayer. Coop remained still, his face red, his pulse throbbing in his neck. Sunlight glinted on the gold rings that wrapped each of his fingers. Joe wondered how much extra weight they added to his hand. His mother had never worn jewelry of any kind.

The voice on the scanner spoke.

"White Dog to Delta. Casualty report."

"Negative."

"Prepare for insertion."

"Delta prepared."

Coop held a pen at the black spot closest to the circled F, watching the radio as if it possessed the power to attack him. His hand quivered. Botree was audible now, a steady murmuring drone.

Frank's voice entered the room. His tone was modulated to an eerie warmth.

"I'm going to read from the Montana Constitution, Article Two, Section Two. 'The people have the right of governing themselves as a free, sovereign, and independent state.'"

Joe stared through the window at the early sun on the slopes. Smoke outlined the mountain peaks, turning the sky crimson and brown, laced with rusty strips of blue.

The scanner spoke.

"White Dog to Delta, stand by for insertion."

"Standing by."

"Go, Delta."

Gunfire sounded from the scanner. The Bills responded with a long barrage of return fire. There was no more talking, only the noise of automatic weapons tearing the air to pieces. The sound rose and fell in waves as the men emptied their clips and reloaded and emptied them again. The pitch of battle increased, and Joe realized that the assault team was nearing the Bills' camp. The noise reverberated in the room, tinny and unreal through the cheap speakers. It reminded Joe of old machinery rattling.

Slowly he realized that the CB had stopped producing sound. All gunfire came from the scanner, short bursts that received no answer. The time between rounds lengthened until the airwaves hushed. A line of cattle walked along a path outside the window. Their heads dipped with each step.

Botree squeezed Joe's hand until it hurt. She was crying. He watched twilight pass to day as he waited for radio sound.

After a long time, a scratchy voice came over the scanner.

"Delta to White Dog. Objective achieved."

"Casualties?"

"Negative."

"Outstanding, Delta. Hostile casualties?"

The voice of the Delta radio man changed tone.

"All, sir. Uh, there was no attempt at retreat."

"How many?"

"Four."

"Repeat, Delta. How many hostile casualties?"

"Four, sir. That's it. There's no army here. No artillery. Just a radio and four dead. It's a mistake, sir. We cut them to bits."

"Terminate radio contact, Delta. Repeat, terminate radio contact."

Coop pushed against the table and stood. He leaned on the windowsill, raising dust that began to settle in the golden light that streamed through the glass.

Abilene yelled for his mother, and Botree hurried to the bathroom, as if grateful for a task. Joe left the room and walked through the house. Johnny lay on the couch. Even in sleep, his face showed stress. Joe felt sorry for him.

He knelt by the fireplace and began twisting old newspaper into tubes of kindling. His mother was probably buried beside his father, who was next to Boyd. There were more empty plots and Joe realized he would never claim his. He wished he'd asked Orben if Rodale's dog had lived.

Joe went to the kitchen, ran water in the sink, and washed the supper dishes. He wondered how far Orben's body would float. When he didn't return, people at home would believe that Joe had killed him. Someone else would come. The faucet dripped. Joe went to the mud room and began searching for a gasket to fix the leak. He felt as if another man had killed Rodale and he was simply held to account. He wondered if town water had reached Blizzard yet.

He should have gone with Ty. Now he'd have to leave anyway, and he didn't know where to go. The prospect of beginning again in a new place filled him with dread, although he couldn't imagine faring much worse than he had in Montana. He decided on Alaska. He would convince Botree to sell her share of the ranch, and they could homestead with the kids. He wished he had the possum.

He bent to retrieve a child's mitten on the floor. It was blue with a hole in the palm, like a pair he'd shared with his brother. He wondered how much Sara's kids had grown. He'd forgotten to ask Orben about his mother's house. The family wouldn't sell it, and Sara preferred the privacy of the hollow. She was probably mad at him for making her responsible for the homeplace. If he had stayed, he could have sold his trailer and moved into his mother's house. He and Abigail would be married by now.

From outside came a steady thump, like gusts of wind slamming a tin roof. He went to a window and watched a dark helicopter descend to the road. Machine-gun barrels on the exterior swiveled with the motion of the pilot's head. Dirt blew from the earth as the helicopter settled. Two men jumped to the ground, carrying rifles. One man ran to the corner of the barn and the other man squatted behind Joe's Jeep.

Joe put his pistol in the freezer. He slipped a white dish towel through the ring on the end of a broom handle. Dust rose from the helicopter's blades, but he could see that the hull was dark green with flat black numbers painted on its side. He opened the front door and poked the broom out. He hoped the men in the yard wouldn't shoot.